PRAISE FOR
PIERRE OUELLETTE'S
THE DEUS MACHINE

"A terrific read . . . the best, and hungriest, predators since *Jurassic Park*. . . . Pierre Ouellette has a sure instinct for clarity and an absolute genius for metaphor . . . an unremittingly inventive work of near-future fiction."

—*Entertainment Weekly*

"Pierre Ouellette hurtles you on a gripping journey into the dark side of technology in the future. An unbeatable read from start to finish."

—Clive Cussler

"Ouellette writes with vivid clarity . . . a genius for description. . . . Ouellette seems the offspring of some reputable influences: Émile Zola, William Gibson, Robert Heinlein, Stephen King, Tom Clancy, and Michael Crichton."

—*The San Diego Union-Tribune*

"One unrelenting horror after another surfaces in *The Deus Machine* . . . simply impossible to put down. . . ."

—*The Oregonian*

"Instantly addictive. . . . Ouellette makes the future sound all too close to home."

—*San Francisco Chronicle*

"In the vein of Tom Clancy, Pierre Ouellette has created a novel of exquisite and sophisticated suspense. . . ."

—*Virginia Pilot*

"A tightly written spellbinder. . . . If you read *The Deus Machine*, get ready for a lot of sleepless nights."

—*South Bend Tribune* (IN)

"Entertaining. . . . Satisfying. . . . The action kicks in at light-speed. . . . You've got to find *The Deus Machine*. It's great. Lie, beg, borrow, or steal to get it."

—*The Crypt* newsletter, CompuServe

"Reads like a Michael Crichton techno-thriller with bits of Stephen King and Dean Koontz added for good measure."

—*The Columbian* (Vancouver, WA)

"Ouellette has taken elements of cutting-edge science fiction and gadget-laden techno-thrillers and synthesized them into a crackerjack new novel. . . . *The Deus Machine* is an absorbing and scary roller coaster of a book, one you will find hard to put down."

—*Bookpage*

Books by Pierre Ouellette

The Deus Machine
The Third Pandemic

Published by POCKET BOOKS

THE THIRD PANDEMIC

A NOVEL

PIERRE OUELLETTE

POCKET STAR BOOKS
New York   London   Toronto   Sydney   Tokyo   Singapore

This book is a work of fiction. Names, characters, places and incidents are products of the author's imagination or are used fictitiously. Any resemblance to actual events or locales or persons, living or dead, is entirely coincidental.

A Pocket Star Book published by
POCKET BOOKS, a division of Simon & Schuster Inc.
1230 Avenue of the Americas, New York, NY 10020

ISBN: 0-671-52536-0

First Pocket Books paperback printing May 1997

10 9 8 7 6 5 4 3 2 1

Cover photo by Custom Medical Stock Photo

Printed in the U.S.A.

Dedicated with love to my wife Nancy

Acknowledgments

When I started work on this book in early 1994, the threat of emerging infectious diseases was still far from the public mind. The exotic viruses that now routinely creep across newsprint and TV screens were still safely tucked away in remote parts of the third world. Since information on the subject was scant, I had to rely heavily on knowledge and advice from many people who were generous both in time given and support rendered. The same is true of all the other technical arcana and theoretical thinking found in this book.

Dr. Mark Loveless, Arthur Anderson, Ph.D., and Fred Heffron, Ph.D., were very helpful in pointing me toward an interesting infectious agent. Dr. Jim Gilbaugh and Sue Reber assisted with their extensive knowledge of general medical practice.

Dr. Stuart Hameroff and Judith Dayoff, Ph.D., provided the theoretical basis for a fascinating approach to molecular computing via the cytoskeletal machinery inside animal cells. Patrick Coleman, Ph.D., at the Centers for Disease Control supplied some very useful insights into the little-known field of biostatistics. Gordon Hoffman furnished valuable technical references in both computer science and biotechnology, and Neil Berglund, Ph.D., pointed out the far frontiers of VLSI technology. Midge Anderson was instrumental in getting me properly connected with the CDC.

For technical details involving aircraft and airport procedures, Larry Jacob lent his experience both as a pilot and engineer. The armament and structure of naval patrol boats came from John Tillman, and Don Meyers contributed heavily in the area of police procedure. Katherine Dunn let me draw on her vast knowledge of serial killers, and David Chen shared his thinking on the impact of a biological catastrophe on business and economics. Wayne Signer was indis-

ACKNOWLEDGMENTS

pensable in introducing me to nuances of international shipping.

Mark Christensen provided both editorial assistance and enthusiasm, and David Kelly repeatedly came to the rescue with excellent editorial advice. Suzanne Amenta did a wonderful job of first-round copyediting to keep the manuscript clean, and John Russell was extremely generous in arranging for a quiet place upstairs to write.

My agent, Richard Pine, gave both creative insight and welcome encouragement; and Emily Bestler, my editor at Pocket Books, supplied patience and humor while guiding me through the dense and often incomprehensible thicket of contemporary popular literature.

Finally, I want to thank all the people at KVO for their solid support and unflagging interest throughout this project.

POSTSCRIPT—In chapter twenty-eight of this book, there is a reference to Bovine Spongiform Encephalopathy (BSE), and the fact that it has crossed over into humans in Europe. This passage was written two years ago as speculative fiction, but may be well on its way to fact. BSE is the infectious agent in the widely reported "Mad Cow Disease," which is now suspected of crossing over into humans in Britain and Europe. Let's hope that the rest of this book stays firmly embedded in the realm of fiction.

Thought I was smart,
The race was won.
And here come the devil,
Doin' a hundred and one.

— Gene Vincent
"Race With the Devil"

PART
ONE

PART

ONE

Prologue

THE METAL DETECTOR SCREECHED NASTILY AS PHILIP PARIS passed through the electronic security portal. The last thing he expected was that the power would still be on here. He paused and looked past the portal's big white arch to the little plastic trays that waited patiently for keys, penknives, bottle openers, and all the other metallic trivia snuggled in the pockets and purses of weary travelers.

But right now, no one would challenge him and check for such items. No green blazers, gray slacks, shiny shoes, and dangling ID tags. No neat hair, vigilant scowls, or irritating delays. Instead, Paris had a clear view down the corridor of one of Sea-Tac Airport's major concourses, a carpeted causeway more than a quarter mile in length.

Empty. Inhabited only by patches of afternoon sun streaming in through the big view windows near the gate areas.

The air-conditioning was off throughout the entire main terminal, and the TV monitors that usually announced arrivals and departures poured out the busy snow of random signal. He could feel the hot, dead air press against the enormous volume of the vacant terminal, and it seemed appropriate, because he was about to stage a solitary funeral march in remembrance of those now baking in the winged silver oven outside.

A trickle of sweat settled over his eyebrows as he drifted past the gates with their vacant check-in counters and scores of empty, black seats. Gate D1. Gate D2. Gate D3. An incremental trek toward a terminal condition, both literally and figuratively, mused Paris. He wanted to hum a dirge of some sort, but the brilliant heat and light made it seem inappropriate. Besides, he didn't know any.

At Gate D4, he first heard the voice and stopped to place

it. A TV. Yes, it was coming from a TV, a broadcast voice, an anxious commentary of some kind. As he continued on, he wondered if someone were actually down there at the end of the terminal, sitting placidly in this empty and horribly dangerous world watching TV.

At Gate D5, he looked out the tinted view windows. The tarmac was a bleached, concrete desert dabbed with brown petroleum stains, but wiped utterly clean of planes and all the little land vehicles that usually swarmed like worker ants around the great, tubular beasts with their razor wings. At Gate D6, a scrolling message marquee remained on, and red digital letters scurried by reminding the vacant walkway that "ALASKA FLIGHT 217 TO SAN FRANCISCO IS CANCELED . . ."

Now Paris saw the origin of the TV sound up ahead, at Gate D8. An overhead monitor dedicated to a news network that catered specifically to air travelers. It struck him as supremely ironic that this particular network should still be alive when airports the world over were so very dead. He could discern two distinct male voices, trading commentary in the universal style of broadcast journalese:

". . . at least three hours, and no sign that the situation is going to change anytime soon."

"Bill, do we have any idea how long this could go on before it gets really critical out there?"

Really critical. Even before he reached the gate and the TV, Paris knew precisely what they were talking about. He found it incredible that after all that had happened, they still did their little verbal tap dance around imminent death.

When he arrived at the gate, the image on the screen was no surprise, either. An extreme telephoto shot through the quivering liquid medium of heat waves rising off the taxiway right here at Sea-Tac. And doing a rubber dance to the tune of the heat was the winged silver oven itself, a Boeing 737 jet airliner. The plane's nose was pointed off to the left of the screen, so the trucks on one side of the plane were clearly revealed, vehicles of the type used to repair power lines, with cherry-picker booms shooting out the rear to hold elevated workers. But now the booms were being put to a

4

very different purpose: to shut off the plane's exits and keep the passengers sealed inside.

Paris sighed as he turned to the view window and pressed his nose gently against the glass. Out on the field, he could see the plane in question on a remote taxiway, with several ribbons of cement and brown grass in the foreground. Alone. Aside from the cherry-picker trucks, no other vehicles were to be seen anywhere.

". . . The real issue now is dehydration. The temperature in the shade here is already in the nineties, so it's got to be something a lot higher out there . . ."

Paris snorted as he listened to the journalistic banter. They were talking in grave and momentous tones, as well they should. Because they were lucky to be here, fortunate to survive what was probably their final assignment. He turned and spotted a bar across the main aisle. He was thirsty, very thirsty from the relentless heat.

As the TV raved on, Paris crossed the aisle, moving behind the bar, and idly tilted a spigot offering a local microbrew. Still worked. So, why not? After all, who was left in the Seattle Police Department to discipline him? He grabbed a glass, poured himself a beer, rounded the bar, and sat where he could see the plane-turned-oven out the window. The glass felt warm, but the beer was cold, an amber ale of some sort. The TV camera now zoomed in supertight so the heat waves contorted the image furiously, but despite this turbulence, Paris and the remnants of the network audience could now discern small white dots in the passenger windows, tiny and troubled icons of humanity.

". . . refuse to comment, and we've just been informed we'll have to shut down within the hour. The chain of command here has become very difficult to figure out, but we have to assume that the governor . . ."

"Cheers," Paris toasted the TV. He took a long pull on his glass and looked back out the window at the hobbled plane. Unlike the journalists, he knew that the tires had been shot out, and the engines disabled by tools tossed into the turbine blades. A winged silver oven, with no air circulation, baking its passengers, patiently sucking out their sustaining fluids.

I should pray for them, he thought. *I should pray for their redemption.* But there was no prayer within him, no spontaneous recitation that would deliver their mortal packaging safe from harm.

Instead, he quietly sipped his beer. And in spite of himself, he wondered how it ever came to this.

1

Port Owendo, Gabon

THE TRIBE CLUNG TO THE FLESHY RIDGES BENEATH THE black, fatty sky and waited with infinite patience for better times. Several million years of survival had taught them to silently absorb the lessons of the past, weather prevailing conditions, and watch diligently for new opportunities.

Such was life inside the muscle tissue of a chicken, which rested in a plastic bag in a freezer compartment on the main deck of the *Tiana Maroo,* a tramp steamer moored just south of Libreville, the capital of Gabon in Central Africa.

The tribe went by the name of *Salmonella,* a form of bacteria legendary for stalking the poultry of the world. But this particular tribe had recently endured a horrific battle against a devious chemical called tetracycline, which crippled, shriveled, and decimated their numbers.

The drug came from a farmer in Bangkok, Thailand, who waged a vigorous campaign to keep his poultry disease-free. Wave after wave of this toxic flood had flowed through the chicken and destroyed the tribal members from the inside out. For the bacteria to carry on their normal business, they relied on internal manufacturing sites called ribosomes to crank out the necessary goods for life at the microbial level. But the tetracycline came thundering in, and its barbarian horde of molecules destroyed these tiny factories by plundering their internal computer centers, which translated the blueprints for life-sustaining products and sent fabrication orders to their manufacturing floors. Soon, the *Salmonella*'s internal economies plunged into complete chaos, and deprived of the currency of life, they expired in enormous numbers.

But not all. A few members of the tribe had a unique weapon in their defensive arsenal, a special chemical that attacked the tetracycline invaders and disassembled them before they ever reached their targets.

And the current tribe, now nestled in this chicken meat, were all descendants of these fortunate few. They were the toughest of the toughest, the survivors of the survivors. Since the 1940s, whole armies of antibiotics had been raised and arrayed against them, and they lost almost every battle, but never the war. A few always slunk off in retreat, carrying away vital defensive knowledge that was passed on to subsequent generations.

And so it was that the tribe proudly carried their shields against tetracycline, and all the drug's immediate relatives.

But that was history. Today, the tribe simply dwelled on the muscle fiber mountains under the fatty sky.

And waited for better times.

"So you see, Captain, I can promise nothing. All I can do is appeal to the proper people and hope they listen."

Captain Stratos nodded gravely at the African man seated on the worn upholstery of a bench in the officers' smoking room of the *Tiana Maroo*. Behind the man, a large porthole framed the shoreline of Port Owendo in the blistering heat of the vernal equinox. Lighterage vessels clustered around the loading facilities where the railhead was located, the terminal point on a railroad track that ran back into the interior to fetch hardwood timber and manganese ore.

By now the lighterage craft should have been bringing tons of the manganese ore out to the *Tiana Maroo,* for loading into her cavernous holds. But there was a problem.

Of course, thought the captain. *There is always a problem.*

And so he continued his series of sober nods as the man proceeded to elaborate upon the difficulty. To do otherwise would be to mock the man, to expose him for the petty bureaucrat he really was. And that would simply escalate the magnitude of "the problem."

"What we may be able to do is take care of your water supplies while the other documents are being processed," continued Omar Amiar, who took a drag on his Marlboro and exhaled a blue-gray cloud that caught the brilliant tropical light. He was a Fang, one of the ten groups of Bantus in Gabon, and the one that made up the ethnic majority. As such, he belonged to Libreville's small and privileged

8

professional class, which populated the clerical arm of the government and business. "If everything goes well, you could probably depart right on schedule."

The captain smiled inwardly. He would be departing all right, but not by boat. His seven-month tour expired tomorrow and he would leave the *Tiana Maroo* anchored here in the Estuaire de Gabon, take a taxi to the airport north of town, and fly back to Athens, where he would have passionate reunions with both his wife and his mistress. Nevertheless, his professional pride demanded that he resolve this situation before he left.

Part of the covert bargaining with Amiar had to do with water. His ship's tanks held nearly two hundred tons of fresh water, which was consumed at the rate of six or seven tons per day. With over one hundred tons still on board, the *Tiana Maroo* could wait until it reached a European port, where the tanks could be topped off for about fifty cents a ton. Here in Africa, fresh water went for more than ten times that amount. Nevertheless, Captain Stratos deemed it prudent to buy an extra hundred tons through the good offices of Omar Amiar, who would most certainly profit handsomely from the transaction.

But now a more overt gesture was required to complete the round of negotiations.

"Mr. Amiar," said the captain, "you've been most helpful, and on behalf of myself and the owner, I would like to express our gratitude."

He pushed a cardboard box across the table. Inside were several cartons of American cigarettes and a dozen bottles of premium Scotch from the ship's bonded locker.

Amiar opened the top of the box and peeked in discreetly without showing any sign of enthusiasm. "If you'd like," continued the captain, "Ramon can stow that in the shuttle boat for you."

"That would be fine," replied Amiar as the Filipino cabin boy came forward and removed the box. "Captain, did I ever tell you about my wife?"

Damn! That should have done it, thought Stratos. But he kept his composure. "No, I don't believe you have."

Amiar broke into a broad grin. "She is the best cook in all Libreville!"

"Is that so?"

"With the proper ingredients, she can perform miracles, as the French say."

Ah, sighed the captain with relief. *So it's food. Simple enough.* "And what sort of ingredients does your wife like to work with?"

Amiar leaned forward across the table to stress the importance of his reply. "Chicken."

"Chicken?"

"Yes. Chicken."

"Well that's a remarkable coincidence."

"It is?" Amiar's eyes widened in mock surprise.

Now it was the captain's turn to lean forward. "Just yesterday, I was talking about provisions with my steward, and we uncovered an odd mistake."

"You did?"

"Yes. As you know, our last port was Bangkok, and our ship chandler there must have been a little tipsy when he inventoried our provisions."

"Why is that?"

The captain smiled craftily. "We received a dozen too many chickens. All dressed and ready for cooking."

"Amazing!"

The captain pushed back his chair and stood. "Mr. Amiar, it would be my pleasure to share a little of our luck with you and your good wife. Let me get the steward."

A minute later, Captain Stratos, Amiar, and the steward descended two flights of stairs to the main deck and out onto the fantail, into the hot shower of afternoon heat. From there they reentered the superstructure, walked down a passageway, jogged right, then left, and stopped before a large metal door, which the steward unlocked with a key from a big noisy key ring. Once inside the door, they stood in the freezer anteroom, with four metal doors set into the wall with heavy hinges and latches, each about four feet high. Behind these doors, refrigerator compartments held foodstuffs at varying temperatures, from deep freezing to moderately cool for items such as cheeses.

The steward pulled hard on the latch to the deep-freeze compartment and swung the door open. Inside, coils of tubing snaked across the walls behind wood shelves, which held mostly meat in plastic bags and cartons. The steward ducked into the compartment while the captain talked idly with Amiar, then returned with a cardboard box containing a half dozen chickens individually wrapped in plastic.

"You run a taut ship, Captain," complimented Amiar as he took the box from the steward.

"I try my best, Mr. Amiar," replied the captain as they stepped back out into the main hallway. The deal was done, and he was anxious to get back up and pack for his trip.

Omar Amiar drove his old GM pickup truck along the Voie Express, heading north toward his home neighborhood in Libreville. It had been a good day. He would make a nice profit off the water deal, which was consummated through a supply company owned by one of his associates.

Plus he had the chicken.

He grinned as he glanced at the cardboard box on the seat next to him. The bid for the chicken had been spontaneous, and he hadn't really expected it to work. Oh, well, you never knew, especially with the foreigners, like Stratos.

Indeed, there were many things that Omar Amiar would never know.

Like the problem with the compressor that drove the ship's freezer. In fact, two compressors drove the ship's freezer system, and they alternated to avoid unrelieved stress on a single machine. But somewhere in the Strait of Malacca, one of them burned a bearing and seized up completely, which meant the freezer was only being cooled half the time. Which in turn meant that the temperature in all the compartments began to rise.

Since the warming was gradual, no one noticed at first. For some reason, the gauges registering the temperatures in the various compartments were down the hall from the freezer itself, so it took an extra effort to associate their readings with the freezer area. Gradually, the needle on the circular gauge for the meat compartment went from minus eighteen degrees centigrade to plus ten degrees.

When some deep-frozen stores began to melt, the steward realized the problem and informed the captain. The remaining compressor was put on full-time duty, and everything that had thawed was moved to one of the warmer compartments, where these goods would be consumed as soon as possible.

But by the time the *Tiana Maroo* pulled into Port Owendo, a dozen chickens were still in the improvised compartment.

Now six of this remaining dozen sat on the seat next to Omar Amiar. And were warming rapidly in the blazing tropical heat.

The tribe stirred as the cool, fatty sky began to warm and promised a new era. It was time to go forth and multiply, to retake the lands of their dead ancestors, to spread out across fibrous peaks of the chicken muscle. (Magnified forty thousand times, a salmonella would have the same shape as a standard pill capsule, a cylinder rounded at each end, with a dozen or so fine threads called flagella projecting from its surface.)

Now, with the new prosperity upon them, the tribe began to divide and conquer, but not in the human sense. Instead, every organism divided and became two, each carrying the heritage of the original, including the great victory over the molecular scourge of tetracycline. So now the growth became exponential. Within a few hours, dozens became millions, then billions.

But eventually, they would overpopulate the muscular peaks and ridges, and the number of deaths would quickly equal the number of births, and their population would stabilize.

Unless, of course, they could find a way to a new world, a bigger world with more promise and greater opportunities.

2

DAVID MULDANE FELT IT AGAIN, AN ODD WAVE OF MUSCU-
lar sensation rolling up his trunk into his head, where it left
a tingling in his scalp. He remembered the first time he had
felt it, as a boy of twelve when he stole into his parents'
bedroom and rifled through the male menagerie of objects
in his stepfather's top dresser drawer. A dead Rolex, a
clutch of stale Percodans, coins of some exotic destination,
three .45 shells, a packet of condoms, expired credit cards,
a crippled electric razor, and other such flotsam from the
latter half of the American century. Even as he slid back
the drawer and heard the quiet rush of wood in the silent
afternoon, he knew it was a forbidden place, and the wave
had rolled up through him then just as it did now.

Because once again, he was doing a naughty thing in a
forbidden place. Only this time, he stood in the brilliant
interior of an operating room full of green gowns, polished
metal, and death in the making. And this time he was the
grown David, the surgeon, the nexus of this carnal theater,
who would attempt to pull the unfortunate patient back
from the mortal brink.

His team encircled the operating table where the seventy-
one-year-old male lay in a nihilistic stupor fueled by an IV
tube that dripped the sedative Versed into his circulatory
system. A surgical nurse checked her tray of sterilized instruments while the anesthesiologist gazed over at the instrumentation that blipped out the little parade of life in a march
of electronic blips. The laser technician fussed with some
settings on his console, while Dr. Wilkes stood back slightly
where she could observe but not obstruct. Back from the
table, an imaging technician sat at a computer console.

"Well," announced David, "let's get to work."

The entry spot on the patient's groin had been shaved of
pubic hair and was covered with the amber stain of disinfec-

tant. David felt for the unmistakable pulse and pushed the sharp point of the introducer into the flesh, right where the groin joined the leg, and angled the instrument so it slid into the right femoral artery.

"Okay, let's have the tube," he ordered without looking up. The optical tube immediately came into his field of vision, fed by the surgical nurse. It was one of the first of this particular design, with a fiber-optic core to transport a laser pulse surrounded by an outer layer that both sent and received normal light. The sent light would illuminate the long, dark journey up the patient's arterial mainstream, while the received light would serve as David's eyes to control the navigation.

The tube's destination was far off, a piece of possible death lodged in a coronary artery, a buildup of plaque that would soon strangle the blood supply to a major hunk of heart muscle and bring the organ to a disastrous halt. The whole point of this perilous trip was to bring the optical tube's inner core face-to-face with the obstructive plaque, so a laser pulse could course through it and evaporate the obstruction.

"Bring it in close," he ordered. The nurse's gloved hand moved the optical tube within an inch or two of his own. In a deft maneuver, he pulled the obturator out of the introducer, plucked the optical tube from the nurse, and pushed it into the open cavity in the introducer. He did it fast enough that only a single pulse of blood gushed out from the artery before the tube resealed the opening left by the withdrawn obturator.

Now that the entry site was secure, he looked up to a TV monitor suspended from a mechanical arm and saw what the business end of the tube saw, only better. A normal visual image would have revealed nothing but the red rush of the blood past the tube's optics, but a real-time image-processing system reworked the picture to reveal the curving surface of the interior wall.

"Okay, let's hit the road." His left hand moved to a toggle pad that allowed him to steer the tube, while his right hand began to feed the tube up the femoral artery toward the iliac bifurcation, where the main aorta splits into the two iliac arteries.

* * *

He had flunked out of medical school on a beautiful spring day. The big cherry tree in the backyard of their rental place was in full and furious bloom, and every little breeze cut loose a tiny blizzard of pale pink and white over the lawn. Carolyn was sitting at the patio table in halter top and cutoffs, her chestnut hair pulled tight into a knot with little streamlined highlights that went gold in the afternoon sun. Sunglasses concealed her eyes of striking blue, but not the elegant lines of her face, as she read a paperback romance of some sort.

"So," she said, not looking up, "what's with you?"

Usually he would have mumbled something and gone inside for a beer. But today, he kept silent and slunk into the weathered patio chair opposite her. Maybe she would pick up on this little aberration from their normal discourse and sense a preview of the trouble to come. But probably not. She flipped a page and her lips held steady at an absolutely neutral angle. Still, she looked great. He wondered how many of his friends wanted to fuck her. More than half, he speculated, based on some paranoid survey that belched up from the darkness below. And how many actually had? He'd like to think none, but he couldn't. It just didn't feel right.

It was a perfect time to speculate on this bit of personal pornography, since his academic testicles had just been completely severed. A gentle gust of warmth blew the perfume of the cherry blossoms across his face.

She had the upper hand, of course. Always. A little better family background, peppered with a senator here and a chief executive officer there. A bit more money, which she expertly siphoned out of mysterious coffers somewhere in the fiscal hinterlands when it suited her fancy. An impeccable social instinct, which let her navigate regally through even the most difficult gatherings. A sensual halo that canonized her sexuality and drew little predatory knots of hopeful males, which amused her greatly.

And now, on this catastrophic, career-busting afternoon, in this moment of grinding pain, he saw the truth of their marriage. Their union was just one more little expedition for her, an amorous venture with no long-term risk. Even the divorce might be kind of fun, in a perverse way. She would go apartment hunting with sympathetic friends, go off on a trip to effect a geographical cure, let the predatory male knots grow tighter and more exciting.

The silence wore on and her mouth held the perfect pitch of complete indifference. As his attempt at a dramatic pause dribbled away into the perfect light of the afternoon, he grew weary and simply blurted it out.

"I flunked. I'm out."

No change. Not for several heartbeats. Then she carefully folded a little triangle on the corner of her book page to save her place, closed it, and looked up while she put it down.

"You what?"

"I flunked out. I'm through. Kaput. Get it?"

And he knew precisely what fueled his anger: that little triangle on the page, the neatly folded corner. Her place in the book had taken precedence over the biggest career reversal in his life. It put a crease into their marriage that would never iron out.

Carolyn exhaled an exasperated sigh and unfolded her legs, sitting square in her chair. "Okay, let's not panic, all right?"

"I'm not panicked. I'm mad. I don't think you give a shit whether I make it or not. No skin off your back, right? Absolutely right. So let's just have a drink and watch me dangle in the wind, shall we? Great fun. Maybe we can get one of the neighbors to help you cut me down after sunset when it gets a little too chilly out here."

"You are one paranoid son of a bitch," she retorted through her five-hundred-dollar sunglasses.

"Wrong! Paranoid is when you *think* something bad is going to happen when it *isn't*. Well, I'm here to tell you the bad thing has already happened, Carolyn."

And the bad thing was very bad, indeed. Three years of sweat, anxiety, and mental exhaustion as he trudged through physiology, bacteriology, virology, and all the ologies that medical schools throw at you. And now he had failed a clutch of spring midterms so miserably there was no hope of redemption by the end of the quarter. Well, at least he was part of a very exclusive club. The attrition rate in medical schools is very, very low. They don't let you in if they don't think you can make it out.

Carolyn recrossed her legs and leaned back, her thighs a perfect extension of her stone-washed denim shorts. It wasn't that she had nice legs so much as the shorts probably cost a couple of hundred dollars and were form-fitted to match her contours. "So what happens now? Can't you take those classes again?"

"Not for a year, a whole fucking year. I'll never last that long."

"What do you mean you won't last that long?"

"Just what I said. I won't last that long."

He knew he should have been speaking in the plural. It wasn't just his medical career that wouldn't make it. It was the two of them. And on both counts, he was right.

On the TV monitor, David saw the tube was approaching the great fork in the patient's arterial river, and he slowed his forward progress to negotiate the upcoming curve.

"Can you steer the tube through a complete three hundred and sixty degrees?" asked Dr. Wilkes.

"Sure can. This toggle pad gives me a full range of control. Watch how we go around the bifurcation into the main aorta so we can head north."

He'd attended several other procedures with Dr. Wilkes and found her likable as well as professional. With some doctors, both male and female, there was always a subterranean pissing contest going on, an implication that one could somehow do it a little better than one's peers. But in Elaine it seemed absent. She was completely focused on the procedure and the technology.

With his left middle finger, David applied a slight bit of pressure to the right as he fed the tube forward with his right hand. On the screen, the view panned right as the tube entered the wider expanse of the main aorta, which snuggles at the base of the spine behind the body's compressed array of internal organs.

In this inner world, they were now tunneling underneath the sigmoid colon and the tight tangle of the small intestines. At odd intervals, there were holes in the wall, the openings to arterial tributaries that nourished the overall system, all the way down to the capillary level.

"We'll pick up some speed now, because it's a straight

shot all the way to the aortic arch," said David as he fed the tube in a little faster.

In the background, the anesthesiologist and the laser technician were talking about golf, something about the grip being everything.

I'm not only not a golfer, I'm not a surgeon, either. So what am I doing here?

He could see it now. The filter of hindsight removed all the emotional noise that had obscured the original signal. Carolyn had been a prize, a very big one. As big as those enormous marlins you saw in pictures from subtropical fishing derbies, where the sun leered down on the ebullient fishermen in their ridiculous caps and ludicrous sport shirts.

At first, she seemed utterly taken with him and happily helped construct a phallic obelisk of staggering height for him to perch on and view the world from a serene and lofty distance. It wasn't until much later he realized that, like the prized marlins, she could wriggle free at any time and disappear into the limitless ocean in a quicksilver flash.

The first hint came shortly after they were married, on a sailboat trip up the inland sound between Vancouver Island and the Canadian mainland. Their boat slid along under a lazy mix of cumulus and sun, and the water was a beautiful hard blue as they drifted among the little islands to the east of the big island. They had the forward cabin and made love frequently on quiet evenings, with the water pushing a sloshed whisper against the hull. From up on deck, they would occasionally hear sharp verbal thrusts coming from Sam and Catherine, the other couple, who had hit a slick spot in the marriage and were skidding a bit.

As the trip wore on, the fallout from Sam and Catherine settled uniformly over everyone. Catherine tended to station herself apart from the rest and lapse into desultory moods where she stared at the little forked pattern traced by dragging a stick in the water. In effect, the four were now three, and a new dynamic emerged, a highly aggravating one from David's point of view. It seemed that Sam was fabricated from the same social template as Carolyn and began to subtly broadcast this fact:

"You were on Corfu that summer? We must have just

missed each other! Hey, you know that little place where the blind guy plays the Stones on the douzouki? . . ."

When decoded, his message was simple: like Carolyn, he, too, was a big fish. A prize that could never really be landed. Big enough to slither off even the largest of decks and swim free through a beautiful trail of silver bubbles.

Carolyn listened carefully to these broadcasts and encouraged them through rapt attention and little shimmering bursts of amused laughter. Or so David thought. That was the hell of it. Was this guy probing the outer perimeter of David's marriage? Was Carolyn giving him helpful hints? Or was David just plain paranoid? Hard to say.

But then the sex stopped. Carolyn trotted out all the timeless excuses of a woman who in truth just wasn't interested. At night, they lay back to back in the little forward cabin, now bisected into two opposing camps.

Silently, David rested his case. Both suspects were guilty of copulating from a distance. The weight of circumstantial evidence left no other conclusion.

Later, after the trip, the sex returned. But it was never quite the same. And then of course, after his catastrophe in medical school, it went away altogether.

The tube was now halfway up the main arterial highway and paused at this little rest stop where there was a major branch to the right renal artery, the one that supplies the kidney. Just inside this smaller cavity, the image processing revealed an inward bulge in the arterial wall where a plaque buildup was beginning to obstruct the flow of blood.

"Look on the right and you'll notice an obstruction coming up," suggested David. "That's a plaque deposit on the way to the renal artery."

"Good call," commented Dr. Wilkes. "I might have missed that."

"Bob, let's switch to an unprocessed picture for a second," David ordered the imaging technician. On the monitor in front of him, the pulsed flow of blood became visible at the arterial junction.

"Look closely and you can see a turbulence pattern set up by the plaque," David said to Elaine. "Sort of like rapids caused by a raised river bottom."

"You know, it's not often I get to see this kind of problem from the inside out," replied Elaine. "I wonder how far occluded that has to get before there's notable loss of renal function."

"Good question." David had no idea what the answer was. "Well, we're about two-thirds there. Let's keep the show on the road. Bob, give me back the processed view." He started the tube moving forward once again, under the liver.

I don't have to be here. I don't have to be doing this. What if they knew? Well, with a little luck, they won't. We'll be through with this thing, and they'll say something like "Nice work, Doctor." And then I'll be a surgeon, a real one. It's not a piece of paper with a gold seal that makes you a good doctor. It's pulling off something like this. Just one chance, that's all I needed. And here it is.

Once again, his stepfather's drawer was open on that silent afternoon, and he saw the old H-P calculator, a 15C, the kind favored by engineers like his stepdad. Only, by this time, his stepfather had drifted up into some dubious stratum of management where golf clubs replaced calculators as the tool of choice. Sometime earlier, when his stepfather still really designed things, he told David proudly about building devices that made airplanes land in fog as thick as a vanilla milk shake. But later, his job became an intangible abstraction, and David could only observe it secondhand, through the symptoms. A couple extra drinks in the evening. An exhausted slump into the easy chair after dinner. A sharp snap at his wife that came out of nowhere.

But sharp snaps were nothing new in their house by then. David was continually testing his stepfather, as though the man was some kind of equipment that could be toggled into a failure mode, a breakdown that would confirm and validate David's periodic fits of contempt. He hurled one confrontation after another at this patient man and drove him well past any reasonable threshold of restraint.

After each engagement, they would back off, both frightened by the ferocity of it, then try the rational approach, searching through David's childhood, collecting pieces and attempting to fit them together. But to form what? There were no clues, no great pictures of revelation. His stepfather was the only father he'd ever known, so why didn't they transcend biology and slip into a comfortable bond? Neither knew.

His stepfather responded by gradually quitting the field of battle and slipping off into the professional high country, where he was respected and admired. And as his stepfather faded out of his life, David felt a great emotional reversal and the ache of loss. As the man moved off, David longed for his love, which by now was like a signal transmitted from a great distance: still there, but full of noise and confusion.

In his late teens, David desperately gathered these tiny scraps of affection and processed and purified them so they became the fuel that powered the doctor dream. Like his stepfather, he would be an engineer, but an engineer of people, not an engineer of golf clubs and 8 P.M. meetings.

The dream's intent was sealed on the Sunday morning some years later when he found his stepfather on the couch. One of his arms hung limp off the side, and the family dog was licking his hand and whimpering. David always wondered if the dog really knew, or if it was just disappointed that it hadn't yet been fed. Within five minutes, the living room was a mass of paramedics, firemen, tanks, tubing, masks, instrument boxes, portable radios. A coronary, it seemed. A massive one. Shock didn't work. Nor chest massage. Nor exotic injections and inhalations.

But something would have worked. And David would find out what that something was and effect a posthumous cure. Someday.

And that day, of course, was today. This was the procedure that would have saved his stepfather, his only father. From a distance, he'd watched developments in the field, studied the literature, and mastered every nuance of the procedure. His credentials were impeccable, and the knowledge gained in medical school helped him thread the bureaucratic maze to perform this particular operation in this most modern and progressive of institutions. The illusion he presented was perfect, and the surgical team greeted him with the kind of regard reserved only for those in the innermost circle of medicine.

I can retire after this. Just one shot. It's all I need.

"Okay, ladies and gentlemen, time for the U-turn."

The tube had now reached the aortic arch, where the main aorta curves up off its track on the inner side of the spine and doubles back down into the heart itself. With care, David changed his finger pressure on the toggle pad and guided the tube around the sharp 180-degree turn. He was now almost at the end of the road, where the main aorta terminated and the heart itself began. And right here, within an inch or two of the heart, the wall of the aorta was covered with numerous tunnels: the openings to coronary arteries, the little tubes that fed fuel to the heart muscles.

"And here's the exit point."

David slowed the travel of the tube and turned it gingerly into one of the tunnels. Now the going got quite a bit tougher. The tube filled nearly half the diameter of the coronary artery, and he had to steer with great care so as not to veer off to the side and injure the arterial wall.

"One more branch and we're in the neighborhood."

Directly ahead, the artery divided into two smaller ones, and David turned to the right.

"And there we have it."

Thanks to the image processing, the arterial plaque was clearly visible, a plump crescent composed of fat and calcium that nearly closed the tunnel in front of the tube. On the far side, the heart muscle was dying from lack of oxygenated blood. Any more decomposition and the patient would soon die along with it.

So the mission was simple enough: use the tube's laser to vaporize the plaque into a liquid that would slosh harmlessly on through the system.

"Okay, let's have the reticle."

A set of cross hairs like those on a gun scope appeared on the monitor image. David positioned them directly in the center of the plaque.

"Jim," David said to the laser technician, "set me at eighty millijoules with a hundred-nanosecond pulses."

"All set," came the reply.

David felt with his right foot and found the pedal that would trigger the laser. "I'm on the trigger. Arm the laser."

"Armed."

From an angiogram done before the operation, David

knew a sharp ninety-degree bend was on the far side of the plaque, where the artery rounded a corner. One or two quick red flashes and they should see it.

"Here we go."

He tapped the foot switch, saw the red flash, and observed a major piece of the plaque simply disappear.

One more hit and I'm a doctor.

He tapped the floor switch a second time.

"Jesus!" exclaimed someone.

The plaque was completely gone now, and they could all see on through. To the big gaping hole in the arterial wall where the blood was already pulsing out into the pericardium, the sack that holds the heart.

And the greedy, thirsty heart muscles were already howling in protest. No blood, no work. No work, no life.

"Blood pressure gone. Pulse gone," announced the anesthesiologist.

No!

David reeled back from the table. He knew immediately what had happened. They all knew what had happened. He had misjudged the strength of the laser beam. The second shot had blasted through the remaining plaque, then bored a neat circular hole right through the arterial wall on the far side, where the blood spurted out in massive quantities.

Elaine Wilkes moved forward and brought her palm down on the patient's sternum in a futile attempt to get the pulse back. Again and again. No luck.

"Well," somebody said with great fatalism, "that's that."

Nobody looked at David or spoke to him as they filed out. Only Elaine remained.

"David, it was an honest mistake. Any number of surgeons would have made the same decision."

"Yeah, sure," he mumbled. Any number.

"There'll be a review. You'll get another chance."

"Yeah, I'll get another chance," repeated David weakly.

Elaine left and David stood alone in the operating theater with the expired patient. He swore he could hear a gurgling from the massive deposit of spent blood pooled within the chest cavity. Normally, a team of cardiac surgeons would have been standing by and would have torn into the chest in a gallant effort to repair the grievously damaged artery.

But of course, this wasn't normal. Not in any sense of the word.

As David pulled off the VR helmet, he felt a warm coat of sweat on his forehead. Same thing with the sensor-studded gloves, which looked damp and wilted from perspiration. Jesus! Months of effort, and it all came down to this. He had spent hundreds of hours on the Internet via the fiber-optic ATM link that fed into his PC with its RISC multiprocessor array, here in the Seattle/King County Department of Public Health, where he was the director of Management Information Systems.

Some time back, he had made the right connections and worked his way into the Virtual Reality Surgery Center out of Stanford. He knew the jargon, he knew the medicine, and he studied each procedure with great care before he participated. Through the standard virtual-reality tools, with their hi-res video, audio, and touch-wired gloves, he was transported into a surgical scenario of great realism, with the patient, the gear, and the room being produced on a supercomputer somewhere in Palo Alto. The surgical team was composed of other people connected via the Internet from across the country, and the supercomputer turned them all into human images that populated the operating room. Prior to the operation, each had furnished a video of himself, so even the facial representations were correct.

In the end, his participation in all this was a clever fraud, but his need to vindicate himself had become obsessive, and the regulations soon seemed more like obstacles, and deceits like transformations.

But now that he had failed, it all seemed criminal, and in a petty kind of way. He was not a doctor. He was an imposter. And not even a good one.

David reached over and turned off the computer. If the people at the Virtual Surgery Center knew the truth of his life, would they forgive him? He hoped so. He yawned and stretched. It was late, very late, and he was drained by the stress and failure of the surgery, but he didn't feel like going home. Instead, he decided to go down to Pioneer Square and have a drink somewhere. Anywhere.

* * *

"You can only love a wooden boat," declared Philip Paris. "A wooden boat is a living thing. A plastic boat is a dead one. If you listen closely to a wooden boat, you can hear it talk to you. Listen to Fiberglas, and all you'll hear is yourself listening. That, sir, is why I will always own the *Cedar Queen*."

Tommy Graziano gave a small nod of concession as Paris raised his glass of Cutty Sark in an undeclared toast to the vessel that held them dear on this, his forty-seventh birthday. Once again, he had successfully defended his ownership of a boat that drained both his time and limited money on a grand scale, nearly as grand as the *Cedar Queen* herself, a Blanchard 36 standardized cruiser.

Tommy Graziano and Bill Bronson sat opposite Paris in the saloon of the *Cedar Queen*, and Steve Larsen sat next to Paris. All cops, just like him.

Tommy and Bill were from the old Homicide Division days, and Larsen was one desk over in Burglary and Theft, where Paris now resided.

"Well, goddamnit, Phil, if the boat makes you happy, so what? I mean, so what?" droned Larsen through a thick booze fog. Larsen was a doughnut cop, maybe fifty pounds overweight, a veteran from the old days when a big box of plain and glazed was a daily fixture at the precinct, the days before everyone started talking about "good" and "bad" cholesterol. But still, he had that bulldog look about him, as if somehow all that flesh might explode into decisive action if sufficiently motivated.

Larsen's skewed comment had diverted the stream of conversation, and for a moment, all four lapsed into silence. From up in the wheelhouse, the easy banter of the wives floated down through this fine summer night on Lake Union in the midst of Seattle. With them was a friend of Bronson's wife, a nice woman in her late thirties, obviously intended for Paris's covert perusal. Nice try. He had to love them for it, but no go.

"Tommeee!" came the nasal call of Phyllis Graziano. "We gotta go, guy. I gotta get up early."

Tommy drained his can of Miller. "Great party, Phil. Thanks."

"Don't thank me, Tommy. You guys put this on. I just

supplied the boat. Dinner cruise for twenty on Lake Union. I'll send you a bill in the morning."

The three cops chuckled politely, but it was a lame joke and Paris knew it. The party was over. At its peak, there were maybe twelve couples, mostly cops and their wives or husbands. All friends, all people who had stuck by Paris through the bad years as well as the good. It was supposed to be a surprise, but Larsen had tipped him off because he knew Paris didn't like surprises, not on the job, not anywhere. Not anymore. And that, of course, was why they had the party on the *Cedar Queen* instead of at a restaurant.

Paris rose from his seat on the padded settee that folded into a double berth. At six foot three, his head barely cleared the gently curved beams of the cabin ceiling. He could feel the tenor of the group change as his physical presence unfolded and took charge. When he was thirty, the feeling would have given him several extra volts of positive charge. But now, it seemed a distant phenomenon whose ownership was more a matter of chance than anything else. Nevertheless, it had its intended effect. Even Larsen slowly stirred and slid out from behind the folding table.

The party was over. Lt. Philip Paris had just declared it so. Philip Paris, once prime candidate for precinct captain, once heir to the throne of the chief himself.

Paris watched the three detectives climb the short set of stairs to the wheelhouse. Good guys, good friends. Probably better than he deserved. As he rounded the table to follow them, he could hear Bronson's wife scolding him for spilling beer on his new sports shirt. Paris chuckled. It was a terrible shirt, with diagonal patterns of mallards climbing into a 40 percent cotton sky. If Bronson was lucky, the shirt was totaled, although Lucy wouldn't see it that way.

Up in the wheelhouse, Paris sniffed the warm summer breeze blowing over the lake as he said his good-byes and took a little extra time with the nice woman who had been towed along with the best of intentions. It wasn't easy for her, he knew that. It was never easy, not for anybody.

As they left the ship and headed toward the marina parking lot, Paris turned back to the wheelhouse, where the cabin lights played over the rosy orange glow of the teak paneling and trim. Beautiful. Just as pretty as the day he and Ginny had first come aboard nearly fourteen years ago.

He extracted two plastic trash bags from a storage cabinet beneath one of the padded seats, turning a brass latch he had installed on one of those quietly glorious weekends long gone past. The empty cans went into one, and the plastic cups into another. Moving down to the main saloon, he repeated the ritual, then stored the remaining booze in the icebox. He liked the ritual of it, the cleansing, the return of a magnificent lady to a high state of dignity.

When he was finished, he moved to the galley, fired up the stove, and made a cup of tea. Looking up through the skylight, he observed the full moon staring down at him in a white blaze of secondhand sunlight, and he liked what he saw. He turned out the interior lights, sat at the folding table in the darkness, and stared at the pale square of moonlight on the wooden deck. As he sipped his tea, the irrepressible buzz of the city floated down the stairs and washed softly against his ears.

When he finished, he rinsed his cup and returned to the wheelhouse. He should have been tired, about forty-seven years' worth, but he wasn't. He slid in behind the wheel with its polished wooden spokes and stared at his reflection in the large, rectangular panes of flat glass in the windshield. A big man, thick through the shoulders, with bushy gray hair cut short and slightly receding. If he didn't know this guy, he would be wary of him, observant and respectful. The overhead light left his eyes in shadow and played up the angular creases on his cheeks and the strong jaw.

He would take her out, he decided. Now.

With a practiced motion, he fished for his keys and fired up the six-cylinder Kermath engine and heard its vigorous burble as it came to life and idled in neutral. After flipping off the wheelhouse lights to kick in his night vision, he moved onto the dock, casting off the moorings, hopped back aboard, slipped into reverse, and added just a touch of throttle to launch the vessel into motion. The *Cedar Queen* was thirty-six feet long, a stately vessel built of Western red cedar over sturdy oak frames. Her strong vertical lines predated streamlining and gave her a regal bearing that her slinky offspring could never match.

Paris's big hands played deftly over the throttle and wheel as he maneuvered the big boat out into the open water of Lake Union. He was at the north end, between the Ship Canal and the mouth of Portage Bay. With a gentle push of throttle, he nudged the big white hull south along the western shore. It was past midnight now, and there was almost no traffic along the one-mile length of lake that stretched out ahead of him and terminated in a dazzling matrix of downtown lights. He reached over the wheel, swung the wheelhouse window open, and felt a soft, warm gush of maritime air flood in.

And in with the air came Ginny.

Right about now, she would come up the stairs from the galley with a cup of coffee hiding a discreet dash of Jack Daniel's. As she put it in the little holder next to him, he would slide his arm around her and draw her close, and she would give him a little peck on the earlobe as they cruised through the quiet evening. After a bit, she would slide away and go back below. No words spoken. None needed. The moment would have a wonderful symmetry all its own.

Seven years. The length of many metaphysical cycles. Seven years. That's how long it had been. A lovely woman, a nurturing woman who ignored her fragility by turning outward to face the world on its own terms, without regret, without fear. An English teacher devoted to her students, whom she symbolically adopted to make up for their own lack of children. Every year, she and Paris would take a few of the chosen ones on a day cruise as a reward for work well done. He could still see her beaming at them as the breeze played through her hair, and the sun caught the premature streaks of gray. They adored her, of course, and so did he.

Yes, and so did he.

Paris looked over at the cars coursing through the night along Westlake Avenue and caught the reflection of the mercury-vapor lamps off the mild dither that spread over the water's black surface. Seven years. Jesus. And the whole thing had happened just a few weeks before his birthday, the worst birthday of all.

She was sick to begin with, and in the end, that made all the difference. Insulin-dependent diabetes, an unusually extreme case that occasionally became unstable and required hospitalization. Not a fatal malady, but definitely a compromise to her health. But Ginny would rather be dead than down, and that was that. So they sailed on as usual, both literally and figuratively. Which is why they went out that night. Nothing special, really. Just a quiet dinner at a little Italian place. A few laughs, some good food, and a little intellectual sparring with a teacher friend and his wife. The guy taught social studies and was fascinated by Paris's job as a cop. After a couple of bottles of Chianti, he was deep into the police "as an alienated urban subculture" or some such thing. Paris could never remember what.

But he clearly remembered his trip to the rest room, even through the pale red buzz of too much wine. And what his cop's eye saw on the way out.

Now Paris rotated the spoked wheel to match the contour of the shore as it curved east at the south end of the lake. Ahead of him, the deep black silhouette of Capitol Hill was framed in subtle contrast against the pale sky glow. Beneath the hill's black horizon, thousands of tiny lights sang their little sparkles into the night. He reached in his shirt pocket, fished out a smoke, and lit it with his Zippo. The flicker from the flame danced off the wheelhouse windows, then expired as he snapped the lighter's lid shut. Only the radiant orange tip of the cigarette remained.

When Paris had come out of the rest room and headed back toward their table, his route took him by the swinging doors to the kitchen. Given his mildly intoxicated state, he might have missed it, but the restaurant's interior was only dimly lit, by squat candles flickering in red holders of cut glass parked on the checkered tablecloths. Every time the kitchen door burst open, it strobed a rude dose of fluorescent kitchen light into the place, so it was difficult to ignore.

When he was maybe twenty feet from the door, it swung open and a man walked out; a quick, black cutout against the white kitchen light. And at that very moment, his cop's instinct told him something was wrong.

But what? Wasn't it just another waiter with another plate piled with pasta? No, it wasn't. The suited figure turned abruptly, his back to Paris, and took off into another section of the restaurant. As Paris continued on, he lost the figure for a moment, but then he came back into view in the dim, red light as he seated himself at a table, his back still to Paris.

So what did it mean? Probably nothing. But Paris did the good cop thing and recorded it on a mental scratch pad reserved for all the little anomalies he noticed. They were like pennies, he thought. Most were worth one cent, but occasionally you snagged a collector's item worth a fortune.

But the incident that Paris collected on that particular night was worth a trip to hell.

In the wheelhouse, Paris could feel the warm vibration from all six cylinders as they leisurely pushed the *Cedar Queen* through the dark waters at around five knots. He stubbed out his cigarette in the beanbag ashtray set between the compass and the depth finder, the boat's one grudging accommodation to modern navigational aids. Off to his right, the streets terraced up toward the interstate freeway on its midnight run to the Canadian border. Paris's eyes made a practiced scan of the lake's surface over 180 degrees. No running lights, no traffic. Unless some fool was out there without any lights. And Paris was in the right business to know what fools could do. Fools and worse. Much worse.

It had been about four in the morning when he rolled out of his slumber and felt the vacancy beside him. Through the open bedroom door, he could see down the hall to the bathroom door where a long, bright sliver stole out from the gap at the bottom.

"Ginny?"

No answer. He brought himself upright and felt a residual ache lurch across his head, an artifact of the wine.

"Ginny?" he called a little louder. Still no answer. He swung his legs over and rose to his feet. He wanted a cigarette, but there weren't any in the bedroom. Ginny drew the line with that, and Paris knew she was right. If he smoked in bed, it'd be no time at all before he reduced himself and her to charcoal.

He sighed, stood, and shuffled down the hall in the dark. So what was going on? Maybe she was downstairs, getting a snack. She did that sometimes. Cheddar on Ritz crackers, and maybe a little glass of apple juice.

He'd try the bathroom once more. "Ginny?" he asked while leaning his tired forehead against the door.

"Phil!" Her cry was tissue thin and barely audible from the other side of the door.

By the time he yanked the door open, he had surged to full wakefulness. She was sitting on the floor hugging her knees through the folds in her nightgown, her back propped against the tub. Her color was nearly gone and she was immersed in a flurry of shivers.

"Jesus, Ginny! What happened?"

"I got a little sick," she whispered. "Then I got a little sick again. And again."

Paris went to full alert. She had that stare, that terrible stare. He'd seen it many times on the street, with gunshot and accident victims. Rather than look you in the face, they froze into a concerned frown and threw their focus out to some deathly horizon far beyond mortal vision.

"Don't move," he commanded as he sprang to his feet and dashed back to the phone in the bedroom. With his big fingers, he stabbed 911 almost hard enough to crack the keypad and delivered his emergency call with great economy and force.

He grabbed a blanket, sprinted back to bathroom, and wrapped it around Ginny.

"It's gonna be all right, love. I got an ambulance coming." He held her gingerly, afraid of squeezing the remaining life out of her.

"Oh, that's all right. I'll be okay. I just need to lie down for a while. That's all."

He felt her forehead. A boiling fever danced over his fingers. Great Jesus! How long had she been like this?

He would never know. Because at that moment, her eyes rolled up and her head fell over onto his chest, and she went into a diabetic coma.

The commotion of the paramedics, the ambulance ride to the hospital, the agony in the emergency room, the long, grim vigil, were all an old show for Paris, a ghastly little vaudeville where the performers changed, but the props and plot forever stayed the same. Sometimes he'd wondered if it would make a tragedy of his own any easier to bear. It didn't.

Ginny's doctor, a nice fellow who'd moved out from New York several years ago, was there in less than thirty minutes. He explained that it appeared to be food poisoning, and how it presented Ginny's already destabilized health with a highly grievous insult, and how she had gone into severe ketoacidosis from the fluid loss, and how they were trying to stabilize her with insulin and intravenous salt injections, and how . . .

The longer the doctor's explanation, Paris knew, the more perilous his wife's condition. And the explanation was very long, indeed. All he asked was to stay with her. And he did, but nothing happened, nothing changed. She remained comatose all night, and into the following morning. Then there were more doctors, more talk, more opinions. The pH levels in her blood had been extremely high, although they were now improved. There was at least some chance of permanent brain damage, just a chance, mind you . . .

Now, ahead and off to starboard, Paris could see the big span where the interstate crossed over the mouth of Portage Bay. He broke into a yawn and sat down on the four-legged wooden stool, the one with the inlaid compass pattern in rosewood and white oak in the seat, the one Ginny had given him for Christmas one year.

He was ready to take the *Cedar Queen* back in and call it a night.

It might have ended with Ginny's coma. That might have been the focal point of his anger and grief, the point from which to measure his recovery. But it wasn't. Not by a long shot.

He took the elevator down to the lobby that terrible morning, then could go no farther. Driving was out of the question. He sank into a chair and felt the lobby recede as he drew inward, to some epicenter of the soul where he might mount a defense against the terrible pain that lurked right behind the numbness. He had to take action, he knew that. If he didn't, he was a stationary target, and the grief would eat him whole. But where to start?

"Paris." He turned. It was Helen Whitmire, a doctor from emergency, sitting down beside him and grasping his hand. Over the years, Paris had spent enough time around emergency rooms that he casually knew the staffs, and Helen was a veteran ER doctor with a quick and cynical wit that Paris had always admired. But the wit was gone now. She looked devastated. "I just got here. They just told me. Phil, I'm so sorry. Can I help? Is there anything I can do?"

She was an angel, but she'd never know that. She gave him reason to act. He put his hand over hers. "Thanks, Helen. I don't know what to tell you. It all happened so fast. She was sick, you knew that. But this . . . I never expected anything like this. Jesus!"

"There's been five more cases since her. *E. coli.* All the same strain. The lab reports are still coming in. The public health people are already on it."

The lobby and the doctor snapped back into sharp focus. "Five cases?"

Helen sighed. "Yeah, and that's just here. So you can bet there's more scattered around town. Where'd you eat last night?"

Paris told her.

"Yeah. Same place as the rest. You eat something different from her?"

Paris didn't answer. He was back in the restaurant, coming out of the rest room, watching the rectangular burst of light from the kitchen, seeing the suited figure come out, tracking him to the table in the dim reaches of the room.

He poisoned them. Poisoned them all. He poisoned Ginny. He killed her brain.

Paris knew it in an instant. Somewhere deep within him was an entire legal system that operated with a brilliance seldom matched by the real thing. Symbolic cops, judges, attorneys, and juries: the staff behind his remarkable intuition.

"Paris?" Helen was looking at him with some alarm. "You need to go home. I'm going to get you a prescription for a sedative, okay?"

"Yeah, sure." But he wouldn't need them. He was already mapping the investigation, the escape route that would let him flee the horde of demons hunting him down, waiting to spear him with despair.

The next week confirmed the worst. Ginny remained in the coma. A neurologist was called in. Tests were run. Wave forms analyzed. The prognosis was not good. She was alive, yes. There was something going on inside her skull, yes, but not much. The hospital could do no more. It was time to look at other "extended care options."

Options? What options? His wife was one of the living dead. That's what they were trying to tell him. And that placed him in an exclusive portion of hell reserved for spouses of the permanently comatose.

At first, people made concerned queries: "How's Ginny?" "Is there any change?" "Don't give up." But then, as the months dragged on, the queries died out, and people politely avoided the subject.

But Paris made it the center of his life. He would find the poisoner, the figure emerging from the kitchen. Using all his considerable powers, he would hunt down the monster who stole his wife's soul and left her useless body to torment him.

From the start, there were problems. He met resistance at the office about opening an official investigation. From a political standpoint, Paris was well positioned in the department, a natural leader, a star performer in the Homicide Division, a top contender for the next chief of detectives. But pressure was coming down from on high. The public health people weren't pleased with the notion of bringing the police into the affair. Worse, his boss, a hard-nosed cop named Albert Carno, was dragging his heels about opening an official investigation.

"I got a problem with this case," said Carno as they sat in his cramped office. "And unfortunately the problem, Phil, is you. Look, here's what we got: We got no physical evidence, we got no motive, we've got no other eyewitnesses. We've only got you, Phil. For all we know, what you saw was some shitfaced schmuck who took a wrong turn on the way to the bathroom. It's just not enough. The DA simply isn't interested." Carno paused and exhaled loudly. "Look, I'm sorry. I'm really sorry. Don't forget I knew Ginny." He stopped as soon as he said it and looked mortified. "Jesus, Phil, I'm sorry. I know she's . . ."

"It's okay. We all know what she is."

"She's a great gal. It must be terrible. Ask me for any other kind of help and you've got it, but I can't do this. I just can't."

Unfortunately, Carno was right. There wasn't near enough evidence. Paris had gone back to the restaurant and talked to everyone on staff who was there that night. The owner was extremely cooperative, and with good reason. If the poisoning was a criminal act, the restaurant was off the hook. But no one had seen a stranger stray into the kitchen. He talked to the waitress who'd handled the area where Paris had seen the man sit down, but she drew a blank.

Paris could go no further without official support. It didn't look good. He was on his own. And that was when the trouble began.

Because he couldn't leave it alone.

He worked nights on it, long, bitter nights. It consumed all his spare time and filled in all the cracks, fissures, ruptures, perforations, and punctures in his heart. And the harder he worked on it, the better he felt. Deep down, he knew he was just staving off the inevitable, the acceptance of her loss, but Paris had never been one to wait things out on the bench. He pressed on.

He persuaded the restaurant owner to give him all the credit card receipts for that night and conned a friend in Records into running the names against criminal records. Interestingly enough, two convicted felons had been eating there that night. One was an embezzler and the other a burglar of long ago. He dug deeper and checked both out, but neither seemed capable of committing so bizarre a crime. So he spread his net wider and started going through the other patrons, one by one, all fifty-three of them.

It was grueling work, especially since he was working the day shift in Homicide. Most of the time, he came to work close to exhaustion. His eyes went hollow and he lost weight to the point where his clothes hung limp and defeated on his big frame. The other cops noticed, but said nothing. He was their friend and he was hurting and they knew why. People who had once looked to Paris as an alpha figure now looked elsewhere as the leader in him retreated deep into shadows.

After many months, he had ground his way through everyone who was traceable to the restaurant that night. Along the way, he had built a profile of the person he was looking for, a psychopath, a criminal first cousin to the serial killer. Unfortunately, no one on his list fit the bill. But he had confidence in his profile. He'd built it with great care and skill that combined his own experience with extensive research. And if he was right, the monster would inevitably strike again.

And the monster did just that.

At the end of month fourteen, a Chinese restaurant on Capitol Hill was the site of an outbreak food poisoning. *E. coli.* The same strain that killed Ginny. Seventeen people were infected. All survived.

Paris was there the same evening, talking to all the help. This time, he drew a complete blank: nobody had seen anything unusual. No one even remembered a male dining alone. The only thing he succeeded in doing was aggravating the public health people, who promptly contacted Carno. And this time, his boss was a lot less sympathetic.

Carno had stood and paced behind his gray metal desk that had dried coffee stains dripping down the front in little brown curtains. "Look, Paris. I know what you're doing. We all know what you're doing. You're looking for a freak, a serial poisoner. I don't buy it, Phil. The DA doesn't buy it. Nobody buys it. The public health people tell me this kind of thing happens all the time. Some bug gets loose. Pops up here. Pops up there. Simple as that. Now here's the deal: There's personal business and there's police business, and you're starting to get them all mixed up. You got to quit. I covered your ass, Phil. I won't cover it again. Hear me?"

"Hear you."

But how could he quit now? His hypothesis had been confirmed by a malicious experiment in the laboratory of crime, and the monster roamed free, feeding like a ravenous glutton on his newest success. Once again, Paris found the restaurant owner more than willing to help, and once again he got his credit card list for the night of the poisoning. He still remembered his excitement as he set out to compare the lists from the two restaurants. A single name on both lists would give him his killer. But it didn't happen. Most likely, the poisoner paid cash.

But by this time, he was getting tired, edging toward a true and final confrontation with the loss of his only love. So now he was running a race against not only the killer, but also against resignation and acceptance. The rage that fueled him was still there, but for the first time, he realized that it was supplied in finite quantities.

And that was when he made an irrevocable error. Exhausted by working the night shift for Ginny and the day shift for Carno, he began to steal police time to search for the poisoner. Not much, just a little—at least at first. But while Paris was a great cop, he made a terrible thief, and soon the scope of his thievery was simply too large to be ignored. He fell hopelessly behind on his caseload.

In retrospect, it could have been a lot worse. Carno took him to lunch instead of confronting him in his office. The old cop seemed genuinely depressed, a man reluctantly pulling the trapdoor lever on the gallows. "Phil, I think you know why we're here. You're in deep shit, my friend. You're a good cop and you're in deep shit," declared Carno as he dunked his French dip into its attendant bowl. "I've thought about it a lot. You can't stay in homicide. Too much chance you'll do some serious damage. But you're lucky. You got friends. A lot of friends. So I cut a deal. You're going over to Burglary and Theft. What do you say?"

"Thanks," replied Phil, who picked idly at a dinner salad.

Carno looked up from his plate and shot a sharp look at Paris. He'd taken it wrong.

"I mean it. Thanks."

Carno seemed satisfied and went back to his sandwich. Paris knew the man was doing him a big favor. Carno could have chopped his head off, had him busted back to patrolman, or made him give a painful accounting of his behavior in a vain attempt to save his job. He did none of these. Instead he'd arranged to tuck Paris in a job where he'd spend most of his time filling out reports on missing boom boxes and cellular phones. During the remainder of lunch, they avoided the subject completely and talked of crooks and crimes long gone by.

Now, Paris brought *Cedar Queen* back into the marina at a slow crawl and expertly nursed the vessel into her slip. As he twisted the key and cut the engine, the silence grew large in the dark wheelhouse. He flipped on a single light, went to the rear deck, grabbed a mooring line, and vaulted over the side onto the dock. He could still make the vault with ease, and he marveled at his strength, which came from nowhere. At his size and age, a lot of men were in full physical retreat, and though he'd done little to stave off the process in himself, he had somehow avoided the consequences. As he finished securing the boat fore and aft, he saw a meteor flash across the summer sky close to the zenith, where the city lights did minimum damage to cosmic clarity. It etched a brilliant crease through the cross of Cygnus and expired as it approached the region of Vulpecula. He paused on the dock for a moment to pay his respects, then looked back at the warm light radiating from the wheelhouse.

He'd stay here tonight.

3

BENNET RIFKIN STOPPED FOR A MOMENT AND LISTENED TO the ocean surf. It was a little angry tonight, hissing and spitting foam up onto the sand below his two-story condominium in La Jolla. Out to sea, the moonless night was sprinkled with the navigation lights of the Third Fleet as it milled on through some massive exercise off the coast of San Diego to the south. A warm breeze shivered the palm fronds next to his deck and shooed him back to work on his laptop computer. He put the earphone back in his right ear and went on reviewing this afternoon's teleconference. On the computer's screen, two windows held video images of middle-aged male executives, and a third displayed a table of financial data. Through the earphone, he could hear one of the executives drone on about potential "channel conflicts" in some remote marketing plan from an obscure corner of Uni's Uni-verse, the global electronic domain that defined the corporation's constantly shifting structure.

In moments like these, Bennet's mind sometimes wandered and dwelled on the paradox that he was nowhere yet everywhere.

To the casual observer, Uni presented all the trappings of a typical large business organization. It maintained a fleet of skyscrapers scattered around the world, with long runs of polished metal and smoked glass thrusting up out of the planet's major commercial centers. Inside, energetic crowds of stylishly attired executives strode about over designer carpets and clustered in glassed-in conference rooms to forge nodes of consensus on pending deals. In more remote locations, the Uni logo was tastefully applied to countless factories, labs, administrative centers, distribution hubs, and transport vehicles the world over.

But a closer examination revealed that Uni was a completely novel entity, one where physical location and standard business hours were precybernetic artifacts, crippling to those who clung to them. The telecomm links of Uni Corporation were now dense enough and rich enough that they formed a new electronic crust over the entire planetary surface. Spatial-temporal considerations had dissolved into a simmering stew of global interaction that cared not a whit where you were—or even when you were there.

Bennet seldom pondered the true nature of Uni because in the end, it was unknowable. Of course, you could surf the company's on-line museums and get a multimedia cosmology of the company's origins, which were anything but humble. Bennet had always thought it ironic that Uni's gestation had taken place in the old cultural milieu of the "desktop revolution" and "personal empowerment" and other such phenomena that focused on the cultural micro scale and rendered changes at the macro scale relatively invisible—which did nothing to stop them from proceeding with massive force.

It had been Bennet's extremely good fortune to be part of the team that originally brought Uni into being. Early in his career, Bennet's keen analytical instincts had landed him a job in a think tank sponsored by one of the world's largest corporations. He was assigned to a team given the daunting task of assessing the impact of computer technology and telecommunications on business operations, especially the kind that affected huge companies engaged in global commerce. To put this project in perspective, Bennet's team started by examining the historical role of computers in business transactions. Early on, computer systems, even large ones, were run primarily in a "batch mode," which meant they spent considerable time in semihibernation, then in a sudden orgy of information processing, produced a day's worth of data. The companies they served thus marched ahead to the diurnal ticks of these massive data-processing clocks. But it was very much a herky-march and did not represent the fact that in larger corporations, business went on twenty-four hours a day, and that many decisions couldn't wait for the old mainframe computer to finish its daily workout.

Over time, these batch-mode systems were driven to extinction and decomposed into networks of computers immersed in a din of continuous conversation that represented the highly fluid nature of modern business, where product life cycles were now reduced from years to months. The popular term to describe such systems was *mission critical,* a term borrowed from military computers that meant that the computer system never had the luxury of failing. To do so would kill or cripple the body it served, be it a cruise missile or an international bank.

Soon, mission-critical systems were performing magnificently as a technology. In fact, they were performing much better than the corporations they served. It quickly became apparent that the problem was in the way the corporations were organized. In the days of the diurnal data tick, the traditional business organization worked well, with each department laboring all day to prepare one course of the mainframe's nightly data meal.

But with the arrival of mission-critical networks, the departmental model was an unprofitable artifact of another age. Instead, smaller multidisciple teams could ride the corporate networks and grab what they needed in real time to keep the products rolling and the customers happy. The arrangement was much more organic, with the teams functioning like animal cells: each independent, yet contributing to the body as a whole.

After a long and thorough assessment, Bennet's team became convinced that the mission-critical model was the ideal solution—even for the largest of organizations. So why hadn't it been universally applied in multinational companies? To seek an answer, they turned to their own corporate sponsor and conducted a careful investigation of its organization. What they found was not surprising: Throughout the company, technology remained subservient to politics, and the higher you went in the organization, the more dominant this fact became. The major departments and divisions were mini-nations that held their sovereignty dear and weren't about to disassemble for the sake of progress. While top management liked the idea of a streamlined mission-critical model, the fear of internecine warfare and the resulting chaos held them in check.

Most of the people on Bennet's team were both brilliant and young and thought themselves professionally immortal. This gave them the courage to present their final report to the corporation's Executive Operations Committee, which saw it as dangerous and progressive thinking and nearly shut them down. But a few of the top people, including the CEO, were still interested and granted them a reprieve to study solutions to the "political" problem.

Their solution was both bold and radical: Instead of ripping apart an existing corporation—with all its political baggage—to implement a true mission-critical organization, why not do it right? Why not build one entirely from scratch? Why not do it on a global scale? Why not create an entirely new megabeast of a company, one that never slept and always ate?

When they began to seriously analyze this concept, a second benefit quickly became apparent: the classic business goal of minimizing risk through diversification. A survey of the top ten multinational corporations quickly revealed that five of them had little competitive overlap. One was strong in the energy sector, another in electronics, and so on.

Since Bennet's think tank was a quasi-independent operation, they were able to share their highly original concept with their fellow business theoreticians around the world. Before long they were receiving discreet interest from key sections of management in various large companies. Soon after, planners from five of these companies were meeting on an informal basis, along with representatives from four of the world's biggest banks. The more serious the meetings became, the tighter the secrecy and security. Meetings in cosmopolitan hotels gave way to gatherings in secluded resorts, with extensive electronic debugging and background checks.

The final blueprint for Uni was unique in the history of

business organizations. Only the top portion was conventional, a board of directors composed of the chairpersons of each of the five participating companies and the four banks. Beneath this level, the radical nature of the company quickly became apparent. Uni's nervous system was a fantastically complex network of computers connected by metal wires, fiber optics, microwave relays, and satellites. Unlike other companies, which used at least some outside sources to carry their signals, the entire Uni network, from satellites to phone lines, was private.

When the Uni proposal was near ratification, Bennet had to present the concept to various management groups within all of the participating companies and banks. Uni was a highly abstract notion, and he struggled to find a conceptual vehicle that would easily explain it to the uninitiated. Finally, he hit upon the scientific entity known as a fractal, the classic example being a coastline. If viewed from many miles up, a coastline has a characteristic ragged and random look about it. Seen from just a mile up, the details of the pattern may change, but the same ragged and random character remains. Seen from a hundred feet up, the same thing happens again, and so on. At successively smaller scales, the same basic pattern is expressed again and again. Only the supporting details change.

And so it was with Uni. At the top, the observer would see a network of five separate circles, all connected to each other. These circles represented four broad business areas: electronics, manufacturing, energy, and "organics," which represented food, medicine, and agriculture. A fifth circle was called CorpServe, which represented the interface between the board and the business areas.

If one looked inside one of the business circles, the basic network pattern would be repeated again, only with more circles. This time, each circle would represent a former corporation from within one of the multinational founders' corporate families.

At the next level, the number of networked circles would expand dramatically and represent small multidiscipline teams within these companies. Additional circles would represent customers and vendors, who would retain open communication links with the many teams.

Every one of Uni's 1.2 million employees was permanently equipped with some kind of computing device that participated in this amazing network. Billions of messages streamed daily over the network and produced a quarter trillion dollars in revenue every year. To complete a product, make a sale, organize a deal, teams and individuals operated with great autonomy and constantly roamed over the system to excavate the required resources. A person could keep their entire file system in a portable computer and use wireless satellite or cellular links to forge communication channels to any other person or resource throughout the company.

Not everyone fared equally well in the Uni-verse. The lack of straightforward structure was maddening to many: no organizational chart, no "boss" in the classical sense, no lengthy lists of goals and objectives. Each operating team was much like a military platoon cut off behind enemy lines—you relied on your immediate team members for survival and continually improvised your tactics to stay alive. If you were lucky, you became hitched to one of the grand coalitions that rose in real time to exploit some new economic opportunity. If not, your career melted slowly, like ice left out to face the dawn.

Since he'd helped design the Uni-verse, Bennet had an unbeatable head start when it came to competing in it. He quickly engineered a position for himself in the group called CorpServe, where he was given a charter to roam the Universe and look for ways that its various segments could cross-pollinate each other.

Now, at thirty-one, he had already justified himself by forming several business alliances that had yielded exceptional returns. He possessed an uncanny knack for reading the shifting, almost organic nature of Uni's business web and then plunging in to extract an economic winner. The venture that catapulted his career was a deal that integrated a chip fabrication plant in Romania, an optics operation in New Delhi, a software group in Ireland, and an assembly plant in Somalia to produce a infant-monitoring system sold to upscale families in urban markets along the Pacific Rim.

Bennet yawned lazily and shut down the laptop where the two executives were droning on from the teleconference.

Unlike Bennet, they were going nowhere. Their ideas were mediocre, their approach something less than bold. Here in La Jolla, Bennet knew intuitively he had a winner, even though he wasn't sure exactly how. The trick right now was to remain unobtrusive with the people at the Webster Foundation, who had good reason to resent his presence. So far, so good.

The main problem with the Webster Foundation was its immature state of integration into the Uni-verse. Over the years, its sources of funding as a nonprofit organization had all but dried up under moribund management, and it was reeling toward extinction when it came to Uni's attention. At CorpServe, Bennet had carefully reviewed the radical technology the foundation had centered its research on and decided it was a worthy toy for him to play with.

The startled board and management at the Foundation had little choice but to accept Uni's offer. In exchange for a stupendous amount of funding, the Foundation would sign over all rights to the technology it produced. In return, Uni would permit the Foundation to function as a largely autonomous unit, albeit under much stricter security than before. The work at the Foundation was assigned to the high-risk portion of Uni's $25-billion annual research and development budget, with Bennet and a small staff appointed as the company's representatives inside the Foundation. Bennet's instructions to his staff were explicit: look but don't touch. At least for now.

This last thought brought a little burp of chuckle to Bennet as he gazed out to sea. With Elaine, he had immediately violated his own command, although the damage seemed to be fairly well contained. They kept a goodly distance at work, and she seldom came over here until later in the evening.

Tonight was a little different. She'd shown up early so she could use his new multiprocessor computer for that virtual-surgery thing she did every month.

Bennet sniffed the sea as he put down the laptop and felt a comfortable fog of lust settle over him. Did she think he was an asshole? Probably. Although Uni's approach was low-key and hands-off at the Foundation, everyone intrinsically understood he was the conqueror and they the vanquished. On a symbolic level, this made her part of the spoils of war, and perhaps this excited her. He wasn't sure. Anyway, it didn't seem to get in the way of their vigorous couplings, so who cared?

Bennet got up and ambled off the deck into the house to the foot of the stairs.

"Elaine?"

No answer. Bennet knew she probably had the VR helmet on and couldn't hear any outside sounds. Oh, well. Best to let her finish slicing up some binary patient. People abruptly yanked out of VR tended to be quite irritated about it. And irritated people were seldom fuckable people, Bennet had learned.

Dr. Elaine Wilkes signed off from the Virtual Surgery Center and slumped in her chair. She knew Bennet was upstairs and would soon be on the prowl, but she was hardly in the mood. She had never been in an operation before where they lost a patient, and even though it was all virtual, the shock of sudden death seemed very real. A bright chill had descended over the operating room as all the displays flatlined, and poor Dr. Muldane had backed away from the table in horror. She'd been in on several other surgeries where David was on the team and always enjoyed working with him. He seemed careful and methodical in his approach, and the last thing he deserved was to blow something like this—especially since there was now a statistical correlation between personal success rates in virtual and real surgery. Luckily, it wouldn't hurt him because he was in public health somewhere. Was it Seattle? She wasn't sure. Anyway, she'd find out later and send him an E-mail to get his spirits back up.

"Elaine?" Bennet's voice stalked her down the stairway.

"Yeah?"

"Anything wrong?"

Goddamnit! The guy had great antennae when it came to mood shifts. No denying it.

"Yeah."

"What is it?"

"We lost a patient tonight."

4 5

"Oh yeah? Who was in charge?" Bennet asked as he padded down the stairs and sprawled on the couch.

"Not me. A guy named Muldane. From Seattle, I think."

"Bad break for him, huh?"

Elaine felt a growl of disgust. The new, improved, empathic Bennet! He was like a Vegas comic working a roomful of rubes. And she was one of them.

"Yeah. Bad break for me, too. We do this as a team, you know."

"Look, uh, maybe you need a little space to work this out. Don't worry about me. I've got plenty to do."

Bennet came off his back with feline grace, using the power of his muscular belly to swing to a sitting position. The peach skin, the almond eyes, and the thick black hair formed an unholy alliance that nearly pierced her gloom. But not quite.

"Are you sure?" *I am.*

"Yeah. I'll be fine." Bennet sprang to his feet, padded silently across the Persian carpet, put his hands on her shoulders, and kissed her on the nape of the neck. "Is there anything I can do?"

Yes, there is. You can tell me to fuck off and never come back.

"Not really." Elaine gave his hands a perfunctory pat, then removed them so she could get up and grab her purse. "I'll be in touch tomorrow."

"Hey," said Bennet as she reached the door and stopped to look back. "It was virtual, right?"

"Of course it was."

"Just keep remembering that, okay? Nobody's dead. You're here. They're there. It's over."

"Yes," sighed Elaine as she turned to go, "it's over."

On the way home, she opened the sunroof on her Saab and the warm marine breeze aimlessly combed her hair. Bennet was clever, yet so was she. His manipulations were utterly transparent to her, yet almost totally disarming. Why?

The streetlights blooped by in a cartoon parade as she worked and turned the answer, trying to round off the offending edges. But they stayed sharp and annoying.

Because, in fact, Bennet was no more than a template, one of many Bennets by different names that sprawled over the last decade. Now, at thirty-one, she had the composite Bennet well articulated. Brash, bright, hyperconfident, self-involved, pursued by a glittering string of women, each a finely cut crystal that quickly dissolved when she became immersed in the inevitable affair.

Yet, I'm honored just to be in the line-up. All the detachment, all the cool assessments, vaporized when one of the Bennet objects turned to her with full attention. He might be across the room at a party or at a conference or on the beach. He might be talking to another woman, a fine-tuned female engine that made her feel like a sputtering wreck. But then he would turn from this woman and launch a smile and a twinkle that would send Elaine soaring. Elaine the pilot would try to keep Elaine the emotional missile from climbing too fast, but the controls were limp and useless.

And after the inevitable crash, Elaine the investigating committee would always reach the same conclusion. It seemed the Bennet object was supplying a missing component, albeit a defective one, that completed her identity. The doctor, the nerd, the scientist in her, grappled feverishly with the lover, the sensualist—and won. And the magnitude of the lover's defeat was measured by the ultimate absurdity of the Bennet objects. They were not necessary. She often picked up interesting broadcasts from any number of men in her social proximity. Good men, kind men, funny men. But under the mysterious operating conditions of courtship, the critical component always failed and left her both disappointed and empty.

She sighed as she turned up the hill to her apartment. Things could be worse. At the Foundation, they were on the verge of a real breakthrough, thanks to the infusion of money from Uni. So far, the company seemed content to grant them almost complete autonomy, although she and everyone else kept waiting for the bomb to drop. It was absorbing work, and the longer she was in it, the less regret she had about taking the research path instead of practicing. The world had now come out of a pleasant fifty-year slumber, when infectious diseases seemed flat on their backs, and awakened to find them making an insidious comeback. So

epidemiology, her field, was once again pushing to the forefront of medicine.

Besides, places like the Virtual Surgery Center let her
practice medicine in a safe and strangely satisfying way. Although the business tonight with the botched operation by
Dr. Muldane was definitely disturbing. Poor guy. He seemed
extremely distressed, but then again, so was she. It was all
just a little too real.

4

Iquitos, Peru

THE LITTLE COLONY IN THE RAT'S THROAT LIVED A COMFORT-
able, stable life. Countless millennia of warfare in other
times with other rats had taught them how to get along in
a hostile world filled with various agents from the immune
system: the macrophages, the lymphocytes, the antibodies.

The key to success was to avoid a ruckus, to stay in the
immediate neighborhood and not exhibit any great territo-
rial ambitions. Of course, not all the bacteria in the colony
adhered to this policy, and those that didn't were promptly
eliminated. But at least some of the *Streptobacillus moniliformis* lived out their lives quite comfortably on the gently
corrugated contours of the throat tissue.

But lately, there was trouble in the colony. A new political
party had emerged, bent on restoring the greatness of the
species, dedicated to waging a seemingly suicidal war against
the vast armies of immunity. And for no good reason.

Why?

The rat peered out the end of its short tunnel with the
same nasty wisdom that had guided its ancestors for aeons
and served them so well. It sniffed the hot, damp air and
felt it cooling in the darkness. Its ears picked up the background of jungle sound as it washed over the dump site and
listened intently to the audio foreground, searching for that

odd sound, that wrong sound, the one that might be attached to something that would kill you and eat you.

But there was no such sound right now, so the rat poked its head out of the hole in the red laterite soil of the Peruvian jungle. It ignored the growing soreness in its throat to concentrate on the timeless imperative of eating. A few sniffs sampled the still air of the dump and identified some likely targets amidst a fantastic panorama of odors. Rotting paper, dead motor oil, decaying fabric, melting paraffin, spent perfume, and a hundred other scents rolled over the rat's nose, introduced themselves, and were rejected purely for business reasons. The commerce of consumption was all that mattered.

Directly overhead, the Southern Cross tattooed the dark sky framed by the round clearing where the makers of the dump had once beat back the jungle canopy. To the north, a faint skyglow frosted the stars with light from the city of Iquitos on the upper reaches of the Amazon River. To the south lay a million years of blackness. Here the jungle still had its way.

Although the rat did not care, the dump would lose. The thick green forest would choke, drown, smother, and ferment it into submission. In its early days, the dump had been a depository for a construction company, which condemned large, spent pieces of machinery and industrial equipment to this spot. But since the site was just off the main road, and visible from it, the dump soon became a target of opportunity for anyone with a truck and a load of trash. Now, the spare skeletons of old bedsprings rested atop rusting engine blocks and control panels.

The rat caught a whiff of something promising, something small and recently dead. It inched its way out of its tunnel and waddled slowly in the direction of the smell. The journey was requiring far more effort than usual because the rat was not well. The swelling and redness in its throat were accelerating, and its body temperature was rising into fever.

In the rat's pharynx, a silent civil war was raging and the old guard losing.

Outwardly, it was impossible to distinguish between opposing forces. Both camps were composed of strep bacteria assembled in serial chains, like a string of wieners. Even inside, the differences were subtle. The interior of all bacterial cells house primitive, undeveloped chemical economies. Absent is the vast diversification and specialization found in animal cells, with their legions of shops, factories, and services. Gone also is the nucleus, the corporate headquarters where all of management reside in the genetic tangle of DNA, which is divided into chromosomes, the administrative departments that enforce genetic policy.

Instead, the bacteria run a primitive import/export business managed by a single string of DNA that floats free in the nucleoid region in the bacterial center. Little renegade loops of DNA, called plasmids, also float about and mostly handle unusual contingencies, like creating chemical worker machines that expel poisons.

Recently, in some of the strep, a strange and unexpected agent had gained chemical entry to their interiors. It had come from the big world, the impossibly huge expanse outside the rat, where an old electrical transformer rested above the rat's tunnel. The transformer was well into the terminal reds and browns of advanced rust, which had penetrated its metal skin and wormed on through to the inner layers, one of which contained a chemical called polychlorinated biphenyl, known globally by the unpleasant acronym of PCB.

The PCB had oozed out into the soil, down into the rat's little hidey-hole, then on into the rat itself.

Eventually, the PCB had found its way to the interior of the *Streptobacillus moniliformis*. Here it insinuated itself into management by inserting new bits of instructions into the bacterial DNA. However, in all but one case, these foreign suggestions to management were either ridiculous or fatal.

But the one case turned out to be very special.

This particular piece of chemical counsel allowed for a vigorous expansion of the import/export trade and dramatic growth. The bacteria that harbored it prospered and was soon ready to pass on the good news by duplicating itself. The new management style was passed along as one became two, then two became four, and so on.

And now, the radicals pushed into the majority of the colony in the rat's throat. It was a time of great upheaval, of death and glory. The rat's immune system, like a large, slumbering bureaucracy, had moved slowly against the disturbance in the colony as long as it stayed contained. But now the radicals were trying to vigorously expand their frontiers, and the immune system responded with a massive mobilization. Antibodies tore through the community and killed millions—just as the colony's elders had feared.

But the radicals saw it as their finest moment, even though they perished right alongside the elders. As the battle raged, they were taking large amounts of territory and flexing their muscle in a way never thought possible. Besides, the war would weed out the weak, the timid, and leave only the toughest of the tough to carry on.

The fever was now blunting the rat's senses, and it stopped on a soggy piece of cardboard to reorient itself. The scent of the edible carcass was now lost in the background, and no other promising smells presented themselves. The rat turned and shuffled back toward its small tunnel under the transformer.

The war in the rat's throat would soon spread to other parts of its body and eventually kill it. Then the new race of hyperaggressive microbe warriors would die along with their host, and the damage would be contained.

At least, that's what would usually happen. But not always.

5

"I'M DISAPPOINTED, BILLY. I FEEL USED."

Barney Cox pushed off from the gray metal desk, and his swivel chair rolled in a tiny thunder across the linoleum floor. It coasted to a halt right in front of the crummy little green table with the double-decker coffeemaker and the open box from Dunkin' Donuts. He fished out a big glazed and looked sympathetically at Billy.

"Sorry. Mind if I eat? It's been a busy morning."

Billy, a fellow inmate in the King County Jail, nodded in agreement. It was all he could do. He sat in a second swivel chair with his hands bound behind his back by a dozen wraps of silver duct tape. His feet were bound to the chair legs in a similar manner, and he was nearly choking on the washrag duct-taped into his mouth.

Barney took a bite of doughnut and watched Billy's bulging blue eyes as he chewed and swallowed.

"Anyway, like I was saying, I feel used. And it's a hurtful feeling, Billy, a hurtful feeling. I would hope that in your life, you never have to endure a hurt such as this. Now, you and I both know there's going to be some hurt coming your way, and when it comes, and you're in the middle of it, I want you to remember that it can never compare with the hurt I feel right now."

Barney heard the sudden change in Billy's respiration as the air roared in and out of the prisoner's nostrils in sudden acceleration.

"Problem is, Billy, you nearly queered a couple of months of righteous labor on my part. And I think you'll agree that I've worked really hard to make this a better place for people like you. Haven't I?"

Billy bobbed his head in wild agreement, tears flowing from his eyes.

"So it's not just me you hurt, Billy. It's *everybody*."

Barney stopped to take another bite of the doughnut.

"If they'd stopped this thing, Billy, a lot of people would have died. Real slow. And nobody would have cared. That's the sad thing, Billy. Nobody would've cared. And that's why your little urge to talk was such an ugly thing. I hope you know that now."

As Billy nodded vigorously through his tears, the phone on the desk rang. Barney rolled back to the desk and grabbed the receiver.

"Cox, here. As a matter of fact, that's *all* we got in here." His laughter exploded into the receiver. "Just a bunch of cocks. Get it?"

"You're a funny man, Mr. Cox," came the even voice over the phone. "A very funny man. At least that's what they tell me. Is it true?"

"I'm sorry. I don't believe I got your name."

"Paris, Barney. Lt. Philip Paris."

"Ah, a *policeman!* Well, Phil, let me start by assuring you that the three officers up here are in no way being harmed. I want to do this thing in good faith."

"I hear you're a man of your word, Barney. So I'm going to trust you on that."

"Have you had a chance to look into the matters I put forth in the memo?"

"I have."

"I'd like to conduct all our business over the phone, but there's certain sensitive issues that shouldn't be exposed to recording devices. Do you agree?"

"Will you personally guarantee my safety if I come in?"

"Yes, I will."

"I'm also going to bring a representative from the health department."

"By all means. When can we expect you?"

"The health guy should be here any minute. I'll let you know."

"Good. See you then."

Barney dropped the phone into the cradle. He ate the last chunk of doughnut, then scanned the desktop and tabletop with a disappointed look.

"No napkins, Billy. Can you believe it? No wonder they got problems in here."

As Barney sucked his fingers clean, he mentally reviewed the framework for his upcoming negotiation with Lt. Philip Paris of the Seattle Police Department. The core of his case came down to two dreadful letters: TB. Until the nineties, tuberculosis had drifted out of public perception in the industrialized world. In some circles, it was even romanticized as the dreamy dispatcher of the suffering artists of ages gone by. Nevertheless, it still served faithfully as the angel of death throughout the rest of the world and regularly dispatched nearly 3 million souls every year.

More importantly to Barney, it was now regularly dispatching souls from the King County Jail. He'd gotten his first hint of this from casual observations of the prison population. Too many men had "chest colds" that never went away. At night, you could hear the ominous symphony of hacking and barking bouncing off the cement walls in the dark. When their fatigue and fever got too bad to write off as a simple virus, they were removed from the general jail population, never to return.

So Barney started doing a little research and uncovered an alarming picture. First of all, by the 1990s, over a third of the world carried the TB bug, a highly resilient little bacteria called, not surprisingly, *M. tuberculosis*. This microscopic bomb lodged deeply in the lungs of its recipients, waiting for the right circumstances to explode into a full-blown disease. And in one in ten, this is exactly what happened—with the germs fanning out on all fronts to turn the lungs into a kind of gray soup. Sometimes it even overran the pulmonary barricades and stormed into the bones, the lymph nodes, and the genitals.

More importantly to Barney was the way TB spreads. When a victim becomes overwhelmed by the bacterial onslaught, a portion of the lung dies and produces a miniature corpse inside the living body. The surrounding lung tissue panics and turns the corpse into a liquid, a putrid broth swarming with TB germs, maybe a billion in a single teaspoon. The victim's lungs fight back by launching a paroxysm of coughing that both atomizes this liquid and expels it into the air, where it rides the winds of chance. In well-ventilated and sparsely populated environments, the germs quickly disperse to the point where infection is highly unlikely. But in confined areas with marginal ventilation, the odds turn very ugly, very quickly.

In other words, in places like jails.

David Muldane followed the young police sergeant as they threaded their way through the throng of officers on the upper floor of the County Courthouse. It looked like a staging area for a major military campaign. Assault rifles, Kevlar vests, helmets, Glock side arms, and combat boots all swam around in an edgy swamp of adrenaline.

So, what the hell am I doing here? David asked himself. Perhaps they wanted a little advice on precautions during food handling. Nope. Not likely.

Five minutes ago, he had been comfortably hunched over his computer in his cubicle in the Seattle/King County Department of Public Health, when young sergeant what's his name had materialized.

"David Muldane?" the sergeant had queried. He looked uncomfortable with all his combat gear on in the middle of this completely benign bureaucracy.

"That's me," responded David, wondering if maybe he had crossed some criminal boundary with his bogus operation at the Virtual Surgery Center last night.

"You've been assigned to a negotiating team. I need you to accompany me immediately."

"Negotiate? Negotiate what? More disk space? Bigger RAM allocations?"

"There's been an incident at the jail," explained the sergeant mechanically. "A negotiating team is being assembled to intervene. The director of public health has authorized your participation."

"A generous fellow," muttered David as he pulled on his jacket. He was sure this went way beyond the bounds of his job description. He was a computer specialist, a manager of information flow. The closest he got to law enforcement was the periodic analysis of citations against eating establishments for food-handling violations. Hardly the stuff of high prison drama.

But here he was, following the sergeant through the speculative buzz of the assembled officers. Now they approached the entrance of an aerial tunnel that ran from the upper floor of the courthouse building and over the administration building to the eighth floor of the jail structure and its twelve hundred inmates. When they reached the security post at the tunnel's entrance, he saw a tall man in a worn suit look up at them, then smile directly at David.

Somehow, he already knew it must be Paris. Tall and slightly stooped, Paris had a big face with a hawk's nose and puffy hemispheres under each of his blue eyes. His receding gray hair differed only a shade or two from his pale skin, and the mouth turned easily into a slightly skewed smile.

"Lieutenant Paris, this is Dave Muldane from public health," the sergeant was saying.

Paris thrust out a big hand and shook David's. "Wish we could've given you time to prepare, but as you can see, it's a little late in the game." Paris pointed with a twist of his hand to the combat-ready officers.

"Sorry, I don't know what's going on," replied David.

A flash of wry humor lit Paris's eyes. "Well, neither do I. My usual line of work is stolen property. But a while back I was selected for hostage-negotiation school, and one thing led to another, and here I am and here you are. Funny world, isn't it?"

"Maybe funny to you, but not me. What's happening here?"

"Well, it appears there's been a temporary change in management up in the jail."

"You mean a riot? Hostages? That kind of thing?"

"I suppose you could look at it that way. But so far, nobody's been hurt, and nobody's going to, either. That's where you come in."

"Me?"

Paris looked at the sergeant and the two other officers standing beside him. "Would you excuse us for a minute?" The men backed off and Paris rested a friendly hand on David's shoulder. "I got a quick briefing on the man who organized this thing inside the jail. Barney Cox. An extremely clever fellow. He's caught the county in a bit of a bind. Seems that all prisoners are supposed to be screened for TB, then isolated if they have it. Also seems that the city and county have been a little sloppy about this. There appears to be quite a few people up there coughing their brains out."

"You checked their records?"

"The records look great. That's the problem. They shouldn't. And Barney knows it."

"So, what's the deal?"

"Barney wants the entire jail evacuated until the ventilation can be upgraded. He also wants total amnesty for himself and what you might call his 'staff.' "

"And in exchange?"

"He'll forget about the problem with the records."

David paused and looked at the floor. He didn't like where this was going. He looked back up at Paris, who was studying him intently. "Lieutenant, let's not forget what I do for a living. I'm in public health. If there's a health threat here, I have an obligation to act on it."

Paris's serious face collapsed into a skewed smile. "I said *Barney* would forget about the problem with the records. I didn't say *I* would forget about it. You've got my word we'll follow through."

David sighed. "Okay. But tell me this: What does this Barney guy get out of it? I mean personally?"

"Simple. Power. He gets power. There's over a thousand prisoners over there. Every one of them will know that Barney backed down City Hall—from inside the slammer. It won't matter if it never makes it to the newspapers. They'll know exactly what happened. And they'll tell their friends."

"So what's the negotiating plan?"

"Nothing to it. We meet his demand."

"So why do you need me?"

"I need you to witness the bargain as a public health official. Since you're the guy that manages the records, you're the perfect candidate. Barney's too sly to take the word of a cop without a third party present. Now, before we go up, there's one thing I need to know. Maybe you can help me."

"What's that?"

Paris's face clouded. "He's got three guards as hostages. They haven't been hurt—at least not directly."

"Directly?"

"Each of them is now in a cell with a prisoner who appears to have advanced TB. Obviously a pressure tactic. So what I want to know is, how long can they be in that situation before they're infected?"

"There's no absolute answer to that. It's a matter of probability. On one hand, they could be in there five minutes and the bug could find a happy home in their pulmonary systems. However, it's highly unlikely. On the other, they could be in there for years and stay clean—also highly unlikely. Your answer is floating around somewhere in between."

Paris shrugged. "Okay. You ready?"

Barney hung up the phone and turned to Billy. "They're on their way over, Billy. And you don't look like the kind of guy who's very good with company."

Barney rose from his chair, ambled over, and crouched down so he was eye level with Billy's gagged and tearstained face. "I'm going to excuse you now, Billy. You're socially disadvantaged, and that just won't do under the circumstances. Now, I don't want you to forget that I'm really hurt by what you did. And sometime, after all this blows over, we'll find some special ways we can pay the hurt back."

He rose and wheeled Billy to an open door and slung him and the swivel chair down the hall, where two men appeared out of an open cell to intercept Billy in the hallway. Then Barney returned to the security post at the jail end of the tunnel and sank back into the desk chair. On the desk, he noticed a pair of Styrofoam dice slung over the extension of the desk lamp, the same kind of dice people once draped over their rearview mirrors for decorative purposes.

People like Jerome.

Even now, twenty years later, Barney could still see the dice bounce in sympathy as Jerome's old pickup loped over the ruts in an old logging road east of Grants Pass, Oregon. And although the sky was on the verge of drizzle, Barney was happy to the brim because Jerome was taking him deer hunting. Right behind Barney in the pickup cab, a 30.06 bolt-action Sears rifle with a cheap scope rested comfortably in the gun rack, awaiting its call to duty. To Barney's left, a couple of six-packs of half-quart Buds partitioned the seat between him and Jerome.

"How soon before we see some deer?" asked Barney in his choirboy, ten-year-old voice.

"No tellin', squirt," replied Jerome as he cracked his first half-quart of Bud. "Don't you worry 'bout it. Just do what I say."

At the first fizz of the beer's pop-top, Barney felt his hopes dissolve into the foam. He knew the drill. One can and Jerome became philosophical: "I'm not your real dad, but I'm about the best deal you're going to find, bucko . . ." Two cans and he was well on the way to ugly. And with good reason. Jerome *was* ugly, both literally and figuratively. An oily brown waterfall of hair tumbled from his beat-up cap and clumped into greasy strands, with pale splotches of neck skin poking through. Recessed eyes peered out of sockets fringed with a pale yellow corona. Stingy little lips creased in a full-time scowl.

Three cans and Jerome started hitting. Nasty little backhand swings that stung the cheek and bloodied the nose.

And lately the hitting was worse because Jerome had lost yet another job because "those fuckheads got no respect for people like me."

But then, when it was almost unbearable, when his mom was getting ready to move them out, a clean and sober Jerome announced that he was taking Barney hunting. They even went out for Chinese that night, and Jerome regaled them with tales of past hunting expeditions. Barney was elated.

But not now, not as the pickup plunged to a halt on the shoulder of a road winding through a patch of second-growth Douglas fir. Jerome stubbed out a Marlboro in the ashtray and drained the dregs of the second can of Bud.

"You know what, chief?" mumbled Jerome as they got out and he reached back in to lift the rifle off the rack. "Seems like every day, I get a little less respect. Seems like I can't get nobody to see it my way."

Barney was worried in the extreme. Lately, Jerome had become obsessed with this "respect" business, and it always ended badly when he started talking about it.

"What about you?" asked Jerome as he plucked a bullet from a box in his shirt pocket and chambered it in the rifle without looking up. "You respect me?"

"Sure I do, Jerome," replied Barney shakily.

"Know what I think?" offered Jerome as he looked up at Barney through those yellow-tinged sockets and slammed the bolt shut. "I think you're a lyin' sack of shit. That's what I think. And up here, that's all that matters. But I tell you what, *I* got respect. For you. Even though you ain't got it for *me*. That's why I'm gonna give ya a head start. Just like they do in the movies."

"Come on, Jerome," pleaded Barney. "This is just too dangerous. Let's go home."

Jerome's face folded into a horrible grin as he raised the rifle and squeezed off a shot about a yard wide of Barney. The explosive report made Barney's ears ring, and his heart raced wildly. Now he knew the truth. Jerome was further out there than ever. The announcement of the trip, the night out for dinner, were just some kind of holding action while the boilers inside Jerome were stoked up to full fury.

Barney darted behind the pickup and crashed downhill

into the woods, too scared to cry. He heard another shot, but it hit nothing in his vicinity. He leaped over a fallen tree and crouched down behind it for cover as yet another shot punched through the woods. As long as he could hear the report of the rifle in the distance, he knew Jerome wasn't close enough to spot him.

And as he huddled, the revelation came to him. There was no justice, not like what they said in school. There was no safety. There were only the rules that men made for themselves. Like the rules Jerome was improvising right now.

And if he was going to survive, it wasn't through the police or the welfare people or the school counselors. It was by devising his own set of rules. A set that would never, ever let anything like this happen to him again.

Eventually, Jerome started yelling to Barney that it was all a joke, that it was okay to come out. Barney carefully circled around to where he could see Jerome and observed the rifle was no longer in his hands. After the longest time, he approached close enough to spot the rifle back in its rack in the cab, and the worried look on Jerome's face as the booze wore off.

All the way home, Jerome lied mightily about how it was all just a game, and that there were just blanks in the rifle, just blanks. But Barney didn't hear him because Barney was hard at work devising his own set of rules, a set that would last him a lifetime.

And it wasn't long before he got to apply them.

Barney had observed that although Jerome was large to a ten-year-old, he was a slight and spindly person in the world of grown-up men. Especially compared to their nearest neighbor, Everett, who lived with his wife in a house trailer nestled in a clump of oaks about a hundred yards up the valley. Everett's thick, sinewy arms seethed with a kind of power that Barney realized could be harnessed, just like you tame wild rapids by building a dam.

Barney also knew a big and bad thing had happened because of Everett's wife up there in the trailer. He had heard his mom and one of the other waitresses talk about it one night while they counted their tickets. Some man had been in the trailer with Everett's wife, and that made Everett very mad, and he hurt the man somehow, although the women were not very explicit about this part.

So one Saturday a few weeks after the horrible hunting incident, Barney was up the damp, graveled road when he saw Everett out working on his Grand Prix.

"Watcha want, Barney?" asked Everett from under the hood.

"Nuthin'."

"Then why ya here?"

"Just want to watch."

Everett made no reply, a signal it was okay to stay if Barney didn't get in the way.

"Does your wife make honey?"

"What?" Everett's head ducked from under the hood.

"Does your wife make honey?"

"Now why you wanna know a thing like that?"

"Well, Jerome borrowed some from her a while back."

Everett's eyes flared red. The muscles on his neck contracted into a topography of pure hate. He grabbed Barney's arms and leaned in close. "Now you tell me exactly what happened. And don't try to bullshit me, or you'll never bullshit again. Understand?"

"Yeah. Well, I came home from school and nobody was home. But then I looked out the window and saw Jerome come out of your trailer. When he got home, I asked him what he was doing, and he laughed and said he'd borrowed a little honey from up the road. That's all."

"Did he know you saw him coming out of the trailer?"

"Nope. Don't think so."

Everett's hands dug deep into Barney's small biceps. "Look, me and you never had this talk. You understand?"

"Yeah, I understand."

"I hope to God you do, boy. I hope to God."

Of course, the details of the murder were never revealed to someone Barney's age. He only knew that they found Jerome in a nearby field, but never learned that Jerome bled to death from castration. Even if Barney had, it wouldn't have mattered, because Barney was enveloped in the thrill of self-discovery. Jerome was gone. Just like that. Jerome, who was bigger, older, meaner, an omnipotent giant from the world of grown-ups. Just a few words, that's all it took.

Of course, it wouldn't always be this easy, but it would always be this exciting. Even now, Barney knew that.

From the tunnel, Barney heard the mechanical rumble of the security doors signal the arrival of Paris and friend.

"Come on in," he yelled cheerfully. "Door's always open." In fact, the heavy steel security door really was open, with the key still inserted.

"Lieutenant Paris! Always a pleasure," gushed Barney as Paris and David walked cautiously into the small office. "Sorry, I don't have a better meeting space, but you know how it is."

"Yes, Barney, we do know how it is," replied Paris. "This is David Muldane from the King County Public Health Department."

Barney came out of his chair with a quickness that startled David and crossed the room to shake his hand. "Mr. Muldane, pleased to meet you."

David was completely disarmed by the dry, firm handshake, and the look of complete sincerity. He'd expected someone with more rodentlike affectations: darting eyes, gaunt cheeks, nervous twitches. Instead, here was this well-groomed man in his late forties who looked like a chief executive officer, with his resolute jaw, clear gray eyes, and slightly receding hairline. Even though he was a prisoner in a big jam, he radiated a perverse kind of authority.

Barney left Paris and Muldane standing by the door and sat on the desk, so he wouldn't negotiate from a lower altitude than his opponents. "Can I assume that Mr. Muldane is familiar with my findings about the prisoners' health?"

"I briefed him on the way up," answered Paris, who leaned back against the wall and propped one foot against it in a casual pose. "Now what do we have to do to settle this thing, Barney?" He folded his arms on his chest.

"Well, to begin with, you've got to set the record straight, so to speak. I want everybody up here to be retested for TB, myself included. Anybody that's got it goes out of here—for good." Barney turned to David. "Can you guarantee that, Mr. Muldane?"

David looked to Paris, who nodded. "I guess we can."

"Then I want amnesty for everybody in here, myself

included. You tell the press it was just a minor incident involving a few prisoners. You launch your obligatory investigation, but it eventually peters out. In return, nobody in here says boo to the press about the records."

"I think we might arrange something like that," said Paris. "How long?"

"Couple of hours." Paris shifted his weight back onto both feet. "You've got my word on it. We take care of the health problems. You and your friends stroll on back to your cells. Okay?"

"Almost," said Barney as he stood up from the desk. "I just want you to answer a single question, Lieutenant."

"What's that?"

"Do you think I've done a bad thing here? Do you really?"

Paris's face set hard as granite. "Based on your record, Mr. Cox, I don't think you've ever done anything else."

Barney broke from Paris's stare and wheeled on David. "And what about you, Mr. Muldane, what do you think?"

"I'm . . . not sure," answered David, taken by surprise. How could this man, this petty criminal, make him feel so uncomfortable?

"Let me put it another way, Mr. Muldane. If I develop an active case of TB from being here, can you fix me? Can you make it go away? Can you make me better?"

"Not necessarily."

"In fact, Mr. Muldane, it's highly unlikely. In fact, I would be almost as good as dead. You might want to classify me as an ambulatory corpse, don't you think?"

It was true. Originally, a trio of drugs called isoniazid, rifampicin, and pyrazinamide were used to kill the TB germ. But like old soldiers with good hearts in failing bodies, they were gradually beaten back by aggressive new strains of TB, some of which took shelter in the shattered immune environments of AIDS patients. First one drug then another failed to beat back the onslaught. By the 1990s, new and disturbing strains of TB emerged that were resistant to at least two drugs in the trio. It was soon found that the fatality rates in these cases were as high as if there had been no treatment at all, which meant 40 to 60 percent of the victims gasped to death while their doctors stood by helplessly. And now these new strains had found their way almost everywhere.

"Barney," interrupted Paris, "you've got a deal. We're outta here." He turned to David. "Let's go."

As they walked back to the courthouse through the tunnel, Paris chuckled as the doors shut. "He had you going, didn't he?"

"Well, I wouldn't say . . ."

"Don't worry. You'll get over it." Paris scratched his thinning hair. "He's a brilliant man. You can't teach someone political instincts like that. Unfortunately, when gifts like that fall to earth, you never know where they're going to land."

"What's he in for?"

"Conspiracy to commit murder. First time the DA's ever been able to nail him. But that's not the real problem."

"Then what is?"

"Wherever Barney goes and whatever Barney does, bad thing happen. Very bad things. I've been a cop a long time, and I'm here to tell you there's bad and then there's evil. And Barney's evil. Don't let this business here fool you. A lot of people inside are going to owe their lives to him, but you can bet that Barney keeps a very careful set of books when it comes to favors. He's way ahead on this deal."

The security doors opened and they faced an expectant crowd of armed officers.

"It's done," announced Paris. "Send up a team to get the guards. And play it cool. We don't want any more trouble than we've already got. Mr. Cox and company are voluntarily returning to their cells."

After some additional consultation, Paris turned to David. "I'm getting hungry. Care for a little lunch? It's on me."

David didn't understand how the man could be hungry, but he agreed. After all, this was the most interesting morning he'd ever spent in the service of the city/county Public Health Department.

"You did good up there, Mr. Muldane, which is to say you did nothing. But now the ball's coming your way." Philip Paris stirred a little vortex of dairy mix into his coffee and looked out the window of Lowells into the blue expanse of Puget Sound as the busboy took away the remains of their lunch. "I want your personal assurance you'll find out how those records got screwed up and fix the problem. Can I count on you?"

"Yeah, you can count on me." David kicked himself inwardly. He'd just made a big-time professional commitment without pausing to consider the consequences. There was something about this Paris guy, some kind of propulsive force that made him hard to resist.

"Good. Now, there's one other thing."

"I don't think—"

"Don't worry. We're through with Barney and the jail and all that. This is a separate matter entirely—although it does involve public health."

"So, what is it?"

Paris stopped and sipped his coffee. Outside, a big double-decker ferry churned its way toward Vashon Island.

"I'm sort of a persona non grata over in your neck of the woods. I had a difference of opinion with some of your people over a couple of food-poisoning incidents. They considered them coincidental. I considered them criminal. Still do."

"What do you mean, 'criminal'?"

Paris took another sip of coffee. "A lot of cops have an unsolved case that sort of turns into a hobby. People always expect it's something big and sensational, like the Green River killer."

David nodded. Paris was referring to a notorious serial-killer case where a single person was believed to have murdered forty-nine victims, mostly prostitutes, over a period of nineteen months. Eventually, the killings tapered off to nothing, and the killer was never apprehended.

"Well, it's not always like that. Not with me, anyway," confessed Paris. "It's more challenging to find something that's damn near invisible, something you've got to look twice to even notice a connection."

"Like?"

"Long time ago, I used to work in arson. Got real interested in pyromania. Not just as a crime, but as a psychological state of mind. Fascinating business. It turns out there are several flavors of arsonist. The scariest are the psychopathic type. They set fires as kids or teenagers, then go on to greater things, like rape and murder. For them, I guess you could think of fires as a form of entertainment. They simply don't see anything wrong with it. But there's another kind that's a little different."

"How's that?"

"It's almost like there are two distinct personalities at work in a single person. One is fully aware that setting fires is a bad thing and may cause destruction and suffering. The other could give a rip and is totally obsessed with going through with it. Firebugs like this report that they just can't help it. Even while they are torching a place, they are hoping that someone will discover the fire and put it out. But at the same time, they don't feel responsible if someone gets hurt or dies. From their perspective, they're just as much victims of their impulsive side as someone who gets burned. I guess you could think of it as a form of schizophrenia, although it's not always diagnosed that way."

"All very interesting, but what's it got to do with public health?"

"To make the connection, you've got to take a closer look at the impulsive side of this kind or arsonist. What drives this segment of the personality to such a drastic act? Nobody seems to agree. But one pretty good bet is a deep desire to overcome feelings of powerlessness, the kind you might get from being in an abusive family situation, things like that. What do you think?"

"Sounds reasonable. But I'm not a shrink."

"Nor am I. But I do have a lot of firsthand experience with people of this sort, and the data I've observed fits the hypothesis pretty well. A big roaring fire can provide a pretty grand feeling of accomplishment. It's a very dramatic personal statement. Anyway, let me answer your original question. Over the past few years, you guys have had two *E. coli.* outbreaks that you traced back to a couple of local restaurants. Clean joints, with no record. And the same strain of bug in both cases. You remember?"

"Yeah, I didn't work on it, but I remember."

"And you could never pinpoint the precise cause, right?"

"You know, we didn't . . . wait a minute. You're not saying . . ."

"No, I'm not saying they were caused by a firebug. But I do think they were caused by someone with the same kind of personality."

"Now hold on. We're talking two separate incidents over maybe a two-year period. And none since. What makes you think it's even the same person?"

"To begin with, it's a rare strain of the bug. Not likely to strike twice, even over that long a time period."

"Anything else?"

"In both cases, you never found the cause. Didn't even come close. Right?"

"I'd have to check."

"I've already checked. And I think whoever's doing this gets the same kind of kinky reward as the dark side of a firebug. A feeling of great personal power. A triumph over all the things that conspire to control him."

David put on a cynical smile. "So what do you do? Stake out every restaurant in greater Seattle and watch for someone that looks a little weird?"

Paris grinned him down. "Something like that. Anyway, I need some unofficial help from someone who can approach this from the public health side."

"Like me?"

"Yeah. Like you."

"But I'm not a doctor."

"But you know the profession, right?"

"Right."

"Good. That's all I ask. Congratulations. You just signed on."

Before David could reply, Paris was up and heading toward the cash register.

6

Iquitos

PETER RANCOVICH KNOWS THE TAXI IS KILLING HIM, BUT doesn't complain. It would do no good. The driver speaks only a few token words of English, and Peter speaks virtually no Spanish, especially the dialects of the upper Amazon Basin used here in Iquitos. The driver, a stocky man of indeterminate age, would not comprehend terms like *exhaust leak* and *carbon monoxide,* which is most surely being issued from a manifold leak and finding its way through a corroded hole in the fire wall to the passenger compartment.

Peter sighs. It must be a slow leak because the driver appears to be in adequate health despite constant exposure for God knows how long. Peter leans back, closes his eyes, and lets the exhaust mingle with the damp rubber, the stale tobacco, and wet rot of upholstery stuffing in the damp jungle heat. At twenty-six, he would regenerate the poisoned tissue and escape even a minor dent in his mortality.

The irony of his approach to healthy living was completely lost on him as the old Toyota whined on down Próspero Street past the string of hotels and hostels. True, he ate very carefully, avoiding the fatty agents of cancer and heart disease, and exercised religiously to stay blissfully oxygenated and toned to the hilt. And his job at the Webster Foundation gave him access to the very best medical counsel on the preservation of his physical self. But then, he would turn right around and do the crazy stuff. Like the time he ripped the wing off the hang glider on a tree branch on the big island in Hawaii. Or had the problem with the regulator when they were diving one hundred feet down in the Caribbean.

If confronted, he would have justified these episodes as a willful offering to the keepers of mortality, whoever they might be. It was one thing to be the passive object of some creeping illness and quite another to be riding high on a spike of adrenaline and have your health ripped away in a high-stakes game of physical chance. Besides, without these moments of supreme risk, he would languish in the secluded labs of the Foundation and rapidly decompose into a sad and paunchy middle age. Of this he was sure.

And because he was, he dedicated two weeks a year to a glorious, senseless, exhilarating adventure. A vacation on the border between heaven and hell.

The taxi slowed for a stoplight, and Peter glanced up at the marquee for the Cine Iquitos. The movie title was in Spanish, but the star billing underneath read "Bruce Lee."

They were close to the market area now, just a couple of blocks, he thought. Still time to call it off, to go back to the hotel, get a good night's sleep, and catch a flight back to Lima in the morning, then on to the States the next day. Diana would be elated.

Diana, that was the problem all right, Diana. She of the piercing green eyes and long auburn hair, the one truly dangerous woman in all his adult life. Even now, her remote image was like a drag chute draining momentum from the current expedition. Often, she mockingly called him "Peter Pancovic" to squelch the frolicking boy in him. But the boy was strong, spirited, and willful and, in the end, had his way about this trip.

However, before he did, their relationship tumbled wildly as she launched an enormous assault across a broad front. But his defense was simple and effective: if she wanted to come along, to share the experience, she was more than welcome. And of course, she didn't. Even at the airport, she pouted and gave him only a cool embrace and desultory peck to send him on his way.

Funny, thought Peter, this was the most benign of all his forays—at least from a physical standpoint—and yet she carried on as if he were stumbling into the heart of the apocalypse. He first got the idea from a guy he met skiing up in Aspen. Like himself, the guy (whose name he'd now forgotten) was a part of a large underground army composed of many different divisions, including so-called slackers and ski bums. Wherever people decided to trade off professional achievement for freedom from responsibility, a new unit was formed. All things considered, it was a fair trade, at least while in the full bloom of youth, when the benefits could still be derived. Anyway, the different divisions communicated regularly over microbrews in taverns, joints at the bottom of remote canyons, wine in bohemian cafés, and mushrooms in the most vacuous of deserts.

In this manner, Peter learned of the shaman, and what the shaman did.

The taxi was in the market area now and took a left onto Abtao Street. At night, nothing remained but the wooden skeletons of stalls, which were filled in the daytime with fish, vegetables, rice, sugar, coffee, gasoline, and the pelts of animals from the jungle. A single streetlight marked the spot where the taxi halted, and the driver turned to Peter while pointing out the windshield.

"Belén."

Peter peered out the windshield and saw only dull orange dots in the blackness outside the feeble light cone from the streetlamp.

"You . . . wait," he said carefully to the driver, who nodded earnestly. Peter opened the door and climbed out into the damp night. Ahead of him was Belén, a huge and rowdy cluster of ragged huts atop balsa rafts that floated up and down with the tide of the Amazon River. As he walked out onto a stubby little dock, he saw that the orange dots originated from lamplight glowing through open windows, and now he heard the lapping water mix with communal dog barks, portable radios, and baby cries. This great waterborne slum had a perverse synergy about it, a life beyond the control of its inhabitants. No matter how wretched their personal fates, Belén itself floated on in the most robust of health.

He checked his watch. Right on time. But then again, what did that mean in this culture? He wasn't sure. And that was part of the fun of it all, the novelty, the release from convention.

He ran his fingers idly through his ash-blond, shoulder-length hair and scratched his thin nose. What did the shaman think of him? Did he see through the surfer-boy good looks and into the center of his soul? Did he see the great vacuum there, the hollow zone scoured out by years of good fortune, family money, and total absence of personal commitment? Or did he maybe see some great and elegant bird winging its way through the hollow zone on an endless and noble flight of self-discovery?

It was hard to say. Two days earlier, he had gone to the shaman's house in a modest, but respectable part of the city. As he approached, he was startled to see an army officer coming out, but then he remembered that the magic of the jungle had no respect for the city limits. In fact, the city was just an illusion, a clever concrete prop to dam the primal power that oozed through the rain forest and down the great swollen river, the Río Amazon.

He was also startled to find the shaman in khaki pants and a Pink Floyd T-shirt. Still, he did have the carved mahogany face of an Indian, with brown eyes just this side of black. Threads of gray laced his straight black hair, which looked as if it had just been sidewalled by a Midwestern barber. Peter was shown into the "consultation" room by a woman he assumed to be the shaman's wife or companion. The shaman sat cross-legged on a mat woven from a yellow fiber and motioned to Peter to sit on a similar mat about a yard away. He then called over Peter's shoulder in Spanish, and a second man entered, who was to act as an interpreter.

As the consultation progressed, Peter stuck to his carefully prepared complaint: his stomach. Every time he felt sad or angry, he sensed a small fire in the pit of his stomach, and the worse he felt, the brighter the fire burned. He had tried conventional drugs, antacids and the like, to quench the fire, but to no avail. So perhaps the drugs were not the answer, perhaps the shaman had the answer.

As he told this tale, he was increasingly unnerved by the shaman's unblinking stare. Every time Peter stopped talking and the interpreter translated, he kept waiting for a compassionate nod from the shaman, a small sign of empathy, a validation of his story, but none came. In truth, his stomach complaint was like one of the outer planets, a small and solid core surrounded by a vast ball of cool, wispy gas. He really did get upset stomachs from time to time, especially if his brain was also upset—but not quite on the order of magnitude he now presented to the shaman.

Did the man think he was lying? Was he quietly subjecting Peter to some kind of spiritual x-ray? No way to know.

When Peter was through expressing his malady, the shaman spoke briefly to the interpreter, never taking his eyes off Peter. There would be a "session" conducted two days hence to treat him. He was to meet the interpreter at the appointed hour in Belén and proceed from there.

Now, as he stood in the hot night, Peter heard the boat before he saw it. The periodic splash of oars dipping into the muddy-brown water. Then a small, narrow vessel glided into the light of the streetlamp and he could see two men, the interpreter and a companion, who was rowing. Peter knelt to catch the boat as it pulled up to the dock, and the interpreter clambered up. Without a word, the rower backed the boat into the night as Peter and the interpreter walked to the taxi, where the interpreter spoke a few words in Spanish to the driver and they were under way.

In just a few blocks, the lights and buildings outside the taxi tapered off into an anxious blackness. The interpreter said nothing to Peter and the taxi filled with the grumpy buzz of the aging engine and that vague stink of exhaust. A short time later, the paved road gave way to gravel, and the taxi's headlights cast a futile little beam into the overwhelming void of the equatorial night.

And now Peter began to realize how truly novel this adventure was to be. All his other expeditions had been characterized by brilliant imagery. Dazzling snow with a diamond ice crust. Angry mobs of silver bubbles framed in ultramarine. Blue sky slammed tight against a jagged green horizon.

But this time, the trip would be inward, across a bridge of blackness to a place he'd never seen.

Fifteen minutes later, the taxi pulled off the gravel road onto a rutted side road, and the driver shifted into low gear to negotiate the bumps. Now the jungle thrust its clutches into the headlight beam, and Peter saw thick clusters of bushes and trees pushing hard to retake the space where the road was. Then he spotted a flickering light ahead, capped by a pale splotch he recognized as lantern light.

The taxi bounced to a halt, and after paying the driver, Peter got out and saw they were in front of a wall-less shelter, with a thatched roof supported by wooden poles and a wooden floor covered with woven mats of some kind. A propane lantern hung in the center and blanketed the scene with a frank and brutal light. In front of the shelter, the shaman squatted over a fire gone to embers with a smoke-stained kettle perched on top. He wore faded Levi's jeans, a plain T-shirt, and a fresh pair of Nike sneakers as he gently stirred the boiling liquid in the kettle. As the taxi pulled away, he turned and nodded briefly to Peter and the interpreter as they approached.

"You may go sit," the interpreter said, in the first words spoken to Peter during the entire session. The man was small and trim, with a flowery sport shirt, ridiculous secondhand polyester pants, and aging sneakers. He stopped to confer with the shaman as Peter went to sit cross-legged in the center of the shelter.

The crude engine sounds of the taxi were gone now, and Peter felt the acoustic shower of jungle noises spill into the shelter over the white hiss of the lantern. Beeps, squawks, hisses, grunts, trills, rustles, and buzzes all wrapped tightly about him. He watched the shaman gingerly remove the kettle from the coals to cool. Its contents were the vehicle for this adventure, and the shaman was the driver.

His research for this trip told him that the shaman was more properly called an *ayahuasquero* and that the preparations for this session had begun several hours ago, with the boiling of a woody vine from the species *Banisteriopsis caapi*. More commonly called ayahuasco, the vine contained three alkaloids called harmine, harmaline, and tetrahydroharmaline, a powerful trio of psychedelic agents with at least the wallop of LSD. While some might see ayahuasco as a psychic toxin, the Amazon shamans perceive it as a valuable tool in treating many forms of illness, not so much as a cure, but as a gateway leading to the underlying cause. In effect, the shaman helped the patients burglarize their own souls, crawling in through a window opened by the drug, then stalking through all the secret rooms and locked doors of the subconscious.

And Peter knew that soon he would be just such a thief, ransacking his inner self. Lost in an adventure entirely of his own making. Literally. Whatever visions crawled out to greet him would be created exclusively within the soul of Peter Rancovich.

But there were many things about this place, these people, that Peter did not know. Not now. Not ever.

Ramon, the interpreter, watched the reflection of the firelight in the shaman's eyes as they waited for the ayahuasco brew to cool. A little *chacruna,* containing a psychoactive agent called DMT, had been added by the shaman to fortify the drink. Now the shaman sat on his haunches before the ruby coals and rocked gently to and fro in a way Ramon had never seen. Something was wrong. Was it the *gringo?* Probably not. They had seen plenty like him before.

Then Ramon saw something that made him shudder. For

just a second, the shaman's eyes quit reflecting the firelight and went as black as the surrounding jungle. No shadow passed over his face to explain it. Nothing moved to block the dying light from the embers. Only the eyes went out. Ramon had seen many strange things in his time with the shaman, but not this thing. It had a bad feel about it, a very bad feel.

At that moment, the shaman stopped rocking. When the glow returned to his eyes an instant later, he turned to Ramon.

"Let us begin," he said quietly in Spanish.

Peter watched the two men by the fire. The shaman must have been going through some preliminary ritual because the interpreter seemed intense and attuned to the shaman's every move. Now the pair got up, and the shaman poured some of the ayahuasco brew into a large earthenware cup, which he cradled gently in both hands and carried into the shelter. When they were all seated, they formed a perfect triangle in the center of the structure with the cup in the middle. The shaman spoke softly to the interpreter, who seemed strangely agitated.

"The time has come for you to take the journey," relayed the interpreter to Peter. "You must go to the place where your illness lives and visit those who live there."

The shaman rose to his haunches, cupped the bowl in his hands, and gave it to Peter. When Peter took it, the shaman looked at the cup, then up at Peter, and nodded his head once. Peter brought the cup to his lips and tasted the warm liquid, which had a bitter alkaline flavor.

So far, so good. I haven't puked yet.

While Peter continued to drink in small swallows, the shaman puckered his lips and began a raspy whistle that seemed to travel at random up and down the tonal register. Sometimes he increased the volume, and a set of rich harmonics marched along with the fundamental tone. Other times, the whistle retreated to the point where it was almost like a frail ghost lost in the jungle's animistic chorus.

The sipping and the whistling went on until the cup was empty, then Peter placed it carefully in front of him, as if it were a sacred object, a psychotropic chalice of some kind.

The interpreter sat cross-legged and absolutely still, staring into the distance.

So when does it hit me?

Suddenly a big shadow flitted over the seated figures and did a mad dance on the bamboo mat, followed by a long series of angry buzzes and bumps from overhead.

Is this it?

Peter looked up and saw a giant winged insect assaulting the lantern glass. Its wings spun in a blur, and its thorax curled toward the light. As it charged madly at the glass, Peter identified it as a giant moth of some kind. While the interpreter started at its presence, the shaman ignored it.

Nope. Just a bug.

Just then, a fistful of nausea hit him hard, sending a bitter bubble of liquid charging up from his stomach. His cheeks ballooned and it was all he could do to keep his face from exploding as he scrambled to the edge of the shelter and retched into the bushes. Then another fist hit him, and another. Soon he was throwing up his composure along with the contents of his stomach.

Jesus! How long can this go on?

When it finally passed, he crawled weakly on all fours back to his place in the seated triangle, a changed man. The shaman and his assistant showed no reaction. Peter closed his eyes and breathed deeply. Maybe this wasn't such a good idea after all.

The shaman came up from his sitting position and produced a *schcapa*, a sheaf of dried jungle leaves bound together with a vine. He began to orbit Peter and shook the sheaf, which gave off dry rustles and rattles. After about a dozen loops, he returned to his sitting spot.

I wonder what time . . .

A string of small waves rippled through the pattern in the mat, as if there were a liquid pad underneath that had suddenly become agitated. No big waves, but definitely there.

Well, okay. Here we go. If this is all there is, then . . .

A great shadow spread over the mat, as big as a thunderhead over a parched desert. The crash of thunder hit him and he shrank before it. The still air came alive with a sawtoothed hum that tickled his ears and made his nose itch. Another crash rolled right through him and turned his belly inside out, followed by a humming that threatened to shake his face apart. The surface of the mat lurched wildly under the great shadow that flickered and slithered with a horrible vigor. It was all coming from above . . .

The lantern burned like a sun gone nova, and its violent light revealed a winged bug the size of a dog crashing madly against the lantern's glass cylinder. Its wings churned the air to hot butter, and its proboscis snapped out and curled shut like a rusted watch spring.

Peter gasped and squelched a scream with his last reserve of bravado. He turned to the interpreter for reassurance and . . .

The man's face was replaced by an insect head, exactly like that of the fluttering monstrosity overhead. Twin snakes shot out of his shirtsleeves and formed folding arms by sinking curved fangs into each other's swollen body. The snake arms would not still and writhed in a green jelly quiver as the head's insect eyes gave Peter a purely predatory appraisal.

Peter turned to the shaman, who looked absolutely normal in this sickening sea of confusion. He was now scared beyond screaming.

Help me, I'm . . .

"What you see will not hurt you," said the shaman. "It carries the power to heal."

How could he understand? Was the shaman speaking in English? In Spanish? Peter could no longer tell. The black shadow from the huge insect flickered mercilessly overhead, and the humming and banging kicked down the doors in Peter's ears so the sound shoved its way right to the center of his head.

The shaman picked up his sheaf of leaves and started to unfold out of the sitting position.

Good. He's going to . . .

But then, without warning, he sat down again. Hard.

The interpreter Ramon watched the shaman carefully in the lantern light, which was disturbed only by an occasional flicker from a gypsy moth probing the glass. The gringo's eyes bulged and he was deathly pale. This was normal.

The shaman's sudden return to the mat was not.

The shaman's eyes closed and he rolled to his right, his head thumping loudly when it hit the mat.

Peter saw the shaman die and knew he was dead before he hit the floor. The skin instantly went from flesh to wax, and something flared out the top of the head before it started its tumble to the mat.

Ramon froze for a moment in panic and disbelief, then rushed to the shaman and put his ear to the man's chest. No breathing. No heart.

Peter saw the insect man embrace the dead body with its horrible snake arms and sink his bug head into the chest. Upon contact with the head, the shaman decomposed into a horde of small snakes that slithered off across the heaving mat under the buzz and roar of the flickering shadow.

The snakes had almost reached Peter when he leaped to his feet and ran. In a panic far beyond blind. In a brilliant Technicolor panic unlike any he had ever known.

Ramon saw the gringo cut and run. Should he try to retrieve him? No. His loyalty was to his departed master. He gently stretched the body out in a dignified pose and knelt to pray over it. It would be a long night.

Peter could see in the dark. That was the hell of it. His tortured optic nerves were at full throttle and pouring a searing overload into the visual centers of his brain. Even in the dark, there were enough photon scraps to build full images.

As he ran down the rutted road, his lungs expanded to the size of water heaters and smashed his entrails down deep into his pelvis. They squeezed his bladder flat and expelled hot urine into his pants as his legs pounded along furiously. The running and the associated physical sensations seemed to damp the visions, and that made him want to run all the faster. Maybe, just maybe, he could outrun the hellish rogue wave that must be right behind him.

And then he felt the wave curl over his head, and the first drops from its breaking crest rained down on him. Big, hot drops that splattered and cratered his exposed skin and scalp. As he came to the end of the rutted road, he turned right, skidded, fell, and sprawled across the gravel. His forearm and knee burst into napalm flame, and a bright orange burst of abrasive pain consumed his vision as he scrambled back to his feet.

They can't get you while you're running. They only get you when you stop.

The pure and timeless wisdom of this thought clung tightly to the controls inside Peter Rancovich and drove him forward. He would run and run. All night if necessary.

Mile after mile, Peter ran through the rain, and as he did, a funny kind of serenity began to mix in with the nightmares. Maybe the rogue wave wasn't back there anymore, with the insect man and disassembled shaman riding its crest. And even if it was, he'd proved to himself he could outrun it in a pinch. He slowed to a jog and felt his sweaty T-shirt and shorts hold him in a soggy embrace. The raindrops were cool now, diamonds of soft ice that melted over him.

Forms and shapes danced more wildly than when he ran at full tilt, but now he clearly made out some rectangular silhouettes off to the left, and a muddy little road leading to them. A house? Shelter? Help? He turned down the road and in less than a minute, entered the dump.

The rat crouched at the entrance to its tunnel under the leaking transformer and looked out into the rainy night that stretched over the dump. It was very sick now, its throat nearly swollen shut, its body temperature far above normal. Movement was difficult, and creeping starvation now compounded its difficulties. The only option left was to stay concealed from predators, hope the illness would pass, and begin to eat once more. Meanwhile, the new and improved generation of *Streptobacillus* surged through its organs and nervous system.

What was it? A farm? Peter could not tell as he slowed to a walk and tried to assess the jumbles of shapes. He tripped and fell over something hard, setting off a crackling display of visual electricity. As he climbed to his feet, his legs felt shaky and his soggy clothes seemed to weigh a ton. Maybe it was time to rest.

A couple of yards away was a little mound, with some kind of cylinder sprawled over its top. Peter stumbled over, turned around, and sat down next to the cylinder.

The rat saw the huge form plow into the dirt just below its tunnel entrance and smelled the leather, rubber, and skin. When the motion stopped, an enormous column of flesh stood less than an inch from its head. Now, in its terminal stupor, the rat's brain issued the wrong instruction. Rather than withdrawing to safety, it attacked and sank its sharp incisors into the skin.

The pain shot up Peter's leg and set off a burning white ball in his head. He leapt to his feet and whirled to face the attacker, but there was none. The white ball burst and turned into millions of smaller balls that spun madly in little whirlpools. The colors! Each ball had its own, and they spilled far beyond the visible spectrum into violets and reds usually reserved for physics. Now the tiny balls washed around Peter like atomized star dust and guided him back toward the main road. The pain was still there, but only like a cheap memento stuffed in a box somewhere in the cellar.

The small band of *Streptobacillus* had never expected to be an expeditionary force. For some time, they had been encamped in the rat's epithelial tissue and periodically set sail in the saliva. They lived as refugees, far from the great immune response raging in the other parts of the rat. But now, the currents of the saliva sea took them out of the rat's mouth and onto a new planet: the subcutaneous tissue of Peter Rancovich, in a small spot just above his Achilles tendon.

The strep had no idea they'd just discovered the New World, and its tremendous expanse of cultivable tissue. For the time being, they concentrated on setting up a beachhead and fighting the local agents of the immune system, which were already beginning to stir.

But soon, they would move out in force.

7

Gabon

MARTIN N'DONG PULLED THE ANCIENT FORD PICKUP OVER TO the shoulder and cut the engine. He slid across the seat and climbed out on the passenger side because the door on the driver's side was missing a handle, with only a grooved metal shaft poking out. He looked up and down the road, listened carefully, but didn't hear the distant rubbery whine of approaching vehicles. Good. He could take a minute and check the parrot.

At twenty-one years old, Martin was muscular and athletically inclined, so he vaulted himself up and into the pickup bed in a single burst of motion. After digging in his pocket, he came up with the key to the padlock secured to the rusty hasp on the plywood toolbox, removed the lock, and opened the splintered lid.

The parrot looked up at him with the disdain of a captured warrior. It was a rare and beautiful bird known as a Jardine's parrot, nearly a foot tall with a green body, black head feathers, and brilliant red markings on the edges of its wings. The makeshift chicken-wire cage seemed a shabby prison for so noble a bird, with its stunning colors and huge beak. It seemed healthy, and that was good, because his uncle Omar would immediately see the value in it and reward Martin appropriately.

Now the distant whisper of an approaching vehicle came to Martin, and he closed the lid, locked it, and vaulted back down to the ground. He was probably being overly cautious, but it was better that way. He climbed back into the truck and pulled onto the road for the last eighty kilometers to Libreville, where Uncle Omar lived. Martin himself had lived his entire life in Mounana, a modest town in the southeastern interior of Gabon, and was thrilled at the prospect of spending some time in Libreville. He had only been to the great coastal city one time before, when he was sixteen, and would never forget the towering buildings, the beautiful shops, the magnificent restaurants.

Ever since that visit, he had continually schemed to find a way back. The centerpiece in all these thought experiments was his uncle, Omar, his mother's brother, who worked in one of those fabulous buildings and spread his patriarchal power out in a rich glaze over the entire city. Omar dealt with the ships in the harbor somehow, although Martin was not sure of the details. But that was only the foundation of his empire. Many people came to Omar's house, both African and European. Some were beautifully dressed and driving cars of their very own. Others were simple people, like Martin, who came in battered old vehicles or on foot. But in every case, Omar showed the same expansive hospitality, serving fine wine and liquors from France, and wonderful meals cooked by his wife, Uma, who barked down orders at the several domestics who assisted her.

During his former visit, Martin had been present at many of Omar's sessions with his callers and was amazed at the variety of dealings that were discussed. Everything from logging mahogany in the interior rain forests to supplying fresh produce to restaurants, to the distribution of medical supplies to clinics in the interior. Even at sixteen, Martin was shrewd enough to understand that while Omar did very little himself, he was like the operator of a switchboard and had the power to connect disparate elements in a mutually profitable way. It wasn't so much the specific nature of the enterprise that counted, as the way Omar packaged it.

So Martin had waited patiently for the right kind of business opportunity to present to his uncle. He was picky and particular in his search because he would have only one chance to get it right with Omar, and if he failed, he would be doomed to the sadly diminished life of the rural laborer, or the short and desperate life of the urban street hustler. Neither seemed a just alternative for a young man with such a righteous entrepreneurial spirit.

In the toolbox, the parrot perched sullenly. Martin would always think he netted the bird through great stealth and personal skill and would never know the truth. In fact, the parrot was ill, its reaction times significantly diminished. In its lungs dwelled a swarm of unwelcome residents technically identified as *Chlamydia psittaci,* the tiniest of the tiniest bacteria, so small that they are nearly beyond the reach of the optical microscope. Hundreds would easily fit into a single red blood cell.

To survive on the mean streets of microbiology, the *Chlamydia* had long ago copied the devious ways of viruses, the ultimate small fry. Instead of loitering between cells, the *Chlamydia* bored through the cell wall and slipped inside, where they tapped into the cell's ancient power plants, the mitochondria. Once established, they formed a vigorous colony where they multiplied rapidly until they burst the cell wall and migrated to new cells, which became reluctant hosts.

Now, as Martin started the truck and pulled back onto the road, a most unusual event occurred deep inside one of the parrot's nasal passages.

One of the migrating *Chlamydia* had just taken up residence in a new cell in the parrot's nasal membrane and was setting up housekeeping when an abrupt shift occurred in its interior, where a circular chain of DNA called a plasmid suddenly snapped open like a broken ring on a shower curtain. And for some unknown reason, the repair job was botched when the loose ends were rejoined, which caused the DNA code to be slightly modified.

A mutation of this kind hadn't occurred for over a million generations in the *Chlamydia* and wouldn't again for another million. And most of the time, it wouldn't matter anyway. But this time, the twist in the code created a chemical condition called an R factor, which protected the *Chlamydia* against the lethal assault of a drug called erythromycin. This common antibiotic attacked the same factories as tetracycline, but specialized in destroying the molecular machinery on the manufacturing floor, the 50S ribosomal subunits, which assembled the final products. By disabling the drug, the R factor allowed the factories to stay in business, and the *Chlamydia* to prosper.

Now the modified *Chlamydia* began to divide and pass the R factor on to offspring. Within a short time, billions would carry the trait, holding it like an ace in the hole. An ace they could play against the vast majority of antibiotics and win hands down.

But would they ever play it? Not likely. In its natural state, the parrot would never have recourse to erythromycin, and the *Chlamydia*'s random inheritance would never be put to the test. And even if the R factor did battle and won, it was still powerless against one last line of defense, one major drug group:

The tetracycline family.

8

VINCENT'S LAST NAME ESCAPES HIM. AT LEAST FOR NOW. BUT he doesn't worry. It will come back. And what if it doesn't? So what?

In the cool dryness of the basement, the arrogant smell of cement mixes with that of aging wood. Before him, the instruments of his true calling rest on the pressboard surface of the workbench, which is illuminated by a single neon fixture that sputters and hums from a broken transformer. To the rear of the bench are two plastic boxes with matrices of little drawers, all shut tightly and labeled in a cramped cursive. A row of dusty textbooks and a ring binder snuggle up to the box on the right.

Vincent no longer requires the knowledge in these texts. He has perfected his process. But he keeps them in place because they add a kind of professional authenticity to the work area. And rightfully so. Because Vincent's work has a significance far beyond that of all those professional people comfortably situated in their well-appointed offices downtown. Unlike many of these people, Vincent would readily admit that his work defines him, rather than the other way around. And in no way does this dehumanize him.

Because Vincent has little reason to think of himself as human at all.

The exterior of Vincent's cheap rental suffers from a sad

case of psoriasis as multiple layers of paint peel away in a depressing display of pentimento. The small front porch sags downward in deference to the street, and the windows are caked with a decade of grime that hides the interior in a cloudy haze on the rare occasions when Vincent opens the blinds.

The main floor of the interior is little better. An empty plain of dirty floorboards stretches across the living and dining rooms, interrupted only by an ancient couch riddled with cotton tunnels chewed by rodents that scamper boldly across the open floor. Their droppings fill the corners in little desiccated heaps. The old wallpaper is going yellow with age and is punctured with holes rimmed in dirty Sheetrock. The tile corners on the kitchen floor curl into angry little flips, and the sink is peppered with a fine mix of dirt and dust. An old refrigerator hums on in the silence, and the stove has three empty sockets where the burners have been gouged out. Near the back door, a plastic trash bag bulges with consumed TV dinners, and a swarm of flies seeks out the moldering contents.

Occasionally, Vincent's work is interrupted by a nameless impulse, which drives him out of the basement and into the bathroom, where he stares into the pitted and fractured mirror. With clinical detachment, he examines his image and wonders who he really is.

There are very few clues.

More precisely, there are three clues, three memories Vincent has of his early childhood. He has not retrieved any of them since the time he got so sick a few years ago and landed on an internal focal plane that snapped his life into brilliant detail.

During this time of minor agony, he lay on an old couch where the fever's breath blew a white-hot cinder through his brain and he played three memories, over and over in a continuous loop.

Memory One. The stink of hot, ancient oil: crankcase drippings soak into crushed gravel and bake brown in the summer sun. His nose pokes through an empty diamond defined by the wire in a corroded chain-link fence. Before him, the snout on the German shepherd is a big black bullet that always points toward the snake, a coiled tube of glistening green and brown. From above, the metal buckle on the waist of a leather motorcycle jacket gives his cheek a chilly brush as its owner sways in agitation. A sandpaper voice rubs itself raw against the rising heat.

"Git that fuckin' snake! Come *on!* Git that fuckin' snake!"

His little fists grip the wire diamonds of the fence and he pushes his face in until it hurts. Beer splashes down onto his T-shirt, and its fermented yellow odor pushes deep into his nostrils.

The dog darts in for a quick sniff and backs off instantly as the snake hisses and its head makes a phallic stab out of the tubular coil.

"God*damn!* Git the fuckin' snake! Bite its fuckin' head off!"

The dog makes two more orbits around this serpentine sun, then noses in for another sniff with the black bullet nose. The snake snaps out of its coil in a green flash, headed straight for the dog's face. The dog dodges and the snake's fangs sink into its shoulder. The dog emits a sharp yelp as the snake's body ripples like a thick rubber rope driven by the dog's jerking retreat.

"Shit! Come *on!* You're dead meat!"

The dog twists its neck violently to draw a bead on the writhing snake. The jaws part and the huge, curved canines flash white in the noon light. They catch the snake in midbody and rip it loose from the wound on the shoulder.

"All *right!* Kill the goddamn thing!"

The dog's fangs sink deep into the snake, and it shakes the serpent in a wild, twisting frenzy mixed with deep and angry growls. The snake's head smashes repeatedly into the gravel and its muscles go slack and lifeless.

But already, the dog's legs are going soft as the venom pushes its way through the animal's veins and into the vital tissues.

Memory Two. The attic forms an elongated triangle of dark, dead lumber with a dry, pungent smell. The bare rafters are studded with porcelain insulators carrying twisted old wires off into the darkness. He stands at one end and the floor planking plays out before him to the far wall, a gable where a small window casts a cold, dirty light. Beside him is a trapdoor with a little rope handle that disappears into holes drilled in the wood.

It is hot. Very hot. The kind of heat that robs your breath and sucks at the center of your chest. The kind that tries to burn you hollow from the inside out.

He panics and drops to his knees in the gray dust and yanks on the rope. The trapdoor will not budge. He yanks over and over, harder and harder, but to no avail. With every yank, the heat hugs him tighter. He rises to his feet, thrusting his head up in search of cooler air, but finds only a boiling fog of scorched oxygen.

He faces the far gable and its small window and explodes into a full run. The sound of his small feet thunder off the rafters. The dusty planking rolls beneath him as he stretches his arms out into a shoving position. Halfway across the attic, he begins to yell, a little-boy yell, a vulnerable soprano sound.

First the gable and then the window fill his world as his hands shatter the glass and he plunges through. As his chest hits the sill, he hears a brittle crash and the city bursts into view crowned by the cool, white sky.

He rebounds to a sitting position on the dusty floor and hears a muffled scream coming from somewhere below.

Memory Three. He lies on his stomach on a mattress with swirling wads of old bedding around him. He is naked except for underpants that smell of urine and is oblivious to the rest of the room except for the TV, which sits atop an orange crate and casts a picture leached of color and speckled with snow.

An old cartoon shows a gang of stunted demons pursuing a hapless rabbit-child through a nightmare forest. As they run, the demons sing a simple existential ballad to the little critter:

> *You're nuthin', you're **nuthin'**.*
> *You haven't got a clue.*
> *You're nuthin', you're nuthin'.*
> *You're not even you.*

When the fever finally abated, and the fluids stopped running, the three memories broke out of their continuous loop and floated free, so Vincent was able to tuck them away in a deep hole. And while he excavated this hole, he tried to review his postchildhood years, but failed completely. As soon as he attempted to peek, the memories blew apart in a colossal internal explosion and hurtled outward so that each became a solitary traveler in a great and solemn space. And as they did so, there was only time to capture a single shard of recollection:

He was a king, and he could feel the press of a cardboard crown upon his forehead as he strutted across the stage and delivered his lines with a force and clarity far beyond his years. From the corner of his eye, he could see his drama teacher beaming at him, her star student. It seemed Vincent was a natural actor, with a nearly flawless instinct for drama. But what the teacher failed to understand was the origin of his gift: Vincent could become any character he chose because there was no real Vincent to get in the way. And now Vincent the king turned to the audience in a sweeping gesture and looked out past the footlights into the dark void in search of his parents; but at that very moment, the space that hid the audience became the negative hollow within him, and this last fragment flew away and disappeared into the distance.

But then, on the last day of his illness, the real Vincent showed up and poured himself into this terrible vacancy. Sitting at the kitchen table in a square patch of sunlight, the real Vincent explained to the old facade that he was much more than just an actor. He was a theatrical genius in every sense of the word, an actor, a playwright, a director, and a producer.

And now, with the sickness finally behind him, it was time for his first production. A work of great power that would go right to the gut of his audience. Literally.

As there had been three memories, there were now three acts. In the first, the stage was set. The germ culture was obtained from his own illness, then appropriate texts were studied and growth environment readied. Soon after, a used microscope was purchased and the supporting cast brought into focus. Seen through the eyepiece, a swarm of *E. coli* rehearsed diligently to perfect their grand finale.

The second act elaborated the action and moved it into a public restaurant, where the sacrament of contamination took place and the microscopic cast mingled freely with the audience. Soon, the entire community bore witness to the drama, and the media dwelled upon every nuance and speculated wildly about the origins of such startlingly original work.

But it was the third act that made the production a true piece of dramatic apotheosis. Like all works of creative genius, it was absurdly simple and required only a single trip to Good Will to purchase the appropriate materials.

Now as he sits in the basement at his workbench, Vincent chuckles to himself about the undeniable brilliance of the third act. It breaks all the rules. For one thing, it is not until now that the lead character appears, which, of course, is Vincent himself. For another, it moves the action to a most unexpected setting. Finally, it resolves the conflict in a stunningly original manner.

Vincent hums to himself as he prepares a slide for viewing. He has taken the sample from the hard surface of the nutrient agar in one of the petri dishes carefully arranged in a row at the rear of the bench top. He snaps the slide into place on the stage of the microscope, flips on the light source, and rotates the lens turret to select the proper objective. He leans over and peers through the twin ocular lenses.

There they are. *E. coli.* Little capsules of intestinal agony, searching for an ideal homeland. They weren't the O157:H7 strain, which occasionally killed as well as tormented, because that would complicate the delicate structure of Vincent's third act. Still, they packed plenty of punch.

Vincent is still humming as he surveys his supporting cast at x1500.

> *You're nuthin', you're nuthin'.*
> *You haven't got a clue.*
> *You're nuthin', you're nuthin'.*
> *You're not even you.*

Each *E. coli* under Vincent's view is about .0004 inch in diameter. If one of them were granted human dimension, the microscope slide would become a glass desert eighteen miles across, and the microscope itself would be a huge tube towering over a hundred miles into the sky.

Vincent pulls the slide out of the microscope and stares at the little poisoned bubble where the germs swarm. They are toxic; yes, they are that.

But never quite as toxic as Vincent himself.

Lately, Paris had begun to think of the relationship between himself and Skip Sloan in terms of international diplomacy, like two sovereign nations that embrace vastly different cultures, but were forced through historic circumstance to become trading partners. Skip was his sister's son; more importantly, his *widowed* sister's son. And so now, as the boy cut a troubled wake through adolescence, Paris was supposed to become some kind of paternal navigation beacon. But precisely what kind of beacon escaped him. He had no kids from which to draw experience, and his own childhood seemed like a mildly earthlike but very distant planet.

Still, his sister, Cathy, was a good woman doing her best with a bad hand, and Paris could not refuse. So once again, on this fine night, this night when he could've done almost anything else, he'd gone on a trade mission to the country of Skip to see if a little business could be done. The Mariners were playing at the Kingdome and it seemed like good neutral territory, a timeless zone somewhere between the Stones and Pornos For Pyro.

During the game, Paris let their minimal conversation stay light and superficial. Stuff about Skip's school, his mom, his musical interests. But Paris was merely setting the stage, lulling Skip and preparing an ambush. It was the only way to get the kid out into the open, even for the briefest of moments. And now, as they sat under lurid neon in a fast-food joint after the game, he squeezed off his opening round:

"So, Skip, you packin'?"

He delivered the line with an optimistic grin, as if he hoped for a positive answer.

Skip was eating pie and milk in a Hawaiian sport shirt, with a porkpie hat pulled tightly over his shaved head. A tiny pearl of milk clung to the extreme end of the little triangular beard under his lower lip. He stopped eating and looked up at Paris from his hunched position over the pie. The drop of milk lost its grip, fell into the pie, and was swallowed by the crust. Skip's dark brown eyes hid his pupils and his mouth gaped open as he stared at Paris, trying to figure what the angle was.

"Don't know what you mean," Skip said flatly.

"I mean what I said. You got a gun? You carry it around sometimes?"

Skip abruptly broke off his stare, plunged his fork back into the pie, and shoveled a small mountain of crust and apple filling into his mouth.

"Or maybe you carry it all the time and just leave it home when you see me. You know, because I'm a cop and all."

Skip's vision remained fixed on his bowl as he finished off the pie, leaving an empty paper wedge. "You think I'm crazy, man? You think I'm gonna tell a cop if I'm packin'?"

"Nope. I don't," said Paris with a twinkle. Now, for the first time all evening, they were having a little fun. "But I thought maybe you might tell your old uncle. I don't think your uncle would bust you. What do you think?"

Skip drained the last of the milk from the little carton and looked straight at Paris. "Whatever you want to do, man. Whatever's cool with you, then that's what you should do."

Paris took a quick but careful look around before he made his next move. Good. They had the place basically to themselves.

"You really want to know what I'm doin'?"

"No. But I bet you're going to tell me anyway." Skip cast a bored look out into the night.

"No, I'm not going to tell you. I'm going to show you." Paris reached under his billowing sport shirt, pulled out a 9mm Glock automatic pistol, and put it on the table between them. "I'm packin'."

Skip's cool persona fractured instantly. "Jesus! What if somebody sees that?" he exclaimed as he twisted around to see if anyone was looking.

"Maybe they'll call the cops. Maybe they'll arrest me. What do you think?"

"Hey, why don't you put it away, okay?" Skip requested nervously.

Paris was pleased with the outcome. If his nephew had been spending time with kids who were really into firearms, he wouldn't even have flinched at the presence of the pistol. "Tell you what. I'll put it away. But I want you to listen to a story. And I don't want you to space out on me while you listen. Okay?"

"Yeah, okay." Skip took another look around, then looked back at Paris, who saw the dawn of respect in the young man's eyes. Amazing. All you had to do was exercise incredibly bad judgment and you had the kid's complete attention.

"Take a guess how long I've been packin'," commanded Paris as he slipped the gun back into the holster under his shirt.

"Probably ever since you started being a cop."

"You got it. That's twenty-two years ago. Now guess how long I went without pulling it out."

"A couple of years?"

"Nope. I went all the way up until two minutes ago."

Skip looked amazed. "You're shittin' me!"

"Nope. I wouldn't do that. There's a lot people out there that are gonna bullshit you, Skip—and I'm not one of them."

"You must have come close."

"Yeah. Real close. More than once."

"Like when?"

"One time I went to arrest a guy who'd killed his wife. He was holed up in a cheap motel room with a pistol aimed at his head. Seemed he was a little remorseful, or something like that. Anyway, he could have jerked the gun off his temple, nailed me, then gone back to doing himself in."

"So what happened?"

"I kept my gun out of sight, sat down, and had a little chat with the guy. Actually, a really long chat." Paris chuckled. "I think he gave up because his arm got tired of holding the gun that high. Anyway, I never pulled my piece. Didn't have to. Mostly, guns cause more trouble than they solve, even for cops."

"So why you carryin' one around? Like tonight?"

"Because there might come a time when you've got no choice. And for me, that time was tonight."

"Tonight?" Skip looked genuinely puzzled.

"Yeah, tonight. Know how long I've been trying to get a direct connection with you?"

"Nope."

"A long time. A very long time. I finally got desperate. I pulled out my piece. And you know why?"

"Nope."

"Because I think you're worth the hassle. And you know why I think that?"

"Nope."

Paris put on just a hint of a grin. "I haven't the slightest idea." He glanced at his watch. "It's getting late, we better go."

As they left, Paris held off on congratulating himself. His surprise attack had left a modest dent in Skip's armor, but the kid was a tough case, a really tough case.

But then again, thought Paris, so was he.

9

ELAINE WILKES LOOKED UP FROM HER DESKTOP COMPUTER and paused to watch the twisting spray from the lawn sprinklers at the Webster Foundation turn a brilliant gold in the setting sun. Normally, she would be gone by now, but they were executing a major run on the system, a test of Agent 57a, and she simply couldn't wait until morning to see the results. The curiosity of the child fueled the inquisitive quest of the scientist, and the child needed an immediate reward to keep the quest worthwhile.

Her flat-panel computer display showed a graphic of a large meter, a throwback to the era of analog instrumentation. Each incremental meter mark represented an hour of compute time, and the marks ran from zero to eight hours, the estimated run time for this particular job. The meter was now at seven and three-quarters, and Elaine was getting a little twitchy with anticipation. You never knew what to expect. That was why they did the runs. Each agent had its own peculiar modus operandi, which produced some surprising twists when you looked at the data.

The actual run was taking place downstairs, in a heavily secured vault with independent power and air-conditioning. To get to the inner sanctum, you passed through two security checkpoints using a retinal-scan device, and even then, you could only observe the computer through thick, bulletproof glass. Inside, you saw several people in white, sterilized bodysuits and hoods, with respirators that filtered the air down into the micron range, and deep green goggles to protect against the flood of ultraviolet rays from the overhead lighting.

Unlike most installations, the respirators were not worn here to protect the people in the suits. Instead, they protected the computer from any organisms that might be exhaled from the lungs of the people maintaining the central machine.

Because, unlike any other computer in the world, this one was composed of living tissue.

Some time back, computer scientists worried that conventional computers might run out of gas as they ascended the performance curve. When integrated circuits became jammed with ever smaller detail, strange things began to happen. Very fine metal traces, the "wires" of the circuit, began to slow the rush of electrons containing the desired signal, much like a narrow stream causes a logjam you wouldn't encounter in a wider river. And alpha particles from cosmic rays scattered electrons like pins before a bowling ball, aborting their electrical mission inside the chip. Finally, at very small scales, quantum mechanics would ultimately turn every electronic transaction into a roll of the dice. Some circuits now conducted certain kinds of business with fewer than a hundred thousand electrons, and it was well known that when this number went down to one hundred, there would be a 10 percent probability of error in each transaction.

So a search began for other ways of computing that might be smaller and faster. There were many possibilities to consider. Essentially, a computer is a chimerical, mathematical beast that can assume any earthly form that allows it to execute a form of mathematics called Boolean algebra.

One such form turned out to be certain kinds of molecules that could be switched between the on and off states required by Boolean equations. Many such molecular paradigms were proposed in theory, but found wanting in practicality. Ironically, they returned computing to the age of the mechanical calculator, albeit at a fantastically reduced scale, and required enormously complex designs involving gears, switches, and levers built from molecules, all interacting mechanically to perform computations.

The Webster Foundation ultimately settled on a molecular circuit. But on a much simpler one. A circuit already designed by none other than nature itself.

For many years, the inside of an animal cell was considered a squishy little ocean where small bags of jelly with different functions floated and squirmed inside the cytoplasm. But eventually, a cellular entity with much greater structure and symmetry was discovered, the cytoskeleton. Like a vertebrate skeleton, it gives the cell shape, but then it goes on to perform many other astonishing feats, such as continually demolishing and rebuilding itself to accommodate the current requirements of the intracellular community. It also acts as a vast distribution and control system, shipping construction materials and tools through its network of fibrous tunnels called microtubules.

All these tiny tunnels have precisely the same design and are constructed from a single type of molecule that comes in two flavors, which can represent the on and off states required for Boolean equations. These molecules form the microtubule tunnel by arranging themselves into a tube that resembles a piece of chicken wire folded into a cylinder about thirteen-billionths of a meter in diameter. Each hexagon in the chicken wire represents a single molecule, and as it turns out, the current flavor of this molecule is dependent on the current flavor of its neighbors. Which in turn means that elaborate patterns of these two flavors, representing digital information, can be made to ripple up and down the walls of the microtubules. Better yet, the microtubules are interconnected by tiny molecular filaments that can also propagate on/off patterns from one tunnel to another.

Thus, the whole system becomes an elaborate circuit capable of functioning as a full-fledged computer system—at fantastic densities and speeds. A single molecule in the system is a scant eight-billionths of a meter in width. The time required to switch a molecule from on to off is about ten picoseconds, or one-hundredth of one billionth of a second. A comparable electronic operation would be twenty to fifty times slower.

As it turned out, nature had designed the microtubules to be self-assembling. They didn't need to be tucked inside a cell to survive. All you had to do was put their chemical building blocks into a nutrient liquid, and they spontaneously organized into elaborate networks capable of truly prodigious feats of computing.

The central security chamber at the Webster Foundation now held what quickly became known as the cytoputer, which dwelled in a bulletproof glass beaker filled with nutrient chemicals to keep its microtubular network alive and well. Much of the rest of the chamber housed elaborate chemical control systems designed to create an optimum living environment for this special set of microtubules and their unprecedented calculating power. It also housed the input/output system, which was constructed from SQUIDS, superconducting quantum interference devices, which converted the molecular activity into electrical signals that could be handled by more conventional computer circuitry. An adjacent chamber held a fast conventional computer whose only purpose was to serve the whims of its organic cousin during the calculating, which routinely shattered every known performance record for computers of any sort.

The meter needle on Elaine's display now showed only two minutes until the session was complete. Good. The run was going to go off without a hitch. A good thing, because Peter Rancovich, the cytoputer's chief technician, was off on vacation in South America doing God knew what.

As always, Elaine felt a tingle of anticipation as she speculated about what they would see. While Agent 57a was not particularly exotic, it had fairly devastating potential, and a relatively high probability of expressing itself in the global biosphere. Thank God they were observing it this way, as a cybernetic threat, instead of a real one.

Speaking of nightmares, she had had one about Bennet the other night. She was at the beach and he buried her up to her neck in sand as the tide came in. As she screamed to be rescued, he sat cross-legged before her with a concerned look and nodded sympathetically as she struggled to free herself, but he did nothing to help.

The dream was one more signpost on her journey out of his life, and she hoped he wouldn't show up tonight, but he probably would. These runs were the Foundation's sole reason for existing, and Bennet loved to see the big action take place. After all, they were witnessing a great advance in epidemiology, one with truly global implications, which explained Uni Corporation's great interest in its success.

Before the Foundation, before the cytoputer, many efforts had been made to study the spread of disease through computer-based modeling. Most were quite ingenious and some produced useful results. To construct a model, the historical behavior of a disease was studied statistically to determine how it acted in the real world. Mathematical tools such as regression analysis allowed investigators to search for links between different traits of a disease. Was its infection rate related to population density? Did it occur only in the winter months? Were only the elderly vulnerable? Or the very young? Was its rate of spread linked to the size of animal or insect populations that carried the disease from person to person?

This statistical analysis then became the raw material for a model that encapsulated the general behavior of the disease. This behavioral model could then be immersed in a database that represented the environment where the disease resided. The database could include such things as the geographic distribution of the population, the age and health profile, climatic fluctuations, and any other measurable phenomena that might play a part.

All of these endeavors shared one thing in common: they used the past behavior of a disease to predict its behavior in the future. But now there was an urgent need to find a different modeling method, because many modern diseases either had no past or were mutating so rapidly that their past was irrelevant. AIDS and the Ebola virus were just two examples of diseases that came out of nowhere. And the sudden, nasty turn of the hantavirus was a prime example of an old disease with a new and deadly disposition.

Finally, there was the highly disturbing problem of two or more diseases intersecting in a way that promoted the virility of one or more of the pathological partners. The intersection of AIDS and tuberculosis provided a tragic illustration. Equally ominous was the exchange of genetic information among bacteria, a dark and powerful underground network in their rebellion against drugs.

So how could you employ computerized techniques to predict the future course of emerging diseases? The solution undertaken by the Webster team was the most complex and ambitious project in the entire history of mathematical biology. The project's name, based on its core technology, was lettered in silver on the glass outside the cytoputer chamber.

EpiSim

In the past, most attempts at predicting the future behavior of diseases boiled down to extrapolation, a concept familiar even to high school students. You start with a graph containing a straight line that slopes from left to right, but then stops somewhere in the middle of the graph space. This stopping point represents the end of the past and the start of the future. To extrapolate the line into the future, you simply extend the straight line on its present course. With more complex math, you can do the same for a wide variety of curved lines. In every case, the line represents some form of behavior, and the past predicts the future.

So to extrapolate something's behavior, you essentially observed its reactions to the world about it and reduced these to a line on a graph that could be extended into the future. If you wanted to predict the action of an auto engine within a particular car, you would observe that if you depressed the accelerator pedal a certain number of degrees, the engine would turn at a certain speed and move the car forward at a predictable velocity. Press the pedal another degree, and the engine speed increases by a certain amount, as does the car speed. After many observations, you would have a graph with a line that described the engine's behavior and its effect on the car's motion. You could then extend this line to predict the car's future behavior, at least within practical limits.

Nevertheless, you would know nothing about the engine itself, only how it behaved. It was a black box; and its innards, which represented the true nature of the thing being modeled, were still a mystery. The same was true when modeling a disease. You would see the symptoms it created, but witness nothing of the great chemical orchestra playing inside the germ as it elaborated its ancient theme of pathos.

Now what if you were designing a brand-new engine? Or dealing with an emerging disease that has never before existed? Could you rely on old black boxes to predict how new ones might operate? Absolutely not. New engines or diseases have their own unique way of doing things. And without a predictive black box, you had no mathematical line of behavior to extend into the future, no way to forecast their behavior.

The only way around the problem was to rip the black box open and replace its mysterious innards with a detailed facsimile of a real engine. You reduce the object being modeled to its most primitive elements and mathematically derive a set of laws describing how they interact.

In the case of the auto engine, you started with the gas pedal as before. But now you modeled how the pedal was linked to the fuel injector, and how the injector mixed air with gas, and how the fuel pump got the gas to the injector, and how the intakes and valves routed the gas into the cylinders, and so on. Now you had a model that rigorously described how the engine produced the behavior in the car, rather than just the behavior itself. And by tweaking the model here and there, you could simulate the behavior of virtually any engine of the same basic design—even one that had never been built.

With these so-called deductive models, you had a much more reliable method of forecasting the future behavior of emerging and mutating diseases, even ones that had no history behind them.

To complete EpiSim's epidemic simulation environment,

many models were involved. First, the team constructed a detailed account of how the infectious agent worked. Its reproduction, its reaction to temperature and pH, its mobility, its synthesis of toxins, its reaction to antibiotics, and many other factors were combined to describe the bug's internal functioning. Next you needed to simulate the human immune system, the delicate dance between the lymphocytes, macrophages, phagocytes, and coordinating chemicals that all mobilized in times of infectious war. You also needed models of the vectors, the creatures that gave the infectious agent an unwitting ride from one place to another. Sometimes these were human, other times they were animals or insects relegated to the role of organic taxis carrying free fares.

Every scientific field has what are often called its grand challenges. And building these simulation models was one of the grand challenges of biological mathematics. Every organism is a hierarchical system, from the whole body down to collections of molecules inside individual cells. The mathematics of this organization were forbiddingly complex, at least until several conceptual breakthroughs occurred in the emerging field of complexity theory. This new knowledge supplied radical and powerful tools to describe how the different parts of the hierarchy related to each other, thus allowing the creation of highly accurate organic simulation models.

In the EpiSim project's simulation environment, the models were the actors; and like all actors, they required a stage. In this case, the stage was a huge database that viewed the world from the standpoint of infectious agents. Compared to the human view, it was a bizarre and distorted landscape. Due to transportation links, the major urban centers of the world were clustered almost in each other's backyards, with smaller cities forming a larger suburban area, and a vast outback representing rural areas. The view was further distorted by differing concentrations of people, seasonal variations, and the distribution of vector populations.

There was also the question of scale. Ideally, the simulation of an epidemic would involve a model of every person in the population and the quirks of their particular immune system. Since this was obviously impossible, the next best thing was to break the population down into groups that shared common traits. For instance, male smokers over sixty-five with a history of lung infections might be a group unto themselves, as would children under twelve with no vaccinations. For the Webster Foundation project, the general simulation model of the immune system was then tweaked to apply these to thousands of specific groups.

Finally, there was the matter of chance. Many earlier attempts at epidemic modeling were hobbled by a lack of computing power that mandated unrealistic assumptions about the behavior of the population under study. It might be assumed that every time an infected person came in contact with an uninfected one, the latter would come down with the disease. Or that everyone in the population is exposed to everyone else at sometime in the course of the epidemic. A better, but more complicated way was to make simulated events much more prone to chance, as they are in reality. Within EpiSim, each time an infected person met a healthy one, a kind of mathematical coin was tossed. Sometimes an infection occurred. Sometimes not.

When an EpiSim simulation actually ran on the cytoputer, it demanded calculations of epic proportion. The database contained billions of records representing the global population, and the interaction of these records rippled out in a grand web as the hypothetical epidemic progressed through space and time. Each interaction required its own stunningly intricate set of calculations as the model of the infectious agent did battle with one of the immune-system models.

As the simulation ran its course, another program acted as a historian and recorded the progress of the epidemic as it crept across the global cyberspace. The resulting data was then refined into a series of reports and graphics that showed the progress of the epidemic. The profiles of individual epidemics varied greatly. Some flared up locally then quickly sputtered out. Others marched slowly but surely across the globe. Still others came in successive waves.

Elaine watched the graphical meter on her screen peg at eight hours. The cytoputer run for infectious Agent 57a was over. In just a minute, she would have a preliminary compilation of the results. She got up, stretched, and walked out the door and into the hall. Empty. Good. She'd expected to see Bennet striding aggressively toward her office, so he could see the results of what he called "the big show." She didn't want to share this moment of discovery with anybody, especially him. Agent 57a was her very own creation, and in just a moment, she would have the godlike experience of seeing how it might alter the entire course of human history—at least in theory.

The creation of Agent 57a itself was a special subset of EpiSim. When the project first started, all its resources were applied to testing the system by running known epidemics and observing how well the simulation matched the actual history. Now the testing was fairly complete, and the next step would be to examine emerging diseases. But another goal of the product was to create agents that had never existed and to observe their impact on the biosphere. These artificial infectious agents would be a valuable tool in studying the dynamics of disease in general.

Rather than develop germs that were totally fictitious, Elaine proposed the creation of diseases that were fairly close to the real thing—but with a bit of internal remodeling, the kind that nature might produce through genetic mutations. Once the budget was approved (with an executive nod from Bennet), Elaine undertook an extended investigation to discover what type of new germ was most likely to make its global debut. Some forms were more likely than others to spontaneously mutate. Others were often in close contact with microbial cousins who could slip them new genetic information. Still others were highly susceptible to man-made mutagens. By sorting through these possibilities and applying various statistical filters, Elaine brought the cytoputer to bear and came up with the most likely candidate of all, Agent 57a, which apparently had a 72 percent chance of becoming a reality within the next decade.

Surprisingly, it wasn't a virus, but a bacteria. Even more surprisingly, it was rarely found in humans. At least, not yet.

Its immediate parent was *Chlamydia psittaci*, usually found in birds.

Once Elaine determined the exact attributes of this odd newcomer to the realm of diseases, she went into EpiSim's bacterial modeling library and began to construct the thing from the inside out. Just last week she had completed testing, and tonight was Agent 57a's debut in the main ring of the EpiSim project.

A synthesized sparrow chirped on her computer. The data was ready.

As she sat back down, the screen brought up three summaries of the simulation: a world map, a line graph, and a table. The map gave the quickest read. It was programmed to show the area affected by the epidemic three months after its onset. The oceans were blue and the continental land masses were brown with purple areas to show the territory conquered by the disease.

And tonight, all the continents were solid purple. In just ninety days, Agent 57a could be everywhere.

10

The City of Iquitos

MARIA SANTOZ CRUISED SLOWLY DOWN THE SIDEWALK ON Brasil Street and watched the neon splatter reds, yellows, and greens across the pavement, which still glistened from an evening rainstorm. In the wake of the downpour, a sodden heat hung in the air, a lustful heat that would be good for business. After six months on the street, Maria understood such things and leveraged them as much as possible. But right now, it was a buyer's market. The rain had driven all the prospects into the bars and hotels, where they launched pitiful little amorous expeditions almost certain to flounder. And to salvage their efforts, they would turn to professionals like her, who occupied strategic positions on barstools and lobby couches.

But Maria could no longer mine these profitable indoor veins of illicit congress. The problem was one of light, and how even modest quantities of it revealed certain flaws in the product she offered. On the street, where the light was more subdued, the defects were not so much an issue. By the time a deal had been struck, and the customer was blind with salacious expectation, quality was seldom an issue.

But now, as she drifted through the wet pools of neon, business matters dissolved into the damp street, and her heart floated up out of a crack in the sidewalk.

And with it came Felix.

Yes, there he was. Felix of the impossible smile. Felix of the amber eyes. Felix of the coffee skin and flat belly. Felix of the large muscular hands moving like a cat gone mad across the frets of his Fender bass.

Felix played world beat. In fact, Felix *was* world beat. Part African, part Portuguese. She still remembered the first time she saw him at the Club Mercury, a bar out on the leading edge of pop culture in Iquitos. The place was packed with local glitterati, sons and daughters of local government and business families who formed the avant-garde of the local aristocracy. Unlike this privileged majority, she belonged to a small minority who wormed into the Club Mercury through a murky assortment of loopholes. Some offered discreet drug purchases. Others were spectacular dancers. Still others had the gift of quick wit. And a few, like Maria, were exceptionally beautiful.

Her perfect skin, thunderous black hair, and taut figure had all arrived in her sixteenth year—and immediately set out to destroy her. In the little shack in Belén, she grew like a perfect flower out of the muck around her and ignited numerous fires far beyond her control. One of her uncles tried to rape her and instead was beaten senseless by her enraged father, who was as envious as he was indignant. A jealous female cousin put a curse on her, which tied her stomach in a knot for several months. A pack of lecherous young men circled her in an endless ballet of predation, just waiting for the right moment to strike.

In response, she developed a two-pronged strategy of self-rescue. First, she leveraged her beauty to harness a willing workforce for the construction of a defensive perimeter about herself. The romantically smitten and the insecure volunteered in droves for the job and went about their work with great passion and dedication.

Second, she looked for a way out. It was already obvious to her that great sexual beauty was a hard currency, one negotiable in virtually every corner of society, from the floating shacks on the muddy river to the penthouses atop the tallest buildings downtown. It was simply a matter of learning the market and how to exploit it.

So when a girlfriend told her about the Club Mercury, she was filled with a giddy mixture of anxiety and expectation. From her admiring court of cousins, sisters, and friends, she borrowed enough clothes to assemble a decent outfit, then spent hours working on her hair. And as she sat before a jagged piece of mirror, Maria sadly realized that she was a romantic proxy for all those other women who would never escape, but would go with her in spirit.

Her insight proved correct when she and her friend arrived that night at the club's entrance. When they reached the front of the line, a rude young man with a crew cut and an earring stood as guardian of the gate in a fashionably floppy sport coat and khaki shorts. After casting a cold, appraising eye on the two of them, he let Maria through and rejected her girlfriend, who gave her a teary hug and slunk back through the city toward the river.

Once inside, Maria knew instantly she had crossed some kind of osmotic barrier that would never let her return to Belén, except as a base camp to assist her in scaling some unknown summit. The elegant people, the fine clothes, the electric chatter, and the flashing lights swirled about her like a galaxy of infinite proportion.

And then the music caught her ear. The singer was the center of attention in the band, to be sure. His dreadlocks flew about in wild synchronicity as he cupped the microphone to his lips. But then, to the side, her eye caught a searing flash of white, and one of Felix's impossibly huge smiles radiated straight to the center of her heart. He bounced and swayed with the rhythm as his hands played over the four steel strings in a supremely sensuous manner. And in that wild moment, Maria knew in her soul that Felix was not playing the bass; he was playing her and coaxing out the most beautiful of melodies.

The magic of this moment elevated her onto a plateau where she stayed for several months. Given her stunning looks, the introduction to Felix seemed almost a foregone conclusion, and their affair predestined by some cosmic mandate. The gloss of the club melted away like candy in the sun, and all that was left was Felix, who bathed her in ecstasy. In the mornings, he would run a feather down her back to awaken her, and they would have a simple breakfast on the balcony of his little apartment that overlooked a park, where they watched all the poor mortals stroll about far beneath them.

But that was months back. Now, on the wet and muggy sidewalk, Maria spied a prospect at the far end of the block, a stocky man in white pants and a sport shirt walking slowly her way. She took a moment to adjust her blond wig with its jumble of artificial curls, and to pull the hem of her miniskirt straight. Next, she checked the available light. Good. At the point where she would intercept him, there was only secondhand street light to illuminate their bargaining session. This meant the customer would not notice the swarms of small pitted scars that crept down her shoulders and neck and disappeared into her bosom under the cotton top piece that covered her breasts. The scars also covered her face, but a liberal application of makeup pretty much hid them from view. Fortunately, her backside had been spared, so if a bargain was struck and they retired to a hotel room, she would disrobe and present only her back and bottom for the customer's perusal during the consummation of the deal. Most customers seem quite satisfied with this arrangement.

Maria knew the cause of the scarring all too well. It was a curse, a hex engineered by someone in Belén and expertly applied by a shaman. Who? Hard to tell. A woman jealous of her beauty, perhaps. Or a spurned suitor. It really didn't matter. Whatever the source, the result was the same. Felix was gone and she was afflicted, her beauty severely compromised.

The curse had fallen upon her in three stages. First, she lost Felix. His band got a gig in Rio, and despite a spectacular display of female hysterics and tears, he wouldn't take her along. However, he did hold her tight and promise that his heart would be with her no matter where he went. In the end, it was scant consolation. There were also more practical matters. Without Felix, she had no room and board, no way to survive in the more prosperous zones of Iquitos. Nevertheless, it would be better to die than to return to Belén and descend back into the smoldering pit of perpetual poverty. Given this attitude, her life as a prostitute was nearly inevitable. At the Club Mercury, she had seen certain young women plying this trade, beautiful, well-dressed girls who arrived in taxis and could afford their own drinks and meals. A few return visits to the club and Maria was quickly in business as a sole proprietor.

Then, just as she was established, the second part of the curse came in the form of chancre sores. With a mirror, she could see one on her left labia, a rimmed crater a half inch in diameter with a smooth, moist, pink plain inside. With her finger, she could feel a second sore higher up inside her vagina. The sores prevented her from working for a month or so, while she prayed for the curse to be lifted and even consulted a shaman for advice, who put her on a very specific regimen of herbs. To her great relief, the herbs apparently worked, and the sores quickly disappeared. The only remaining disease was the huge hole in her heart left by Felix.

Then, less than a month later, the curse returned with horrific velocity. Her fever shot up to 102 degrees and tried to boil all the fluids out of her body as she lay stricken in her tiny apartment. The lymph nodes in her groin, neck, and armpits swelled to the size of golf balls, and she broke out with swarms of little scabs that eventually pitted her skin with scar tissue. At this point, she turned to conventional medicine and had a friend bring her antibiotics purchased off the street. In Maria's mind, there was no distinct line of demarcation between science and superstition. The drugs were just another kind of charm to ward off the terrible curse that had descended upon her. The little capsules were like beads on a ceremonial necklace fashioned by spirits deep in the jungle. Unfortunately, they also contained no antibiotics. The unregulated street trade in medicinal drugs made it impossible to know what held the power to heal in addition to the power to hope. In this case, only hope survived.

Soon, the curse reached its point of maximum density and the disease took total possession of her as she lay on the soaked sheets and shivered violently.

It was at this very moment that she had the vision. The grimy ceiling fell away, and she saw Felix sitting at a table in an outdoor café clutching an iced tea. Behind him was a beautiful little town bleached white by a sun that hovered directly overhead. He flashed his impossible smile at her.

"Don't go, my love. Find me. Come to me."

By morning, the fever had broken. She sipped some tea, drank some soup, and held tightly to the vision of Felix, preserving every detail.

Now, on the sidewalk, the man was very close and glanced over at her. Maria locked onto his eyes in a bold gesture that signaled her availability. The man failed to reciprocate and walked on past into the muggy night.

Very lucky. He had just avoided a potential encounter with a spirochete called *Treponema pallidum,* which now had taken up permanent residence inside Maria. *T. pallidum* is the infectious agent of syphilis, and in Maria, the disease had now completed its secondary stage and temporarily faded into the physiological background. Nevertheless, it maintained a thriving germ population inside her, a horde of tiny spiraled rods very eager to invest in fresh tissue.

Marie walked on without looking back. She was relieved that there was no sale. It gave her more time to think about how she would find Felix and stay with him always.

"It looks like maybe you were right," admitted David Muldane as he stood before Paris's metal desk and its mess of unprocessed paperwork. It was noon, and most of the other desks in Burglary and Theft were deserted.

"About what?" Paris asked.

"About the poisoner."

Paris managed a grim smile. "Of course I was right. No maybes about it. I was right the first time, too. And the second time." He leaned back in his office chair and clasped his big arms behind his head. "Sit down. Tell me about it."

"It'll be in the paper by tonight," said David as he sat down in the dilapidated straight-back chair. "We've got two dozen confirmed cases, six in the hospital. There's probably a few more who just toughed it out and didn't go to the doctor."

"Anybody seriously sick?"

"Nope. We've got the usual dehydration and severe nausea, but nobody's at death's door. Same as the other times.

It's *E. coli,* and it's exactly the same strain. The lab just confirmed it."

"What are you going to tell the press?"

"Just the facts. No speculation about the cause."

"Good!" exclaimed Paris. "We've got enough problems without our boy knowing we're onto him."

"What makes you so sure it's a male? Shouldn't we keep an open mind about this?"

Paris twinkled. "Could be a woman. But not likely. It's a style thing. Style's all wrong for a woman. Just like you seldom run into female serial killers, you hardly ever have a woman pyromaniac. The evil that men do tends to be done by men and men alone."

"So men are the root of all evil?" David asked, a little defensively.

"Hardly. Like I said, it's just a matter of style. Let me tell you a story. One time out on the street, I saw three kids about ten years old, two boys and a girl. One of the boys was throwing rocks at an abandoned car. The car was already a goner, so I hung back to watch them before they could spot me. The kid throwing the rocks was a born vandal and had this kind of burning glee. Real aggressive, real violent. The other boy watched the vandal and did nothing—at first, anyway. Then he began to watch the girl. And then he began to watch how the girl watched the vandal. She was totally seduced. Even at that age. You should have seen the adoring look in her eyes. She loved the energy. She loved the action. So, guess what happened."

"The other boy started throwing rocks to impress the girl?"

"You got it. Now that's a crime of passion, a crime that'll never be on the books, but a crime nevertheless. Probably first committed a million years ago. But that's not the kind of thing our particular criminal would be interested in."

"Okay, let's assume this is a male crime. How do we locate the particular male who's doing it?"

"What's the name of the food joint this time?"

"It's called the Western Family Steakhouse. It's in South Seattle. Just a run-of-the-mill place. No previous violations. I took a quick look at it and didn't see anything that looked unsanitary. We're running checks on the employees right now, but they're all coming up clean. Just like all the other times."

"Doesn't leave us much, does it?"

"No. It doesn't."

"Well, let me tell you what I would do with this case if it was my job, and not a sideline," said Paris.

"And what is that?"

"I'd do it the hard way, just like I did before. I'd go back to every restaurant, starting with the most recent. I'd talk to everybody who was working there the day of the bug, and to all the victims. I'd try to find out if they noticed anything unusual. Like somebody spilling something or wandering into the kitchen. I'd also check to see if anybody could be traced on paper to all the places. Like a common employee."

"Let's back up a little. First of all, you were right about something else: you don't have a lot of friends over in public health. I asked around and the word is that you're a little off the deep end." David stopped and cast a nervous look at Paris. "Why didn't you tell me about your wife? I mean, that's got to be at least part of it for you, doesn't it?"

"You're right. It's got to be part of it. But not all of it. Not by a long shot. There's a guy out there poisoning people. A very patient guy. And so far, he's winning big, because there isn't even official recognition that he exists. Your people in public health may be great detectives when it comes to germs, but that's where it ends. It's going to take a real cop to find him."

"So where does that leave us? I thought you wanted my help. But I'm not a cop."

"No, you're not. But you're sharp and you're knowledgeable. You know the medical end of this thing. I don't. So I want you to think. I know there's a way to crack this thing. It might be scientific. It might be intuitive. It might be a combination of both. So just keep on thinking about it. You know, in those odd moments. Like when you're zipping up your trousers. Times like that. Sooner or later, we'll get lucky. In the meantime, let me know what's going on. I can't show my face around your office without catching a whole lot of shit, so you need to tell me how the case unfolds."

"Sounds like you want me to be a spy. I'm not sure if I like that."

Paris leaned forward. "You know why you came down here? You know why you're sitting there?"

"Why?" said David in a tone that implied he already knew the answer.

"Because deep down in your gut, you know I'm right. You know that guy's out there. You can feel it. I know you can."

David stood. "You're right, I guess. Okay. I'll let you know what's going on."

"Good."

"One other thing."

"What's that?"

"I'm sorry about your wife. My whole career is trying to prevent things like that from happening."

"Thanks. I appreciate that."

As David left, Paris sank back in his chair. He wasn't surprised that the poisoner had emerged once more. But he was surprised by his attitude about it. He'd expected that the news would reignite the terrible passion that had consumed so much of his life since Ginny's coma. Instead, it hit him at a much more oblique angle, and a large part of the hurt simply bounced off. He would carry on his search, but he wouldn't let it throw him around and smash him against hard surfaces, like his job and his health.

As Paris climbed to his feet, he surveyed the empty desks and they formed a gray metal chorus that told him it was time to get out for a bit.

And that's exactly what he did.

11

"SO, ELAINE, WHY DON'T YOU GIVE US A QUICK EXECUTIVE summary of Agent 57a?"

Bennet's voice drifted out of the stereo speakers in

Elaine's desktop computer as she watched a portrait-size image of him on her screen. There were similar images of Mr. Jiminez, a balding man in his forties, and Ms. Hokuro, an Asian woman in her fifties. She also saw a picture of herself, produced by the cyclopean videocam eye at the top of her flat-panel display, with the obnoxious little red LED underneath to remind her she was onstage.

During the introductions, Bennet had explained that both these other people worked in Uni's Organics Sector, Mr. Jiminez in sales and marketing, and Ms. Hokuro in research and development. No other explanations were given. They could be involved in anything from fertilizer to baby formula to antiviral therapies.

Obviously, Bennet was being his usual cryptic self about what all this might mean. Elaine was still annoyed that he had popped up on her screen not five minutes after the simulation was complete, asking a multitude of questions about the potential consequences of an epidemic fueled by Agent 57a. It seemed he had been monitoring the entire run from his office on the fourth floor and saw the results at the same moment she had. What could she say? When it came right down to it, there would be no runs at all without Bennet to champion the Webster Foundation's work to the arcane corners of the Uni-verse that funded their project.

"It's a variation on an organism called *Chlamydia psittaci*," said Elaine.

"*Chlamydia?*" said Jiminez. "Does that have something to do with venereal disease? Some kind of thing that women get?"

"There's more than one kind of *Chlamydia*," explained Elaine. "You're thinking of a kind called *Chlamydia trachomatis*. And it's not just women that get it. Men get it, too—and spread it. It causes symptoms similar to gonorrhea, with a lot of pain and infection. Anyway, both forms of *Chlamydia* are a type of organism known as rickettsia."

"Not exactly," said Ms. Hokuro in excellent English. "They are a very close cousin, but not precisely the same as rickettsia."

"That's correct," conceded Elaine. Aha. Ms. Horuko was showing a little professional ankle. She obviously had at least some knowledge in the field of microbiology. "But for our purposes, the differences are not of any consequence."

"So what's so special about this kind of bug?" asked Jiminez.

"Well, for starters, it's extremely small. In fact, it's the smallest thing that's truly alive—unless you consider viruses to be living things, which most people don't. It's at the very limit of what you can see with an optical microscope. It's also a parasite. It needs the energy machinery inside animal cells to survive. It burrows into living cells and reproduces until it destroys its host, and then all its babies drift off to look for new homes."

"Yuk," said Jiminez.

"You can't judge the microbial world using human values, Mr. Jiminez," Elaine responded. "It exists unto itself and couldn't care less what we think of it. Anyway, the form of *Chlamydia* we used to create Agent 57a causes a type of pneumonia called psittacosis. In the U.S. it's pretty rare. You only see about sixty to seventy cases per year. But if you get it, it can be a very nasty business. First of all, it's hard to diagnose. You have to culture it in living tissue, which means taking a sputum sample, staining the cell, then searching for the bug with a microscope. The other way is through serological tests, which hunt for antibodies the immune system produces when it tries to stomp out the little critters. Once it's detected, the standard treatment is tetracycline; but even then, it takes a while to recover completely. And if you don't receive treatment, you've got about a twenty percent chance of dying from it."

"So, how might you get something like this?" inquired Mr. Jiminez with a slight hint of anxiety.

"From birds."

"Birds?"

"Yes, birds. The entire psittacine family is susceptible to it. Parrots, pigeons, chickens, turkeys, and seagulls, among others. All it takes are the right circumstances. In the 1970s, there was an outbreak in a turkey packing plant in Nebraska. Twenty-seven people got it all at once. You can also get it from other people."

"That's very interesting," said Ms. Hokuro. "But let's get

back to Agent 57a. Why did you choose *Chlamydia psittaci* as its progenitor?"

"Some of the reasons are mathematically complex, but some are just common sense. First of all, there are several qualities a bug can have that make it a prime candidate for an epidemic. One is being transmitted in aerosol form through the air, like TB or the flu. It's the quickest way to spread something where there are high concentrations of people."

"You mean like in buildings in cities?" asked Jiminez.

"Exactly. Another important quality is the disease's incubation period. The longer you carry it around and shed the germs before you know you're sick, the more people you're likely to infect. In the case of psittacosis, you can carry it for up to two weeks before you know you're ill, so you've got a long time to infect the people around you."

"What could be worse?" asked Jiminez.

"Vectors."

"What do you mean 'vectors'?"

"In this case, it's the birds. A vector is any organism that carries the germs from one place to another. When the bubonic plague hit Europe, the plague bacteria was carried by rats and fleas, which together made a highly efficient vector team. The germs resided in the fleas, which hitched a ride on the rats for long-distance hauls. They could then hop off and find a nearby human to bite. With *Chlamydia psittaci*, you've got birds capable of flying great distances and then transmitting the disease through airborne particles when they reach their destination."

"So, Dr. Wilkes," interjected Ms. Hokuro, "if psittacosis has these qualities, why haven't we already seen an epidemic of it?"

"That's where Agent 57a and EpiSim come in. It appears that the current strain of *Chlamydia* is not virulent enough to cause an epidemic. However, that doesn't mean it couldn't become so through mutation. And *Chlamydia* does indeed mutate. There are already six known serotypes in birds."

" 'Serotypes'?" asked Jiminez.

"When an organism enters your body," interjected Ms. Hokuro, "your immune system identifies it by subtle characteristics of its molecular makeup called antigens. The system then manufactures antibodies that are specifically customized to fit these antigens in a way that destroys the invading organism. By checking for specific antibodies in your blood—or in a bird's blood—you can identify an infectious agent very precisely. These very exact identifications are called serotypes."

"Couldn't have said it better myself," commented Elaine. She was already a little less than objective about Ms. Hokuro. "In this case, ninety-five percent of the samples fall into one serotype, and that's the one we used to engineer Agent 57a. One thing we needed to do was take this basic *Chlamydia* model and make it more aggressive, so that it would have a much higher hit rate when it went to infect a bird or a human. This turned out to be fairly simple. Only three chromosome sites needed to be modified, and not by much. Next, we boosted its resistance to antibiotics. Once again, this wasn't too tough. The only drug that is really effective against it is the tetracycline family, and all we had to do was modify a single plasmid to render it impotent. There are other drugs that work, but not as well. In a real-world situation, they would be sort of a last line of defense."

"You mean there's no cure for this thing?" asked Jiminez.

"Nope. Not really. Your only defense is your own immune system. But that's not much consolation. When we ran our model against all our subtypes of human immune systems, the bug did much better than the humans. About seventy-five percent of the simulated infections resulted in death. But don't get too worried—at least not yet. You've got to remember that 57a only exists as a model inside a computer. At least for now."

"But what about later?" Jiminez asked warily.

"That's a different story. The most difficult part of the project with 57a was to determine how likely it was for a thing like this to actually come into existence. It involved some very sophisticated statistical analyses. There were thousands of other candidates besides 57a, and we had to narrow down the pack through a great deal of mathematical filtering. But in the end, good old 57a came out the winner. We calculate a seventy-two percent probability that it will emerge within the next ten years."

"I'd like to see a detailed description of your methodology," said Ms. Hokuro.

"No problem," said Bennet before Elaine could protest. "We'll get you everything you need."

Elaine glared at the little image of Bennet on her screen. The son of a bitch just gave away several years of her life to someone she didn't even know. She'd never quite made the adjustment to the fact that the Foundation was now a commercial entity and not an academic one.

"Now let's talk about tonight's run. What happened?" Bennet asked Elaine.

"Well, in a word, we set Agent 57a loose in the simulated world to see what would happen. We selected a spot at random between fifteen degrees north and south latitude and let it do its thing."

"Why that particular region?" asked Ms. Hokuro.

"Several reasons. For one, you've got the largest concentration of psittacine birds in this zone, and they're the reservoir for the infection. Also, the tropics have the greatest amount of biological activity per square foot of land, so it's just more likely that things will happen here."

"So what happened?" asked Jiminez.

"Well, you've all seen the map," said Elaine, referring to the world map of continents painted purple with disease. "Let's move on to the graph." She issued a command that brought up a graph with four curved lines that ran its length. Simultaneously, the graph was appearing on everyone else's screen. The lines represented the S, I, R, and D groups, the four classic categories used in the study of epidemics. *S* stood for susceptible, which referred to healthy people who did not yet have the disease. *I* signified the infected, those who were sick. *R* were those who had gotten sick and recovered. *D* meant deceased.

On this particular graph, the S line plunged down a steep slope as the population rapidly became infected, and the I line came up to meet it. Most ominously, the D line arched sharply upward as a seventy-five percent fatality rate took hold within the infected group. At the far end of the graph, at the twelve-month mark in the epidemic's history, the D line was more than halfway to the top, with the R line somewhat lower. Sixty percent of the planet's total population had died.

"A sixty percent fatality rate? In just twelve months? Are you sure?" asked Ms. Hokuro. For the first time, her scientific persona yielded to a touch of fear.

"That's what it appears," responded Elaine. "And remember: This is a graph of the world population, about five and a half billion people. So you're looking at how the disease progresses across the entire planet. In any one locality, especially cities, the time scale is quite compressed. You might see the whole cycle occur in just two to three months."

"How soon can we expect a full report?" inquired Ms. Hokuro.

"I can have both the executive summary and the supporting data ready later this evening. The sooner we get this to the Centers for Disease Control and the World Health Organization, the better."

All three of the little video portraits on her screen stared at her in a moment of silence, which Bennet broke.

"Yes, I think we've all got a lot of work to do," he said gravely. "Elaine, thanks for your incredible effort. Let's meet again tomorrow at oh two hundred Universal time. See you all later.'"

One by one, the little portraits disappeared, until only the map and the graph were left on Elaine's screen. She slumped in her chair, tired but agitated. They had obviously gotten weird when she mentioned the public health people. Why?

Bennet fought to control the expanding dome of excitement that threatened to fill him and expel his normal caution and common sense.

The business opportunities offered by Agent 57a were overwhelming. As he sprinted through one scheme, another would flash before him, and he would tear off to see what new treasures it might offer. Then another, and another.

At the same time, he forced himself to go through the mechanics needed to set up the proper forces inside Uni. The first action item was to get on his machine immediately and call Jiminez and Hokuro back into conference. There was much to discuss, and most of it was not suitable for the ears of Elaine Wilkes. Pity about her. A good mind, a fine lover. But not a player. Never a real player.

So now Bennet reached out through his speculative buzz to set up the teleconference—and made a small error. The teleconferencing program allowed you to define "groups," specific sets of people that you wanted to tie into a single teleconference session. This way, you didn't have to enter all their names and cyber addresses every time you set up a conference. The computer did all the dialing and arranging. Further, you could break groups down into "active" and "monitor" participants. Active were those whose video and audio appeared on each other's screen and speaker. Monitor were those who weren't actually displayed, but could see and hear the active participants.

Now, in his excitement, Bennet slid down a menu and selected a group simply called "57a—sim2." What he forgot was the difference between "57a—sim1" and "57a—sim2." The former included only Bennet, Jiminez, and Hokuro. The latter also included Elaine Wilkes as a monitor; a silent, invisible witness.

The chime on her computer pulled Elaine out of her brooding. The icon for an impending teleconference was winking on and off and counting down from fifteen seconds. What the hell was going on? Bennet had said they weren't going to reconvene until tomorrow, and she had no other meetings scheduled. As the count sank beneath ten seconds, big flashing red letters shouted "MONITOR ONLY" to remind her she sat in the silent outer ring in this meeting. With the count beneath five, she saw the portrait images of Bennet, Jiminez, and Hokuro appear like playing cards dealt in a game of stud poker.

"Thanks for coming back on short notice," Bennet said. "We've got some basic issues we should discuss right now, before this thing gets more widely known."

"The first issue is security," said Jiminez. "What about this business with CDC and the WHO? We can't let that happen. It'll throw the whole thing into the public spotlight and we'll look like shit if we don't share the data with everyone and their brother."

"I agree." Bennet nodded. "I'll take appropriate measures to ensure it doesn't become a problem."

"What kind of measures?" asked Ms. Hokuro.

"You're just going to have to trust me on this. Let's remember who made this opportunity available in the first place, shall we? I've got as much at stake here as anybody and probably more. Now, let's look at the basics. Here is the core proposition as I see it: First, we know 57a will probably hit sometime in the next ten years. Maybe sooner. Maybe later. Second, we've got a model of the infectious agent that's accurate down to the chromosomal level."

"I want to reserve judgment on that until I see the algorithm," threw in Ms. Hokuro.

"Okay, fine," said Bennet impatiently. "But for now, let's assume it's accurate. Now you tell me: How long will it take you to develop a new antibiotic that's specific to this bug?"

"Well, the first thing we have to do is find a suitable molecular target. Since the thing has already mutated around all the major drug compounds, this might take a while. I'm going to guess—and it's only a guess—that we can do it in two years."

"That fast?" said Jiminez.

"You've got to remember that in the past, a lot of drug research was simple trial and error," said Ms. Hokuro. "It's only recently that we've been able to really work at the molecular level with new computer techniques. We're already seeing some spectacular results from the labs in Singapore and Palo Alto. But none of them have been publicly released or gone to clinical trials."

"Well, for now, let's assume we've got a couple of years to get a workable product," said Bennet. "Odds are we'll get the drug done and inventories built before the disease hits. So let's move on to marketing."

"What marketing?" said Jiminez. "It's a dream. All we'll have to do is process the orders. When this thing hits and a couple of million people go down in the first month, there isn't a government on earth that's going to get fussy about clinical trials. The only thing we'll have to do is keep the price within reason. If we look like we're profiteering, the political fallout could be really nasty. We'd probably want to immediately license it out to competitors. It'll dilute the revenue stream, but it could save us a lot of grief down the road."

"What about distribution?" asked Bennet.

"The existing channels can handle it just fine. We'll stock-pile the stuff at strategic sites around the world."

"How will we explain why we had such massive quantities of a drug on hand that hadn't even gone through clinical trials?" asked Bennet.

"We won't," said Jiminez. "An epidemic this size will cause an incredible panic, and people will just thank God that we have what we have."

"Okay, here's my take," said Bennet decisively. "One—the disease is for real. Two—we can probably beat it to the punch. Three—if we don't appear too greedy, we can make this an enormously profitable exercise. Anybody disagree?"

"What about funding?" asked Ms. Hokuro.

"Don't worry about it. That's my problem. I'll arrange the required capital flow matrix through CorpServe. Well, that's about it for now. I'll check back in tomorrow after our two o'clock meeting. See you later."

Elaine watched the images of Bennet and the two execu-tives disappear off her screen. Unbelievable. Why had Ben-net let her monitor it? There must have been some kind of mistake.

Then she caught herself. Of course, there was a mistake: Bennet. A mistake right from the start. For selfish reasons, she had run him through a carefully constructed emotional filter that removed the avarice, the rabid narcissism, the wanton lust for power.

But now, in this digitally linked theater-in-the-round, she had just watched Bennet producing his magnum opus, a work of fantastic callousness and conceit. The EpiSim run of Agent 57a might be the greatest work in the history of epidemiology. With the foresight provided by the simulation, a horrifying epidemic could be snuffed at its source. The appropriate antibiotic could be developed and immediately applied to the first known case, which would be rapidly iden-tified because authorities would be watching for it in ad-vance, just like a policeman on the beat with a mug shot of a murder suspect.

But not in Bennet's scenario. A few million deaths and the resulting panic would punch the product's unit price through the ozone layer as the stampede of demand rolled in. She thought back to the dream of Bennet at the beach, with his mask of empathy as the water crept toward her. And now she remembered the rest of the dream. Bennet had reached up and casually ripped his face mask off, and underneath was exactly the same face. He repeated this act again, with the same result. Soon the sand was littered with the masks, and she could feel the cold tickle of sea foam on her cheek. Then she woke up.

And now she woke up again. For good.

As the jet ascended into the clear night and banked to the north, Elaine could see the lights of the San Diego harbor recede into the distance. The plane was sparsely populated on this last run up the coast, with a quick stop in Los Angeles and on up to Seattle. The insistent whisper of the fan jets soothed her, and she felt a delicious drowsiness begin to creep over her. It seemed strange that she could be so relaxed after shattering her entire career in a single stroke. It was a lonely feeling, but a good one. Perhaps courage was its own consolation.

In the overhead bin above her was a suitcase with twenty magneto-optical discs. Collectively, they told the entire tale of Agent 57a as it crept across the globe and went about its horrible business. The world had a right to know.

In her purse was all the cash that a couple ATM machines would give her. Plus she had her credit cards, and one suitcase full of clothes in the baggage compartment. She had packed quickly and immediately called a taxi for the airport. She wanted to be on the plane before her resolution faltered and she slid back into the cool, muddy waters of compromise.

She kept waiting for the undertow of regret to pull at her, to knock her off her feet, and drown her with recrimination. But strangely, it never came. Instead, she felt a sense of direction and velocity that was exhilarating. And also ironic. Because she really had little idea what her next move was. She had never been to Seattle and had no idea what to expect outside of vague images of ferryboats, water, and mountains.

In truth, Seattle had only one thing that mattered. Dr. David Muldane lived there, and from their shared time in virtual surgery, she knew he was in public health. And soon she would present Dr. Muldane with the deadliest public health scenario in over six hundred years. She had chosen this strategy because the Webster Foundation had little interface with the medical or scientific community in general, especially since Uni took over. Not a single paper had been published on EpiSim, so she would have to build her case from scratch. To do this, she would need an advocate, and Dr. Muldane seemed the most logical candidate.

Elaine sank back and closed her eyes. As the plane knifed through the star-studded blackness, she had a vision of it melting away until only she and her seat were left, sailing gracefully through the night. She became a microscopic dot tracing a beautiful arc across the globe, a curved line of perfect grace and dignity.

12

Iquitos

"HERE. *ALTO*. HERE."

Peter Rancovich pointed to the street corner at the intersection of Arica and Brasil. The wet street outside shrieked a flood of color at him through the open window of the old flatbed truck. The colors twisted about each other and fornicated wildly, procreating hues he had never imagined possible.

"*Alto. Sí.*" The old Indian driving the truck cracked a smile that stretched into a carnivorous array of white set against the copper glow of the man's skin. Peter felt a sickening lurch as his brain continued on even though the truck had come to a stop.

"*Gracias.*" It was the best he could do. He was soaking wet and held tight in the psychedelic vise of the ayahuasco, although he now accepted its intrusive power and drifted where it took him. He opened the door and gingerly stepped onto the wet pavement, which looked as if it might be the surface of a bottomless liquid. He shut the door behind him and the truck lumbered off, a huge metal galleon sailing through the tropical night in a sputter of fumes and noise.

The street was deserted, and he surmised it must be very late. There was no telling how long he had walked down the jungle road before the truck had come along and the driver had been kind enough to stop and give him a ride. Somehow, Peter had chosen the right street, and his hotel was at the end of the block. It would be a long and difficult journey on legs that were numb stumps, so he would have to sail the remaining distance, sail on a sea of wet color that filled the canal that had once been a sidewalk.

As Peter embarked on this voyage, he was unaware that a second conspirator was now present and actively plotting with the ayahuasco. The rat-bite-fever bacteria were probing his system and testing their new virility. And the results were spectacular. Already the infection was rampant and his temperature had climbed to 102 degrees.

But Peter was oblivious to the germs, and as the specter of the shaman's death slipped away, a peaceful radiance settled in. Soon he would reach port and be safe.

It was then that he saw the angel.

She was sailing on a course that would momentarily bring them together, and already he could feel the waves of love lap gently against him. If she had been a native of earth, she would have been the most beautiful woman in all creation. The blond hair gleaming gold in perfect tumbles of curl. The eyes glowing like sunsets from the dawn of time. The sweet curves of her lips converging in perfect innocence. Because she was a virgin, untouched and untainted. He knew that intuitively, and it nearly brought him to tears as the distance between them diminished to a few feet.

And then her eyes met his, and their luminance nearly paralyzed him with joy. Her lips parted and she spoke, but he heard not a word, nor did he hear his reply.

Before he knew it, they were ascending the stairs inside his hotel, to the next world, and all its promise.

Then they were in his room, but it wasn't his room anymore. The ceiling was gone and replaced by a glowing mist high above. His bed was a vast purple expanse of sumptuous material that softly caressed him as his back sunk into it. He closed his eyes and saw the primal red of an apocalyptic sun and felt his wet clothes slide off and his skin breathe deeply. When he opened his eyes again, she hovered over him and he felt an ache of desire unlike any other in his entire life. He was instantly erect and would die if he didn't have her. The magnitude of his lust meshed perfectly with the perfection of her virginity. She could kill him instantly if she withdrew, but she didn't. Instead, she gently guided him in and brought her breasts down onto his chest. Her magnificent face loomed high above him, like some monument carved in the hillside of another world. Immediately he felt himself emptying, draining huge reservoirs that had accumulated a lifetime of desire.

And as the last drop expelled, he felt himself go out along with it.

Maria Santoz waited an obligatory moment or two before she climbed off the customer. Something was wrong with him. He felt hot and wet and weird. Now he seemed to be in some kind of rapture or something, with his eyes shut and his breathing shallow. Oh, well, that was his business. She had done what she always did in these situations. She thought of Felix.

She grabbed her clothes and shoes and went to the tiny bathroom and shut the door. As she sat on the toilet and waited impatiently for the usual fluid drainage, she spotted an object on the shelf below the mirror that made her heart leap. It was the thing she had hoped and prayed for all these months, the way back to Felix, and now it was a single grasp away.

The wallet of Peter Rancovich.

She grabbed it, opened it, and couldn't believe her luck. Two hundred U.S. dollars in twenty-dollar bills and a flock of credit cards stacked symmetrically in their leather slots. Some were foreign to her, but not the Visa and the American Express. She'd seen plenty of these at the Club Mercury and knew exactly how they worked.

With great stealth, she dressed and prayed that her luck

would hold. She parted the bathroom door and saw the customer still out cold on the bed. She stole across the room and out into the hall.

Free! Free of this nasty occupation! Free of Belén! Free of Iquitos itself! And most of all, free to find Felix, who had called to her from the dream and beckoned her on his journey.

As Maria descended the stairs, a most unusual event was occurring within her, an international conference of sorts. During her coupling with Peter, a small abrasion on his penis had acted as a portal for the *Streptobacillus moniliformis* and launched them into her vagina, which bore its own small abrasion at the tender site where the chancre sore had recently resided. As these two tiny wounds came into contact, the *Streptobacillus* germs had jumped ship and crossed over into Maria, where they quickly found their way to the local transportation network, the minute capillaries at the far end of the circulatory system.

For the time being, they were tourists seeing the sights. But soon they would be ready to take up residence and do business.

13

"So, MY MAN," SAID PARIS, "LOOKS LIKE YOU'VE GOT YOURSELF into a bit of jam."

Skip looked down at the dull squares of linoleum on the floor in front of Paris's desk in Burglary and Theft. Paris could feel the heat of the kid's shame from four feet away.

"Yeah. You're right. I got in a jam." He looked up at Paris with the eyes of a cow that had just caught a whiff of the slaughterhouse. "But I wasn't looking for trouble. You gotta know that."

Paris leaned back in his swivel chair. "Yeah, I know that. It's not your style. But it's definitely the style of your good old buddy Adam. He's a real noble guy, that Adam. I understand he took the fall. What a prince!"

Paris already had a rundown from Shavers in Juvenile. Last night, Skip and Adam had been stopped in downtown when a patrol car had spotted a car sprinting at full acceleration from one light to the next down on First Avenue. The car was Adam's dad's, a brand-new sports sedan, loaded to the hilt with ridiculous options. Adam's dad was gone on a business trip. So was Adam's mom.

Paris had seen Adam with Skip a couple of times at his sister's house. The kid had a stooped, vulturelike way about him that had always repelled Paris. He was tall and curled, not a warrior, but a carrion eater. His eyes swept the room looking for dead things to eat, and also for things that might soon be dead. His relationship with Skip was totally unfathomable.

Adam had hyperprofessional parents who had long ago been swallowed by their careers and were already partially digested. Their lives were a Gordian knot of business trips, teleconferences, and back-to-back meetings, which allowed them to manage their marriage quite easily because there was really no marriage to manage. As Adam had grown beyond nanny range, he raised himself in accordance with the norms presented by the mass media, which made him a special kind of monster, completely understandable yet totally repugnant.

A search of the dad's car had turned up a veritable smorgasbord of recreational drugs, both organics and synthetics. So naturally, Paris had received a frantic call from his sister, Cathy. The kids had been busted. At 4 A.M. Adam was at the station downtown. Would he pick Skip up? Yes, of course he would. A quick phone call to the office confirmed that only Adam had been charged and detained. Paris arranged to have the desk sergeant keep an eye on Skip, then he went back to sleep. It would be better if Skip had a little time to meditate on the heart of darkness before Paris showed up.

"Adam's okay," said Skip with little enthusiasm as he shifted uneasily in his chair and resumed his rapport with the linoleum floor.

"We'll see about that. This is only chapter one in this particular tale. In chapter two, Adam's parents fly home—

one of them, anyway. And that parent expends some of the IRA nest egg to get a high-priced lawyer. In chapter three, the lawyer suggests to Adam that he wasn't the owner of all that dope. That he got it from his low-rent buddy from the wrong part of town. His sleazy pal, Skip Sloan of South Seattle, who is corrupting the young nobleman Adam of Bellevue. Like the story so far?"

"Nope."

"Neither do I. So let's write a happy ending. Know how it goes?"

"Nope."

"You keep your young ass away from the dope, away from Adam, and all that Adam represents. He's a rotten rich kid, which gives him the worst stink of all. Stick around him and it'll rub off on you so bad it'll never come off. Got it?"

"Got it."

"Here's a buck for the bus. Police stations are for cops and crooks. You're neither. Get out of here."

Skip made a wordless exit just as Larsen was coming in for the morning shift with his retrograde box of doughnuts. "Who's that?" he asked as he bisected a maple bar in a single bite.

"My nephew. My errant nephew." Paris pursed his lips and surveyed the big stack of printouts beside his PC, an old 286 with eight megs and a hundred-meg hard drive. At least the monitor was decent. It came from some new enterprise in South Africa that had blindsided the market with a cheaper, better product. The Koreans weren't happy about it at all.

But today, as Paris powered the machine up, his mind was not on global economics. It was on the report he would have to complete today, the first of its kind in his career. Within days of using his elegant discretion with firearms as an object lesson for Skip, he'd pulled out his piece and shot somebody. Outside of the fact that he was still alive and uninjured, Paris wasn't very happy about it.

It had all started when Gooden got sick. She was assigned to a daytime stakeout, but then she came down with appendicitis of all things, so Paris was pulled in to cover for her. He was paired with Gooden's regular partner, Kolwoski, to cover a warehouse down near the docks in West Seattle, the site of a suspected fencing operation. It was a small, windowless building set close to the street with a loading dock and a single door at street level. They had been lucky enough to grab a deserted second-story space in a building directly across the street, where they set up a video camera, some lawn furniture, a portable TV, and a trash bag to collect the refuse from the pizza and Chinese takeout. For now, all they had to do was videotape the traffic appearing at the loading dock, so they could collect faces and license plates for a major bust.

Simple enough. Kolwoski was a taciturn fellow who watched soap operas during Paris's turn at the window, but Paris didn't mind. Because on Kolwoski's watches, he could read back issues of *Wooden Boat* without being obligated to contribute conversation.

Then, on Kolwoski's watch, it happened. An Econoline van pulled up, backed into the loading dock, and two men got out, both in black jeans and T-shirts, one with a ponytail, the other with a buzz cut.

"Here we go," announced Kolwoski, who flipped on the camera, zoomed in on the license plate, and then backed off to track the men. Paris approached the window, but stayed back far enough to be invisible from outside. He saw the ponytail approach the door and ring the buzzer, while the buzz cut vaulted up onto the dock. The door opened, revealing a fat man who looked like a biker, with a bulging belly and long, frizzy hair restrained by a dirty headband. The ponytail went inside, the door shut, and a moment later, the big sliding door to the loading dock rolled up, revealing a dim, rectangular cavern with the vague outline of boxes stacked near the rear. The ponytail and the buzz cut started carrying boxes in from the van and off to the right side somewhere. Paris shifted his view over to a video monitor connected to the camera, where Kolwoski had brought the lens in tight on the operation. The boxes sported logos of various TV manufacturers.

"Ah," sighed Paris. "Wholesale electronics. Famous brands now available in limited quantities at fabulous discounts."

Kolwoski said nothing. Five minutes later, the biker closed

the loading door. Then ten empty minutes. Then the other door opened, and the ponytail and the buzz cut walked out and headed for the truck, carrying a cigar box.

"It's all wrong," declared Paris. "We need backup. Right now."

"Whadaya mean?" Kolwoski had a hatchet face with dark brown eyes bunched too close for comfort, and now these eyes blew twin barrels of disgust at Paris.

"The box. Got to be money. And not theirs."

"Bullshit."

Before Paris could assemble a rebuttal, it happened. Across the way, the ponytail opened the door on the far side of the van, and buzz cut opened the driver's-side door. Just then, the biker appeared at the open warehouse door, his T-shirt soaked with blood.

"Shit!" exclaimed Kolwoski.

Before this expletive was even complete, the wounded biker steadied himself against the doorframe, swung a shotgun into view, and fired into the backside of the buzz cut, who was not ten feet away and halfway into the van. The shot pattern caught him in the back just below the neck. The impact propelled him forward with enough force that his head struck and shattered the door window before he slumped to the ground.

Before the buzz cut hit the ground, Paris was sprinting for the door, where a set of outside stairs dropped down to street level.

"What are ya doin'?" yelled Kolwoski, as if some explanation were required.

Paris ate up the stairs several steps at a time and hit the street at a dead run. By this time, the ponytail had reached into the van, pulled out a shotgun of his own, and was walking toward the rear of the van, where he would have a clean shot at the biker, who remained slumped against the doorframe.

As Paris crossed the street, the ponytail disappeared behind the van. Paris heard the huge thump of the shotgun and saw a hand-sized blister of red appear on the biker's thigh. A second thump tore a fist-sized chunk of red out of the biker's biceps, but not before he got off a shot of his own.

Instinctively, Paris raced around the far side of the van, so he would come up behind the ponytail and not risk getting caught in a crossfire.

Suddenly, he noticed that his 9mm was out of its holster and in his hand. In this furious storm of adrenaline, he wasn't even conscious of deciding to draw it. It was a primal, hardwired decision, not a soft and reasoned one.

He caught a rear view of the ponytail just before the man loosed a fourth blast that caught the biker in the face, reducing it to a bubbling riot of smeared red. Automatically, Paris crouched into a shooting stance, grasped his 9mm automatic pistol with both hands, and aimed it heart-level at the ponytail.

"Police! Drop the weapon!" Paris thundered. He had a voice with the heft of a good-size artillery piece, and more than once it had resolved the issue with no further show of force. But not now.

Because the ponytail had just been inducted into a very exclusive subset of humanity. He had survived a face-to-face gun battle where neither side held an intrinsic advantage. The outcome was a cast of the divine dice, and its good fortune flooded him with a feeling of invincibility. He turned sideways but made no move to drop the weapon.

"Put it down!" boomed Paris.

The ponytail smiled and looked down at his shotgun. Empty. The hollow metal orifice of the chamber stared up at him. No matter. He would simply reload.

Paris could not believe what was happening. He had this man's life squarely in his sights, and the fool was calmly reaching into his pocket and plucking out a shotgun shell and pushing it into the chamber. As soon as he slammed the bolt shut, it would once again be an even game.

Only a fool or saint would wait that long, and Paris was neither. He squeezed off three quick rounds in a deafening blast, and the ponytail spun around once, then fell to the ground, his shotgun bouncing off the pavement, which chambered the round and discharged it into the back of the van.

Now, as Paris completed the report, the thing he remembered most was the ringing in his ears. It was one thing to shoot a large-caliber pistol while wearing hearing protectors on the firing range, and quite another to discharge it in the immediate vicinity of a naked pair of eardrums. He had barely understood Kolwoski's shouting through the nonstop avalanche of white noise that stayed with him for days afterward. It turned out that the ponytail had lived, but with the stakeout's videotape as evidence, the state would probably take up where the biker had left off.

With the report finished, Paris turned to the unkempt community of paperwork that littered his desk. Where to begin? Larsen solved the problem for him.

"Check this out," he said as he threw a photocopied paper onto Paris's desk on his way for coffee to wash down a plain glazed. "Babes in crimeland. Your very own personal copy."

Paris picked up the paper and settled back in his chair. It was a flyer, one of hundreds they got every month over the network from the National Crime Information Center, or NCIC. Each described a suspected criminal from some other jurisdiction who was wanted for this or that. Here in Burglary and Theft, the only flyers that hit their desks were those involving some kind of larceny. What made this one different was the picture of the suspect. An attractive woman in her midthirties or so, with a sleek professional look about her. The product of generous genes combined with a surfeit of discretionary income. Not the usual suspect, not by a long shot.

So Paris read on. The suspect's name was Elaine Wilkes. The flyer originated from the San Diego district attorney's office, and the arrest warrant charged her with grand theft.

Paris looked at the picture again. Even through the veil of an image transmitted at a coarse resolution with no contrast control, her intelligence punched through and caught his eye. White-collar crime. Had to be. Probably an interesting tale behind it.

Paris tossed it onto the pile. Fat chance anything this juicy would come his way. He picked up the next report he had to complete. Someone had taken a crowbar to a condom machine in a tavern rest room and made off with a pound and a half of quarters.

Now that was more like it.

It was happening again.
Betty Williams exercised a special kind of fright. Physi-

cally, she was weak, but relatively comfortable. The nurses had adjusted her bed to a tolerable height, and she barely noticed the IV tube taped to the white underside of her forearm. She was even regaining her dignity after the urgent trips to the toilet to relieve the cruel blasts of fluid that shot from her. The doctor said her dehydration was on the mend, and the fever from the infection was gone.

But she wasn't safe. She knew that. Because of Tim.

She would never forget that day nine years ago, when he went into this same hospital in Seattle to have a routine operation for a routine ailment. He'd had a sinus problem that just wouldn't quit, one that inflated little bags of pain in the center of his face and nibbled away at his sense of well-being. So it was decided that a little corrective surgery would do the trick.

She would never forget the day he was admitted, the last day he was the Tim she loved and remembered. A stocky man of thirty-one, with receding hair, big shoulders, and a quick smile. Ironically, his sinuses weren't even bothering him on that particular day. He joked about having a construction project going on inside his face and gave her a big hug when she left him that evening in his room.

The next morning, the surgery went off without a hitch. The surgeon told her it was a good thing they'd gone in, because the problem would've only gotten worse. By noon, he was groggy, but grinning. Another day and he'd be out. A good thing, because she already felt a little lonesome. They had no children and had expanded to fill each other's universes in a warm and comfy kind of way. She went back that evening and watched TV with him, then went down to buy him a copy of *Sports Illustrated*. When she left, he looked pretty weary and weak, but she supposed that was to be expected.

She got the call early in the morning and it sent a lance of panic through her. *There's been a complication with your husband. Could you get over here as soon as possible?*

He was no longer in the nice little room with the TV and magazines. He was in the intensive care unit, with a respirator tube shoved down his throat and a terrible garden of tubes and wires growing out of him. His eyes were smashed shut and his skin had gone to bread dough. All the little instruments in the room flickered in a dance of imminent death.

The family doctor was there, and he took her to a conference room, where she collapsed in shock and tears. *What was happening? What went wrong?*

The doctor, a man about Tim's age, explained that it had nothing to with the surgery. It was pneumonia.

Pneumonia? How did he get pneumonia?

As the doctor began his explanation, his guarded tone set off a new alarm circuit within her. It seemed there were many kinds of pneumonia, but the lab had already identified the particular cause of Tim's, a bacteria called *Staphylococcus,* the one that caused all those "staph infections" you heard about. It also seemed that these staph bugs had a real affinity for hospitals and were hard to control. They ignored many disinfectants and settled in for good, like unwelcome relatives. Worse yet, they preyed upon people who were in a weakened state of health. People who had just undergone a physical trauma from disease or surgery. People like Tim.

She felt a small surge of hope. Staph was a bug, right? And you can cure a bug, right? It's not like cancer, not like a virus.

You can give him a drug and make him Tim again, right?

The doctor hesitated as he collected his thoughts. We used to treat staph infections with drugs like methicillin, he began. They would go in and burst the cell wall, and all the bug's chromosomal material would pop out in an explosion of liquid thread. But slowly, over several decades, the staph bugs worked their way around the problem. But it didn't matter because there were other drugs, like the aminoglycosides and chloramphenicol. But the hordes of staph wouldn't quit, despite enormous losses. Soon medicine was down to its last line of defense, a drug called vancomycin, which did the old methicillin trick and punched a fatal hole into the bug's cell wall. But then it happened. Not too long ago. Several locations reported a staph strain that vancomycin wouldn't touch. And here it was. Right here in this hospital. Right here in Tim.

He'd lasted another two days. And Betty had lasted another nine years, so far. After his death, she had gone to the library to do research on *Staphylococcus.* She wanted to stare the killer in the face. She was surprised at how benign it appeared, a little round ball that grew in clusters that looked like a mountainous landscape of grapes. Try as she would, she could not make any visceral connection between those piles of grapes and her dead husband.

After that, she lived modestly in a little apartment and managed her money carefully. Most of the time she shopped the specials and cooked enough to make leftovers for the next night. But once a week, she splurged and went out. And so it was that she went to the Western Family Steakhouse and caught a bit of intestinal hell. She was too weak to make it to the doctor, so they called an ambulance and here she was.

It's happening all over again. Only this time it's me.

Her doctor had reassured her that there was no connection between her ailment and that of her deceased husband. But she could feel the sickness all around her, thick in the air she was breathing.

"Ms. Williams?"

A gentle, compassionate voice tugged her away from her troubled gaze out the window, where the city lights twinkled in the fading light. She turned and saw the clerical collar first, and then the man attached to it. He smiled. "Sorry it took so long to get around to seeing you, but like Robert Frost said, I've got miles to go before I sleep." He opened his smile a stop wider. "I heard you had quite an adventure in dining."

Betty's anxiety faded into the background as she smiled back at the man. She was glad that clergymen were wearing collars again these days. It showed a kind of pride and devotion she admired, especially in someone like a hospital chaplain, who faced an endless parade of strangers in physical distress.

"Yes," she said, smiling back weakly, "as a matter of fact, I did."

"And it doesn't look like you needed to lose any weight!" he commented cheerfully as he sat down beside her.

"Well," she ventured modestly, "maybe a pound or two." He was young, younger than her anyway, and kind of cute.

"Well, I hope you didn't suffer much to do it." The chaplain's face took a serious turn, and his eyes went from blue to gray. Her pain was his pain.

"The truth is, it was the worst agony I ever even imagined. It felt like I was going to explode, but I never did."

He put his hand on hers. "But it's over now, right?"

"Right."

"You know, it's funny how something like this can change our lives in a positive way—if we let it. You'll be out of here in a day or two—and none the worse for wear. You've been given the gift of recovery, and as you know, it's not given to all." He stood to leave and gave her hand a warm squeeze before he let go. "My advice is, put that gift to work."

With a grin and a wink, he was gone.

Betty sank a little farther into her pillow as some of the tension went out of her neck. She felt a little better now. Maybe she'd read or watch some TV.

In the elevator down to the hospital lobby, Vincent closed his eyes and stroked the starched curve of the clerical collar. He hoped that during the visit, his sport coat had covered his erection.

The third act was over.

At least for today. But how lovely it was! How exquisite to see that woman so frail and pale, so vulnerable and malleable! A perfect monument to his handiwork! And to hear her describe her suffering! When she alluded to explosions, he'd nearly climaxed, but was glad he didn't because he wanted to savor every precious moment of the experience without distraction.

Well worth the risk. And besides, the danger was minimal. He simply entered the hospital wearing the collar, went to the information desk, and said he was there to visit the admission from the food poisoning, the one in the papers. A hospital was an efficient rumor mill, and if one of the victims was here, the information person inevitably knew about it. If not, Vincent said he must have made a mistake and was off before any damage was done.

When he reached the proper floor and the nurses' station, he sailed right by without suspicion. Just another clergyman doing his duty. The victims, of course, assumed he was the hospital chaplain, and he never stayed long enough to arouse any suspicion. It was a perfect arrangement, like a well-crafted business deal. Everyone was pleased and derived some sort of profit.

Outside, in the parking lot, he sucked in the cool night air and walked briskly toward his car. There were several more victims in a handful of hospitals throughout the city. And who better than he to comfort them during their time of pain and suffering?

14

JOHN MERKIN HOVERS ON THE PRECIPICE OF DEBILITATING shame as he lunges down the hallway in the basement of the Webster Foundation next to Bennet Rifkin, for whom he has a great purity of hate.

Merkin is fat. Grossly so. One hundred extra pounds cling tenaciously to his frame, where they have found the perfect homeland, because John is quite comfortable with their presence. At fifty-two, he has chosen to lead a "life of the mind"—as he calls it—where his physical self is simply baggage along for the ride. At dinnertime, he shovels in a mountain of fats and sugars while watching *Jeopardy* on the little TV perched above the microwave. He is good at beating the contestants to the correct answer as he dips into his deft memory and scoops out the required information. On nights when he wins the game, he rewards himself with a quart of premium ice cream and retires to his computer, where he composes beautiful tracts of code dedicated to mathematical gymnastics of the most abstract sort.

But right now, the muscles in his stubby legs burn and scream as he tries to keep pace with Bennet, who is striding furiously down the hall toward the data center. Merkin knows that if Bennet picks up the pace even slightly, he will be forced to break into a jog to keep up. He can already visualize the ludicrous scene of this trim, muscular corporate executive sailing along with this sweating, wheezing fat man trotting at his side. He wants badly to retreat to the world of mental abstraction, where he could quickly bring Bennet to heel, but the pain of the exertion blocks his withdrawal.

Mr. Merkin's physical stature and outlook are in complete harmony with his occupation. He is the director of computer services for the Webster Foundation and has ultimate responsibility for the care and feeding of the cytoputer and all its supporting hardware and software. In his head, he carries a detailed representation of the computer complex, and during administrative meetings he can extract large chunks of this model and hurl them at opponents, who are stunned and crushed by their sheer mass.

But tonight, his expanse of knowledge about the system is a liability. Less than an hour ago, Rifkin had phoned just as Merkin was excavating the top of a carton of vanilla-fudge ice cream. It just wasn't fair. *Jeopardy* had ended hours ago, and although John had won handily, he exercised a rare burst of restraint and put off his reward for several hours. Now here was Rifkin, demanding that he immediately get down to the Foundation, just as he was about shovel a quart of frozen heaven into his mouth.

Bennet slows slightly as they reach the end of the hall. To avoid the impression of panting, Merkin breathes through his slightly opened mouth. Bennet puts a magnetic card to the panel on the wall, and the sliding glass doors part to admit them. Inside is a small anteroom where a woman sits at a counter desk with a large vault behind her. Its thick steel door hangs open to reveal rows of disk drives of many sizes and designs, and the energetic blinking of hundreds of LED indicator lights, a mad carnival of dancing data. The woman eyes Rifkin with a mixture of clerical fear and institutional suspicion as he approaches her desk with John slightly behind.

"You know Dr. Wilkes?" Bennet demands.

"Dr. Wilkes?" the woman repeats. John can tell from her tone that she is simply delaying the inevitable.

"Yes, Dr. Wilkes," spits Bennet. "Where's the log? When's the last time she had a transaction?"

"Oh, yes—Dr. Wilkes," says the woman as she clicks away at her console. "That's right. She was down here a couple of hours ago." The woman glances at Merkin, for whom she works, but sees no redemption.

John now knows something is definitely wrong. So far, Bennet has offered no explanation of why John was yanked down here on such short notice. But here it comes.

"And what, precisely, did she do down here a couple of hours ago?" asked Bennet.

"Well, it seems she needed the results of a simulation run that was conducted today." She clicks away once more. "It was for an agent . . ."

"57a," snaps Bennet. "What did she want?" He knows that the vault behind the woman contains all the data from all the simulation runs and is held under extreme security. It is bombproof, fireproof, and even shielded from electromagnetic interference. All data from the cytoputer is instantaneously transmitted to this site over fiber-optic lines from upstairs and held for distribution on a need-to-know basis only.

"She, uh, requested the entire output of the simulation. Not just the summaries."

"So. What did you give her?"

The woman's hands came off the keyboard and she began to knead her fingers into nervous little knots. "We gave her the backups—she was cleared for that. She needed them for some kind of report that's due by tomorrow."

Bennet froze as he thought about the consequences. After the conference with Jiminez and Hokuro he had paced his office in a flood of excitement. It wasn't until he went to review the record of their conference that he discovered his horrible mistake. The teleconference log said it all: "Monitor 1: E. Wilkes," and confirmed that she had logged on during the meeting. She had heard the whole damn thing, all of it. He had raced downstairs, but by that time she was gone. He immediately tried her both at home and at his place, but with no luck. What was she going to do? She was such a goddamn idealist, it was hard to tell. But the more he thought about it, the more he knew. She was going to do exactly what she had said in the meeting. She was going to report Agent 57a to the public health people—whether he authorized it or not. She was going to steal the company's private property and spill it like cheap slop into the public trough.

And now she had the goods to do the spilling. The way the system worked, the data went immediately onto a high-speed, high-capacity hard disk; then an automatic system promptly created backups on magneto-optical disks, which were small and portable so they could be loaded onto desktop machines. Elaine now had the entire set of these disks.

What could be worse? Only one thing. He turned to Merkin.

"What about the original files?" he demanded while pointing at the vault. "In there. On the hard drive. There's no way, right?"

Merkin's pulse rocketed back up to where it had been during the trip down the hall. "Well, under normal procedures, there wouldn't be any problem. I think . . ."

"What about under *ab*normal procedures? What then, Mr. Merkin?"

"Well, key project managers have read/write access. That's the way we've always—"

"You're telling me she could have erased them, right? That's what you're telling me, right?" hissed Bennet.

"Well, under certain circumstances, that could happen. We can most certainly check on that," replied Merkin with the optimism of the damned.

"Well, then, let's start checking," commanded Bennet quietly. His fury condensed into a small ball with enormous explosive potential as Merkin and the clerk scurried into the vault.

She'd fucked him. She'd fucked him big time. She had the disks and had his balls right along with them. But what if she'd destroyed the whole simulation? What then? It was nearly unthinkable.

When Merkin emerged from the vault, Bennet was imagining Elaine in prison with very big women with very short hair and very uncomfortable penetration devices.

"It appears that she did erase the main simulation record on the hard disk, and also the model of Agent 57a." As Bennet's face began its flex into contortions of rage, Merkin quickly added, "But I don't think she was aware of the archival service. It's a clerical procedure and doesn't involve the staff, so most of them don't pay attention to it."

"The archival service?"

"We back up everything once a day and store it off-site on a completely independent system. Which means we have all the models you need to re-create the simulation, including Agent 57a."

Bennet stared at Merkin and the clerk with disgust. They had the anxious yet hopeful look of penitents seeking absolution. But before absolution, there had to be penance.

"How long will it take to get it back?"

Merkin beamed and the woman looked hopeful. "We can have it over by courier first thing in the morning."

"How long to rerun the simulation?"

Merkin's beam vanished. "We're going to need some technical help for that. The system has to be reconfigured and the models recompiled before we can simulate again. The person who usually does that is on vacation this week."

"And who might that be?"

"Peter. Peter Rancovich. We, uh, believe he's somewhere in South America."

"Can't anybody else do it?"

"Not at this time," answered Merkin weakly. He was in the horrible position of technical managers everywhere. Now that he was an administrator, he no longer dealt with the system on a daily basis. And as it evolved, little changes crept in here and there. Little changes with large consequences. So while he had an impressive conceptual grasp of the computing vehicle he managed, he could no longer safely drive it.

"Then at *what* time?"

Merkin felt Bennet's question claw at his innards. "We'll contact security and see if there isn't some way to contact him. If not, he's back by next Monday."

Bennet relaxed. His shoulders fell several inches, his arms dangled loosely, and a smile washed all the nasty little lines out of his face.

Merkin was terrified.

Bennet strode over, put an arm around the stubby little man, and walked him a few steps down the hall for a confidential chat.

"You know what, John?"

"No. I don't," squeaked Merkin.

"Monday could be your last day. Your very last day at this very fat job, this job that's almost as fat as you are. Especially if the simulation isn't done before then."

Bennet smiled, patted Merkin on the back, and strode off down the hall. One fire was nearly extinguished, but another was burning out of control. Elaine was out there somewhere with all those disks, the disks of the biological apocalypse. They held the key to millions, maybe billions, of dollars in business. If they became public or fell into the wrong hands, the loss to Uni and Bennet's coalition would be staggering.

He couldn't let that happen.

Bennet Rifkin cracked a grim smile as he looked at the notepad next to the phone on the bedside table in Elaine's bedroom. She might be a great scientist, he thought, but she was going to make a lousy felon. He'd driven here straight from Uni, and it had only taken him a couple of minutes to figure out where she was off to.

For starters, she'd obviously forgotten that she'd given him a key to her condo sometime back, when the blaze of lust was still bright and warm. He went straight to the bedroom because he knew she'd pack at least something, probably a single suitcase that she could easily carry. He went to the closet first and saw a full suite of clothes still hanging there. The big suitcase was there, too, the one she'd taken when they went to Italy last summer, a large beast of soft black leather lacerated by multiple zippers of dubious utility.

Then he spotted the notepad. The term "456Q" was written in Elaine's tight scrawl.

It was an airline flight. No doubt about it. Probably Alaska. Since he flew all the time, he was master of the airline network. He got on the phone to Alaska and simply asked what time Flight 456Q got into Denver. After a brief pause, the cheerful and helpful person at the desk came back on and informed him that 456Q didn't go to Denver, but had arrived in Seattle several hours ago.

Bennet thanked her, hung up, and went out to his car in the parking area. This next call would best be made from the cellular phone in his vehicle. He slid in, closed the door, and turned the key to activate the car's electrical system. As the instrument panel lit up, nothing indicated that car was equipped with an ingenious encryption system for turning telephone calls into a hopeless tangle of digital garbage as they passed through the telephone system on their way to the intended receiver, where they would be converted back into a normal voice.

First, he punched a button that selected an audio CD from the number one slot in the remote player in the trunk. This particular compact disc was a copy of Aaron Copland's Symphony No. 3 and ran about thirty-eight minutes. When it was loaded and ready to play, he dialed a residential number in Seattle, the home of an attorney named Robert Fancher, who was retained as a lobbyist for Uni.

Fancher answered on the third ring. "Hello." He had a permanent hint of annoyance in his voice, as if you were probably wasting his time, and that no matter what your business, it was barely worth his attention.

"Three."

"Hold on," commanded Fancher.

Bennet knew exactly what the attorney was doing. Three was the code for the Symphony No. 3 CD, which he was slipping into a CD player at his end.

"Okay," said Fancher as he came back on.

The connection was now set, and the system enabled. Both Bennet's phone and Fancher's included a chip called an ASIC, short for Application Specific Integrated Circuit. The chip used a silicon technology called .03 micron CMOS, which allowed over a million logic elements to be compressed into a space half the size of a postage stamp. Together, these logic elements worked as a program that listened simultaneously to both the callers and the CD.

On Bennet's end, as the music played, the CD produced a continuous stream of ones and zeros that were shipped into the chip in batches of many millions at a time. The chip's program then stirred this binary stew even further by rearranging the digits of the original CD bit stream into a highly scrambled sequence, which if listened to would produce only an incomprehensible hiss. At the same time, the program listened for Bennet's voice and converted it into a second binary stream, which it laid down next to the scrambled CD stream in the chip's internal memory. Each binary digit had a counterpart in the opposite stream, like pairs of marchers in a parade just two columns wide; and these two digits were then combined using an operation called an XOR to create a third digit.

Now the parade was three columns wide and marching to a regular cadence through time. The first column of bits represented Bennet's original voice. The second was the profoundly scrambled binary stew, and the third was the XOR product of the first two. This third column of bits was then sent over the public phone circuitry to Fancher's phone system. For all practical purposes, it appeared completely random, and not even the most sophisticated computer was capable of breaking it. But at Fancher's end, his system had both the ASIC-based program and the same CD, so the column of binary stew used at Bennet's end could be precisely duplicated. This duplicate column was then paired with the column coming in over the public phone system, and once again, the XOR operation was applied to create a third column. And this third column was none other than original data for Bennet's voice. In a final operation, the ASIC turned the digital voice data into an analog wave that came out of the phone receiver.

The system not only created a code that was unbreakable by eavesdroppers during transmission, but also one that was largely immune to espionage. If the ASIC chip in the phone was stolen, the thieves had only attained the mix master that created the second bit-stream column in the encoding process—but not the ingredients, which came from the audio CD. And at any time, the CD title could be changed to any album in existence, so long as both parties agreed on what it was. Uni had added yet another layer of complication by having a number of different albums in use at any given time, each identified by a number, which the caller and receiver could agree upon. In a brilliant stroke of arrogance, the current list of albums was always available in an Internet newsgroup called "alt.music.albums.timeless."

"Robert, I do believe we're clear now," said Bennet. "Sorry to bother you at home, but it couldn't wait."

"No bother. What's on your mind?" Bennet could feel the arrogant frost in the voice and pictured Fancher in his den overlooking Lake Washington. Bennet could see the high forehead, the aristocratic nose, the bright blue eyes, the nasty little scowl welded onto the pale, starved lips. Fancher was Uni's lobbyist in Washington, where the company owned numerous operations in aerospace and computers. As such, he was generously compensated, and because of the magnitude of this generosity, he was expected to deliver a broad spectrum of services, some formally specified, some not.

"I have a problem down here that I need your help with. It's a criminal matter."

"A criminal matter? Bennet, my good man, there are many thousands of criminal lawyers in your immediate proximity. Why me?"

Bennet was always annoyed by Fancher's condescending tone, especially since Fancher was the vendor in this relationship. Worse yet, he was already backing Bennet into a cul-de-sac. "First of all, it's crime against the corporation. Theft of proprietary information. Secondly, I have good reason to believe that the person who committed the crime has fled to your jurisdiction."

"Really? And what's the precise nature of the crime?"

"I can't divulge that at this time. It's data from a highly classified project, and it's packaged on a set of magneto-optical disks. The guilty party took off with it just a few hours ago on a plane to Seattle."

"Well, if we can't discuss the crime, maybe we can discuss the criminal."

"That we can. It's a scientist, a woman named Elaine Wilkes. At this point, her motivation for the theft is somewhat ambiguous, but I suspect she'd like to sell the data to potential competitors."

"And what might it be worth?"

"Difficult to say. But I'd guess it would be in the multiple millions."

"Ah," mocked Fancher, "the good old multiple millions. In that case, I suppose you'll be wanting your property back in a timely manner."

"You suppose right." Bennet's agitation was mounting. He remembered a party at Fancher's house, where the host had loaded them on his sailboat and taken them for a ride past the Bill Gates mansion. He'd conducted the tour like a high priest revealing the wonders of the great temple to a group of gawking peasants.

"Very well, then. Here's what we do. First, you need to contact the San Diego police and report the crime immediately—tonight. Tell them you have reason to believe that Ms. Wilkes might be in Seattle. They'll issue a warrant and contact the Seattle police."

"And what happens then?"

"Normally, not much. Grand theft isn't a threat to public safety—especially when it's white-collar crime. So it won't be a high-priority item for the cops here. They'll take their time."

"We don't have time."

"Right, Bennet. But you do have me, now. Don't you?"

"Yes, Robert. We do have you," admitted Bennet, who now felt his opposing molars trying to annihilate each other.

"And I will deliver. On time. There's only one other thing I need from you."

"What's that?"

"Get a hacker and check the major cards. We might get lucky." Fancher was referring to freelance help with the skills to penetrate the major credit-card databases and get a trail of transactions to the fugitive.

"No problem."

"Good. Just one more thing."

"What's that?"

"What if I need to explore other options? What should I do?"

"That's very simple, Robert. You should do whatever you think is proper under the circumstances."

"All right then. I'll be in touch soon. Good night, Bennet."

"Good night, Robert." Bennet broke the connection. The man was an asshole, but a clever and resourceful one. Like he'd said, he always delivered. Bennet put the matter behind him. He had a date tonight and was already running late.

Robert Fancher hung up the phone and turned up the CD, which was still running even though its role as an encrypt/decrypt machine was now complete. The second movement, allegro molto, was under way, with its aerial bursts of brass and paternal boom of timpani. It spoke of power, of great mechanical energies brought to bear, of mythical gears and levers set into inexorable motion.

And Robert's mood meshed perfectly with the music because power was his native tongue. He would now create inexorable motions of his very own.

Peter Rancovich shivered violently as he sat cross-legged on the futon with a blanket wrapped around him. The drug should have let go by now, but it hadn't. The hallucinations were gone, but he still felt high and weird as he looked out the window of his apartment into the San Diego night. He suspected he had a fever, but didn't have a thermometer in the place to check it out. He'd never needed one before.

His apartment was that of the itinerant student. A brick-and-plank bookshelf held his stereo, small TV, and paperbacks. Iconoclastic posters decorated the walls, and his ten-speed bike rested along a wall by the door. A single lamp, set on a big, wooden wire spool that served as an end table, dimly illuminated the living room. This place seemed at once familiar and utterly alien to him as he struggled to sort out the recent past. Iquitos, the shaman, the angel. They took turns bubbling up out of a boiling soup of memories. And then the crisis. No wallet, no money, no nothing. Fortunately, he had found his ticket and passport still in his backpack. The business at the airport was still a muddy blur, and the plane trips were tormented stretches of skewed dreaming, but eventually he had found himself in the terminal at San Diego, broke and spaced. He had thought about giving Diana a call to come and get him, but she would only gloat over what a mess he'd made of his vacation. So he walked. And walked. On legs that turned to fibrous jelly the farther he went.

Now he was home, but it didn't seem like home. It was strangely distorted in the heat of the fever.

The electronic warble of the phone yanked him out of his stupor. The receiver felt hard and cold as ice in his grip as he answered the call.

"Hello?"

"Peter, it's John. John Merkin. Boy, it's lucky I found you."

"Yeah?" Peter's mouth hung open.

"I thought you'd still be gone. Listen, old buddy. We've got a problem. A very big problem."

"We do?"

"Yep. You're not gonna believe this. Elaine Wilkes took off with the entire run on Agent 57a. Stole it and split. Even deleted the central files and all the models. Rifkin is going nuts. We've got to go into the backup and rerun the whole thing. Pronto."

"Look," Peter said feebly, "I'm not feeling very good right now."

"You'll have to save your not feeling good for later. This is bad shit. Really bad shit. Take a cab. Charge it to the Foundation. I'll see you in half an hour."

Damn! thought Peter as Merkin hung up. *The fat little fuck is sticking his dick right into the middle of my vacation.*

He rolled off the couch and felt dizzy as he got to his feet. His trip to hell was still a work in progress.

"Jesus! You look like shit! What happened down there?"

Peter was in no state to tolerate John Merkin on a night like this. He stood at the entrance to the control room in his tropical shorts, dirty T-shirt, sandals, and temperature heading toward 103 degrees. "Just let me get it done and let me get out of here, okay? I'm going to set it up and start it and go home."

"Maybe you ought to think about going to the doctor, old buddy."

"Maybe I should. Please leave. Let me alone so I can get it done."

"Okay, okay. I'm outta here. I'm in my office if you need me." Merkin seemed quite jolly, which only added to Peter's irritation. Peter disliked all people who managed other people, and especially those who managed him, like Merkin.

As Merkin waddled down the hall, Peter shut the door and felt the air-conditioning paint a coat of ice on his skin. One hour. That's all he had to last. One hour.

Fifty-five minutes later, he hit a snag. By that time, the CRT display was a dancing flood of alphanumerics, well on their way to becoming meaningless symbols to his fevered brain. To rerun the simulation, he had to recompile all the simulation models into an exotic code that would run on the cytoputer. As in software projects everywhere, programmers had made different versions of the models through debugging and performance improvements. Every time the simulation was run, a log was made of which versions were used to build it. Version 3 of this model, version 5.2 of this model, and so on.

And now the log was telling Peter that the last run of the simulation had used version 8.1 of the model for Agent 57a. However, the most recent version he could find was 8.0, and a warning message was shouting something about "a configuration error."

But right now, Peter Rancovich was losing it. Eight dot oh, eight dot shmo. The hot fever wind sailed him right past the point of caring. He loaded the old version of Agent 57a and started the simulation on its way through untold billions of calculations.

Without even calling Merkin, he wobbled down the hall, up the elevator, and out into the warm night where the taxi was patiently waiting for its fat corporate fare. He'd already forgotten about the configuration error caused by version 8.0 of the model for Agent 57a. By now, he knew he needed medical attention, and nothing else mattered as his universe constricted to meet the urgency of the current situation. He did not know or care that the final and correct model for Agent 57a, version 8.1, existed only on a magneto-optical disk over nine hundred miles away in Seattle.

A minute later, he slid into the back of the taxi for the last car ride of his life.

PART
TWO

15

Libreville and São Tomé

THE PARROT'S TALONS WRAPPED IN AN ANGRY CURL ABOUT the wooded dowel that served as the perch in its cage, which twisted slowly in the weak breeze threading through the neatly tended shrubs in Omar Amiar's backyard. The cage hung from the frame of a gazebo sporting a fresh coat of white paint grudgingly applied by Omar's minions under the imperious supervision of his wife.

Two small portholes interrupted the smooth curve of the parrot's beak and marked the location of its nostrils, and down these tiny tunnels stretched a lining called the nasal membrane, which connected to the interior of the beak and the throat and lungs. And within this membrane, the new and improved *Chlamydia* had settled in and quickly set up their beachhead. Already, they were fighting countless skirmishes with the local authorities, and occasionally they would produce enough immune reaction to increase the local mucous output and cause the parrot to sneeze to clear its breathing passages.

Now, in the bright green heat of the tropical afternoon, the parrot swayed sullenly on its perch and peered through rusted bars at the house in the distance, where the big kitchen windows were wide open to provide what little ventilation might come their way. A layer of window screen stretched on a frame over each window to prevent airborne insects from foraging within the kitchen, where several pieces of chicken rested on a wooden chopping block—the very same chicken that Omar had wrested from the gullible Greek in his clever negotiations aboard the *Tiana Maroo*. The very same chicken riddled with the *Salmonella*, which were now thriving once more in the rising temperature.

At this same moment, a housefly landed on the screen's enormous grid of woven wire, and its sensors picked up the odor of the chicken within, which prompted it to start a random search for some kind of ingress, some way to navigate to this newly discovered food source. And luck was with it. After two inches of travel, it came upon a hole the size of a dime, with a jagged tangle of severed wire around its circumference. It easily hopped through the tangle and took flight into the kitchen guided by an olfactory radar that provided a rough but adequate image of the target area. Its irritating buzz went unnoticed in the empty kitchen, which the cook had left to make a phone call to her cousin, who was once again pregnant and none too happy about it.

The fly swooped down and landed on a chicken leg. It took a moment to survey the pale yellow plain with its subtle undercurrents of blue and purple. The fatty surface shone weakly and was interrupted by a wild scattering of bumps that had rooted feathers in the bird's better days. The fly's peripheral vision saw no motion and no threat, so it slashed into the fat and began piping pulverized flesh down its digestive tract. Soon, it had torn up an entire excavation site, and bits of the churned chicken skin clung to its barbed legs.

From their newly prosperous enclaves buried in the bird's flesh, the *Salmonella* saw the day of reckoning descend upon them as the fatty sky of black exploded and let in a blast of brilliant light. The sky then boiled and churned into pink clouds, which sucked up entire bacterial communities and carried them off wholesale. And some of these communities now found themselves bound inextricably to a leg of the fly, the monstrous angel of their private Armageddon.

Soon the fly was satiated and took flight once more. The way out was a puzzle of enormous difficulty, a maze of hard, flat surfaces that seemed to undergo endless perpendicular intersections with other hard, flat surfaces. But then the cook opened the door as the fly lighted upon it, and it seized the opportunity to fly into a hallway, where an open doorway to the backyard painted a huge rectangle of salvation for the tiny insect.

Outside, the fly easily rode on the small thermals rising off the lawn and headed for a large, bright object that dominated the scene played out in each facet of its segmented eyes. Once there, it spotted a smaller, suspended object that presented a good landing spot.

The parrot did not see the fly land in the bottom of the

cage. Nor did it care as the fly crept over its food, an assortment of seeds in a shallow, earthen bowl. And its vision was not nearly acute enough to see the fly negotiate the pitted, abrasive surface of one certain seed, where tiny chunks of the chicken flesh scraped off and secured to the seed's outer skin. But the buzzing departure of the fly did snatch the parrot out of its heated stupor and cause it to thrust its beak into the bowl and snap up this very same seed, along with several others.

The violent gnashing inside the parrot's beak was murder in the dark, where the offspring of several plant species were thoroughly crushed and devoured. And during this, little specks of chicken meat were continually thrust to the side along the inner lining of the beak. Some of these specks were flung into a remote location where the nasal passages intersected with the interior of the beak. A place of adventure and opportunity for those with the stamina to cross it, like the *Salmonella* who now wandered off the meat and onward toward a destiny unique in the history of their species.

"And then they will take you to the basement and tie your ankles to a table and insert a large gourd up your rectum. This will hurt very badly, but if you scream, they will only put it in further. If you ask why they are doing this, they will say it is part of the standard search procedure when someone is caught smuggling."

Martin N'Dong listened carefully to the man, who spoke with great conviction and authority. In the last light of day, they could see a compressed black sliver on the ocean's edge against the setting sun, which poured blood and copper into the maritime sky. Martin knew the sliver was a profile of São Tomé, an island about 150 miles off the coast of Gabon, and a small but sovereign nation. From the deck of the ferry where he stood, he estimated they would be there in less than two hours, and suddenly, he didn't want to be there at all. All because of the man next to him, the old man with white hair and beard, who spoke with an authority that Martin had heard only from his uncle, Omar Amiar.

"And how many do you suppose they catch?" Martin asked cautiously.

The old man stroked his iron beard and looked out toward São Tomé for a moment before answering. "Many. Dozens every day. Fools, all of them."

As the old man spoke, Martin felt his patiently constructed plan collapsing into a heap of rubble. He would never get the parrot past customs. Of that he was now sure. The old man was a citizen of this island nation and obviously had an intimate knowledge of the way it operated. On the day-long ferry trip from Libreville, Martin had begun to realize the true magnitude of the risk he was taking—and why his uncle Omar had reached his elevated station in life.

When he had first brought the parrot to Omar's house, his uncle had seemed unimpressed and even slightly amused by Martin's initiative. In a very African gesture of hospitality, he let the boy stay on and apparently forgot about the bird entirely, even though it launched an occasional blood-curdling screech from its cage in the backyard. Then yesterday, he had called Martin into his den with its desk and the first personal computer Martin had ever seen.

He told Martin that there was a man on São Tomé who would very much like a parrot as a domestic pet and would pay handsomely to get one. If Martin would be willing to take the parrot to the man, Omar would split the profit with Martin. And perhaps if all this went well, there would be other business dealings that he could entrust to Martin.

This last statement suffused Martin with a flood of elation that severely fogged the last part of Omar's proposition: It seemed that it was slightly illegal to bring parrots onto São Tomé, but that customs were really just a kind of joke on this tiny island, a mere formality. If you didn't flaunt your transgressions, you weren't bothered. It was that simple.

But now, as he stood at the ferry railing less than two hours from customs, Martin was severely bothered. For this first time, he understood that he was taking all the risk, which might be considerable, and getting only half the profit. Omar, who had done nothing but make a contact, would pocket the other half. Martin might have found this tolerable under some circumstances, but definitely not under those the old man had described. He could all but feel the gourd right now, and he involuntarily clenched his buttocks into a defensive position.

He excused himself to the old man, entered a passageway, and went down two decks to the small cabin that came with the ticket Omar had bought him. He unlocked the door, entered quickly, and closed it before flipping on the light, which sprouted naked out of its overhead fixture. The old metal trunk on the floor was painted olive drab and splotched with rust. It looked innocent enough, unless you got close enough to notice the small holes drilled discreetly near the edges. Martin unlocked the trunk and looked at the parrot, which stared back at him contemptuously. It had already undergone the indignity of being rendered unconscious for the trip on board, and now Martin would have to repeat the process for the upcoming passage through customs.

Martin got out the rag, the leather gloves, and the bottle of ether from a cardboard box inside the trunk. He lifted the cage out of the trunk and placed it on the metal floor, where it vibrated in sympathy with the ship's engines and filled the room with an irritating metallic buzz. As he put on the gloves, he paused and stared at the bird and the cage and realized that he himself might be a bird in a much nastier kind of cage if he was caught. He pictured the customs men in their starched khakis and military dress caps, their eyes obscured with jet-black aviator sunglasses. Big men with broad faces, pinched lips, powerful forearms, and 9mm automatics slung sullenly in their holsters of polished leather. Men with whom even his uncle could not negotiate, let alone himself. Men with handcuffs, basement tables, and gourds.

With that, he put down the ether bottle, pulled a spare shirt out of the trunk, and draped it over the birdcage. He opened the door and looked up and down the passageway. All clear. Two decks later, he reached the railing in the last light of dusk.

Inside the parrot's nostrils, the evening sea breeze flowed over the nasal membranes, where the *Chlamydia* were now living in cohabitation with the *Salmonella*. And as these two cultures intermingled, a burgeoning market had come to life, with genetic material as the medium of exchange. All chromosome purchases were made on a caveat emptor basis— you never knew what you were receiving. Sometimes it was trash, sometimes it was poison, but sometimes it was of great value. And occasionally it was priceless.

And tonight a great and rare bargain was being struck. Here and there, *Salmonella* bacteria were dying and their innards spilling out as their cell walls disintegrated. And part of the molecular flotsam that spewed forth were fragments of DNA, the most basic of genetic currencies.

Many of these fragments drifted aimlessly and eventually dissolved into a meaningless horde of nucleic acids. But a few were snapped up by the *Chlamydia,* who took them in through their cell walls, giving them a new home and a new lease on life. And of these chosen few, some carried the code for how to ward off the horrible scourge of tetracycline, the notorious burster of bacterial bubbles.

The *Chlamydia* that struck this fateful bargain already carried the genetic defense against erythromycin, one of their two mortal enemies from the drug world. And now they had acquired complete immunity to their other adversary, tetracycline. At last, they were free of the chemical persecutions that descended from the macro world, the big world of scientists, technicians, and laboratories. Soon they would pass this trait on to their children, and in a few generations, it would become a permanent entry in the local lexicon of drug resistance, taking its rightful place as the definitive description of self-defense.

In this way, the small microbial community inside the parrot's nose became a biological bomb with a power greater than the world's combined nuclear arsenal.

And now Martin balanced the cage on the deck railing, opened the door with gloved hands, and flung this feathered bomb out into the humid, salty air.

As he squinted into the fading light, he could see it flying off on a steady course toward the island of São Tomé.

16

"LIEUTENANT PARIS?"

Paris swung around from his PC, which was currently protesting that its hard disk was full, and saw a tall man standing before his desk in a tailored summer suit of a tight cotton weave. Lawyer. Had to be.

"Yeah?"

"My name's Robert Fancher. I'm an attorney. Mind if I sit down?"

"Go ahead." As Fancher handed Paris his card, Paris noticed the man's permanent leer, as if all his facial flesh had been pulled an inch too tight and gathered into a little ponytail of scalp at the back of his head.

"Thanks. I'm not here on official business. But I do have some information you might be interested in. It's regarding a warrant on a grand theft charge."

"Client of yours?"

"No. Not yet, anyway. Although I would provide legal representation if recommended."

Paris didn't buy it. The guy didn't seem like the kind of lawyer who would be hustling business from the bottom up. His tie looked like a week's take-home for the average cop. So why the ambulance-chasing routine?

"Any particular reason you picked me to talk to, Mr. Fancher?"

Fancher forced out a polite laugh. "Actually, no. I came to Burglary and Theft because of the nature of the warrant. You just happened to be available." Fancher cast a glance over at Larsen, who was wolfing down a chocolate-covered doughnut dusted with pink speckles. "Your associates all appeared to be occupied."

"Forgive us, Mr. Fancher. We do the best we can with the resources available."

"I'm sure you do. Anyway, the warrant is from San Diego

and the suspect is a woman named Elaine Wilkes. The case is a bit unusual. She's a medical doctor, a researcher."

Paris immediately remembered the flyer, and the woman with the intelligent eyes. "A doctor? Wanted for grand theft?"

"You've got it. I believe its some kind of white-collar crime."

"So what should I do, Mr. Fancher? Fly to San Diego and arrange for a physical?"

"That won't be necessary. She's right here. In Seattle. Just checked into the Sheraton. That's what I came to tell you."

"And just what made you go and do a thing like that, Counselor?" asked Paris with an amused smile.

"It's a business matter, Lieutenant. And a rather complicated one." Fancher rose to leave. "I won't bore you with the details. If I can help, give me a call. Good luck."

Paris watched Fancher stride briskly between the desks and out into the hall. What was his real angle? No way to tell. At least not yet. He looked at his desk with the eye of a paper archaeologist and began to peal back various strata in a search for the flyer from San Diego. There it was. The woman now looked more intriguing than ever. He got up and put on his coat.

"Where you goin'?" asked Larsen.

"I'm going to meet an attractive young woman in a hotel room."

"Oh, yeah? Well, be a good boy, now." Larsen licked a smear of chocolate frosting off the inside lid of the empty doughnut box.

Robert Fancher felt a little worried as he walked the two steep blocks up James Street to his next destination. There was a problem with the Wilkes thing, a potentially big one. After leaving Paris, Fancher had made a few discreet queries at the district attorney's office and discovered that an extradition back to San Diego on a white-collar crime charge was something less than a sure thing. Most people assumed that if you committed a crime and fled to another city far away, the proverbial long arm of the law would hunt you down and bring you back. Not true. Extradition arrangements turned out to be slippery and flexible affairs that depended on the nature of the crime, the distance, the available human resources, and much more. Commit a murder in San Diego and run off to Portland, Maine, and they'd inevitably come and get you. But commit a car theft in Oklahoma City and run off to Phoenix, and the outcome was definitely in doubt. It wasn't unusual for a suspected fugitive to be picked up in a distant city and have the original jurisdiction decline their right to extradite—in which case the suspect was simply set free, no questions asked.

Which meant that the Wilkes woman, along with her stolen property, might suddenly be released. He couldn't let that happen. His retainer with Uni was the foundation of his current lifestyle. Besides the lakeside home, it included a nice little A-frame up on Mt. Rainier, a summer home on Orcas Island, three late-model luxury cars, tuition for two kids to Ivy League schools, and an apartment for his mistress downtown.

His client, Bennet Rifkin, was a key player in the Uni system, a randomly folded mass of spaghettilike connections that Fancher only vaguely understood. But he did understand that if he failed Bennet, waves of negative polarity would ripple through the connections, and the retainer might evaporate as suddenly as it had appeared. In the event of such a catastrophe, he would have only one major source of income, a source that made him as uncomfortable as it made him prosperous.

And now he entered the executive suite of this source, the King County Jail.

In recent years Barney had become a profitable client for Fancher, with a maze of business dealings that required nearly continuous attention. But up until now, he had carefully insulated himself from the dark side of Barney, where money turned to blood, dark coagulated blood that stuck hard and fast if it touched you. When Barney had become ensnared in his present difficulty, Fancher had recommended the best available talent in criminal law and quickly bowed out of the matter.

But the Wilkes case was forcing his hand. In an elliptical kind of way, Bennet had been quite clear about the situation: *You should do whatever you think is proper under the circumstances.* And given the present circumstances, with the

Wilkes woman likely to go free, a visit to Barney was not only proper, but the only reasonable option.

When Fancher arrived at the visiting room, Barney was already waiting in one of the little booths and stared at Fancher with faint amusement as the lawyer sat down in front of the glass window and picked up the phone.

"Bob! I'm surprised and honored," said Barney cheerfully. "Are you taking up criminal law as a hobby?"

Fancher forced a self-effacing laugh. "No, I don't think so. How've you been, Barney?"

"How do you think I've been?" asked Barney with a poisonous hiss. "I've been shitty, Bob. Really shitty."

"There may be something we can do to change that. That's why I'm here."

"Like what?"

"There's a potential deal where I might act as a middleman between you and one of my corporate clients."

"Like who?"

"I can't say, but I can tell you that I'm empowered to negotiate for them."

"Negotiate what?"

"Well, it seems that a certain woman stole some very valuable research data from them, and they want it back. I've made arrangements for the police here to pick her up, but there's a problem. She probably won't be extradited back to the original jurisdiction, so she may very well go scot-free."

"That's a sad tale, Bob," said Barney wistfully. "And how might I help this major corporation?"

"The woman's name is Elaine Wilkes. And there's a high possibility she'll be booked in here before the day is over. She needs to be persuaded that it's in her best interest to surrender the stolen property—even if she's set free. In that case, all she has to do is walk out and fail to claim the disks on which the data is stored."

Barney smiled. "Just walk, huh?"

"That's right."

"I'd like to just walk, too, Bob. I'd like that a lot."

"Well, to a limited extent, that may just be possible. That's the offer I make on behalf of the other party. Certain arrangements might be engineered where your bail might be reconsidered, then the funds for the bail might be made available—at no expense to you, personally."

"That would be a very kind and generous gesture on the part of your client. I like it. It would be one business organization recognizing the plight of another and reaching out during a time of need."

"That would be an elegant way to think of it. Can we call it a deal?"

Barney sighed. "You know, Bob, I shouldn't just cave in. I should treat this offer as a starting point and negotiate. But I'm tired. I'm tired of being unjustly confined. Do you understand?"

"I do indeed."

"Good-bye, Bob."

"Good-bye." As Fancher turned to leave, he could feel Barney staring at his back though the glass, which was half an inch thick and bulletproof.

Even so, he felt a slight prickle creep along the back of his neck.

17

"You must compliment Dr. Wilkes and her team. The model for 57a is a fine piece of work. And a very interesting one."

Bennet looked at the small video picture of Dr. Ahmadi on the screen of his laptop computer. It seemed a little ironic to have this serious little Pakistani in the foreground of his vision, while not a hundred yards away, a flock of bronzed kids played volleyball on the beach below his deck in La Jolla. The doctor's image was flanked by video images of Mr. Jiminez and Ms. Hokuro, and together they formed a strange corporate triptych that only the Uni-verse would have allowed.

"Thank you, Doctor," said Bennet. "I'll be sure and pass on the compliment." He had already created a shaky fabrication about Elaine's absence from this meeting. It seemed her mother had taken ill, and she was off to Arizona for a few days. With a little luck, he could make this fictitious mother gradually grow worse and extend his lie until it no longer mattered.

Right now, it still mattered greatly. He'd already set all the machinery in motion to find her and get the disks back, but he knew with a sickening certainty that the longer she was loose, the higher the likelihood that she'd made copies. If so, she was probably slinging them across the globe, like little UFOs on a mission of truth and justice. Fortunately, most of them were worthless because they were unreadable without the cytoputer technology here at the Foundation, which had the only software and hardware capable of understanding their content. But those with the final reports and summaries were readable with several common desktop applications that ran on garden-variety computers, and they contained enough sensitive matter to launch a long and embarrassing string of official inquiries.

Bennet turned his attention back to the teleconference where Ms. Hokuro was admitting, with her usual reservations, that she "couldn't find any holes" after reviewing Elaine's work. It was difficult to imagine what this woman did for fun.

"That's good," said Dr. Ahmadi, "because we've almost completed the genetic reconstruction. And based on what we see so far, there are several possibilities for an effective drug therapy."

"Are any of them commercially available?" asked Jiminez.

"No. They're all still in R and D. One here, one in Rio, and another in Prague. Of course, we can't give you a definite answer until the work is complete, but at this point, I'd say we've probably got something to work with."

Dr. Ahmadi's group was a self-contained unit charged with developing new antibiotics through biomolecular engineering, and the mechanics of their work were suitably baffling to people outside the profession. Bennet had learned just enough to make informed decisions—at least he liked to think they were informed.

To understand Dr. Ahmadi's group, one had to understand that from the very start, the history of antibiotics was built on fortuitous circumstance. Fleming's discovery of the first antibiotic, penicillin, was based on a casual observation that bacteria in a culture dish failed to grow where there were little dots of mold that naturally produced the drug. Over the years, many other drugs were also discovered in natural substances, then refined or isolated in the laboratory. To locate these substances, research teams scoured the globe, often relying on local medical traditions to point the way.

In any case, the pattern remained largely the same for over fifty years. First you discovered the compound, then you observed how efficient it was in killing particular species of bacteria. Through the microscope, you could observe the specific kind of damage it was doing inside the bug, like ripping holes in the cell wall or disassembling the nucleoid or knocking out the ribosomes.

But you never saw what really happened. You never glimpsed the true cause of the microbial genocide being played out, because the real battles were occurring several orders of magnitude below. In the end, these tiny conflicts were molecular battles, where the molecules of the drug staged assaults on the various atomic assemblies that constituted the organism itself. Chemical bonds were ripped open, proteins violently unfolded, and unholy atomic alliances formed.

Even after many years of research, the molecular targets inside a bug, the soft spots in the microbial fortress, were often still a mystery. All you knew was that the drug worked, and what the aftermath of the battle looked like. But you never saw the battle itself, or how the drug won it.

But now there were groups like Dr. Ahmadi's, groups aided by high-speed, submicron computers that let them set sail through the vast molecular seas where the battles were fought. On these voyages, they carefully observed how the conflicts evolved, how the drugs worked their way around defensive fortifications patiently engineered over millions of years of evolution. Once they had this information, they could design drugs that were battle-hardened even though they had never seen combat, drugs that knew all the little nasty tricks required to sneak in and bring the organism down.

In the case of Agent 57a, Dr. Ahmadi's group would inspect its molecular fortifications and seek out weak spots vulnerable to attack. Then very specific combat engines could be engineered to breach these spots and cause the kind of strategic chaos that would ultimately destroy the organism.

But first, they had to build a new representation of Agent 57a, one quite different from EpiSim's, which was designed specifically to operate in the statistical realm and not the molecular one. To build their statistical model, Elaine's team had gone from the specific to the general. They had started with a detailed profile of the bug's genes, about 3,500 of them spelled out in over 3 million nucleotide letters. Each of these genes performed a certain function, such as repair and maintenance of the cell wall. For every gene, Elaine's group then wrote a computer program that did the same thing, except in an abstract and somewhat simplified manner. Instead of a real cell wall, there was a section of a database that represented the wall, and the program operated in this data. So in all, there were 3,500 programs that represented the entire genome, and a complex set of rules that coordinated their behavior as they came together in the mysterious dance of life.

In constructing Agent 57a, Elaine had borrowed many genes wholesale from the original *Chlamydia,* the one found in nature. But she had also made numerous modifications to many other genes. So now, Dr. Ahmadi's group had to analyze the programs representing all these genes and turn them back into the original genetic programs spelled out in DNA sequences and executed by the legions of natural biocomputers inside the bacterial cell. It had been an arduous task and required the use of advanced computer systems on three continents that were connected through high-speed communication links. But now, the biological model of Agent 57a was nearly complete, and Dr. Ahmadi and his team could walk the bug's ramparts and see the soft spots, the molecular targets, where certain chemicals might punch through.

"I have to give credit to Dr. Wilkes for her design work," said Dr. Ahmadi. "There is not any existing antibiotic that would have been effective against this thing. With the Tet^R gene inserted on the third plasmid, tetracycline would have bounced right off it."

"So how long before you can test these new compounds?" asked Bennet.

"Well," speculated Dr. Ahmadi, "we'll be able to run the formal verifications on the computer in a few weeks. I'm sure at least one of the new compounds will do the trick. Of course, beyond that, we have a unique situation. There's no real organism to test the compounds on, so that part will just have to wait until it emerges from the environment. But given our success in past projects involving real organisms, I'd say we have a very high chance of complete success."

"Doctor, thank you very much," said Bennet. "You're making a great contribution and we're pleased to have you on the team."

"Thank you, Mr. Rifkin. I'm glad to be of service."

I'm sure you are, thought Bennet as the doctor's image winked off on his screen. *If everything goes right, this is going to make you a very rich man.*

"Any questions, Mr. Jiminez?" asked Bennet.

"Well, what if one of these new drugs *doesn't* work? What then?"

"There are things we can do to guarantee they will work—beyond any reasonable doubt," said Ms. Hokuro.

"What things?" asked Jiminez.

"I'm not able to discuss that, Mr. Jiminez."

"Well, then, I'm off to my next meeting. Check you later." The image of Jiminez faded from Bennet's screen.

"So he's not cleared for LifeForce?" Bennet asked Hokuro.

"No. There's no reason he needs to know, especially about something that's still highly experimental. The first trials haven't even been conducted yet."

"But you could do it if you had to?"

"I'm sure we could. If the situation warranted it."

Bennet hoped so. LifeForce was the result of advanced research in laboratory robotics, which allowed the customized assembly of long strands of DNA. For the first time, it would be possible to construct entire sets of artificial genes. The technique was still limited to gene sets of under

5 million base pairs, but this capacity was more than adequate to construct the complete genomes of many bacteria, and most certainly that of *Chlamydia*. And once you could make the genes, the next step was to manufacture an organism defined by the genes. In many cases, this was still a forbiddingly complex exercise, but not in those cases where the new thing was a slightly mutated version of the old thing. In these cases, you went into the bug and removed the nucleoid and the plasmids and replaced them with artificial ones carrying the new genes. With a little luck, the new genes would act like a reformed government that could institute change, yet still manage the organism—but without introducing revolutionary actions that might tear it apart. Agent 57a would be a prime candidate for this process, which would yank it out of the cyberworld and blow the breath of God into it. Then the live version of Agent 57a could be made to multiply, and the resultant hordes would become microbial guinea pigs to test the new antibiotics. In theory, at least. As Hokuro had noted, the system had never really been used yet. But a project with potential income the size of Bennet's could most certainly act as a catalyst to move things along.

As Ms. Hokuro signed off, Bennet shut down his computer and took a minute to inhale the balmy marine air off the beach. He watched the kids playing volleyball, their hard brown bodies pumping into the clear blue sky to bat the ball with open palms. Thanks to him, thanks to Uni, they would live to be old.

At least, most of them.

18

The South Atlantic

IT WAS THE CLUMSIEST OF ASSASSINS, A WANDERING BLOB with a license to kill any nonresidents it happened to bump into. And now, in the yellow and liquid interior of the liver of Maria Santoz, it did a silly thing.

The macrophage did not kill with deft chemical blows, artfully aimed missiles, or savage invasions. Instead, it smothered its victims by enveloping them in its billowing protein folds, which became a prison that denied them the nourishment they needed to survive. Although some invaders were clever enough to go into suspended animation when captured this way, they still lost their freedom of movement and faced a life of permanent confinement.

This particular macrophage had been on a routine patrol when it encountered one of the syphilis spirochetes that were now permanent citizens of Maria's physical self. In a slow but steady motion, it pushed forward so the offending germ was shoved in a pocket of jelly, much like a finger pushed into bread dough. The germ offered no resistance. In the microbial world, the split-second violent encounters of the animal kingdom give way to prolonged actions where neither predator nor prey is capable of calculated action.

Eventually, the macrophage would complete the job and close in behind the pocket holding the spirochete. But now, in a rare event, it collided with a second offender, one of the rat-bite-fever germs inherited from Peter Rancovich. This lone *Streptobacillus moniliformis* was one of the few survivors of a pitched battle fought near the point of entry in Maria's vagina. Unlike the massive invasion of Peter through the bite wound gouged by the rat, only a small number of the strep germs had entered Maria. And while they were virulent warriors, they faced a massive and overwhelming force from the immune system, which went immediately to maximum war footing. In the ensuing battle, only a handful of survivors managed to escape through the circulatory system, which had brought this particular survivor to the liver.

Now both the strep germ and the syphilis spirochete were crowded into the same small pocket, with the macrophage wall slowly closing behind them. The strep germ, already wounded by antibody attacks in the great invasion battle, chose this moment to expire, leaving the spirochete imprisoned with a leaky corpse. Fissures in the dead strep's cell wall allowed its innards to pour into the pocket, and part of this gusher was a flood of genetic material, threads and rings of DNA.

Given the confines of the macrophage prison, the spirochete had no choice but to take in some of these refugee chromosomes and incorporate them into its own power structure. And then, just before the prison walls closed forever, the spirochete struggled free of the macrophage and floated into the liver, where it soon divided and primed a reproductive chain that would send the newly acquired genes far and wide.

So the legacy of the mutated strep germ, its hypervirulence, its will to wreak massive destruction on living tissue, was passed on to the syphilis community inside Maria Santoz. But within this community, the new trait would not be put into immediate action, because these patient microbes were in a passive stage, waiting to explode into tertiary syphilis some years hence. Instead, they would act as a living vault to store this potential for microbial ultraviolence and keep it safe for generations yet to come.

Maria was oblivious to the microscopic drama playing out inside her as she settled back into the padded leather of the first-class seat and looked out the window. In the near distance, a thunderhead pushed a huge white cauliflower of cumulus in the ice blue sky, with flashes of lightning flaring on its dark underside. She sipped her wine and stroked the expensive silk blouse she'd bought a few days earlier before boarding a plane in Iquitos. When she had arrived in Rio, the scale of the city nearly crushed her resolve, but the quest for Felix pushed her on. After going to a few nightclubs, she learned that his band, a sensation of Iquitos, was unknown in this great metropolis, where there seemed to be a band everywhere you turned. Then, at the point of desperation, she found a bartender who remembered them.

"Those guys? Yeah. Played world beat. Played it real good."

You remember the bass player? The one with the big smile?

"Yeah, man, I remember him. Said he was goin' home."

Home?

"Yeah. Those guys broke up and said he was goin' back home. Some island somewhere."

São Tomé?

"Somethin' like that."

São Tomé. It had to be. The place in her fever dream, the place Felix had described with such affection. She went to the airport, bought the ticket, then chucked the stolen credit cards into a garbage can before they turned from a short-term asset into a criminal liability.

São Tomé. She turned the place over in her mind as she watched the thunderhead out the window. An island right on the equator with only 150,000 people.

And one of them was Felix.

19

PARIS KNOCKED DISCREETLY ON THE DOOR OF ROOM 1237 AT the Sheraton Inn. Most of the time, it went just about like this, a quiet affair with little dramatic or cinematic content. The public, which watched an endless parade of wild street scenes on "live action" cop shows, no longer realized they were watching the small minority of police arrests. When Paris had worked in Homicide, he found this doubly true; by the time the police were involved, the central act of violence was over, its intrinsic energy dissipated, and the investigators worked in a depressing cloud of emotional exhaust to solve the crime.

"Yes?" A woman's voice, laced with a strong dose of reservation.

"Lt. Philip Paris. Seattle police. We need to talk." Paris knew that interval between his words and the door's opening would have a direct bearing on how difficult the ensuing events would be. The longer, the tougher. Fortunately, the door opened almost immediately.

It was her. No doubt. The same bright eyes.

"Elaine Wilkes?" asked Paris as he held out his ID for her inspection.

"That's me." She turned and walked back into the room with a curiously relaxed stride, ignoring him completely.

Still, he didn't feel snubbed. She was an angular, attractive woman, in her midthirties, with short blond hair carefully and expensively shaped.

As he followed her into the room, she sat at a little round table by the window, which looked out on the rowdy march of big buildings down to Elliott Bay, where several big container ships pushed toward the docks to the south. He took the chair opposite her and observed her profile as she stared out at the scene. "I take it you know why I'm here," he said.

"I'm a little surprised that you found me so fast." She turned toward him. "Couldn't be that you had a little help, could it?"

"As a matter of fact, we did," said Paris in a carefully neutral tone.

"I'm sorry, Officer—what was your name again?"

"Paris. Lt. Philip Paris."

"I would like to ask something of you, Lieutenant Paris. We both know why you're here, but I don't think you have any idea why I'm here. Not really. Before you arrest me, I'd like to tell you."

"In that case, Ms. Wilkes, we better kick this off with rights: You have the right to remain silent—"

"If I remained silent, Lieutenant, it would be the biggest crime of all. Possibly the biggest crime of all time. Therefore, in the interest of humanity at large, I waive my rights."

"That's quite generous of you, Ms. Wilkes." Paris settled back in his chair. This was definitely more fun than filling out theft reports. He'd give it a little time before he hauled her in. "Now, where would you like to begin?"

She inhaled deeply and exhaled slowly, in the way people often do before telling a difficult thing. "Suppose I told you that over half of the world would be dead within the next ten years."

Paris grinned. "Which half? Mine or yours?"

Elaine turned and eyed him sharply. For the first time, she realized Paris was going to be more than a listening device on the far side of the confessional screen. "Until a few days ago, I worked at a place called the Webster Foundation. You've probably never heard of it. It's a relatively small institution that was purchased a few years ago by Uni Corporation."

"And it's in San Diego?"

"Yes. Anyway, the Foundation was struggling to create a new simulation technology which could forecast the onset of epidemics. Then Uni poured in enough money to make it work. I won't bore you with all the technical details. The important thing is that all the tests indicate these simulations are highly accurate."

"Have they actually predicted an epidemic?"

"Not yet. We used historical epidemics for the tests. One was the Spanish flu which started in 1918. We recreated global conditions at that time in history and set the disease lose. The results were a very close match to the real thing."

"Sounds like a big deal. A very big deal. Why haven't the media glommed on to it?"

"We stopped publishing when Uni took over. The agreement was that we wouldn't resume publishing until all work on the technology was complete and made public to the business community. In other words, we couldn't say anything until Uni figured out how to wring maximum profit out of the technology."

"So how do you fit into all this?" Paris didn't like where this was going. It was going toward germs, toward the poisoner. Toward Ginny.

"The technology's called EpiSim. My role in it was a project to build a computerized model of a certain kind of germ, a new infectious agent, one that doesn't currently exist, but is very likely to emerge in the near future."

"Sounds highly theoretical."

"So was the atom bomb—until they exploded one. Unfortunately, this is a bit worse than that."

"You're sure about that?" She had to be kidding.

"I wish I wasn't. But there's about seventy percent probability this thing will emerge in the real world in the next ten years. It's a mutated form of *Chlamydia psittaci*. Highly virile and completely drug resistant. Nothing will stop it."

Through pure luck, Paris knew the bug she was referring to. A few years back, one of the public health people told him about it. They had a case here in Seattle where a woman came down with psittacosis after working in a pet shop with a large stock of parrots. It took months of drug therapy for her to recover.

"So, have you run a simulation based on this new bug?"

"We just did. A few nights ago. In just a year, it would kill over half the world's population."

Paris couldn't help but lapse into an incredulous smile. "That's a fairly ambitious statement."

"Not if you go back in history. It's already happened. Twice."

"So tell me about it." Paris was suspended between repulsion and fascination.

And so she told him. In both cases, the culprit was the same, a bacteria named *Yersinia pestis,* the microbial agent of bubonic plague. For reasons unknown, the germ awoke from a comfortable slumber in the bellies of fleas and poured out in a rage that covered the entire known world. The fleas used rats for transportation—at least until they died; then they looked for a new ride, which often turned out to be human. A black, gangrene-like pustule formed at the point where the flea took its fateful bite and injected the germ. Soon, the lymph nodes in the arms, neck, and legs swelled dramatically as the body frantically tried to mount a defense. Then the buboes showed up, the purple blotches of hemorrhage that gave the plague its name. In more than half the cases, the next step was madness and death as the disease poured a flood of toxin into the nervous system. Sometimes the process took a week, sometimes only a day.

The first incidence of bubonic plague was in the reign of the Emperor Justinian, A.D. 541, when the disease marched out of Egypt and then forked like a serpent tongue to scour both Europe and Asia. The second was in 1340, the time of the Black Plague, when it originated in Asia and made its way along the trade routes to Europe. Both times, between 30 and 50 percent of the world population was killed. No other catastrophes in all human history came anywhere close.

"So in the past," she concluded, "we've had two truly great pandemics. I guess you could say that this new outbreak will be the third great pandemic."

"Very interesting. So over half of us are going to buy the farm sometime real soon?"

"That's correct."

"It's a pretty big pill to swallow," declared Paris as he shifted his weight in the chair.

"The problem is there isn't any pill to swallow. Agent 57a is totally immune to all antibiotics. We're completely defenseless against it. We might be able to use some kind of inhalant to relieve the symptoms a little, but not for long. No matter what, your lungs are going to fill up with fluid, and after that, there's a good chance the disease will go systemic."

"Systemic?" said Paris, whose grin was now down to compound low.

"When a disease strikes your body, it usually hits a specific site, like your lungs, your ears, or your intestines. Most of the time, your immune system swings into action and keeps it confined to this area. But occasionally, it will break out and get into your bloodstream, which takes it throughout your body. Then it becomes a free-for-all. All your organs can become afflicted and you suffer a massive physical collapse."

"You die?"

"You die. Horribly."

"Are you a doctor?" Paris had heard enough about the disease. It was time to change the subject.

"Yes, I am."

"And would you stake your professional reputation on this work?"

Elaine sighed. "I've already gone a little further than that. Two days ago, I completely destroyed my professional reputation over this."

"Why?"

"By accident, I found out the company has no intention of sharing this information with the public. They're going to use it to make a huge windfall in the pharmaceutical business—and maybe let several million people die to build up demand."

"They're going to make a new drug?"

"They're going to try."

"And so you stole your own research?"

"In a word, yes. I copied the entire simulation onto a set of disks, then erased the original files. I took the disk set and got on a plane. Simple as that."

"Simple as that. And where is the stolen property?"

Elaine walked over to the smaller of the two suitcases resting on the bed and unzipped a pouch on the side. She pulled out a cartridge that contained a disk about the size of an audio CD. "This particular disk is a summary. There are dozens of other disks in the bag, if you'd like to see them."

Elaine brought the disk over to the table and sat down. "Do you believe me?"

"About what?"

"About all of this."

"Does it matter?"

"Yes, it does. Because I'm going to ask a rather large favor of you."

"And what's that?"

Although she didn't show it, Elaine was unsettled by this policeman, this Philip Paris. He was tough, very tough, but not menacing. In fact, there seemed to be a weary kind of gentleness about him. Nevertheless, he now held absolute power over her, and she resented that immensely. But right now was hardly the time to work it out. His presence had thrown her completely off track, and she'd just have to improvise. Before he'd showed up, she'd intended to go to David Muldane's office at the public health department, where they could run some of the report and summary disks on a personal computer so Muldane could get a sense of how truly devastating Agent 57a could be. After that, she'd hoped he would help her get the disks copied and off to people at the National Institutes for Health and Centers for Disease Control.

But no longer, not with Paris here. How had he found her so fast? She'd only checked in a couple of hours ago. Bennet? Uni? Paris had hinted that the police received some help in tracking her down, so she had to assume the company was already in hot pursuit, even hotter than she'd imagined possible. Was Paris himself involved? Not likely. Like it or not, she'd just have to trust him. It was her last chance to get the disks into public view. As soon as she went to jail, the disks would become evidence, and since they were stolen, they'd undoubtedly be returned to Uni.

Elaine put the disk down on the table between them. "I'd

be very grateful if you'd give this one disk to a contact I have here in the King County Public Health Department. Go ahead and book the other disks as evidence, or whatever it is you do in these cases, but give the world a break and deliver this to the public health guy."

"Who's your contact here?"

"A doctor named David Muldane."

Muldane? A doctor? Not the last time Paris checked. Somebody was scamming somebody, but he'd sort that out later.

"How do you know him?"

"We both participated in remote surgical procedures at the Virtual Surgery Center. It's a computer environment where you can practice for the real thing, even if you're not a licensed surgeon yet."

Paris got up and watched a seagull climb in a long, slow spiral between the skyscrapers. He should stay out of this. Completely. He was like the bird out there, slowly spiraling up out of a pit of grief and obsession, getting a little higher on each revolution. Just lately, he'd put the hunt for the poisoner into a better perspective, one that didn't plunge him into a self-consumption that gnawed at the vital tissues of his soul. The last thing he needed was another infectious agent in his life.

But he believed her. That was the problem. She wasn't lying. He had a practiced eye for all the discontinuities that criminals presented to cops in vain attempts to squirm free: the simple facts versus the convoluted excuses, the indignation of the innocent versus the arrogant strut of the truly disaffected, the pleas for compassion versus the violence done to the victim. They were all absent here. Besides, no business would have gone to this much trouble to get their property back unless it was extremely valuable.

"Before I do something rash," Paris said, "let's see if I can sum this thing up. The world's largest business has a very accurate forecast of a major plague. But they don't wish to share this information with the public health community. Instead, they plan to use it to develop a new antibiotic, which they can sell at premium pries when the disease actually hits. And to make sure that demand goes through the roof, they'll wait until a couple of million people die before releasing it."

"You got it."

"And because you're slightly upset about a couple million potential murders, you quit your job in the middle of the night and stole the data."

"That's right."

Paris sighed. "Tell you what I'm going to do. I'm going to meet you halfway." He pointed to the disk on the table. "Can this thing be copied?"

"Yes, it can."

"I'm going to let Muldane have this long enough to make a copy then give the original back to me so I can book it. I'll book the rest of the disks right now. Fair enough?"

"More than fair. Thanks." She smiled at him, a big hug of a smile that got through his defensive perimeter and poured down into the trenches like a warm spring breeze. But the sentries were sharp inside Philip Paris, and they sounded the alarm and contained the intrusion.

"You're under arrest. Do you understand that?"

"Perfectly. So what do we do now?"

"We take you to the King County Jail and book you. Then I notify the San Diego DA's office, and they arrange for extradition."

"How long will that take?"

"Hard to say. A week, maybe. When we get you back down there, you can retain an attorney and get out on bail."

"And then what?"

Paris shrugged. "I'm a cop, not a lawyer."

"And I'm a doctor, not criminal."

"Then we're even. Let's go."

As Paris went to get her bags, Elaine suddenly realized the true depth of her predicament. Since climbing on the plane in San Diego, she'd harbored a tacit assumption that her altruism would act like a moral force field that would protect her against hostile projectiles, legal and otherwise. But now she could envision a courtroom, a prison cell, and the vindictive glare of Bennet as he made her suffer the maximum pain the law would allow—and maybe more if he could get away with it.

Still, would she have done it any other way? Not really.

Paris opened the door to the hallway, put the bags outside, and gestured for her to follow. "After you."

He must have seen the anxiety in her face because his expression softened and he put his hand gently on her shoulder as she passed through the door.

The warm touch of his hand felt better than she could ever admit.

20

Island of São Tomé

OSCAR SILVA REVOLVED THE BAR RAG IN LAZY CIRCLES OVER the wooden surface buried under multiple coats of varnish that Oscar himself had lovingly laid down a decade and a half ago, when he took over ownership of the Paradiso from his father. Located on the Avenida Conceição in São Tomé, the island's only full-fledged town, the Paradiso was a popular drinking spot, especially in the evenings when workers streamed off the docks where the cocoa beans went out and just about everything else came in.

The Paradiso occupied half of a one-story stucco building and was a fat rectangle with an open front that was secured after closing with a security gate that collapsed into an accordion fold during business hours. The bar ran the length of the back wall, so Oscar faced a blinding box of tropical light reflected off the faded pastel surfaces of the two-story buildings across the street. To his right along one wall was the little plywood bandstand where local musicians played three nights a week for drinks and tips. The rest of the place was populated by little tables with bright red plastic tablecloths and metal folding chairs. When the band played, Oscar employed two large laborers to ensure that the occupants of these tables got their drinks from the bar, and not from accomplices loitering outside the exposed end of the room.

But right now, in the punishing afternoon heat, no occupants were at the tables, where the tablecloths nearly melted. In fact, there was only one customer, and she was a great delight to Oscar, who had quite an eye for the ladies for both professional and personal reasons. On the business side, he knew the universal law of drinking establishments was to draw the women first. The men would always follow. On the personal side, he had had more than his share of indulgences with impressionable young women who were bedazzled by his role as an impresario of the local night life. So many that on several occasions, his wife had volunteered to remove the engine that drove him to these senseless and disgraceful acts.

For the time being, the professional side was applauding the lone customer. Even though her features were obscured in shadow, he could tell she was a real stunner. A woman this beautiful would be a tremendous attraction, especially in a town where new faces, even ugly ones, were few and far between. As for personal potential, his sexual antennae had already told him that this was a highly unproductive target. She seemed quite distant and distracted and simply sat at the far end of the bar and drank cans of imported beer. Oscar wondered about her ethnic origin, but didn't pry. She was an exotic hybrid of some kind, and on this island, that was the rule rather than the exception. He himself was a *filos das terras,* a person of mixed blood whose ancestry came from a commingling of African slaves and the Portuguese over a period of four hundred years.

When she had first sat down, she asked him about some bass player named Felix, but he knew of no such person and told her so. She had not said a word since and simply raised her finger when she wanted another drink.

All she did was sit there and stare at the parrot.

Oscar thought it to be quite good fortune that the parrot and the woman had shown up just within a few days of each other. When he woke up earlier in the week, the parrot had been perched on a branch outside his bedroom in the little backyard. It was nibbling away at the seeds from a thistle bush and looked quite at home. Always the businessman, Oscar saw great opportunity in this large, colorful bird. It would become a living ornament at the Paradiso and add another chapter in the rich lore surrounding his establishment, such as the time the young European woman pulled off her tank top and danced topless for a delighted clientele. In a way, it was sad that the bird should be such a big deal. For many decades, São Tomé's sister island, Príncipe, had been downright famous for the gorgeous parrots that came from its volcanic slopes. But profit and greed had formed their usual partnership, and now the island was completely denuded of the beautiful birds.

As he had slipped out of bed, Oscar wondered briefly where this particular specimen had come from. But it really didn't matter. It was now within the sovereignty of his tiny backyard, and that made it his.

He quietly circled around to a shed, where he had a weighted fishing net designed to be thrown from an open boat and spread over the water. He'd never used it on land, but saw no reason why it wouldn't snare a bird as easily as a fish, especially since he was expert at casting it. Fortunately, the bird was roosted on an exposed spot where the net would have room to expand and envelop it. He got it on the first cast, and the thing put up a horrible struggle, with feathers flying about and an endless train of murderous screeches that gathered several of the neighbors to watch the spectacle. When he finished, he held up the subdued bird and accepted a round of applause that was befitting a man of his stature.

Finding the cage was not that difficult, either. In the heyday of the parrot trade on Príncipe, cages had been a common item, and now they lingered on as artifacts of a time come and gone. He found a used one at the general store on the Rua Patrice Lumumba and quickly talked the clerk down to just a few dobras. When he'd opened earlier today, he'd brought the parrot with him and proudly hung the cage from a piece of nylon rope suspended from the rafters.

Between the parrot and the woman, tongues would wag, and business would be good.

Maria stared at the can of beer from East Germany. In her purse, there was enough money left for a few more drinks and another night or two at the Bar Bahia in the center of town. When she'd first arrived in São Tomé, her spirits were sagging because she had felt a little nauseated and feverish on the plane ride from Lisbon. But the illness quickly passed and she was thrilled to see the town of her dream, the town of Felix. The place looked like a beautiful old Portuguese village transplanted onto a tropical island. The streets were lined with two-story buildings of teal and beige stucco, the people were cheerful and friendly, and she could smell the sea in the air.

But now, several days later, the quest for Felix was once again winding down into failure. And this time, the failure seemed terminal, because it would dissolve the vision of the dream, and her slim balance of hope along with it. São Tomé, with its thirty-five thousand people, was the only place on the island big enough to support a musician, and only a handful of nightclubs had music. The Paradiso was the last such place on her list, and she was nearly out of money. There was now the distinct possibility that she might have to resume her old career simply to stay alive.

She was on her fourth beer as she looked at the parrot, which was perched stoically in its cage. It was a magnificent bird and had a depth of primal wisdom about its features that she found attractive. She could learn from this bird, especially now at this pivotal moment in her life. So she reached out through the fuzzy cloud of four beers and put her fingers through the cage to touch it.

There was a frantic flush of feathers, a blur of color, then a sharp linear burn across the tip of her index finger. She yanked her finger out, but a bubble of blood was already on the flesh where the parrot's beak had nipped.

Oscar heard the angry flutter in the cage and turned just in time to see the girl staring at her bloody finger. He knew right away the parrot had bitten her, and he rushed over to offer his sympathy in Portuguese. The girl seemed more stunned than angry and mumbled something in Spanish, which Oscar did not understand. He took the girl's hand and examined the finger. Fortunately, it was a superficial wound, so he brought a clean bar towel and a Band-Aid to help her dress it. She seemed dazed but grateful, especially when he made it clear that she would not have to pay for any more drinks.

A few minutes later, Oscar and Maria went back to their previous stations in the afternoon heat inside the Paradiso.

Neither could possibly understand the significance of the wound on Maria's finger.

21

DR. ELAINE WILKES WAS BEGINNING TO LOSE IT. PARIS COULD tell. He also knew she would never let on if he asked her, so he didn't bother. He'd trusted his judgment and not bothered to handcuff her, so the true shock of incarceration hadn't hit her until just a minute ago, when they walked through the entrance to the King County Jail. He recalled reading somewhere that people don't spend their lives in fear of their deaths, because it is an unimaginable event, a phenomenon beyond their mental engineering capacity. Experience had taught him the same thing was true of upper-middle-class people and jail. For most, it was a catastrophe far beyond reckoning, like a two-dimensional creature trying to comprehend an event in the third dimension.

Now, as they stopped at the booking desk and waited for the clerk to unglue herself from her computer screen, Elaine turned to him and he saw the fear in her eyes.

"Will I be okay?" she asked in a voice that somehow remained steady.

And the moment she spoke, a huge fissure opened in the bureaucratic bulkhead of Philip Paris, and a flood of compassion rolled in. The weight of it caught him by surprise and he struggled to maintain his composure as the sudden feeling sloshed around unchecked inside him. He knew what she must be going through, and he also knew she was utterly alone in a strange town, and that he was her only source of consolation.

"Yeah. You'll be okay," he answered as his throat tightened a notch. "I'll check on you if you like." *Bad form,* he thought, *bad cop.*

"I'd like that. And thanks for your help. It means a lot to me," said Elaine as the matron walked up to take her away and Paris waited for the clerk.

He was still kicking himself about it when he reached the property room to check in her two suitcases. She'd hit a switch and closed a contact that hadn't carried any current in a very long time, and the heat and energy were now flowing freely. Worse yet, it felt good, like some narcotic that lit you up now, but would snuff you out later.

He shrugged it off and opened the bigger of the two suitcases and kicked himself yet again. He was embarrassed to be going through her things. If he'd just kept the proper clinical distance, this wouldn't be a problem, but now it was. The search was a routine examination for contraband: drugs, guns, explosives, that sort of thing. He pawed quickly through her clothes and toiletries and a copy of *Vanity Fair*, which still had the receipt from a gift shop at the San Diego airport stuck inside. There was also a snapshot album, which he left untouched.

He unzipped the smaller suitcase and found more clothes plus two paper boxes, which he removed and opened, and there were the disks, just as she'd said. A couple dozen of them, with no labeling other than some kind of ID numbers scrawled on one side with a red felt-tip pen.

He held up one of the disks and looked at the little arcs of rainbow that danced on its shiny surface. Half the world's population she'd said. He wondered what chapter in the chronicle of doom he was now holding. It was just a bit too much to wrap his brain around. He put the disk back in the box and zipped up the suitcase.

Several stories above, a female trustee pushed a mop past an empty cubicle and stopped long enough to get a good look at the image on a computer display. The trustee had been around long enough to know what she was looking at. It was the jail's link to the National Crime Information Center, and the trustee was delighted at the transaction now on display. It was from San Diego, a verification of the warrant for the arrest of one Elaine Wilkes. The trustee smiled at the picture of the Wilkes woman. *Some classy babe, all right. Just like they said she'd be. And now that babe is right in here with the rest of us fine ladies,* the trustee thought. *Maybe she can teach us some manners. Maybe not.* The trustee really didn't care. All she had to do was pass the news along, and she'd get a real special package, a big piece of the rock. She could already feel the crystalline smoke hitting her lungs and the ignition kicking in. Perfect. Because when you're doing time, altitude and attitude are very often interlocked in a waltz of their own.

As Paris walked back to the large anteroom on the main floor of the jail building, he searched for a distraction and found it in the poisoner. He'd managed to move the poisoner down several notches in his priority queue lately and prided himself on this accomplishment. He could afford to be patient. The crimes occurred at wide intervals and left little visible evidence. He was now convinced that this case was not a war of investigative attrition, as so many were. Instead, it was a matter of intellect and imagination. Somewhere out there in a vast swamp of speculation, the key to the puzzle of the poisoner was crouched in concealment. And from experience, Paris knew he wouldn't recognize it until it suddenly appeared before him in the most full-blown and literal manner.

Just then, it did just that. It walked through the main entrance, not ten yards from him.

Paris would later marvel at the coincidence. If he hadn't been working on the puzzle, he would never have made the connection. Paris was walking along slowly, his hands dug in his pockets and his eyes focused inward as he went over the profile of the biological pyromaniac yet another time. The monster had to have some way to revel in the power of his labors, some way to come into communion with the crime. But somehow it eluded Paris. He grudgingly agreed with Muldane's position that it wasn't an inside job. David had made a good case. The killer didn't get his jollies by slinking along the paper trail within the public health department. But that left only the victims themselves, and once again, he had had to agree with Muldane. That option seemed downright suicidal. And suicide, literal or figurative, didn't fit the profile.

It was at that very moment that Paris looked up and saw the priest.

* * *

Elaine missed her watch. It would have given her a way to count her time toward getting out of this horrible place, but they'd confiscated it along with everything else when they processed her.

She'd just traded a career in medicine, a comfortable condominium, bushels of stylish clothes, and a sleek car for a pullover cotton dress and some dirty slippers. If you took several million possible deaths out of the equation, it seemed like a very poor exchange. And even if you left them in, it didn't seem very equitable at the present moment.

Oh, well, at least she was learning new things. Like how you had to roll your fingers just so to get a good impression on the record during fingerprinting. And how you had to keep your chin straight and level when they snapped the front and back views with the Polaroid.

She sat on the bottom bunk in a cell that held five other bunks and eleven other women, all clothed in the same cotton dresses and dirty slippers. They seemed to be of all possible sizes, shapes, races, and hairstyles and swam curiously about the space, like tropical fish in an aquarium, forming short-lived clusters, which dissolved and reassembled in new combinations. The cement floors and ceiling cast all the voices into a hard, bright pool of reverberation that merged them into an incomprehensible din. Then suddenly, a voice floated close enough to break out and be heard.

"I got small hands, honey. That's all I got to work with. So I got to do my best with the nails. Know what I mean?"

Elaine had no idea what this meant. All she knew was that a short, slight woman with a wilted shock of curly red hair had sat down next to her. The woman's pale skin was lightly freckled and her green eyes peered out from under lashes of pale rust. She stared into the distance as she spoke.

"You're a kind of pretty gal, yourself. So maybe you don't know what I mean. I mean some of us has just got to work with what we got. I got tiny tits, tiny feet, and tiny hands. Now the feet you can hide, and the tits you can fake, but the hands are definitely a problem. Yes, they are. So that leaves me with just the nails. That's all. Just the nails."

The redhead held up her left hand and examined it studiously. She was right. It was small, slender, and splashed with freckles on the backside. The fingers were weak and pale sprouts, all red and scaly in the regions of the knuckles. The smallest no bigger than the diameter of a cigarette.

But the nails were perfect. Each a shiny teardrop rounded to a graceful curve at the top.

Elaine looked away and up at the barred window. It was night. Sometime at night. Sometime during a wretched night of minimum velocity and terminal drag. The redhead kept going.

"You can't grow 'em long in here. Might be weapons then. But I push it. I always push it."

"I'm sure you do," agreed Elaine, hoping her reaction might end the encounter.

"Well, like I said, you're sort of a pretty gal. So it probably doesn't matter much to you." The redhead turned her green eyes on Elaine, and they seemed almost transparent. "But it matters a whole lot to me."

The redhead floated to her feet and drifted off. Elaine felt very tired. She parked herself on the bunk and quickly dozed off.

The pressure hit Elaine in several places simultaneously, in her mouth, her shins, and her forearms. Her eyes snapped open and she saw the cell light was out. The only illumination came from a dim and recessed light somewhere outside the bars. The hollow din of voices still carried on, but from a far distance down the corridor.

She couldn't see her attacker, who held her from behind, but she felt the heft of a large, plump arm that encircled her chest, pinning one of her arms to her side and clamping the other with a strong hand. The opposite hand had stuffed a wad of something in her mouth, so that her breathing rocketed in pure panic up and down her nostrils. She felt an enormous padded mass up and down her backside and the weight of the huge calves pinning her shins together.

A second figure joined them and knelt gingerly beside the bed near Elaine's face. The redhead. She could tell by the outline of curly hair and skinny neck against the dim and distant light.

"All right, darlin'. Let's get with it." The voice from behind was husky, and it blew the hot, rotten stink of tobacco and bad teeth all over Elaine's face.

The redhead put out her slender hand, which was clenched into a fist, and unfurled her little finger, with its perfect nail. And with great care and precision, she inserted this finger and its finely honed nail into Elaine's right nostril.

Every muscle in Elaine's body jerked to attention, but met an equal and overwhelming reaction from the hidden mass of fat and muscle that pinned her.

The interior of the nostril is exceptionally rich in nerve endings, and soon the sharp edges of the nail began to invade the narrow portion of the nasal passage and deliver an almost unimaginable stab of pain.

As the tears poured out of Elaine's eyes, the voice and the stink came back again and addressed the redhead. "You got where you want it now?"

"Yep," said the redhead in quiet voice. "Right about there."

The nail was jammed in as far as possible without tearing the nasal tissue open, and the pain exploded in a continuous red wave through Elaine's head.

"Okay, honey," said the voice into Elaine's ear. "Now you listen up. Seems like you checked into this here hotel with a couple of suitcases. Now if you check outta here, you best forget about them bags. You best just grab your purse and head straight for the door. You hear?" The grip on Elaine's jaw relaxed just enough to let her get off a slight nod. "I gotta tell you our little friend here's really an amateur at this kinda work. If you wind up totin' them bags, the next folks you meet is gonna do it all over again with a darning needle and a hammer. You got it?"

Once again, the hand relaxed slightly on Elaine's jaw and she managed a slight nod. "Well, that's real good then," said the voice through a putrid cloud of odor. "You just don't forget." Then the voice turned away to the redhead. "Okay, honey. You go ahead and pull your little pinkie on outta there."

The redhead removed her finger and drifted out of sight, but the phantom of the terrible pain continued to scour the inflamed surface of Elaine's nasal membrane. Then the big arms and legs suddenly let loose, and Elaine's hands instinctively came together in a pose of frantic prayer to protect her nose. Just then, a foot slammed into her back with enough force to knock her out of the bunk and onto the floor. She lay facedown and petrified, afraid to move. Eventually she turned her head toward the center of the room and the empty cement floor. Through the amorphous blur of tears, the bunks towered like great metal insects, waiting patiently behind the cell's long row of white bars. Nothing moved. Distant voices fused with the rush of industrial volumes of air through invisible vents. The right side of her nose screamed and screamed.

Eventually, she climbed off the floor and back into the bottom bunk. It was funny. She couldn't tell if the tears were an involuntary reaction to the nasal insult or plain old grief and fear. And in her present condition, she no longer really cared.

"You're sure?" asked Paris. He was tired, but a rush of excitement was building inside him.

"Yes, I'm sure, Lieutenant," snapped the head nurse. "After all, I *am* in the people business. Just like you." She was over fifty, both in age and excess pounds, the empress of all she surveyed, and completely unimpressed with a police officer.

"Ms. Nelson, I have no doubt that you're very good at what you do," said Paris with a smile as they stood by the counter that connected two long, parallel corridors of rooms. Traffic in corridors was sparse at this hour as the night shift moved methodically through their routines.

Paris thanked Nurse Nelson and headed for the elevator, slightly annoyed that he couldn't charm her into even a hint of a smile. This was the third hospital tonight, and the answer was always the same. Tomorrow he'd work on corroboration through the victims. Muldane could help with that.

On the way down, Paris leaned against the elevator wall and felt its mechanical shudder massage his tired spine. He smiled into the empty cube of wood and metal. After years of plodding, he was within closing distance.

22

OSCAR WATCHES THE BAND SET UP ON THE PARADISO'S TINY stage. He is always amazed that they can fit onto the little plywood platform that elevates them a foot or so off the floor. Electric bass, Stratocaster guitar, Casio synthesizer, and two percussionists all go together like a spatial puzzle with only a single solution. The place is filling up and the cash register along with it, which lifts Oscar out of his late-afternoon funk. The parrot cage now has a sign taped on it that reads "Hands off!" in *forro,* the island's Creole language. Since it bit the girl, Oscar is worried that it might became a legal liability instead of a stellar attraction. And on top of that, the girl is gone. She had crawled off her barstool late in the day and headed for the street. Oscar had made a last-ditch effort to convince her that all drinks would be free forever, and she should stay, but to no avail. She wobbled off into the street and was lost in the fading light, which comes on suddenly in the equatorial regions.

But now, the band launches into a happy romp based on a simple two-chord riff that hangs on the tonic and occasionally departs to the dominant. Two lovely young women spring up from the little tables, pulling their males onto the small space reserved for dancing. Soon the place is enveloped in a flowing tapestry of sound and motion as others take to the floor. And still others order more drinks. Because it is hot in here. The only circulation is a wooden overhead fan that symbolically churns the air, but accomplishes little in the way of relief. The only source of air replenishment is the open end of the building, but it offers no cross-ventilation to create a current that would move air quickly in and out. So the dancers melt into the heat and lose themselves in it. And the others find insulation in the form of repeated rounds of alcohol consumption.

The parrot watches the scene with the disdain of captured

nobility. He can be confined, but never humbled. Now and again, he is torn out of his stoic pose by a spasmodic twitch. It starts with his head pitching down, then coming up and sideways, and finally returning to normal, all in the space of a single second.

The cause of the spasm is the avian equivalent of a sneeze. And the source of the sneeze is the outcome of a microbial encounter unlike any other in all of history.

Earlier this afternoon, the blood from the finger of Maria Santoz resided in the beak of the parrot, and within this blood was a large and aggressive fleet of the invigorated syphilis germs, which owed their energized behavior to the genetic infusion from the rat-bite fever. As the parrot fed, the train of food spread this blood back into the rear recesses of the beak where the nasal passages connected, and a tiny droplet was deposited onto the nasal membrane. All the while, the parrot's breathing created turbulent eddies of air that swept over the nasal lining, microscopic tornadoes that sucked loose material off the mucous plane of the nose. In this way, the blood droplet, with its syphilitic fleet, was carried off on a violent and atomized journey down the bronchial tubes into the bird's lungs, where it lodged in the alveoli, the little pink bubbles that infuse oxygen into the bloodstream.

The journey scattered the fleet into small battle groups that roamed within many thousands of alveoli, which were already hosting the *Chlamydia.* At this point, it was nearly inevitable that the two cultures would come into contact. It happened when pulmonary macrophages, the blob police, attempted to arrest and execute the syphilis germs by enveloping them. But these new germs fought back viciously, and the result was often mutual destruction. The macrophage was shredded to pieces and the syphilis bacteria had gaping holes in its flanks where the macrophage had launched a fusillade of enzyme missiles.

Out of these ragged cavities in the germ floated the bugs' genetic mother lode, including the strep's new and improved capacity for massive tissue destruction. As these explosive strings of DNA drifted in the fluid of the alveoli, some were absorbed by migrating *Chlamydia,* which had been searching for new cellular homelands in the pink interior of the alveoli.

Each *Chlamydia* that received this genetic infusion became an infectious engine of formidable power. In addition to complete resistance to all known antibiotics, they now possessed a nasty streak that compelled them to plunder the body's healthy tissue and reduce it to a putrid mass of runny garbage. And as these new *Chlamydia* went through their life cycle, they multiplied rapidly and passed these ugly traits on to their offspring, which soon swarmed like an angry mob in the parrot's lungs and caused excessive fluid to accumulate in a last-ditch defense.

To breathe properly, the parrot cleared the fluid through spasmodic sneezing, which expelled it as a fine aerosol with millions of microscopic droplets that floated randomly in the hot, confined air of the Paradiso.

Within an hour, the hot air near the cage drifted slowly toward the cooler air at the open end of the room, and the expelled droplets formed an invisible fog over the entire establishment. And the patrons sucked this horrible fog into their lungs with every breath as they laughed, danced, and drank their way into libidinous recesses of the night.

Although no one knew it, they were the pathological apostles of a new age.

23

"WILKES?" ASKED THE CLERK.

"Yeah. Elaine Wilkes," repeated Paris as he leaned against the counter in the Fugitive Unit and sipped on his morning coffee. He'd promised he'd check on her, and God damn it, that's exactly what he was doing, even though it was action at a distance. In truth, it was as close as he wanted to get.

"Okay, here we are," announced the clerk as he stared at a computer display hidden from Paris's view, then looked up. "You said you're Paris? The arresting officer?"

"Yup."

"We E-mailed San Diego last night that we had her. Didn't get an answer back until this morning. They won't extradite. No reason given."

Paris wasn't surprised. It was a long way to come for a little white-collar theft. *Lucky lady,* he thought. "You notify the jail yet?"

"Notified them an hour ago. She's a free little birdie by now."

"Thanks." Good. He'd kept his word and checked on her, and now he was off the hook. But he couldn't help but feel a little stab of disappointment. She'd been a pleasant diversion from petty burglars and car thieves, and maybe something more than that, although he refused to carry the thought any further.

Anyway, she wasn't completely disconnected from his life, at least not yet. There was still the matter of the disks, and their horrific prediction. In retrospect, it all seemed a little fantastic, but her story about her research had survived his cop's nose for detecting a lie and left him with an uncomfortable feeling that maybe she was right. He was seeing Muldane tonight after work, and he would pass on the disks and her story, just as he'd promised.

Bennet Rifkin fought to maintain the thread of phone conversation while he frantically manipulated the graphical interface on his desktop computer. Fortunately he'd anticipated what was happening and was now launching a contingency plan, which went over the Webster Foundation's local area network, through a router and out to a wide-area network, then on to a remote site, which would be untraceable to himself or the company. Just a few more pushes of some virtual buttons, and he'd have it humming.

"Elaine," he said in a smooth, yet bifurcated manner, "you've got to be reasonable about this. I mean, why did you bother to call at all? Think about that. Why are we even having this conversation? I think you want to negotiate. That's what I think. So why don't we just start with that assumption and take it from there?"

"Fuck you, Bennet," came Elaine's voice over the receiver in a very deliberate cadence. "I think we ought to start with the assumption that I want to hurt you, that I want to plant a big, shiny knife right between your shoulder blades. Now I know that I may not seem entirely rational, and that's because I'm not. But let me proceed anyway. Get ready to wince a little, Bennet, because here's the truth. You were almost off the hook, lover. Yesterday afternoon, I was sitting in a nice hotel room and wondering if this whole thing was worth throwing away my quite comfy little life. And you know what, Bennet? I was seriously thinking that it probably wasn't, that maybe I ought to just give back the goods and walk. But then I spent a night in jail and had a nasal resection without benefit of anesthetic. And as a result, Bennet, I am no longer my good old self, and now I have a religious commitment to screwing you and your precious fucking company as hard and as deep as humanly possible. So *that's* the assumption I think we should start with."

"Elaine," responded Bennet as he pushed the last virtual button, "when people are working through a ruptured relationship, counselors usually advise that they stick to the issues. In this case, I think that's pretty good advice. Now let me tell you what I did do, and what I didn't do. You stole company property, so, yes, I did have you charged with a crime. Further, I traced you to Seattle and arranged to have the police there informed as to your whereabouts. But that's it. That's where it stopped."

"It may be where you stopped, old buddy, but it's not where I stop. Seattle's a big town, Bennet. A high-tech town. Full of disk-duping facilities. So I'm going into the software packaging and distribution business. After all, I've got the hottest game title of the century: 'The Germ That Ended the World.' By the time I'm through, every public health agency in the world will know how to play. Who knows, Bennet, I might even get rich!"

Bennet paused in silence, as though seriously wounded. She would want that. And right now, it was supremely important to give her exactly what she wanted. "You're right, you could get rich. At my expense. But that's not your problem, is it? Now let's talk business. Dropping the charges against you won't take any more than a phone call. The money part will take only a little bit longer. I'm sure the company will offer a very generous severance package. We have an attorney named Robert Fancher who represents us in Seattle. Remember that name, Robert Fancher. He's got an office downtown. All you've got to do is take our property directly to his office and return it. By the time you get there, we'll have the financial and legal details all worked out. We're talking seven figures, Elaine—multiples thereof. You're free. You walk, I clean up the mess. What could be better?"

"What could be better, Bennet, is for you to walk in the mess, and then crawl in the mess, and then drown in the mess. That would be much, much better."

The phone clicked off and Bennet leaned back and looked at his computer display, which had gone into a kind of temporal limbo while a hoard of algorithms churned toward a logical conclusion across the networks. He wasn't surprised by her call, but her attitude had seemed a bit extreme. So what had happened to her in jail? No telling, really. A lot of bad and strange things happened when people were incarcerated, so it wasn't unreasonable to expect that one of these things had happened to her. She'd made a reference to her nose being hurt, and that was too bad. He'd really hoped it would be a sexual thing of some kind.

Bennet's rumination was interrupted by a video image of a bald man wearing round wire-frame glasses, which appeared in the area of the display where the virtual buttons had resided. A second image appeared alongside the man and depicted a map of a portion of Puget Sound around the Seattle area.

"Got what you wanted," said the man. "She called from a phone booth at the ferry slip at the northern end of Vashon Island." A cursor blinked on the map to indicate the location. It was directly west of Seattle across the Sound, a twenty-minute ride by ferry.

"What about the hotel?" asked Bennet. "Is she still registered?"

"Still registered. All on the same card. You want the card number? It's got another four point four K of headroom on it."

"No thanks. Good work. See you later."

The image of the man and the map disappeared. Bennet considered the information. Odds were she would take the ferry back to Seattle.

Fancher would need to know that.

*   *   *

Elaine looked out to the end of the dock where the big ferry aligned its hulking mass of white, green, and black with the dock, and the deckhands stood at the ready to secure thick lines of braided hemp to the mooring posts. She was still furious, still shaking, which made her all the more angry. She'd thought that if she unloaded on Bennet, it would dissipate the rage accumulated during the horrible night in jail. She could still smell the stinking breath and feel the fingernail gouging its way toward the center of her head.

After that awful episode, she'd stayed awake the entire night and made up her mind: she would fight back, any way she could. And her first opportunity came the next morning when they released her. She reclaimed her bags, and as soon as she was outside, she sat on a park bench and carefully accounted for every single disk. They were now more than the salvation of the world, they were also the key to her revenge.

But on the ferry ride over to this island, some of her anger had begun to transmute into fear. What had the big arms and stinking breath said? Something about invading her nose all over again with a darning needle? Was it just a threat? For the first time, she accepted she might be in mortal danger.

Around the ferry, a flock of seagulls screeched and battled the prevailing breeze with its primordial sea smell of creatures from the depths. The wind whipped her hair as she walked over the wooden planks. It didn't matter if Bennet traced her here because she had chosen this spot at random and would not be returning.

As she walked, she stared over the railing and down into the green murk where the light was bent and dissolved into liquid, a dark and predatory liquid that would rinse the flesh off your bones if given the chance. And atop the liquid, she saw her own troubled reflection staring down into the depths.

"I don't want to seem insulting," apologized David Muldane as he sat at the foldout table in the saloon of the *Cedar Queen*. "But it seems a little odd that you'd own something like this on a cop's salary."

Paris grinned as he opened a cabinet in the galley and pulled out two glasses and a bottle of premium bourbon. "Don't worry. I never take it personally. It's a logical first impression. And I'll tell you exactly how I do it on a cop's salary: barely. Just barely."

David felt the cool evening air descend down the companionway as Paris poured out two drinks and brought them to the table. They were moored at the last slip at a marina in Lake Union, and through the port-side windows, David could see the city lights wink on as night fell over Seattle. Paris was different here, David observed, but he wasn't sure why. "So why did you call this meeting?" he asked as Paris sat down across from him.

"I've got a progress report on the search for the serial poisoner." Paris took a sip of whiskey. "I think you'll find it quite interesting."

"Oh, yeah?"

"Oh, yeah. First, let's go back to my firebug theory, and the idea that the poisoner fits the same profile. Now what really gets a firebug off? I ask you. What really gives him his jollies?"

"Hard to say."

"Not hard at all: He wants to see what he did. He wants to roll around in it and feel it. Because what he did is what he is. And the bigger and grander that thing is, the bigger and grander he is."

"So he goes back to the fire?"

"He goes back to the fire. And so how does a food poisoner go back to the fire?"

"He has to see his victims. He has to experience their suffering."

Paris went to full grin. "Seems most likely, doesn't it? Now, if that's the case, then how does he make contact?"

David thought for a moment. "That's a little tough. The papers never print the names of the victims, and physicians wouldn't give out that kind of information. I suppose he could go back to the restaurants and hang around the bar to see if any of the patrons knew any of the victims—but that'd be pretty dangerous, wouldn't it?"

"Sure would."

"Or he could go to the hospitals where they were admitted, but that seems almost suicidal."

"Yes, it does."

"So where does that leave us?"

"An inside job."

"An inside job?" repeated David.

"Suppose the poisoner has access to the records in your department."

"In our department?"

"You're the information officer for the whole department. So you tell me. Don't you keep files that include at least basic information on all the victims?"

"Well, yeah, we do, but . . ."

"So couldn't you identify everyone who had access to them?"

David considered this. The information was in a database, or a "server," a computer on a network that serviced other computers, including those on people's desktops. The network was quite large, with literally hundreds of participating machines and users, and with more than one level of access, so it was difficult to tell who could peek at what. The problem was not unique to his department. Many government agencies had systems that were notoriously leaky. Almost everyone had a story about how a "friend" in the state department of motor vehicles was able to pull supposedly confidential information on unsuspecting citizens. The same principle applied to county and city governments as well.

"Let me put it this way," said David. "In theory we could. We'd wind up with a formalized list of who could see what. But in practice, it would tell us nothing. People are people. People need favors. Know what I mean?"

"I know exactly what you mean. And I came to exactly the same conclusion."

"So where does that leave us? Sounds like nowhere." David was getting slightly annoyed with Paris's peripheral approach to this whole matter.

"Except that you made a mistake. Same mistake I made."

"And what's that?"

"You immediately wrote off the possibility of visits to the hospital."

"And why was that a mistake?"

Paris paused, took another sip, then continued. "I went to the hospitals where the victims were admitted and started asking the staff if they remembered any of the visitors. Seemed like it might work. When you get a celebrity victim like that, the staff's more likely to remember what went on with them. Sure enough, at three separate hospitals, they all remembered a clergyman coming by. Nice young guy wearing the collar. Same description at all three places. They all assumed it was the victim's pastor. They assumed wrong."

"How do you know for sure?"

"I got in touch with two of the victims. They all remember the same guy. They thought he was the hospital chaplain." Paris raised his glass to David. "So, congratulations. We've done it."

"That's incredible," mumbled David. He couldn't believe their luck. Or was it more than that? He put off that debate for later. As a child, he remembered seeing pictures of a roundhouse, a huge place where they took locomotives off one track and put them on another. He had this feeling that over the past week, his life had entered such a switching house, where engines of unimaginable power were driving gears of momentous proportion to install him on a new route, destination unknown. "So, what's the next step?"

"Now that I've got witnesses, I might be able to open a formal investigation, but that wouldn't help much. It's a waiting game now. Probably the best move is to develop a contingency plan for the next round of poisoning. It'll probably happen sooner than later. It's like serial killing. Over time, the intervals between the crimes tend to get smaller. When it happens, we route the victims to hospitals where we've got our people standing by. With a little luck, the guy drops right into our laps."

"Sounds good to me. Meeting adjourned?"

"Nope. One more thing." Paris absently sloshed his drink. "Were you an MD before you went into the computer side of things?"

David tensed. No use lying. He might as well get it all out on the table right now. "Almost. I dropped out in my third year of medical school. It was a bad time. My marriage was going to hell and I couldn't hack the pressure. Anyway,

I still wanted to make a contribution, and public health seemed a good way to do it. So here I am."

"You know a doctor named Elaine Wilkes from San Diego?"

David's stomach constricted several notches and shot a big lump of anxiety up into his throat. Paris must know. He must know about the famous Dr. Muldane, the virtual heart surgeon who blew the big one. He looked across the table at Paris, who always came across as massive, but now rocketed up the paternal scale to monumental proportions. Paris's blue eyes hit him with a calm, expectant look.

"Yes," began David a little unevenly, "I know Elaine Wilkes. She was on a team with me at the Virtual Surgery Center. It's a computer simulation of the real thing. A highly realistic simulation. We performed several operations together. But she probably already told you about that, right?"

"Nope. Never said anything about it." Paris took another little sip of the bourbon and felt the amber glow paint the back of his throat.

"She didn't?"

"No, but she was a little stressed, so I could see where she might have left that out."

"A little stressed?"

"Yeah. I arrested her for grand theft yesterday."

"You're kidding!" David sank back on the settee as he felt the spotlight move on in search of a more convenient target. "You arrested Dr. Wilkes?"

"Sure did," said Paris as he stared down into his glass, then up at David. "Any reason she'd think you're a doctor?"

David felt his heart slam hard against his sternum. He'd been set up by a master, just like a terrified rodent on the wrong end of a cat's paw. The fatal blow was the one you least expected. The truth came bounding out before he had any say in the matter. "Yeah, there is. I faked a doctor's credentials so I could participate in the surgery. No harm done, really. After all, it's only a high-class game, not the real thing. The truth is, I wanted to prove to myself that I could've cut it as a doctor, as a surgeon."

"Well . . . did you?" Paris seemed genuinely interested, but David would never again take the man at face value.

"No. As a matter of fact, I wound up blowing it. But that's another story."

Paris looked back down at his drink. "Yeah. I suppose it is." He reached into an old leather briefcase beside him on the settee and pulled out the magneto-optical disk from Elaine. "After the arrest, Dr. Wilkes gave me this disk and said it was extremely important that you review its contents as soon as possible."

"Where is she now?"

"We booked her, but she got off the hook on a technicality. She was staying at the Sheraton downtown last I heard." Paris handed the disk across to David. "Anyway, I'm out of it. It's your move now."

At the gate out of the marina, David paused to look back at the *Cedar Queen,* which was partially visible in its end slip. It was getting dark and he could see the light spilling out of the string of portholes that rode high on the vessel's big white hull. He could feel Paris in there, going through some unknown rituals of boat maintenance, and he mulled over the interrogative trap he'd blundered into. When he had come clean, something in him wanted to come even cleaner yet, to seek a perfect purity, a state that would grant him complete immunity from further moral infection. But from somewhere inside, a sluice gate had crashed down and stopped the wild and muddy flow of guilt. Funny how that worked.

He looked down at the disk in his hand and thought of Elaine Wilkes. It seemed highly ironic that she was now the criminal and he the morally refurbished one. He headed on up the ramp to his car.

Paris had barely put down his briefcase when the phone rang. Loudly. It was late and he was tired, but he was also a cop, which made it imperative that he answer the god-damned thing. He crossed through the living room, flipped on the kitchen light, and plucked the receiver off the wall.

"Paris," he said with a flat, obligatory tonality.

"Lieutenant, this is Elaine Wilkes. I think you probably remember me."

"Yeah, I remember you," he said, a little more abruptly

than intended. But he couldn't help it. After several years, he was finally on a roll with the poisoner case—and this woman was on a roll in a radically different direction, to some compass point far off the standard charts.

"I'm sorry to bother you. Did I get you up?"

"No. I just got home. What can I do for you?"

"Did you deliver the disk I gave you for Dr. Muldane?"

"Yep. That was the deal and that's what I did."

"Thank God. Did he say when he'd review it?"

"Not that I recall."

"Well, let's hope it's sooner that later."

"Look, I talked to the people in our Fugitive Unit. They told me you were released. So you're free. You're off the hook. Why don't you just talk to Muldane yourself?"

"I'd like to do that. But I can't. I may be free, but I'm definitely not off the hook."

"What do mean?"

"I think I've got a problem. A very big problem."

Paris chuckled in tired amusement. "So now what's happened?"

"For starters, I was physically assaulted in jail."

Paris restrained himself. Jesus! Just what kind of incubator did she live in? Yuppie heaven? "Well, Dr. Wilkes," he said sarcastically, "occasionally the justice system fails to function in a way that fully honors the rights of the accused. When one is incarcerated with members of the criminal class, there is at least some possibility of violence."

"You can cut the crap, Lieutenant. If that's all there was to it, I wouldn't be talking to you."

Her sudden anger made Paris regret his sarcasm. Something was really wrong here. "All right. So what happened?"

"You recall our conversation at the time of my arrest?"

"Pretty much. You predicted a monster plague and stole the forecast from your employer. It's worth a ton of money because of the pharmaceutical deals that could be spun off. How am I doing?"

"You're doing a lot better than I am. Last night, somebody very large held me down while somebody smaller tried to stick their finger up my nose and on into my brain."

"Sorry about that. But like I said, it happens."

"I'm sure it does. But while the little person did her thing, the big person whispered a little something in my ear. It seems I was supposed to leave the suitcase with the disks in the property room when I checked out of jail. If I didn't, then some other nice people would repeat the nasal maneuver with something longer and sharper."

"You didn't get a look at your assailants?"

"I saw the small one."

"Did you tell the guards?"

"I'm a very quick study, Lieutenant. That would've been a serious breach of prison etiquette."

"You're right, it would've been just that. Anything else?"

"Today I phoned the company and let them have it between the eyes. That probably wasn't the smartest of moves, but I was just a little angry. Anyway, they denied any involvement, and then in the next breath, they tried to buy me off."

"How much?"

"At least a million. It was left open. I was supposed to deliver the disks to an attorney here in town, some guy named Robert Fancher. Do you know him?"

Fancher. Paris never forgot a name. And this particular name launched a curious string of associations. Fancher was the lawyer who had given him the tip on Elaine in the first place. Now it sounded as if he was party to an extortion, although you could never prove it. How'd they get to her inside the jail? How'd they know she'd beat the extradition and walk?

And the more he thought, the madder he became. Fancher had used him, used him as a tool in the commission of a crime.

He returned his attention to Elaine. "Where are you now?"

"I'm at a phone booth in the Pike Place Market, right at the end of Pike Street. There's lots of lights here. And lots of people. Suddenly, I'm attracted to that."

"Stay in plain sight. I'm coming to get you. This time of night, it shouldn't take more than fifteen minutes or so."

"I'm very scared. Can you tell?" asked Elaine.

In truth, Paris could not. The subdued light smoothed her lean, angular features as she looked at him with a frankness he wasn't used to. They were sitting at a table in Place Pigalle, a little restaurant in the Pike Place Market. Paris wasn't even quite sure why they were here. He'd parked over on Pine, walked to the market entrance, and spotted her immediately. As they met, he realized he had no real plan of action, so he carried her bags and they walked down into the market and wandered into this place.

"So what are you scared of? The nasty jail ladies? Uni Corporation? The plague? Me?"

She flowered into a lovely smile. "I'm not scared of you. In fact, if things were different, you'd make me laugh."

"Oh, yeah? I'm not renowned as a comedian." Paris tried to dodge the radiant fallout from her smile. Whatever his interest in this woman had been before, it was now cop business again. "Okay, here's what we've got to do. First, I've got to get you out of sight. That'll buy us some time. Then I'm going to do some checking on Fancher. I want to know how he pulled strings inside the jail. That bothers me. A lot."

"Have you got a theory?"

"Yeah, but I'd rather not discuss it right now. You can stay at my place tonight. Then we'll move you to a more obscure location."

"What about your family? I don't want to intrude."

"There is no family. My wife is in a permanent coma and institutionalized."

"I'm sorry."

Paris took a sip of his bourbon. "So am I."

Elaine felt the spiked halo of pain and changed the subject. "Why are you doing all this? I'm not sure I understand."

"I could say I'm doing it all for you, but I'm a lousy liar. The truth is I've been used. Fancher was the one who gave me the tip you were in town and where to find you. I don't like being used. It's as simple as that."

Elaine leveled a knowing smile at him. "Nothing's ever as simple as that."

Paris stubbed his cigarette out in the cut-glass ashtray he'd brought in from the living room. The bedroom was illuminated by a ghost dance of TV glow, which came from a

Japanese monster movie. He shouldn't be smoking in here. Ginny had been right about that, and up to now, he'd honored her wish. So why now? Did it have something to do with another woman sleeping just down the hall? He was a highly skilled interrogator, but not when confronting himself, so he let it go. On TV, the talons on the paw of the monster hooked an elevated train and sent its cars sailing through slow motion and bad light. It made Paris think of large catastrophes. What if this Wilkes woman was right about this plague? He decided it was like nuclear war: too big to worry about, but just likely enough to cause a vague anxiety.

He took the ashtray back to the living room before he went to sleep.

As Elaine lay awake in the little guest room, she heard the sound of Paris padding down the hall with slow, heavy footsteps. For just an instant, she suffered a flare of paranoia and thought he was coming her way, that the door would open and she'd be plunged into yet another physical crisis. But then the footsteps faded off into some other part of the house. The incident in the jail had severely wrenched her worldview.

She turned over and looked out the window, where a throng of maple leaves thrashed the glow of a streetlamp as a small breeze rustled through the night. The truth was she felt safe here, and it annoyed her. In all her adult life, she'd never been dependent on anybody for her basic security. But here she was in the house of this man she hardly knew, and his presence might be the only thing that was keeping her alive. She should resent him for it, but somehow that was hard to do. He didn't seem to revel in his power or gloat over her dependency. He had a kind of instinctive intelligence that she had to admire, a way of sizing you up, but then feeling compassion for your predicament. It seemed as if he understood her fear and uncertainty in every nuance, and somehow that made her feel better.

As the leaves outside rustled on into the night, she heard the footsteps return and his bedroom door shut.

David Muldane sat transfixed in his cubicle. At this hour, even the cleaning people were gone, so he had this terrifying moment of revelation all to himself. He wanted to phone Paris, to phone the director of public health, to phone Larry King; but it was too late at night.

As he looked at the data on his computer display, one question after another tumbled through his mind. Where did Dr. Wilkes find a computer that could even attempt something like this? How did they build the models? Why hadn't everyone in public health heard about this? What was on the rest of the disks? Why hadn't Paris told him more?

What he was looking at was a forecast, a forecast of disease instead of weather. And it was an ominous forecast. A variation on psittacosis that would spill out of the tropics and devastate the entire world. The maps, the graphs, the tables—all pointed toward the largest and most deadly epidemic in modern history—maybe in all of history.

The disk presented a summary of the simulation, and a sample of how the methodology was applied across a sample geographic area, a portion of Indonesia. The richness and complexity of the data convinced him that the simulation was far beyond any kind of shallow fakery. Without a doubt, Dr. Wilkes had a tool here that would revolutionize the practice of public health worldwide. The only question left was the most basic one of all: Did it work? Had they tested it using historical epidemics? Probably. David doubted that Elaine Wilkes would undergo an arrest for something that didn't work.

David's mind had been racing far too fast to settle on a course of action, but now a combination of physical and mental fatigue slowed him down to the point of practicality. First, he'd talk to Paris, who'd told him little about the origins of the disk and the circumstances surrounding it. Then, once he had enough information, he'd make a copy and send it to Dr. John Smali in New York. Smali, of all people, would realize the significance of this fascinating yet horrifying forecast of global pestilence.

"They really fucked me over, man. I didn't even know the guy. I just met him at a joint down the street. We stopped to get some smokes, that's all. Just stopped to get some smokes."

Prisoner 11233 wore a faded paisley bandanna as a head-

band that held his hair out of his eyes. His eyebrows were
nearly absent and he had a mustache and goatee that were
no more than an anemic whimper. The broken nose gave
his voice the nasal whine of the chronically oppressed.

Barney Cox nodded at discreet intervals as he sat across
from the prisoner, who occupied the bottom bunk, one of
only two bunks in Barney's cell. Through complex arrangements, Barney never had more than one cellmate at a time.

"Next thing I know, the store guy's got a hole in his gut.
Jesus, it was ugly! Looked like he was taking a red piss out
his stomach. And guess what? My new buddy? He's gone.
And so's the money. And so's his car. So that just leaves
me and this guy with the hole in his gut. Now, what would
you do, huh? I'll tell you. You'd take off. As fast as you
could. And that's what I did. But the fuckin' pigs got me,
and guess what?"

"They never got the other guy?" speculated Barney.

"You got it. And you know what? I don't think they ever
even looked for him. No, sir, I don't. Now ain't that the
shits?"

"It's worse than that. It's the kind of injustice that's going
to kill this country dead. And then the rest of the world is
going to feed on our big fat corpse. And worst of all, they're
going to feed on you and me right along with the people
who deserve it. All the pigs, all the judges, all the fat cats.
Are you proud to be a citizen of this country?"

"That I am."

"And well you should be. Because most of the people
here are good people like yourself. People just struggling to
get by. And let me tell you, there's dignity in your struggle.
You're a hero, friend. And so are all your brothers and
sisters out there on those mean streets. You do what you
do just to survive, just to stay alive from one day to the
next. Now I ask you, how can any man quarrel with that?
How can any man pass judgment on your fundamental right
to survive? Well, the sad truth is that those with the money
and the power think they can, and they pervert the legal
system to keep people like you in your place. They're out
there right now, sitting poolside at their fancy houses and
moaning about how the world is going to shit. And they're
right. It is going to shit. And they're the very reason it's

going to shit. Only they don't know it. And you know what?"

The prisoner was transfixed. "What?"

"Sooner or later, someone is going to have to explain it to them. In a way they can understand."

"And what way is that?"

"Like this." Barney hissed through clenched teeth as he smacked his right fist into his left palm. "You see, smart people just don't understand what's really going on. They make everything too complicated. So you have to make your explanations very simple and direct. Then they'll get it. Believe me, they'll get it."

"Makes sense to me."

"It makes sense to a lot of people. Both inside and out. More all the time. You got any buddies up here in King County?"

"Can't say that I do."

"Well, I'm going to have you meet some people. You're a straight-up guy. I can tell that about people. You deserve a break, and if we all stick together, maybe I can get you one."

"Thanks, man." The prisoner nodded and seemed genuinely touched.

"No trouble, no trouble at all." Barney cut the conversation short by swinging to his bunk and staring at the ceiling. The real magnitude of his political gift was now coming to the forefront, and he saw himself not as a prisoner, but as a political exile, as Napoleon on Elba, as Mao on the Long March, as Trotsky in Mexico. And with this realization came a kind of mystical consolidation inside him. The criminal and the politician within him were merging into a single entity with far more potential than either had independently. He would build the New Order, a hard and brutish one, yet resilient and strong. And he would build it upon the folly of the existing order, which had become so thoroughly corrupt and self-indulgent. He would build it on the smoldering fury and frustration of the children of the street, who were permanently locked out of the good life, and whose numbers now swelled to nearly equal the majority. He would shape and direct the fire in their hearts and use it to consolidate his cause. All he needed was some kind of social blasting cap to ignite the conflagration.

Right now, it was hard to imagine how such a blaze might start. The steel and glass of the downtown skyline symbolized a continuity of power that seemed as if it might go on forever. Business and government as usual.

However, until the ignition came to pass, tactical details had to be taken care of. Like securing his freedom. He was disappointed in the actions of the Wilkes woman. She hadn't responded to a reasonable and straightforward proposition put forth by his associates. When Fancher had visited today, Barney had explained his disappointment to the attorney and accepted full responsibility. Moreover, he went on to explain how he still planned to honor his end of the bargain: the disks would be retrieved, no matter what the cost. In return, he expected Uni's financial and political resources to catapult him out of this dismal place and onto the political trajectory he now saw as his manifest destiny.

And it was Uni. He knew that for a fact. He'd commissioned a little research that showed that Uni employed Elaine Wilkes through a place called the Webster Foundation. Further, Uni was a major client of Fancher's.

Barney smiled into the darkness above him. Fancher had been alarmed by Barney's warranty on his work with Elaine. He'd told Barney to forget the whole business, that they would find some other way to spring him.

Fuck Fancher. He was a high-priced pawn, safely installed in his big house on the lake with his showboat wife, who was always off to a new clinic for a tuck here or a pad there. Barney had been to the house a couple of times, but always as a solitary guest, never as part of a social function: no way Barney was going to be tossed into the social blender with high-tech chieftains, money people, and the politically anointed. Fancher had been patronizing and his wife had poured her best sorority smile all over him, but it was rigidly pro forma. However, Barney was more amused than shamed or annoyed. Even then, he knew there'd be a day of reckoning, a day when Fancher would pay dearly.

Something was coming. Something big. He could feel it in the clammy cavern where his heart should have been.

24

The Eastern Atlantic Ocean

"So what do you think?" asks Melody Linkford as she gestures toward the surf. "Does it suit your fancy?"

The pounding waves spew a delicate white fog that merges into a sky of clean oceanic blue. From his reclined position on the blanket, Steve Henry surveys the beach with its impeccable expanse of sand. He takes a sip of rum from his glass, then twists it into the sand next to their blanket.

"Do you want to know what really suits my fancy?" His eyes sweep over her firm brown body, held in check by only the skimpiest of string bikinis. Behind her in the distance is a church spire sprouting from the small Portuguese fishing village. A feisty little cloud struts in front of the sun, putting them into momentary shadow and stirring up a breeze that wiggles the small hoop of an earring dangling from her tanned lobe.

"Don't tell me," she teases. "I think I already know." She comes off her side and kneels over him. Her hands are already behind her, and he sees her generous breasts come out just in time to greet the return of the sun. She deftly pulls a knot high on her hip and tugs the string bottom off in a single motion, then twirls it about her index finger.

"And now," she says, "for the main attraction." As she straddles him, the roar of the surf notches up and envelops them in sound.

"Enri?" The voice punches a rude hole in the moment. A clerk's voice. An agitated clerk, one bent on bureaucratic perfection. "Mr. Steven Enri. Isn't that right?"

Highly agitated, Steve turns toward the voice. "For fuck's sake, it's Henry. H-E-N-R-Y. Not Enri. Get it?" He turns back toward Melody. Gone. He looks down the beach behind him. Not a sign. Not even any tracks in the sand.

He sighs, settles back down on the blanket, and closes his eyes. All that's left is the roar of the waves.

The wave roar melded into plane roar, and Steven Henry opened his eyes and looked out the window and down at the Strait of Gibraltar thirty-four thousand feet below. He was semitumid and closed his eyes in a groggy attempt to recapture Melody Linkford. It didn't work. He sighed and looked back out the window again. It was the goddamn "Enri" business. That's what ruined it. First, it screwed up his trip, and now it was screwing up his dreams.

When he got back to the States, he would have the clerk fired. That's what he would do. He would phone the owner of the travel agency and insist on it as a condition of doing any further business. Of course, there would be the usual barrage of excuses, like she was new with the firm or just coming down with shingles or her car had expired in the middle of rush hour. But he wouldn't buy it. Because whatever the clerk's problems, they didn't compare with his.

It all started a month ago, when the clerk took the information over the phone to book his trip. When she asked his last name, he clearly enunciated "Henry"; but incredibly, when he got the tickets, they were made out to Steven "Enri." By then, it was too late to repair the damage. He worked for a successful soft-drink company and was blazing new markets on a long and complex trip that took him through several locations in Africa, then on into Europe. He had no choice but to go and run the gauntlet of problems he would encounter with customs officials along the way.

And sure enough, at one port of entry after another, the local officials had caught the discrepancy between the name on the tickets and that on his passport. Sometimes he was able to settle the problem with the discreet application of American dollars in the proper palms. Other times, he had to miss flights, sit idle in airports from hell, and retreat to shabby hotel rooms, where he sat in a liberal coating of existentialist sweat like the heroes of novels of decades gone by.

His troubles hit their nadir two days ago in Libreville. He winced as the official at the customs counter looked at the ticket, then at his passport, then back at the ticket. The official was thin as a whippet and looked at Steve with maximum reproach.

"Big problem." With his spidery fingers, he held up the

ticket in one hand and the passport in the other. "One name passport. Other name on ticket," he announced in broken English. He looked expectantly at Steve with a pinched, sadistic grin that can only be properly applied by a third-world customs official.

"I know about that," started Steve, who by now had his answer down to a ritualistic chant. "The name on the ticket is wrong. There was a mistake made when it was issued, but it was too late to change it. The name on the passport is correct. I have a lot of other ID that verifies my identity." He dug into his hip pocket, hauled out his wallet, and started to extract his driver's license from its leather slot, but the customs man raised his hand to halt this action.

"You come back tomorrow. Then we see."

Steve dove into a sweaty funk as the man tucked the passport and ticket into a drawer and looked over Steve's shoulder to the next person in line. "But I have a flight to Rome that leaves this afternoon. Isn't there *anything* that we can do to straighten this out?" It might cost him some money, but so what? After three weeks in Africa, he just wanted out.

The customs man completely ignored him and raised his chin to beckon the next person forward. The muscles of the man's long neck pitched and rolled through his taught black skin where it intersected the sharp press of his khaki collar. For whatever mysterious reason, a bribe was not going to work. At least not right now. Steve knew it was time to retreat before he did even more damage to his cause.

To cover his departure, he stopped at all the airline counters and sought passage to Europe by any means available. His original flight had been to Rome, but anywhere would do. It turned out that all flights to Europe for the next week were completely booked, with no relief in sight. Then, at the last counter, a possible rescue. They pointed him toward a local airline, Air Gabon, which had a flight the next day to the island of São Tomé. From there, there was a direct flight the following day to Lisbon.

A quick check with Air Gabon confirmed the São Tomé solution. The next day, he was back before the customs official with an envelope that would provide "supporting documentation" to clear up the ticket name problem. The official held the envelope below eyesight, lifted the flap, and noted the three twenty-dollar bills. Without a word, he stamped Steve's exit papers and returned his passport and ticket. Two hours later, the plane was approaching the airport north of São Tomé, and Steve managed a weary smile as he looked down on the town. His fortunes were shifting. It looked to be a jewel of a place. Luckily, he'd gotten a tourist visa during his last afternoon in Libreville.

That afternoon, he walked the clean, sunny streets, then settled in for the night at the Hotel Miramar. Before turning in, he wandered down to the bar for a nightcap, and in the attenuated light, he saw a beautiful young woman sitting alone in a booth nursing a mixed drink. She had mountains of curly black hair and appeared to be Latin, so he assumed she was of Portuguese descent with a touch of African thrown in. She locked onto his stare and wouldn't let go, and he realized she was for sale as he sat at the bar and ordered a rum and Coke. In other times, it would have been a go, a definite go. Years ago, a frosty crevasse had opened between him and his wife, and the marriage now operated on the implicit assumption that he was a philanderer; as long as he kept it compartmentalized, it would be tolerated. For the sake of the children or some such thing. Of what he was no longer sure.

But tonight, his fidelity came from a lustful speculation. He had already decided to make a major project out of Melody Linkford, who worked in the company's Lisbon office. She was single, sassy, and flung her sexuality about with a reckless abandon that scared many men, but which Steve found irresistible. He'd flirted with her on two previous trips to Europe and had been rewarded with a steady stream of provocative innuendo. An ample breast brushing against his arm. A warm hand folding over his at lunch. An unsolicited stare from across the room during a meeting. Yes, it would be a grand game. He'd already phoned the Rome office and informed them that he would be working out of Lisbon instead, at least for a few weeks before he rebooked his travel back to Seattle.

Steve looked out the airliner window once more. They were six hours out of São Tomé and about an hour from Lisbon. Most of the passengers were lost in the fitful sleep of the air traveler or were reading. The air seemed a bit stuffy, so he reached up, twisted the ventilating knob over his seat, and felt the nasal blast of cooler air buffet his forehead. The man next to him twitched in his sleep and tossed his head to the side before settling back down. He was a Spaniard, a construction foreman, a trim man slightly gray at the temples. Earlier, he had told Steve of his final nocturnal adventure on the island before leaving for Madrid by way of Lisbon. It seemed there was this place called the Paradiso, which had cheap drinks, hot music, and women to match. He had targeted two lovely young ladies, a pair of *Angolares,* then bought many rounds of beer and danced many dances. Late in the evening, as the heat bound them close and the music boldly stoked the flesh, he suggested a ménage à trois in a roundabout and upbeat way. His proposal met with a good-natured flood of giggles. Then the ladies got up and sailed off into the night, leaving him drunk and alone. So here he was, hungover and glad to be heading home.

Steve reached up once more and turned the ventilation knob to full blast. Its raspy rush of air merged with the general circulatory roar of the plane as a whole.

This monotonous blast masked what was a spirited controversy about air circulation inside jet airliners. The mechanics of a jet's air-circulation system were relatively simple. First, outside air was sucked in through the engine intakes, where it wound its way through dozens of rotating blades, which compressed it for use by the business end of the engine, which sucked it through a second stage of compression, then mixed it with jet fuel and ignited it in a combustion chamber for a rocket ride through a turbine, then out the back. Near the end of the second compression stage, part of this highly condensed air was bled off before it reached the combustion chamber and routed through the wing to cooling packs, which were necessary because compressed air is also hot air; an immutable rule of nature dictates that whenever a gas is squeezed into a smaller volume, its temperature rises; in this case, to over 300 degrees F. Once the air was cooled, it was piped throughout the cabin via the side and overhead circulation ducts.

All that was fine and good. It was the air's return trip

that prompted the debate. After the air flowed throughout the cabin, it was pulled out through return ducts near the floor level on the sides of the fuselage. And here, the debate was focused. In older planes, all of this exhausted air was blown out into the atmosphere to make way for fresh air coming in via the engines. But by the mid-1980s, fuel consumption became the undisputed dictator of airliner design, and it decreed that compromises in air circulation would improve fuel efficiency. When compressed air from the engines was bled off for the cabin, less of it was available for combustion, and to make up the deficit in terms of thrust, a little extra fuel had to be continually squirted into the turbine so you could spin the compressor faster and bring in the extra air.

The design solution was simple. Half of the exhausted air from the cabin was blown out into the atmosphere, but the other half was mixed with incoming air from the engines to provide the cabin's total air circulation. This way, the amount of compressed air routed away from the engines was reduced by 50 percent, and fuel efficiency was notably increased.

The net effect was a 50 percent drop in fresh air reaching the passengers. To counter this, recirculated air was passed through HEPA (High Efficiency Particulate Air) filters, which remove 99 percent of all airborne particles, including all those with a diameter of over 0.3 micrometers, which includes most bacteria.

But what about other infectious agents? The kind expelled in the airborne fluids of sick passengers? Things smaller than 0.3 micrometers? Things that made the HEPA filter look like a volleyball net to a flea? Things like viruses, which range down to 0.027 micrometer? Or *Chlamydia,* which average 0.25 micrometers?

Where did they go?

The answer is back into the cabin. When all was said and done, it took from four to seven minutes before the used air was completely replaced by outside air. And during those seven minutes of freedom, the sub-HEPA organisms rode the internal currents on dubious journeys. Most went back out the exhaust ducts. But some stuck to surfaces of clothing. Some latched onto upholstery or carpeting.

Others clung to people. And that was the core of the controversy.

As Steve settled back after adjusting the ventilator knob, he glanced over at the sleeping Spaniard, whose face was tilted in his direction. The man's mouth was wide open, his bottom teeth presenting a little fortress of ivory above his slack lower lip.

And if it weren't for all the plane noise, Steve would swear he heard a distinct wheezing noise every time the man exhaled.

25

"MY GOD! IT'S BEAUTIFUL!" EXCLAIMED ELAINE.

Paris beamed. When first acquainted with the *Cedar Queen*, most people were polite or diplomatically enthusiastic, but inevitably launched into the stock comments about how much work an old boat must be, etc. However, he could tell from Elaine's spontaneous adoration that this time, it was a case of unconditional love. Before he could offer to help, she was up the little stair set and jumping down onto the deck. Paris followed with her suitcases as she went into the wheelhouse and examined all the instrumentation. Then he remembered that she was a doctor, a scientist, a person at ease with the mechanical aspects of the world. Although she was emotionally touched by the *Cedar Queen*'s beauty, she also saw it as a system, a set of functional devices united through design into common purpose.

"You want to drive it?" he asked as her hands played over the spoked wooden wheel.

"Not now. But later—absolutely."

"Let's get you set up," he said, unlocking the door down to the main saloon. The sun was groping its way through the soft morning overcast, and air was still on the damp side. It promised to be a beautiful summer day, and he regretted having to go to work.

Paris walked down the companionway, through the saloon and galley, and into the forward berths, where the hull converged with a bed on either side. He stowed the suitcases in a cabinet underneath the starboard berth and went back into the galley where Elaine was looking at the cooking gear.

"The stove's kerosene. The original was a wood burner, but I'm not that big a purist. There's a little store right up across the road where you can stock up a little." He looked around. "It's not the Ritz, but it's not bad either."

"It's better than the Ritz. Was it like this when you got it?"

"Not quite. We put in a lot of sweat and more money than we should have. But I got no regrets. Not really."

Elaine looked at Paris as he gazed up and out the skylight over the stove. His eyes were bordered by a fine network of random channels, and the burn-off streaming through the skylight ignited them into a violent blue.

He turned from the light and caught her appraising look. For a moment, their eyes stayed locked, neither yielding ground. And in the heated flush of that moment, Elaine realized that the past few days were simply a prelude to this instant of no retreat, here in the belly of this beautiful vessel. For some reason, Paris's house hadn't been a catalyst; but just a few moments on this boat, and there was a quantum shift in the emotional landscape.

The standoff ended as quickly as it had started, and the silence in the cabin was filled with the gentle lapping of the lake water against the venerable wood of the hull.

Paris spoke first. "I've got to get to work. Things are piling up, and I can't afford to let that happen. As soon as I can bust loose, I'll contact Mr. Fancher and see what he has to say. I'll check in on you later this afternoon or this evening. Okay?"

"Okay. And thanks. I appreciate the favor. And so does the sixty percent of the world that might pull through if we can get this forecast out into the open."

"If I was you, I'd withhold my applause for a bit," said Paris with wry smile. "See you later."

He turned and walked up the companionway stairs, his big frame temporarily blocking all the light entering the wheelhouse.

*   *   *

"If I was to say to you 'Robert Fancher,' what would you say to me?" asked Paris.

"Easy one," replied Lt. Bud Franklin of the Organized Crime Task Force. "I'd say Barney Cox."

Franklin scratched his crew cut and waved a hand toward the computer on his desk. Paris noted with some envy that it was powered by a Super-RISC processor and probably had ten gigabytes of hard-disk storage. Big crime demanded big machines, he supposed. "I could cross-reference it ten different ways in the database," declared Franklin, "and the answer would always come up Barney Cox. He's Barney's lead attorney."

"Oh, yeah? How come I haven't seen him involved in the murder conspiracy?"

"He stays in the background. Takes care of all the organization's business affairs. He's undoubtedly pulling the strings of the trial lawyers. Thanks to Barney, he lives quite well. Has a big house on Lake Washington over by Gates."

"That's nice. Is he connected to any other notable clients?"

"Well, for the most part, that's not going to be a matter of public record, but let's see." Franklin swung around and jockeyed the mouse to bring up a window into which he typed brief bursts of data into waiting fields. "Ah, yes. He's a registered lobbyist for the biggest daddy of them all, Uni Corporation."

"Well, how fortunate," commented Paris with open sarcasm. "A real success story."

"Not really." Franklin leaned back in his swivel chair and clasped his hands behind his head. "Barney's bought him. And all Barney's acquisitions come with a lifetime warranty. He's fucked. Every week, every month, Barney will tighten the clamps another notch, and no amount of begging or screaming will change that. But you should know that. Didn't you handle that little disturbance with Mr. Cox over at the jail? That thing about the TB records?"

"You're not supposed to know about the records part."

Franklin laughed. "Of course I'm not. So what else is new?"

"Tell me this. What odds are they giving over at the DA's

office that they'll get a conviction on the conspiracy charge?"

The residue from the laugh slid off Franklin's face. "Not good. He's going to beat it, Phil. And that pisses me off."

"And you're a fairly jaded fellow, Bud. So why does he have this effect on you?"

"Let me give you a little background. To begin with, most career criminals are very conservative."

"You mean they vote Republican and play golf on Thursday afternoons?"

Franklin laughed. "Not quite. But they do believe in a very traditional and structured way of doing things. They may play by a pretty awful set of rules, but they stick by them."

"You mean like killing your boss to get his job?"

"Absolutely. Also, their operations and methods are very rigid and change very little over time. What all this means is that to be successful in the business, you serve a lengthy apprenticeship to establish your credentials. When power changes hands, it seldom moves very far from the original source. Like you said, you eventually kill your boss to get the final promotion."

"So what's all this got to do with Barney?"

"He came from nowhere."

"Came from nowhere?"

"Yeah. As far as we can tell, he never served in middle management. And we know for a fact that he was never arrested. He showed up full grown. And then he broke all the rules."

"He did?"

"In a very big way. The guy's a fucking genius, Phil. A genius from another planet. And a monster. He reads voraciously. He's made a study of business management theory, and then stirred it in with his own shit, and he's been wildly successful. He makes the crime families in New York look like lost children. It's only a fluke that we've got our clutches on him right now."

"So where does he go from here? The presidency?"

"That's what scares me, Phil. He could do it. Easy. He could run the White House. He could run a major corporation. No sweat."

"Swell."

"To put it in perspective, let me fill you in on the murder that landed him here. You heard about the victim?"

"Yeah. Wasn't it some guy that owned an auto parts distribution company?"

"Yup. A real tough son of a bitch. Used to be a biker in his younger days. Not the kind of guy that was going to bow down to anybody. Anyway, what you didn't hear were the details of the murder. He was burned to death with a blowtorch. Just a bit at a time. Little black craters all over him. The body looked like the surface of the moon. He died of dehydration from the burns, which means he lived on for some time during the process. They suspended the body from a rope in his warehouse, so all his employees got the message. It was so gross that none of the media wanted to run with it."

"Not so nice."

"Not at all. Now imagine the same guy in the governor's chair. Or a Senate seat. Or running Boeing. All he needs is the right set of circumstances to cross over."

Paris laughed. "That's gonna be one hell of a set of circumstances."

Franklin shrugged. "It's a big world. A lot can happen."

"Yeah, I guess it is."

"You're not going to believe it," said David Muldane as he plunked down in the chair in front of Paris's desk.

Paris had just returned to his desk from talking with Franklin and had been lost in thought. They had undoubtedly gotten to Elaine through Barney. She might be in a lot more difficulty than he'd originally suspected. And now, he suspected, David was going to tell him exactly why.

"Believe what?" Paris asked innocently.

"Remember the disk you gave me that you got from Dr. Wilkes?"

"Yes."

"I'll spare you the technical details, but it's a forecast, a disease forecast of a global plague. It's incredible."

"That's fine. But is it also bullshit?"

"Don't think so. It's some kind of extremely advanced simulation technology. And the data is too consistent for anyone to have fabricated it as a deception. Where did all this come from? Didn't she work at a research foundation somewhere?"

"Yeah, a place called the Webster Foundation. She stole it."

"You're kidding."

"Nope. You've only got the demo disk. There's a whole suitcase more where that came from."

"Can you get it? Can you get Dr. Wilkes? We've got to talk. We've got to get this in front of the NIH or the CDC."

"I'll see what I can do." Given the emerging circumstances, there was no use telling David any more than he needed to know. "But if you think it's real, why don't you go ahead and see what you can do."

"There's a guy in New York, a doctor named John Smali, who works for NIH. He's the perfect person for this. I've seen him at a couple of conferences on computing and public health. He's putting together some kind of global network for disease reporting."

"Sounds perfect. Let me know how it goes."

26

DR. JOHN SMALI LEAFED THROUGH THE PILE OF FAX MATERIAL from David Muldane with his free hand as he held the phone receiver in the other. He pulled out the one page with the graph showing the S, I, R, and D lines. As he stared at it, he listened to a Mr. Bennet Rifkin at the Webster Foundation, who seemed to be the person in charge of this EpiSim thing. He concentrated on the D line. Over 60 percent dead. Utterly fantastic. Even the Black Plague hadn't killed that many people. Still, there had been even nastier killers roaming the planet in even more recent times. The famous Ebola virus delivered a brand of hemorrhagic fever with a fatality rate that exceeded 70 percent. And then was AIDS, the final nightmare, with a death toll close to

100 percent. But Ebola had been contained, and AIDS was a slow-motion catastrophe that consumed its victims over several years. This Agent 57a was a biological blowup, a wildfire that would explode across the landscape faster than you could run to escape it.

"Now, I'm sure, Mr. Muldane has the best of intentions," Bennet was saying. "But he's obviously not familiar with the source of the material. We're talking about an employee that no longer has both oars in the water. She quit without notice and committed a fairly serious crime in the process. If you look at the circumstances and then at the data, I think you'll see it takes a real leap of faith to get serious about it."

"I see," said Dr. Smali. But he did not. John Smali was a careful and methodical person. When he was a little fellow of four, and going through the monster phase, his mom did special motherly things to help him through it, like putting his jammies in the dryer at the last minute so they would still be warm when he put them on and would drift him off to sleep before the canted yellow eyes and razor teeth showed up. But it was John himself who erected the most effective ramparts. With some help from his dad, he arranged a series of lamps in his room that cast light in a pattern that left not a single shadow. He put a piece of masking tape down the window to block out a gap left between the curtains. He dutifully checked under the bed with a little penlight every night, and he kept his best plastic ray gun under the blankets in a specific location. He added an extra pillow so his head was elevated to give him a better field of view as his lids got heavy. And it worked. The monsters were utterly exhausted by his precautions and gave up after just a few weeks.

And ever since, Dr. Smali had been extremely careful about monsters, including the kinds that could fuel epidemics. He could not rest until every possible contingency had been considered, analyzed, and acted upon. So, no matter what Mr. Rifkin was saying, he would take the time to consider both sides of the case.

"I know it seems a little odd that we haven't published anything on this methodology," said Bennet, "but it's like I said. EpiSim's still a highly theoretical project, and that makes it all pretty flaky. People here all agree that results just aren't stable enough yet to go out and talk about them. Right now, we can run the same simulation three times and get three completely different answers. So what you've got in front of you is a highly academic exercise. We've got high hopes for the future, but that's then and this is now. Having one of our staff go gonzo hasn't helped any, but you'll probably be seeing some papers from us in another year or two."

"Well, all right, Mr. Rifkin. I'll be looking forward to that. Thanks for your time."

"No problem. Good luck with your work."

As Dr. Smali hung up, he was already weighing the various factors in this bizarre business. He didn't know David Muldane all that well, but the man seemed like a responsible sort. They had met at a symposium on the application of computer technology to public health issues and discussed several topics of mutual interest. From time to time, they had exchanged information of interest via E-mail on the Internet. At any rate, Muldane didn't strike him as someone who would deliberately jeopardize his professional standing by supporting criminal activity committed by a colleague.

And there was the material itself. There was something strangely compelling about it. It *felt* right. But then again, a lot of scientists had been derailed by things that felt right, but turned out to be dead wrong. And then there was the Webster Foundation. He'd never heard of them, and after asking around, he couldn't find anyone else that had either. Rifkin's explanation of their low profile seemed quite reasonable, but it did nothing to further their scientific credibility. And finally, there was this strange business about the staff person gone bonkers and running off with the data. Not a good endorsement for the validity of the project.

Smali stuffed all this data into a cluttered mental algorithm that calculated the importance of Agent 57a and EpiSim in the broader scheme of things. In the doctor's world, priorities were established by the spatial location of the paperwork for competing items. A ranking of zero put it in the wastebasket. An immediate trip to the "misc." folder in his filing cabinet was only slightly better. If a document never left his computer nor was made into hard copy, it was in about the same place. If it succeeded in getting into a folder labeled by subject matter, it stood a somewhat improved chance. If it went onto the periphery of his desk, where papers and publications swirled like the arms of a spiral galaxy, then its ranking was greatly improved. The center of his desk was the center of his universe; it was hardwired through his optic nerves to his short-term memory.

With the calculation now complete, Smali was just about to file Muldane's fax in the "misc." folder when he recalled something that changed his mind. A few weeks back, he'd participated in a video conference over the net. One of the presentations was on an emerging form of *Chlamydia* called *Chlamydia pneumonia* (TWAR). The thing had been isolated several years back from throat and sputum cultures, and the "TWAR" handle came from the first two isolates, TW-138 from Taiwan and AR(acute respiratory)-39. It caused fever, cough, myalgias, sore throat, and sinusitus, but all in all was a relatively mild illness—unlike its close relative *Chlamydia psittaci*, which caused serious and sometimes fatal pneumonia. Cases of the TWAR strain were now popping up all over the world, and it appeared to be spread from person to person through inhalation of infectious germs. Fortunately, tetracycline and erythromycin were still quite effective against it, but there was no telling how long that would last. In microbiology, the trend was now clear; sooner or later, the germs would step around the drugs and go their own way inside their unfortunate victims.

All of this made him reconsider Agent 57a in the purloined report from Muldane, which was supposed to be a mutation of the more vicious *Chlamydia psittaci* strain. Based on current experience with the TWAR strain, maybe something like this could go around the world, and very rapidly at that. The two strains differed only at the molecular level, so the mode of transmission from one host to another was probably exactly the same in both cases.

He leaned back in his chair and sighed as he looked at the graph from Muldane's report. The idea of a monumental epidemic like this was fascinating in a morbid kind of way. But it was so large, it created a wall of incomprehension that was hard to scale. Of more immediate interest was the EpiSim tool. He simply couldn't afford to believe it was real, because of the horrible disappointment that would descend on him if it wasn't. A technology like this would be the crown jewel in his Emerging Diseases Information Network. Right now, EDIN was like a global collection of weather stations that could observe and report the current conditions in their immediate areas. These reports could be merged to point out developing trends, but they could not look very far into the future. With a tool like EpiSim, you would have the same kind of forecasting capability the weather services had and be able to alert stations to imminent pathogens before they ever even presented themselves. It would dramatically boost the efficiency of EDIN and ultimately change the whole course of epidemiology.

He put the sheaf of fax paper back onto the periphery of his desk. It was difficult to believe that something like this could have been developed without the knowledge of the public health community—unless it was still in an untested and embryonic stage, just as Mr. Rifkin at Uni had said. He was going to have to confront Muldane with Rifkin's debunking of the Agent 57a forecast, and that wasn't going to be pleasant. About the only way Muldane could get off the hook and convince him was to produce the entire output of the simulation, which would undoubtedly come to thousands of gigabytes of data.

But then again, maybe Muldane would come through. Maybe it was Rifkin who was blowing smoke. He made a note to call Muldane.

27

São Tomé

DR. EMANUEL DA COSTA TOOK A SIP OF COFFEE AND ILLUMInated the X ray clipped to the neon panel in front of him. It presented an interesting puzzle, and Dr. da Costa loved a good puzzle. His aggressive curiosity had propelled him through school here on the island of São Tomé and eventually won him a scholarship to study medicine in Lisbon, where he graduated near the top of his class. After a brief flirtation with research, he was drawn back here by his unrelenting affection for the island and its people. Compared to the ongoing horrors in Central Africa, São Tomé was a tiny beacon of optimism, protected by its insularity, and Dr. da Costa felt an obligation to keep it that way. The country had a long tradition of exceptional health care, dating back to the Portuguese occupation, which, although cruel and exploitative, had a policy of providing excellent medical attention for laborers. Nine years ago, he had joined the staff of the Hospital Adriano Moreira and enjoyed every day of it since.

The X ray depicted the interior of the lungs of a gentleman named Oscar Silva, who owned a place called the Paradiso. Dr. da Costa had heard of it but had never been there. It was reputed to be a bit on the wild side, and the doctor leaned more to the mild side, often reading T. S. Eliot or Cervantes before retiring after a busy day. Mr. Silva had come to the hospital without an appointment two days ago and was clearly a sick man. His temperature was 101 degrees and he was shivering from chills when Dr. da Costa examined him. He complained of a splitting headache and severe muscle pain in his arms and legs. It had all started a week or two before, when he picked up a little chest cold that brought on a wheeze and an occasional dry cough. It didn't get any worse, so he ignored it; then two days ago, the coughing became more violent and sputum-filled, and his temperature shot up, so he came to the hospital, where he was now bedridden downstairs.

The doctor peered at the X ray, an old but still highly useful technology, especially in the detection of pneumonia, which was almost certainly what Mr. Silva had. You didn't even need a trained eye to recognize the soft, milky haze inside the chest cavity where the fluid was building up. On an X ray, the pure black areas represented places where the rays had roared on through without obstruction on their way to the film. The lighter areas showed where the rays had been obstructed by something, and large concentrations of fluid were fairly good obstructors. In the lungs, the high fluid levels usually came from an immune reaction to an infectious agent.

But which infectious agent? The pattern on the X ray was highly suggestive of bacterial pneumonia, and that was a problem. In up to 50 percent of these cases, the pathogenic agent was never identified. One way to try is to collect a coughed-up sputum sample, culture it, and look for suspicious microorganisms through a microscope. Dr. da Costa had already done that and run into the usual roadblock: contamination. When a glob of mucus forms in the bronchial passages, it is rich with the offending organism; but to come out the mouth, it must traverse the upper air passages that play host to a teaming variety of flora. By the time the sputum is collected, the original germs are lost in the madding crowd.

The other way to go about it was through the blood, with antibody tests that sought out the molecular kinks of particular germs. But serological assays of this sort required extensive laboratory work, and no facility on the island provided this service.

So for the first time in a long time, Dr. da Costa was thinking about calling in outside help. Because one aspect of the particular marauder inside Mr. Silva's lungs was very troubling. Most forms of bacterial pneumonia respond well to treatment with tetracycline or erythromycin. Administer one to two grams a day at six-hour intervals and the worst of the symptoms should pass within forty-eight to seventy-two hours. And that was precisely what Dr. da Costa had done with Mr. Silva.

But as of last evening, seventy-two hours had come and gone, and Mr. Silva was getting worse instead of better. Much worse. The coughing spasms were violent enough that he moved the patient out of the ward and into an isolated room and put him on oxygen.

Dr. da Costa kept staring at the X ray, searching for some nuance that would give him a clue as to what he was dealing with. Before the antibiotics had failed, he had Q fever on the suspect list, since most of its symptoms matched quite nicely with those of the patient. But tetracycline easily defeats Q fever, and here it didn't even make a dent.

As he thought about it, another possibility occurred to him. Q fever was caused by a form of rickettsia, and one other form of this organism also caused pneumonia, and that was *Chlamydia.* And come to think of it, the symptoms were strikingly similar in both diseases, causing many documented cases of mistaken diagnosis. Last time he'd checked, there were two types of *Chlamydia* that caused pneumonia. One was the TWAR type, but that was relatively mild and never produced symptoms like those he was seeing here. The other type caused psittacosis, and that could definitely produce some serious symptoms, especially if it was an exceptionally virulent strain. In some instances fatality rates went above 30 percent in untreated cases.

The older doctors around the hospital occasionally mentioned cases of psittacosis. Parrots carried it and there had once been a large parrot population in São Tomé because of the parrot trade on Príncipe. But the parrots were completely gone now, and in all his time here, he couldn't recall a single case. Besides, psittacosis responded well to tetracycline, which appeared completely impotent in the case of Mr. Silva. Still, he had to wonder. Maybe it had worked its way around the drugs.

"Dr. da Costa." The ward nurse at his office door yanked him out of his speculative adventure. "I think you'll want to take a look at Mr. Silva."

It must be bad, he thought as he followed the nurse out. She knew he was scheduled to start his rounds in half an hour and wouldn't have bothered him if it wasn't big trouble.

And it was. The moment he entered the isolation room, his hand automatically went for the germ mask in his lab coat. Oscar lay on his back, with the tubing of the cannula sending a silent stream of oxygen up his nostrils. An energetic mob of little twitches scrambled up and down his limbs. His eyes had gone to glass, and a steady rope of red ran from his mouth down to the pillow where it collected into a crimson lake. Moist, angry eruptions of dark pink rose all over his visible flesh, and his mouth formed a desperate oval, trying to suck in the air that would not come. A young nurse stood a few feet from the bed with her mask on, clearly afraid to approach any nearer. In the quiet, they could hear the faint and terrible rattle of the pulmonary system nearing a catastrophic collapse.

Dr. da Costa turned to the ward nurse. "It's gone systemic. We're going to lose him. Does he have relatives?"

"His wife came to see him yesterday." The nurse's eyes were locked on the patient and flush with fear. She was an experienced hand and knew that something was terribly wrong here.

"She'd better be notified, but she can't see him. I'm declaring this room completely off-limits. You two had better leave now."

The two nurses took one more helpless look at Oscar Silva and left. Dr. da Costa moved closer and looked into the patient's drained eyes. He wondered if a glimmer of sentience still remained inside this poor soul. Maybe the man was riding a shock wave of unbearable pain out into the black void, with no way to dismount and walk away in peace. It didn't seem right. Not in this case, not in any case.

He left the room, went to the dispensary, and got a syringe and a sealed vial containing 20 cc of morphine. On the way back, he could see the two nurses talking to other nurses in the hall. When they noticed his approach, they fell silent and stepped aside, their eyes begging for reassurance, which he could not give.

Back in the room, he took the syringe and the drug to a bedside table and looked at the patient, who was lost in delicate tremors. Clearly the nervous system was under siege, but it was entirely possible that the damage didn't extend to the brain. He took the vial of morphine, removed the metal top, swabbed the rubber gasket with alcohol, jabbed the syringe in, drew back the plunger, and extracted fifteen milligrams of the drug from the vial. He then withdrew the syringe, shot out the air, and moved to the port in the IV tubing leading down the man's arm. He inserted the syringe into the port and depressed the plunger, sending the drug directly into the circulatory system. In just a second or two, the tremors died down. He put his stethoscope to the man's heart and heard it struggle vainly against the massive insult of the infection. Mr. Silva's time was clearly at hand. There was nothing more he could do.

He stepped back from the bed and looked out the window, where the world was normal, and realized that he was enveloped in a blue zone of fear. God only knew what hideous swarm of pathogens had been expelled from the man's lungs and were held in check only by the doors and the windows.

In the hall, he told the ward nurse not to let anyone enter, and to administer 1-cc doses of morphine at sixty-minute intervals. He ran back up the stairs on a jet of adrenaline and headed for the office next to his, which was occupied by a Dr. Raphael Munoz, a craggy, gray-haired relic from the Portuguese days.

"Dr. Munoz, I'm going to need a little help with my rounds. I've got an emergency down in Room B."

"Already heard," replied Munoz as he swung in his chair to face da Costa. "Some kind of pneumonia is it?"

"A really bad kind. Antibiotics won't touch it, and it's gone systemic. The guy will be dead in an hour."

"What do you think?"

"At first I thought it was Q fever, but now I suspect it's some new strain of psittacosis."

Dr. Munoz raised his hand. "Don't tell me. The patient had a little chest cold that hung on for couple of weeks, with a dry cough. Then all of a sudden, his lungs were filled with goop and his temperature shot up. You took an X ray and found full-blown atypical pneumonia."

"You've got it."

"Of course I've got it." Munoz laughed. "I've got two cases. Both came in yesterday afternoon."

"Great Jesus! Where are they now?"

"Down in the ward. Where else?"

"They've got to go into isolation immediately."

"That serious?" Dr. Munoz's laugh was gone.

"Come on, I'll show you."

"Holy mother of God!" said Dr. Munoz as the pair looked at the ravaged hulk of Oscar Silva. "What makes you think it's psittacosis?"

"Mostly process of elimination. I'm sending a blood sample to the WHO lab in Zurich. While we're waiting, I'm going to try to find out if he came in contact with any psittacine birds, especially parrots."

As the taxi cruised down Rua Calxa toward the Paradiso, Dr. da Costa tried to grasp the magnitude of the problem.

How infectious was this thing? Was it airborne? It sure seemed to be. Was it a case of birds to humans? Or was it human-to-human, which was rare but possible with psittacosis? Before leaving, Dr. Munoz had talked with the other two patients, both males in their thirties, and found a common factor. They were regular patrons of the Paradiso and went there several times a week in the evening. Dr. da Costa had seen the frightened look in their eyes as they were wheeled into the isolation area and felt both horror and compassion for them. If Mr. Silva's case was any indication, they were within a few dozen hours of total physical devastation.

The taxi stopped and he saw the front of the Paradiso. The name was painted in soft blue over the beige stucco on the front, which was open to the street and protected by a metal accordion gate. The late-morning sun raked the stucco surface at a severe angle, sending the rough surface into a fury of shadowy texture. The gate was pushed open and a padlock dangled from it, its dirty casing leering in the sun against the blackness inside.

As the doctor got out and approached the opening, a small boy appeared, a Tonga, the offspring of migrant laborers from the continent. He was shoeless and wore a white T-shirt and baggy shorts and held a frayed broom as he looked suspiciously at Dr. da Costa. When the doctor reached the entrance, the boy retreated a yard or so into the interior, but then held his ground.

Dr. da Costa peered in and waited for his eyes to adjust to the dim interior. There appeared to be a bar along the back wall, and to the right he saw something catch the light, something of metal wire. Before he ventured another step, he pulled out the surgical mask he'd brought and donned it. The boy now grasped the broom handle in the manner of a potential weapon, but da Costa ignored him and started toward the back. Ten more feet told the story. It was a cage. A large, empty birdcage, with a little sign taped to it that said "Hands off!"

He walked back outside, removed his mask, and motioned to the boy, who came as far as the entrance and glared at him.

"There's a birdcage in there," said da Costa, pointing to the front. "Was there a bird in the cage?"

"Parrot," replied the boy in a heavy equatorial accent. "Big parrot."

"What happened to the parrot? Do you know?"

"Parrot die."

"How long ago?"

"Don't know. Two weeks. Maybe three."

"You work here?"

"Sometimes. Mr. Silva the boss."

"Yes, I know Mr. Silva. How are you feeling? You been sick?"

The boy shook his head. "Feel fine."

"Look," said da Costa as he knelt down to the boy's level, "I've talked to Mr. Silva, and he asked me to lock this place up and send you on home."

The boy looked suspicious, but didn't interfere as da Costa padlocked the gate, then drew several dobras from his pocket. "He said to pay you for a whole month, and you would give me the key." He held out the money. The boy hesitated, then retrieved the key from his shorts and handed it over as he grabbed the money and ran.

Da Costa watched him disappear around the corner. Would he live? Would he die? No telling. At least not yet. Da Costa climbed in the taxi and headed back to the hospital.

As soon as he walked through the front entrance and saw the receptionist, he knew what was happening. Panic. A restrained and muted panic, but ripe and ready to burst into a billion screams. The girl was wearing a surgical mask, as were the clerks who glided in and out behind her.

He went immediately to the ward nurse's station and asked about Mr. Silva. Dead. About twenty minutes ago. He looked out into the main ward. Many of the nurses were gone from their stations, and the beds of some of the ambulatory patients were suddenly empty. He thought to check Room B with the two other patients, but decided to check in with Dr. Munoz and the rest of the staff first.

It seemed quiet at the top of the stairs, and walking down the corridor to Munoz's office, he saw only two of the fifteen doctors in, both wearing surgical masks. When he reached

Munoz's office, he saw the old doctor snapping his briefcase and getting ready to depart.

Munoz looked up at da Costa. "Seven more cases. We've got them on oxygen and pumped full of tetracycline. Not much more we can do."

"Where are they?"

"We opened the spare room in the old wing." Munoz stood up. "Got to be going now. I'll check in later." He said it in his best professional intonation, but da Costa knew it was a lie.

In his office, Dr. da Costa thought briefly and intensely about his loyalties and obligations. He was a doctor. He was a responsible citizen. He was the father of three young children, but he was still bound by the Hippocratic oath to do what he could to treat the sick.

He walked down the hall to the little room where the EDIN equipment was set up. The staff management had made him the designated operator, and he'd dutifully looked at the manuals and gone through a practice session or two. As he booted the personal computer and the windows came up, he remembered it wasn't that hard. In fifteen minutes, he had entered all the data about Mr. Silva, and the sudden appearance of nine more cases. He scanned in an X ray of the patient and noted that a blood sample had gone to Zurich. After reviewing everything once, he committed it to disk and left the machine running. At a predetermined time, it would convert this information into a serial stream, which would snake out from the PC to a radio transmitter unit, then up to the satellite that would pass overhead and collect it into a memory buffer than would retain it for a download to New York later in the day.

At this point, it was all he could do. It was all anyone could do.

Martin N'Dong alternated between cursing himself, taking a sip of beer, and then hurling an epithet at his uncle Omar, who was comfortably seated in his house over 150 miles away in Libreville. Martin's sneakers were canted upward so the balls of his feet dug two little craters in the dirt floor of the dingy bar on Avenida Marginal in the port district northeast of town center. He poured the remainder of the bottle of Rosema into his glass and stared through the amber filter at the cargo ship. There he had spent the morning as a stevedore loading hundred-pound bags of coffee off the trucks that hauled it from the *roças,* the big plantations in the island's jungle interior. The burlap on the bags rubbed his shoulder raw, and the salt from his sweat in the hot sun stoked a great fire in the abrasion. And for eight hours of this torture, he had made the equivalent of three U.S. dollars, half of which he would now spend for two bottles of Rosema. It was the best he could do. He was here on a tourist visa and had no work permit, so he had to work for cash under the table and hope to save enough for a ferry ticket back to Gabon.

In the wide-angle distortion of the glass, he saw two figures stretch into view. He looked up and saw it was Jean and Raul, two fellow natives of Gabon who worked as *servicais,* contract laborers. Without a word, they sat at the table.

"You should have stuck around this morning," said Martin. "They had work."

"We got work," replied Jean, the taller of the two, with a thin face and bony forearms. He lapsed into a sullen silence and stared down at the table.

"You don't seem very happy about it." Neither man spoke. To Martin, they seemed troubled and distant. "Well—how much did you make?"

"Four thousand dobras," said Jean without looking up. The equivalent of twenty U.S. dollars.

"Apiece?" asked Martin in amazement.

"Apiece," replied Jean.

"That's fantastic! What did you do to get that kind of money?"

"It wasn't worth it," Raul stated flatly.

"Was it a crime?" Martin asked with great interest.

"No crime," said Jean.

"Well, then, what?" asked Martin in exasperation.

"We started for the docks today, but stopped for beer," said Jean. "By the time we started again, it was afternoon. Then it was lunch. Then we got to the docks. That's when the ambulance men showed up."

"Was someone hurt?"

"No. They were from the hospital. They had the white

uniforms. They were looking for someone to do a job," said Jean. "They were looking for someone who could drive."

"I can drive," said Raul with a note of pride.

"So we got the job," said Jean.

"And what *was* the job?" inquired Martin with diminishing patience.

"The men said they had a special meeting they had to go to, so they would miss a pickup at the hospital," said Jean. "It was a body, they said. They asked if we were scared of a body. We said maybe. They said four thousand dobras each. We said okay. All we had to do was drive it to the morgue and drop it off, and then take the ambulance back to the men."

"So what happened?"

"So we dropped the men off at this restaurant for their meeting. And drove to the hospital," said Jean.

"*I* drove," interjected Raul.

"We told them we were there for the body," continued Jean, "and they sent us around to the back. Something was wrong. I knew it right away."

"How could you tell?"

"They all had masks on. I've been to hospitals before. Nobody had masks. Here everybody had masks. It wasn't right."

"Then we got the stretcher and they took us down this hall," offered Raul. "There was a closed door. They said the body was in there. And then they left. Real fast."

"That's all they said?"

"That's all," said Jean. "We went in and the body was in a rubber bag on the bed. Just like the men said it would be."

"Only they didn't tell us there would be blood all over the bed," said Raul. "It was horrible. We put the bag on the stretcher and left as fast as we could."

"We went to the morgue. And then it really got weird," said Jean. "We told them who we were, and they knew all about the body. But they didn't want it."

"Didn't want it?"

"That's what they said. We asked what to do. They said it wasn't their problem. So we left and took the ambulance back to the restaurant. We met them inside, and they paid us and we left. We went to a bar down the street. From the window we could still see the ambulance where it was parked. The men came out and looked in the back. I'm sure they saw the body was still there. But you know what they did?"

"What?"

"They walked away. And they never came back."

"How do you know?"

"We stayed and had beers with our money. Maybe two hours. They never came back."

"Way too strange," stated Raul. "It wasn't worth it."

"Maybe not," said Martin, "but you're rich. So buy me a beer."

28

ROBERT FANCHER LOOKED OUT THE WINDOW OF HIS OFFICE as he put the cipher CD for secure conversations into the drive on his desk. From the seventy-third floor of the Seafirst Building on Fifth Avenue, he peered down on the main ferry terminal, where one of the big vessels was just pulling in to disgorge its load of cars into downtown.

With a little convoy of beeps the system engaged, and the LCD display identified the caller from Uni as Bennet Rifkin. He knew what the call would be about, and it positively ruined the magnificent view rolled out before him.

"Fancher?"

A bad start. Bennet almost always addressed him as "Bob."

"Yes, Bennet. How are you?"

"I'm not well. Can you guess why?"

"I'd prefer not to, Bennet. Can you tell me?"

"I recently received a call from a doctor named John Smali at the National Institutes for Health. It seems the good doctor has at least a cursory idea of the concept behind the stolen property that you assured me you would recover. It seems this information was supplied to him by someone in public health in Seattle. So my question to you, Bob, is a very simple one. What in the fuck is going on?"

It took Fancher just a single beat to recover, which in his particular position was an entire beat too long. Rifkin had him on the run. "Okay, here's the situation as of now. I succeeded in having the Wilkes woman arrested and your property committed to the evidence locker. Then I checked with people inside the DA's office and found she might walk, along with your property. So certain resources inside the jail tried to persuade her to leave the property there if she checked out."

"I didn't hear that last part, Fancher."

"Of course not. And you'll never hear the rest of what I'm about to tell you. The bottom line is, it didn't work. She took the property with her when she left."

"And where did she go?"

"Who knows? Maybe she's already back in San Diego."

"Fine. That's the end of it. It's a public relations problem now. I've got other ways of handling it. You're fired."

"What?"

"I said you're fired. Send us a prorated bill for the current portion of this month and go fuck yourself."

"I think you better hear me out before you do something very stupid, Mr. Rifkin. The resources I used inside the jail take great pride in the quality of their work. They were very disappointed when she ran off with your property. They fully intend to honor their commitment—no matter who you tell to get fucked."

"Okay then, call off your dogs and you're not fired—unless, of course, your dogs have bigger balls than you do. How's that?"

"For now, Mr. Rifkin, that will be acceptable. I'll be in touch."

"I'm sure you will."

A series of beeps terminated the cipher process, and Fancher could hear the unfiltered audio on the CD, which was a reissue of an obscure album by a band called Don and the Goodtimes.

Just then, his office door opened, and his administrative assistant poked her young head in. "Mr. Fancher, there's a

Lieutenant Paris here from the Seattle police. He doesn't have an appointment, but he says it's important."

Fancher cringed and stared out the window, where the sun was drooping toward a cloud bank covering the Olympic mountain range. "Tell him I'm—"

"I think you better tell me yourself, Mr. Fancher."

Fancher whirled to see Paris's big frame coming through the door as the assistant went flat against the doorjamb to make room.

Fancher shot to his feet. "Lieutenant, you don't have any right—"

Paris turned to the stunned girl. "Thank you. You're excused."

To Fancher's supreme irritation, she gave a numb nod, backed out, and shut the door. It was clear to her that the solitary beacon of authority in the room was Paris.

Paris crossed the large room in a couple of easy strides and seated himself before Fancher, who slowly melted back into his chair.

"You set me up," Paris declared as he caught Fancher's darting eyes and wrestled them into submission.

"What do you mean 'I set you up'?"

"How quickly we forget," mocked Paris. "You gave me a tip on a woman named Elaine Wilkes. So I did your bidding. I arrested her. While she was in jail, she got worked over and was warned to part with her luggage. That's called extortion, but being a high-priced corporate lawyer, maybe you forgot."

"So what's that got to do with me?"

"Everything. The only person who could've set her up inside the jail is your esteemed client Barney Cox."

Fancher smiled. "That's a very ambitious assumption, Lieutenant."

"In court of law, yes. But we're not in a court of law now. We're just two guys talking business. And here's my proposition to you and Mr. Cox. Fuck off. Right now."

Fancher stood to terminate the encounter. At least he might get in the last move. "Is that all?"

"Not quite." Paris stood, grasped the outer lip of Fancher's desktop, and upended the entire structure as Fancher frantically danced backward to avoid being hit. Four hundred pounds of premium Philippine mahogany crashed to the floor, followed by an avalanche of executive gimcracks roaring down the steeply tilted surface and onto the antique Persian carpet.

"Now we're done," announced Paris. Then he left.

Technically, the roll was less than one-half a degree, and to Elaine it constituted nothing more than a weak signal from the semicircular canals of her inner ears. After reaching its apex, the roll reversed itself in a corrective action, reached the horizontal neutrality defined by planetary gravity, overshot, then rolled back to a slightly negative position. This cycle was repeated as a series of wave actions with diminishing amplitudes as she thumbed through an old copy of *Esquire* while reclining in one of the forward berths on the *Cedar Queen*.

She would have dismissed it as random wave action, but then it started all over again, and a quick pulse of anxiety rolled through her. Several people were coming aboard, and she was feeling the weight they applied to the deck railing as they came over the side. Then she looked at her watch and relaxed. It was Paris, who'd told her he'd stop in after work. She stretched, pulled herself out of the berth, and headed toward the main saloon. Maybe he had some news about David Muldane and the sample disk.

As soon as she saw the legs and the shorts coming down the stairs from the wheelhouse, she was hit by a sharp shot of fear. This was not Paris.

She froze in place as the man appeared before her. He had a broad, powerful face with a meanly trimmed mustache, and the darkest of eyes. His arms and hands were a controlled chaos of muscle that spilled from a cotton print sport shirt.

"Hi," he said, smiling, "how are you today?"

The boat still rocked. He wasn't alone. Someone else was up in the wheelhouse. The heated air went still and thick. Still, she clung to the ridiculous hope that it was some kind of mistake.

"I'm fine, thank you. Can I help you?"

"Well, I sure hope so." The man parked himself on one

of the settees, blocking her escape up the companionway stairs. He looked around. "Neat boat! Belong to you?"

"It belongs to my husband and me," said Elaine, who felt her knees start to shake. "He'll be back in just a second."

"He will, huh?" said the man with a look of pleasant surprise. "Well, I guess that doesn't leave us much time, does it?"

"Look, I don't like this," said Elaine shakily. "You're going to have to leave. Now."

Just then, she heard the *Cedar Queen*'s engine jump to life, sending a mild rumble through the hull. *My God!* They were going to take her away, take her into some horrible and unknowable zone. A place where mercy and reason had been torched out of existence.

The man ignored her for the moment and looked at the folded wings of the table in the main saloon. He quickly saw how they folded out and extended them to form the full table surface.

Elaine glanced out a porthole and saw the sterns of other boats march by. Soon they'd be in the open lake and she'd be in terrible trouble.

The man looked up from the table and smiled his awful smile. He gestured to the spot across the table from him. "Sit down."

"I'll stand," said Elaine firmly. She was on slightly better ground now. A career professional, she thoroughly understood the psychological dimension of power, and its symbolic thrusts and parries. It was the physical dimension that was new to her, and supremely frightening. In this one instant, all the media myths of female physical empowerment faded away, all the hard body workouts, all the lightning karate kicks to the crotch, all the cleverly concealed canisters of pepper mace. In truth, few women were a match for a large, well-trained male intent on inflicting bodily harm.

"Okay," he said agreeably. Then he reached into the waistband of his shorts, plucked out a yellow darning needle, and placed it on the table. "You don't happen to have a hammer, do you?"

As Elaine stared in horror at the slender, plastic needle, she saw the point had been sharpened. The jail, the rotten stink of the invisible voice, the slim little finger with its deadly nail, all came rushing back.

The man leaned back on the settee and clasped his hands behind his head. "I'll tell you what. Let's forget about the hammer for a minute. Maybe we can work something out."

Elaine's hopes soared. For the first time, there was talk of reason, of negotiation. She swayed to the stern as the boat accelerated and headed west in the open water.

The man reached onto the table, picked up the darning needle, and rolled it between his thumb and forefinger. "I understand that you're in possession of some stolen property. I bet it's here on the boat, isn't it?"

Elaine's mind raced. They were going to find it anyway if they searched. So why deny it? "Yes."

The man's face brightened. "Good!" He pulled out what looked like a cellular phone, extended the aerial, pressed a button, and put it down on the table. "Now, before you go fetch it, I want you to tell me all about it."

Elaine slowly nodded. It would buy her time. And time was all she had left.

"We've got a problem," said Robert Fancher through the reinforced glass of the visitor's booth. "It's the Wilkes woman. There's a complication with the police."

"You mean with Paris?" asked Barney.

"So you know?"

"You'd be surprised what I know. They don't call it the information age for nothing. And there's a corollary, Bob, that says, 'You never know enough.' And that's how I feel right now. I've been thinking about the stolen property from Uni Corporation, and I've been wondering why they're so willing to deal with a common criminal like myself to get it back. No matter what deductive path I follow, I always reach the same conclusion. It must be extraordinarily valuable. Am I right?"

"You're right about its being Uni. Beyond that, I have no idea what the nature of the property is. Nor do I care. But I do know this. The deal is off. I've been in touch with them and received specific instructions to end this operation. And now there's more reason than ever. Lieutenant Paris just showed up at my office and seemed a little angry about your treatment of Wilkes. If it continues, he's determined to make it a police matter."

Barney smiled maliciously. "Lieutenant Paris? I negotiated with him a while back—and to tell you the truth, I had to admire the man. Real leadership potential there. You don't see that very often anymore, and that's why I got curious and did a little checking on him."

"And what did you find?"

"He has a rather large credibility problem inside the department. Seems he spent a lot of official time chasing some phantom poisoner and wound up far down the food chain. So he better have one hell of tale to tell before he takes on a project like this one, and I don't think he does."

"I don't think you heard what I'm telling you. Paris or not, the deal is off. No deal with the DA. No money. No nothing."

"And I don't think you heard what I'm telling *you*," hissed Barney. "The deal is on. And it stays on until I say it's off. And it's not off until I'm out of here. Good day, Bob."

Fancher watched Barney rise abruptly and stalk off, taking the entirety of Fancher's future along with him.

Paris bolted through the marina parking lot with angry crunches of gravel spraying at every step. He could barely believe what he'd seen just seconds before as he approached the main gate leading down to the marina's main dock. As he'd reached for his key to the gate, his eye caught the motion of a big boat pulling out, and as he looked up, he saw the *Cedar Queen* heading for open water. Even at that distance, he could tell that the person at the wheel was not Elaine, but a stocky male wearing shorts and a baseball cap. As soon as the boat had cleared the marina, it turned west and headed straight for the Washington Ship Canal.

Now Paris reached his car, jammed the key into the door lock, and ripped the door open to climb inside. Then he spotted his cellular phone on the passenger seat and made a quick calculation. He'd take the time to phone for help. As he reached in and pulled the phone out, he watched the *Cedar Queen* continue at a moderate speed directly toward the canal, which confirmed his suspicions. First, they were making a break for the open Sound, where they had hundreds of square miles of water to hide in. Second, they had Elaine. Nobody would steal the boat for its own sake. Only a handful of thirty-six-foot Blanchards were left in the world, and it would be impossible to trade or sell without detection.

Third, they were going to kill her after they got what they wanted. No one would leave witnesses to a kidnapping.

Paris stabbed the power button on the phone, then watched the display flutter to life and issue a blinking BATT message. Shit! The batteries were dead! In the confusion of the last few days, he'd forgotten to swap them with the ones sitting in the charger at home.

He tossed the phone into the car, swung behind the wheel, and started the engine. He backed up in a spray of gravel as he slammed the door shut. Bits of rock pinged off the van parked next to him, but he didn't notice. He was already planning his next move. To get to the Sound, they had to go through the locks, and with a little luck, he'd get there before they did.

For all the boats harbored in Lake Washington and Lake Union, the path to the open waters of Puget Sound funneled down to a single choke point, the Lake Washington ship canal and the locks at its west end near the Sound. The boats had to enter one of the locks, which was then sealed shut by huge gates, and wait while the water was drained down to make up the twenty-six-foot difference between the water level in the lakes and that in the Sound. Then they could float free and make the run for open water.

But the boats had to wait and go through in batches. They were lined up in rows and secured to the side of the lock during the draining, which took up to five minutes. And this was Paris's advantage. It would take another ten minutes to secure the boats before drainage, giving him a total of fifteen minutes to reach the locks and intercept the *Cedar Queen*.

The tires on Paris's two-door sedan sounded an anguished screech as they left the gravel of the parking lot and bit into the pavement. Paris jammed on the accelerator and raced the car up the hill to Thirty-fourth Street, where he made a wild left turn, just avoiding an oncoming truck. As he roared under the shadow of the Aurora Bridge, he swung out to pass a minivan and blew his horn to clear the way. He was pushing seventy in a 35-mph zone. The driver of the minivan retaliated and tried to match his speed. Paris pulled in front and cut him off, and the minivan leveled several indignant horn blasts at him.

At the intersection with Thirty-fourth and Leary Way, he rocketed through a yellow light and heard the terrified screech of braking rubber as somebody went into a panic stop to avoid him. At Fifteenth and Leary, he leaned on his horn and pulled around a line of cars stopped for the light. A burly man in a truck gave him the finger as he pulled in front of the pack, found a hole in the cross traffic, and darted through on the red. A few blocks later, the street curved north and he went into a controlled slide that took him around a city bus with his accelerator jammed all the way to the floor.

At the intersection with Market Street, he slammed on the brakes to make a shallow left through a green light, then caught a frantic blue flash in his rearview mirror. Good. A cop car was finally after him. He roared down Market, darting and weaving through traffic with the whooping of the cop's siren providing an urgent score to the action.

As Market turned into Fifty-fourth Street, he could see the cop had gained some ground, so the timing would be perfect. At Thirty-second Avenue, he cranked a hard left that swung him into a wild fishtail that he corrected just as he bounced over the railroad tracks and skidded to a stop at the entrance to the locks facility.

He jumped out, flung open his wallet to display his badge, and was already running back to the cop car as it pulled up right behind him, lights flashing like blue quasars gone mad. "Police officer!" he yelled at the cop, who was stepping out with one hand on his gun. "We've got a hostage situation down at the locks! Call for backup!"

He turned and ran toward the entrance, hoping the patrolman was wise enough not to shoot him in the back.

Inside the *Cedar Queen*, the man with the broad face and thick mustache had a suitcase open and was casually sorting through the disks. He didn't even bother to look over at Elaine when he talked. "So, what you're telling me is that these disks describe some kind of fantastic new disease. And that they give enough information to make a drug that would cure it." He whistled respectfully. "Boy! I bet something like this could be worth a fortune." He abruptly looked over at Elaine, his face a cruel mask, and she winced inside. "What do you think?"

"I think the world needs to know. If it doesn't find out, then money's no longer going to matter much."

"I see," said the man, returning his attention to the disk. "Do you have anything else to add?"

"Yes, I do." Her eyes darted to the nearest porthole. Some kind of cement wall was going past. Where were they?

"Well," said the man quietly, "you'll just have to save it for later." He rose from the table and turned to Elaine. "A whole lot later."

As he came forward, his eyes went to glass and the smile bent into a sneer. His face became simply an excuse to stretch flesh over the hard bones of the skull.

Elaine's mind roared in a fit of wild calculation. She instinctively backed toward the forward berths, but knew they narrowed down into a pit of no escape. Should she fight? It might send him into a new and unknown mode of rage. Should she simply surrender? Outside, the boat had slowed to a stop, and through the internal roar of fear, she vaguely heard voices. Would the voices come and help? *God, please let the voices come and help.*

She would fight, she decided in a highly compressed moment. He would kill her anyway, but she wouldn't make it easy. His arm shot out and caught her high on the chest, knocking her to the narrow deck space between the berths. From the floor, she aimed a kick at his crotch, but he caught her leg and clamped her ankle with enormous strength. She kicked with the other leg, but he twisted and avoided the majority of the blow.

Then she thought to scream. The voices would hear. But he saw the scream in her eyes before it formed in her throat. A backhand blow came out of nowhere, and his knuckles collided with her mouth and propelled a shock wave all the way through her skull. She was dimly aware that her teeth were loose in the region of the impact and that her lips had become superheated balloons.

Then the hand grabbed the waistband of her shorts and ripped them down her thighs.

Paris sprinted down the walkway and past the administration building. He already had his pistol out, and at the sight of it, the horde of summer tourists parted like a school of agitated fish. There! He could see it! The *Cedar Queen* was the third boat out in the second row. But the water was already draining in the locks, and the level was down almost ten feet from the sidewalk, which put the boat decks down about six feet.

Didn't matter. He vaulted over the railing and down onto the rear deck of a cabin cruiser. The force of his big frame hitting the boat from that height rocked it violently as he dropped to his knees and put out a hand to the deck to regain his balance.

"Hey!" came the angry protest of an older man in a cheap yachtsman's cap, who poked his head through the cabin door. His eyes bulged at the sight of the pistol and he disappeared back into the interior of the boat as Paris bounded up, jumped onto the railing, then onto the deck of the next boat, where a small, flabby man in loud shorts raised his hands in surrender. Paris ignored him and crossed to where the boat was secured to the *Cedar Queen.* He put one foot gingerly on the deck railing of his boat and then the other, so it wouldn't announce his presence.

Paris crouched and moved across the rear deck toward the open door of the wheelhouse. He reached the doorframe and saw a man squatting down in the door to the companionway. The man's buttocks strained at the seat of his brown shorts, and his calf muscles pushed outward from the pressure of his folded upper legs. He was completely absorbed by something belowdecks and didn't even notice Paris.

"Police!" he thundered, and the man's body jumped in surprise. Paris saw the right elbow flex and knew the man was going for a gun in his waistband, so he leveled his pistol with both hands for a killing shot. Sure enough, the man pivoted on one foot with surprising speed and almost got a line on Paris before Paris fired.

Through the explosion of muzzle blast, Paris saw the round hit the man in a perfect heart shot and knock him into the companionway, where he crumpled down two stair steps to the interior deck.

As the body tumbled, Paris took one large step and crouched where he had a direct view through the interior door, and all the way through the vessel. Near the bow, he saw a figure move, but in the contrast between the bright summer day and the modest light belowdecks, he couldn't make out who it was.

In an instant saturated with adrenaline, he reached a decision. The man he'd just shot was watching something, like a Peeping Tom. He was watching something sexual. He was watching an assault on Elaine. The moving figure was her assailant. If Elaine could move, she would scream. And she didn't.

But what if he was wrong?

In the cabin, the man's erection had wilted before it could find its target. He reached down into the pocket of his shorts for a compact automatic pistol and whirled just as Paris's shot exploded and the body of the wheelman tumbled down the stairs. He brought the weapon around into the bright rectangle of daylight framed by the cabin door and saw Paris move in to complete the composition. The sight of his barrel arrived in the center of Paris a fraction of a second later, and he started to squeeze the trigger.

Elaine was still woozy from the blow to her face, but heard Paris's voice and the shot. She saw her attacker draw the pistol from his dropped shorts and turn his back on her. As soon as he stopped in place, she kicked him in the small of the back, a weak kick with one leg, but strong enough throw his aim off just as his weapon discharged. The shot went wild and buried itself in the rear cabin wall.

In response to the muzzle flash, Paris fired three shots into the center of the space framed by the cabin door. The first hit the man in the sternum, which shattered like brittle clay and sent a spray of ossified shrapnel into his heart. The second collided with the fifth rib, which snapped under the impact, then burrowed through the lower lobe of the lung and into the liver, where the heavy liquid content absorbed the round's remaining momentum.

The third shot hit in the soft tissue between the rib cage and the pelvis and farther out on the periphery of the trunk.

On entry, it shredded a hole in the internal abdominal oblique, punctured the colon, and exited the trunk through the rear portion of the oblique muscle. So far, it had encountered minimum resistance and had safely hoarded the majority of its destructive potential.

But two feet later, it found a terminal depository in the upper body of Elaine Wilkes. She'd raised herself on her elbows to deliver the kick, which put her chest at a forty-five-degree angle to the deck. When combined with the downward trajectory of the round, the path was nearly horizontal as the bullet entered between the ribs and carved a horrible little tunnel through the upper portion of a lung and nicked the subclavian artery before lodging in the muscle tissue just to the side of the spine.

Paris could hear the screaming sirens out on Forty-fifth Street as he cautiously descended the stairs with his pistol still extended in the firing position. As he stepped over the body, his eyes adjusted to the interior light. In the forward berth, the man with the flat face was sprawled on his side with his shirt soaked with blood and his shorts pulled down around his ankles, exposing his shriveled penis.

"Jesus!" Paris rushed forward, pulled the man's body off Elaine, and saw the chest wound. He grabbed a pillow off one of the berths and slid it under her head. "Can you hear me?"

"Hear you," she said softly through bruised and swollen lips. "Hear you."

"Stay with me," he said in a low voice. He was sick with grief and rage, but stuffed it away to deal with the imperatives of the moment. "We'll get you through this. Just stay with me."

"Stay with you," she whispered as she slid into deep shock.

29

DR. JOHN SMALI POUNDED HIS FIST ON THE DESK IN A SPASM of self-recrimination, but nobody was left in the office to hear the angry thud. It was 8:30 P.M. on Friday, and he'd just blown a diplomatic mission of the highest order. He was supposed to have met his ex-wife for dinner to see if they could renegotiate her alimony without recourse to a carnivorous pack of attorneys. He'd picked a nice little Italian place in midtown because she was highly susceptible to a good Chianti, which might lubricate the discussion in a positive manner. But the dinner was seven-thirty, which meant it was no use even to phone and see if she was still there. He could picture her now, a glowing ember of rage adorned in Bloomingdale's best, riding uptown in a taxi while constructing horrible scenarios of vengeance.

There was only one thing to do. He scampered onto a higher plane of reason, where this nasty little business shrank to a manageable perspective. He was dedicated to the global struggle against disease, and his EDIN system had recently sounded a troubling alarm. It didn't fit the standard fictional scenario, where the evil virus climbed out of the primordial tropical ooze and insidiously worked its way into the prosperous and insulated temperate zones.

Instead, it involved cows. In Europe. For some time, the cow world had been cursed by a thing called bovine spongiform encephalopathy (BSE) agent. Nobody really knew what it was. It had never been isolated. But recent serological tests could ferret out its presence in the blood of infected cows, where it gradually destroyed their brains from the inside out. There had been an epidemic in England in 1990, and also cases in France and Switzerland, but then it faded away.

But now it was back. In people. His network had reported ten cases scattered around Europe over the past eighteen months. At first, the reports were tentative, with only clinical descriptions of symptoms and no conclusions about the infectious agent. The symptoms seemed quite similar to certain other neurological diseases: gradual loss of motor control, slow onset of dementia, and eventual death from respiratory failure as the autonomic system became infected. But the new blood tests were able to pinpoint BSE agent as the pathogen involved.

Dr. Smali was quite proud that his network had detected the outbreak, then distributed information about the new blood tests, so the disease could be properly identified. But a thousand questions remained. How had it crossed over from cows into humans? What was the mode of transmission? Was it carried by a vector? What did the victims have in common? Was there a clue there? Would it establish a beachhead in the human population, or was it a temporary phenomenon?

The mystery of BSE had become so absorbing that he was about a week behind in monitoring other summary reports generated by the network's central computer here in New York. This irritated him. He was understaffed and couldn't do it all alone, but the budget just wouldn't support another full-time doctor, so he did the best he could.

He sighed and picked up a bound volume of hard copy that was a digest of the last seven days and scanned the first page, which gave an index of the rest of the material:

PERIOD 12, Week 2

LOCATION	SUSPECTED AGENT	NO. CASES THIS WEEK	TOTAL THIS PERIOD
Bangkok	Hepatitis C	1	1
Buenos Aires	Rotavirus	2	3
Cairo	Hantavirus	1	14
Calcutta	O157:H7	5	32
Hong Kong	HTLV-1	2	11
Los Angeles	HHV-6	1	5
New York	Parvovirus B19	3	21
Rome	Toxoplasma	1	1
São Tomé	*Chlamydia psittaci*	10	10

His eye rocketed straight down to the last entry. *Chlamydia.* Ten cases of psittacosis inside of a single week. Very odd. In the whole United States, with over 250 million people, you might see sixty or seventy cases in an entire year. He grabbed an international reference book and checked on São Tomé. Yes, here it was. São Tomé and Príncipe. Almost right on the equator off western Africa. About 150,000 people.

Then he remembered it. They'd set up a reporting station there. A nice fellow named da Costa. It had slipped his mind because they'd never had a report from this location. So what the hell was going on? A place with only 150,000 people suddenly had ten cases in a week. Highly unusual. Worth taking a longer look at.

He flipped from the index page to the section that gave the detailed report from São Tomé and grew increasingly alarmed as he read it. Total resistance to standard antibiotics. First patient already dead by systemic infection. Two others extremely ill. Seven more already admitted. And the data was already several days old.

Bad. Very bad. He brought up his contact database on his PC and checked the details on the São Tomé station. It was located at the Hospital Adriano Moreira. A time-zone field next to the phone number told him it was 2:30 A.M. there. Still, there must be someone on night duty. He selected the phone number with his cursor, and the PC dialed the number as he picked up the receiver to listen.

As the phone rang repeatedly, he looked out his window into the night at the sparse matrix of lit office windows. Something was bugging him about this whole business, something besides this disturbing report.

He let the phone ring into the night over a dozen times. No answer. He hung up, and the night somehow seemed blacker than ever. Then he hit it. He knew what was gnawing at him.

Agent 57a.

That whole EpiSim scenario from David Muldane had been based on a supervirulent version of *Chlamydia psittaci.* And it started just about like this thing was starting. His eyes raced over the paper sprawl on his desk, and he started fishing in the area where he'd last seen the fax pages. Ah, there they were.

He pulled out a page with the summary graph. It contained a single paragraph of text that described the overall results: 60 percent deceased. Both birds and humans as carriers, possibly even cats. (Cats? He hadn't noticed that before.) Aerosol transmission. Antibiotics useless.

Dr. Smali got up and paced as he considered his options. First, he had to follow up immediately on São Tomé. In a few hours, he should be able to talk to the hospital or to the health authorities in the national government. Second, he needed to follow up immediately with David Muldane about EpiSim. It was past five in Seattle, so he'd have to get him at home. He grabbed the phone and dialed information. Thank God, his number was listed.

"Hello."

"Dave, this is John Smali, from New York. Remember the stuff you faxed me on EpiSim?"

"John who?"

"John Smali. *Doctor* Smali. We've got to talk. It looks like that stuff you sent me was right on the money. There's an outbreak on an island in western equatorial Africa. They've got ten cases of psittacosis. One is already dead, two are critical, and antibiotics won't touch it. Sound familiar?"

Silence on the other end.

"Dave, are you there?"

Silence.

"Who is this?" demanded Smali. "Who am I talking to?"

The line clicked dead.

Shit! thought Smali as he listened to the dial tone. What a horrible time to get a wrong number. He'd just have to wait and get Muldane in the office in the morning.

His mind raced on. What he needed now was to see the real data on the real disks. The report from São Tomé would certainly get the attention of the WHO and the CDC, but not the emergency attention it deserved if EpiSim was correct. He'd need to get the complete data in front of the right people as fast as possible.

He stopped and caught his mental breath. The only thing he could do right now was to leave voice mail and E-mail with Muldane at his office in Seattle that explained the situation and requested that the data be air-expressed first thing in the morning.

As he did so, Smali looked out the window and down at the yellow surge of taxis responding to a green light, and the little figures inching along the sidewalks.

Just as if everything were all right.

30

ELAINE HAD TO WONDER IF SHE LOOKED AS STRICKEN AS Paris did. His face looked like a building under the wrecking ball as he stood next to her bed.

"I'm sorry," he said. "God, am I sorry. Did they tell you what happened?"

"Not exactly," she answered through a medicinal nebula of painkillers and antibiotics. "I kicked him. I remember that. And there was a shot. Then I'm not sure."

"I shot him. He's dead. And one of my shots hit you, too."

"So what would you do different?"

"Nothing," he sighed. "Nothing at all."

"Well, there you are," she said with a weak smile. She hadn't known about the origins of the shot, but the surgeon had already explained its consequences to her in some detail. The lung damage was a nuisance, but the real crisis zone was the damage to the subclavian artery, the main feed from the heart to the arm. The tunnel had torn the artery's outer muscle layers and caused an aneurysm, a deadly balloon of tissue stretched taut like bubble gum at full inflation. If the aneurysm had burst, she would have bled to death in just a few minutes.

And that's what might have happened. But Paris used a phone on the boat, and a helicopter had plucked her off within ten minutes and delivered her to the emergency room, where the imaging team spotted the problem and summoned the cardiac surgeon, who had just finished another procedure. The surgeon and his team went in and gingerly repaired the damage and here she was.

"Well, believe it or not," said Paris, "I have some good news. Your friend Muldane reviewed your work on the summary disk, and he was completely blown away. He's got a friend high up in the NIH. Somebody like you that's specialized in computers and epidemics. He told the guy what you're up to, and they're very interested. They've already seen a fax of the executive summary and now they want the real thing, so Muldane is going to air-express them the entire set immediately."

"Did you give Muldane the rest of the disks yet?" A long, slow wave of pain accompanied her talking. She'd be glad when this was over.

"Not yet."

"You've got to sort through them. There's one labeled '57a.' Give him all the rest, but keep that one. Don't let it go."

"Something special on it?"

"Yeah. It's the actual computer model for the plague germ. It's the key to making an antibiotic. It's worth millions. It's the reason I'm lying here. We can't let it go without copying it first. If everything goes well, we'll send them the copy. But right now, I'm just a little paranoid, if you know what I mean."

Paris smiled. "I know exactly what you mean." The smile faded. "I've got to ask you what happened out there before I showed up. You up for it?"

"No. But here goes. There were two of them. Only one came down into the cabin. He had a thing that looked like a portable phone. He not only wanted the disks, he wanted their entire history."

"Did you give it to him?"

"Hell, yes, I gave it to him. It's what I've been trying to give to anyone who would listen ever since I left San Diego. So what's it all mean, Detective?"

"It means that Uni isn't the only one interested in what you've got. It means there's someone right here in our fair city who's on your case. We recovered the device you saw on the boat. It was a transmitter with a link to some kind of exotic telecommunications system. The lab people traced its output to a geosynchronous satellite, but that's as far as they got. It gets international after that, but I'm sure the signal came right back down to somewhere here in Seattle."

"You know who it is, don't you?"

Paris looked down at the floor for a moment, then back up. "Yeah. I do. But there's no use talking about it right now. Don't worry. I'll handle it." He curled his big hand around hers and smiled. "You just get well."

"And you stay well." Elaine's eyes closed as she drifted off to sleep.

The two young men are smooth of face and hard of muscle, and the punishing rays of the summer sun hold no fear for them. The driver's long hair blows back over his sunburned ears, driven nearly horizontal by the speed of the big boat as it smacks the water of Andrews Bay on the western shore of Lake Washington. The boat has the look of a devil's snout, with all the hull lines converging into a nasty little point at the bow. In its Fiberglas belly, steel, oil, gas, and spark collide in a mechanical orgy that shoves the boat through the green water at unholy speeds. The young men like it this way. Both are draining their fourth beers and float on an alcoholic cushion generously inflated with marijuana.

The driver spots the geese first. An armada of big Canadian honkers, bobbing on the gentle waves off the shore of Seward Park. He jerks the wheel a quarter turn, putting the boat on a collision course with the birds.

The geese detect the threat coming from the north and go to a state of high alert. They are big birds, many over ten pounds, fat on the generous supply of grains found in the Seattle area. In an instant, they calculate the closing rate of the boat and realize they must act immediately to avoid being hit. In unison, they smash the air with their huge wings and flutter into a low-angle takeoff.

The young men look on with great approval. The passenger, Skip Sloan, goes below to get more beer.

The geese take their rage south and lumber off into the summer sky.

David Muldane taps his fingers in time to a tune on the radio as he drives along the short stretch of highway connecting Sea-Tac Airport to the main freeway north into downtown. In his ears, he can still hear the swell of excitation in Dr. Smali's voice as they conversed on the phone this morning. Clearly, John Smali was convinced; and now there was this outbreak in equatorial Africa to confirm the validity of the EpiSim technology. The timing was perfect. With a little luck, they'd contain the epidemic on that remote island, and the world would survive to see the enormous value of the forecast. And he had a part in it all. Not a big part, but an absolutely vital part. Paris had brought the disks to the office, and David immediately repacked them in a shipping container that would prevent environmental damage. Next, he zipped out a quick E-mail to Smali to let him know the shipment was on its way, then sped out to the airport, where he carried the container to the air-express carrier and booked it on the next flight to New York.

Now he hums along with the radio as he pulls onto the main freeway north into downtown. The music feels good. He feels good. He owes Paris a favor. When he gets to the office, he will spend some serious time on this serial poisoner thing.

The geese labor through the air on a course to the southwest. Their big wings have elevated them to an altitude of two hundred feet as they cross over Twenty-fourth Avenue, with the city rolling away beneath them. They are still twenty miles from American Lake, their final destination. Over twenty birds strong, the flock is arrayed in a classic V formation as it moves along at a steady and noble speed.

Skip Sloan comes up out of the cabin with two more beers as the big boat bashes its way south through the slightly choppy water of Andrews Bay. He is as high as the summer sky, with its scattered patches of cloud drifting under a lazy sun. He sways slightly as he hands a beer to the driver, then looks to the south, where a big jet is dipping down toward the horizon.

In the cockpit of the DC-10, the crew has been cleared to land on Runway 18 and has completed the landing checklist. The pilot hears a periodic buzz emanate from the instrument panel, accompanied by the synchronous flashing of a blue light. He has reached the outer marker, defined by a narrow radio beam of three degrees that shoots into the sky about five miles from the airport. He maneuvers the big plane into the center of the glide slope, an imaginary line that descends from their present position at fifteen hundred feet to the touchdown point on the runway. The engines are throttled back and the flaps extend to provide the low-speed lift required for landing. On this clear summer afternoon, the airport and the runway are already clearly visible out the front windshield.

The air-freight plane, an old Boeing 707, pulls out onto the taxiway with Elaine's disks secured in its belly. The crew runs down its checklist and receives instructions from ground control as they roll along toward the end of the main runway, where they will pour power to all four engines and embark on a nonstop flight to New York. It looks like a milk run, with good weather all the way.

In the approaching plane, the pilot hears the panel buzz again to inform him that he has reached the middle marker, twenty-five hundred feet from the tip of the runway. He checks the glide-slope needle and sees they are perfectly aligned for a textbook landing. By now the wheels are down and the flaps are fully extended, which means the slats on the front of the wing have also been extended by hydraulic arms that push them out into the wind blast. The slats serve a special function. An airplane wing generates lift by bending the air over its upper surface into an invisible suction cup that holds the wing—and the plane—up. The wing makes the best possible suction cup when it meets the air head-on. When the wing is tilted back, as it is during landing, the airflow becomes more turbulent and the suction power is diminished. Less lift makes for faster drops and harder landings. Enter the slats. When the wing is tilted up during landing, the slats channel air over its upper surface in a way that smoothes it out and the wings provide maximum lift during the critical touchdown period.

In the moment the pilot looks down at the glide-slope needle, he misses the birds. At 170 miles per hour, he couldn't have avoided them anyway, but at least he would have known the cause of a sudden shudder through the fuselage.

Outside, in the clear summer air, the left engine has just scooped up not one, but half a dozen Canadian geese, turning the compressor stage of the engine into a reluctant butcher shop. The big blades rip the birds into blood, fat, bone, and muscle, and, in the process, they themselves are destroyed. As they rip loose from the central shaft, they in turn destroy more compressor blades. The engine surges as the delicate pressure ratios between its various stages are permanently destroyed. Bits of blade are now tearing through the second compressor stage and making their way to the combustion chamber.

The pilot looks at the gauges that measure the engine pressure ratios and sees the needle for the number one engine oscillate crazily. As he reaches to feather the engine, he feels a sudden bump, and the shuddering stops.

As the broken blades of the first compressor section spew their wreckage throughout the engine, the compressor seizes up entirely. At the moment of seizure, the tremendous energy of its spinning motion is suddenly transferred to the engine as a whole. The result is an extremely violent twisting action that tugs mightily on the pylon, the structure that connects the engine to the wing. But the pylon and engine have been designed to part ways in just such an emergency. They are connected by fuse links, which now shear away and break the grip between the engine and the plane. As the engine departs, it bangs the underside of the outer wing surface and ruptures the hydraulics that keep the outer wing slat extended. The slat immediately collapses back into the wing.

The renegade engine now becomes an aircraft unto itself, an eight-thousand-pound cylinder hurtling forward under its own thrust provided by the surviving combustion and turbine sections. It screams along two hundred feet above the ground at 170 miles per hour and curves to the left as it loses altitude from a lack of aerodynamic lift. After traveling nearly a quarter of a mile, it hits the paved surface of the south taxiway, takes a crazy bounce, and smashes into the left wing of the air cargo plane.

The old 707 is fully fueled, so the wing erupts in a big

explosion that instantly blows the plane into several pieces, completely destroying the cargo hold. In a stroke of good fortune, the nose section is separated from the main portion of the fuselage and blown clear. The crew, badly shaken but not seriously hurt, crawl out through the sheared metal.

In the other plane, the pilot does everything he can. He pours power to the remaining engines while yelling at the crew to cut the fuel flow to number one engine. From his forward position in the cockpit, he cannot see back to the engine's location and figure out what has happened. All he knows is that some kind of catastrophic failure has occurred. As the first officer hits the fire-extinguisher control for the number one engine, the flight officer calls over the radio to announce a missed approach and a go-around. By now, they are two hundred feet up and two thousand feet down the runway, and the plane is pulling to the left even as the pilot tugs the controls desperately in the other direction.

It won't work. The outer slat on the left wing was permanently retracted by the damaged engine, which means the wing's lifting power is badly crippled, so it dips toward the ground as the superior lift of the undamaged right wing rolls the plane over. This rolling action automatically sends the plane into a banking turn.

Right toward the control tower in the center of the terminal.

The plane's giant left wing hits the base of the control tower and clips it as close as a shaved whisker. The energy of the collision instantly ignites the seven thousand pounds of aviation fuel in the left wing tanks. The truncated tower structure is blown into thousands of pieces that shower down over a radius of several hundred yards and start a rash of secondary fires. Fifty-two die here, including all those who control the approach and departure of aircraft from the floors directly beneath the glassed-in top of the tower. Steel, flesh, and silicon fly in every direction as the fireball expands.

The fuselage and right wing continue on. Relieved of the weight of the left wing, the plane rolls to the right and comes down into the multilevel parking structure behind the terminal. Several tons of fuel now explode into a rumpled balloon of black and orange that rolls like a mobile purgatory through the upper levels of the lot. Here, 785 people die, including all 312 on the plane.

From the boat, Skips sees the fireball erupt over the tree line, followed by a dense cloud of black smoke.

"Hey, man, look at that. Wow!"

The driver pays no attention and cranks the boat into a tight turn that nearly knocks Skip over. "You fucker!" yells Skip as he playfully hits the driver on the upper arm.

Behind them, the smoke climbs ever higher into the summer sky.

In the recreation area of the King County Jail, all eyes were riveted on the TV, which hung like a bloodshot and phosphorous eye because of its big metal harness mounted in the ceiling. The images alternated between real-time reports framed against the furious flashing of emergency lights in the deepening dusk, and earlier footage of the conflagration when it was still at full boil. Now and then, a computer-generated animation presented a speculative view of how the disaster might have unfolded, and several pieces of home video showed people running and screaming down corridors alive with smoke, flame, and fear.

Barney Cox sat in the back, and while he watched the TV, he listened to a tape though a portable cassette player connected to small earphones. The disaster at the airport was interesting, but not nearly as interesting as the contents of the tape, which had been smuggled in to him only an hour ago, after having traveled a convoluted path of wireless communications starting from the cabin of the *Cedar Queen*. He pressed rewind and listened once again.

What he heard was Elaine's voice as she explained what the true nature of Uni's lost "property" was. He found the account of the epidemic interesting, but the part about the antibiotic was truly fascinating. The pharmaceutical business was a mystery to him; however, the fundamental laws of supply and demand dictated that any drug of this sort would be worth a large fortune.

And right here in Seattle, out on that old wooden boat,

was the only recipe in existence to make such a drug. No wonder Uni was so anxious to get it back.

The tape ended with Paris's booming voice and gunfire. He was a clever man, thought Barney as he pushed the stop button, but also a stubborn and principled one. He should have played ball, should have kept his nose clean and stayed out of it. But people like Paris never did, and that's why they stayed little and never crawled any higher up the food chain.

Barney idly watched the horrible images on the TV and smiled. According to the Wilkes woman, this new germ wasn't going to show up for a while, so he had a little time. Good. He needed a hobby, and this bombastic detective and wayward doctor with her fantastic little prize would do nicely.

31

STEVEN HENRY STARES AT THE LITTLE GREEN PATCH OF CAR-pet between his feet. He knows it well. There is small triangle of silver gum wrapper with its telltale serrated edge. And three small crumbs, each maybe two millimeters in diameter and light brown. All have a porous texture, and the largest tends toward a potato shape. Together, they form the vertices of an invisible isosceles triangle of about two centimeters on a side. But his most subtle discovery is the little patch of stain, offset by just a ghost of a shade from the rest of the carpet, with a tiny hint of brown to it. It has an oval shape, with a wobbly circumference that suggests the benign violence of the original spilling action.

Steve knows these things because he has sat on his haunches for hours now. All in this same spot with his back against the wall in this major concourse of Kennedy Airport, which looks like a refugee camp. Every seat is taken with slumped, exhausted travelers lost in a disturbed and transient sleep. The aisles are filled with streams of humanity walking around on those curious and aimless missions that always seem to attend large-scale calamities.

On either side of Steve sit businessmen not unlike himself, warriors of the global economy dressed in suits and ties and fifty-dollar haircuts. They seem sullen and immersed in their bad fortune. It seems there had been a catastrophic plane crash in Seattle. They got the news not from the airlines, but from CNN in the airport bar. It showed a huge and prolonged belch of black smoke punctuated by sheets of flame erupting from buildings in the distance, and it spoke of massive damage to the main airport complex, including the tower and the air traffic control center. Nearby, Boeing Field was taking flights with no fuel to reroute, but all other flights were being vectored to other airports. Within hours, the ripple effect propagated this anomaly through the entire air transportation grid and brought the whole system close to gridlock. Kennedy was crammed with instant refugees.

But Steve feels no sympathy for them because this is a temporary turn for most. Not so for him. The first hint of trouble was over a week back in Lisbon, when he began his cheerful sparring match of mutual consent with Melody Linkford. She looked even better than he remembered and greeted him warmly at the first meeting, with her fingertips gliding softly over the back of his hand. For Steve, this single action erased weeks of steaming tropical airports, surly customs officials, and the bureaucratic stigma of "Mr. Enri." Her ruby smile unfolded into an implied promise that thrilled him and quite frankly scared him a little at the same time. She was single. He was in a state of geographical divorce. Let the games begin.

It took him a couple of days to engineer the proper naturalistic encounter, so it wouldn't have the appearance of a "date" about it. It seemed she was working on some contracts in the Middle East that might influence his business in Cape Town. Could they discuss it? He just didn't have the time until after six. Booked solid. Hey, what if they had a quick drink after work somewhere and ran it down from there? Shouldn't take too long.

He listened with great care to her reply and got the encrypted response he was looking for. If she wanted to shut him down and walk away, she would've said yes, but I've got to be somewhere else by seven-thirty. Instead, she said fine and left the entire field of encounter wide open.

He won the first skirmish handily at a little bar down along the Tejo River, where they had a couple of rum and Cokes and let the conversation stray from the business of business to the business of life. A chuckle and a laugh erupted here and there, and as her teeth flashed white in the dusky light, he felt a definite thrust to it all. Say, do you have dinner plans? No? Well, I've always heard about this little place called the Príncipe Real. Let's give it a try. Okay?

Of course it was okay. At dinner, she listened attentively, her chin resting comfortably on crossed fingers as he put on his best presentation. In the rest room between acts, he turned to the mirror while zipping up and surveyed his assets. The thick and curly hair, the aggressive jaw, the naughty eyes, the liberal sprinkling of smart-ass about the mouth. All deployed along a lazy erotic arc that terminated who knew where? Her apartment? His hotel? Didn't really matter.

Time to dance. They both knew it. Pretty soon, they're in the Bairro Alto, a little drunk, heading into a disco. Bear-size woofers and shrew-size tweeters batter the dance floor, and arpeggios of winking lights perforate the darkness and illuminate the dancers. They get the little table where lips and ears must come perilously close to breach the wall of sound. Perfect. He reaches over to grab her hand and head onto the dance floor. And as he does so, he has the thought, the bad thought, and feels the night slide away under his feet.

He knew the dance was for ritual effect and not anchored in his soul. The rhythm held no real sway over his belly or his loins. It was a means to an end and he accepted this. Because he knew it was really a dance within a dance, the larger and more intricate dance of seduction. And that he also accepted. But then he wondered if perhaps this dance of seduction was a dance inside a larger dance, one he could not grasp. And in turn, perhaps that dance was locked within yet another even larger dance and . . .

The notion disturbed him greatly. A great and invisible shutter clicked and froze the whole scene about him and discarded the resulting snapshot as utterly trivial.

And Melody Linkford instantly read the click of that terrible shutter as its ghostly shadow raced over his face. And Melody Linkford did not like what she saw. Her opponent had stumbled and lost his erotic footing during a crucial maneuver, which instantly disqualified him according to her innermost rule book.

They danced, of course. A solitary and mechanical dance. Back at the table, she put a crowning yawn on the evening and spoke of how much she had to do tomorrow. He knew it was lost, but kept up the sporting facade even as she climbed out of the taxi and headed up the stairs alone to her apartment. Then he slumped in the seat and felt very tired.

In fact, he even felt a little sick.

A small chest cold, a gentle, but persistent squeeze in his upper chest, a minor contraction of the bronchial tubes. As the taxi pulled up to his hotel, he convulsed into a string of three dry coughs, and that seemed to take care of it.

But now in JFK Airport, the cough is wet, and his lungs speak the liquid panic of drowning. Not too loudly, but enough to be a source of constant discomfort. A fever chill has broken out on his forehead as he stares at the fragment of gum wrapper on the carpet. He wishes he were home.

Then he coughs. A big, saturated spasm that stirs the liquid in his internal air passages and breaks loose the mucus and expels it through his mouth.

He raises his hand to block the cough, but halts it about an inch from his mouth. The violence of the cough has vaporized the sputum into tiny aerosol droplets that race around his fist and into the surrounding air. Hundreds of thousands of particles, most around ten micrometers in diameter.

Each droplet is largely water and has a large surface area compared to its interior volume. So all over this surface, the liquid molecules are lost to the surrounding atmosphere until the vapor pressure equals the surrounding atmospheric pressure. And once this barometric truce is reached, the droplets are only slightly heavier than the air they float in. In an absolutely still room, they would float to the ground at the stately rate of one-half inch per minute.

But the concourse at Kennedy is not still. It is alive with subtle currents and thermals that keep the droplets airborne until they are eventually removed through ventilation. And Steven Henry has coughed not just this once, but dozens of times over the past few hours. And now the collective output of these coughs is an enormous squadron of pathogenic droplets, many millions strong. Each carries a load of the new and improved *Chlamydia psittaci* that swim restlessly in these microscopic spheres.

And all it takes is one of them to start an infection.

PART
THREE

32

São Tomé

DR. DA COSTA STANDS AND GAZES OUT HIS OFFICE WINDOW in the hospital. On the street below, hundreds of people mill about in spite of the curfew, some standing, some walking, most sitting. If he looks straight down, he can see the entrance to the hospital and a squad of armed soldiers in surgical masks. He snorts at their presence, because they are guarding an empty promise. Nothing inside here offers the crowd any hope at all. No known antibiotic has even the slightest effect on what is now known locally as the bird bug.

Early on, the government flew in an exotic arsenal of drugs from Europe in the hopes that one of them would somehow hit the biochemical jackpot. All failed.

The hospital is quiet. All the ambulatory patients fled long ago to seek their individual fates in the town or the countryside. The bedridden ill were left without care as the staff fled in a panicked stampede when the bird bug's horrific rate of contagion became apparent. It was an awful sight to look into the ward and see the occasional populated bed and know that its occupant's fate was sealed by a disease that had nothing to do with the original ailment. One old nurse remained on duty, and Dr. da Costa made sure she was heavily armed with pain medication to keep these sad souls comfortable. Ironically, she hadn't come down with the plague, as if she had some kind of divine dispensation that let her care for all these poor people.

Dr. da Costa turns from the window and coughs. It is still the dry cough, but he knows it will eventually become the wet one. At first, it had disturbed and distracted him, but now it was more of a nuisance than anything else, a boring salute to his mortality. He had been a doctor long enough to know that what most people really fear is not death itself, but the physical process of dying. A simple thought experiment proved it. Suppose you lived in a world where death came in an instant, where you simply winked out. No sickness, no violence, no accidents. Just here, then gone. Would you fear it and dread it? Probably not. Because there would be nothing to sink your imaginary teeth into, no gruesome scenarios of physical decline, no descent into the very private world of the seriously sick, no painful alienation from the living.

The course of his own illness would be somewhat different. He simply didn't believe in needless suffering, not for his patients, and now, not for himself. The road out of town didn't have to be filled with potholes of agony. He had set aside a generous amount of powerful painkillers that he could self-administer to buffer his decline, and when he'd had enough, he would administer the terminal dose. The process of his death would be preordained and painless, and it was a process he could accept without fear.

He sits down at his desk and thinks back to the events of that first day of plague. After making the report to EDIN, he had left immediately for home and struggled in a constricting net of fear. Did he have it? It was definitely airborne, and the ten cases must have spread it all over the entire hospital. The building was old and didn't have sophisticated ventilation that would void things like this to the outside. He'd spent many hours inside and probably had maximum exposure.

By the time he got home, he'd temporarily put the issue aside over concern for his family. He could still see the shrill terror in his wife's eyes as he calmly explained that a highly contagious and fatal illness was afoot on the island, and that they must leave at once and not tell anybody why. Her anxiety only increased when he explained that he himself couldn't leave quite yet, but would follow later. The bug was wildly contagious and he had been severely exposed. If he was infected, then the longer he was in their proximity, the more likely they would get it, too. They would just have to wait and make sure he was clean.

As his wife packed a single bag for each of the children and herself, he wondered if maybe they weren't too late already. Rumors spread at a blinding rate, and the number of flights off the island was definitely limited. At the airport, he was relieved to find he could still get them on a flight to

Libreville that left in half an hour, and from there, on to Lisbon, to his sister's home.

And as they waited, he saw the parade of paranoia begin right before him. People he knew from the hospital began to appear at the ticket counter, most with their families in tow. Within ten minutes, the flight was sold-out. Those who remained avoided looking at each other, and da Costa knew why. They were already suffering from survivor's guilt. In a single stroke, they had become both the anointed and the damned.

He hugged his family as close to his heart as he could get them, put them on the plane, and left.

Back home, he looked out at the sea and the eastern horizon toward Africa. Would it spread to the continent? Almost certainly. With an incubation period of up to two weeks, it would probably spread to almost everywhere in the world. He ached for his family and wondered if he should have gone with them. Maybe it was hopeless for all of them, and if so, he could have spent a few more precious weeks with them before the end. But then again, maybe they had a fighting chance if the quarantine barriers went up fast enough in Europe. He oscillated slowly between these opposing views, and then madly, until he was mentally exhausted and a merciful wave of fatigue moved in and carried him off to sleep.

When he awoke, the sunlight was fading, and the barrier between sea and sky had merged into a neutral gray. He turned on the radio at news time to see if there was any mention of the disease on the island's three stations. Nothing. Either they hadn't officially recognized the problem, or they were withholding it from the public to avoid panic.

This would be the last day, he realized, the last day in the current biological epoch on São Tomé, the last day of relative normalcy. So he went for a walk into town on this fine tropical evening and drank in the people and the places with a burning thirst. He stopped at a little bar and sat at an outside table where he wouldn't be as infectious if indeed he had the disease. He watched the handsome young men and women flirt with each other and wondered who would live and who would die in the terrible days to come, the days of absolute justice in the court of nature, where caprice was the only law. Breathe here and live. Breathe there and die. Simple as that.

The next morning he was awakened by a cough. His very own cough, a dry one that ran a fine grade of abrasive over his air passages. He went from complete panic to absolute denial in a single burst of speculation, then tucked the symptoms under the covers and got up without them. A brisk walk on the beach was what he needed to recover. But during the walk he accepted it for what it was, a flight, an escape, a break for freedom that was already lost. On the way back to the house, the next little burst of coughs hit, and he felt the phantom grip on his lungs.

He spent the morning writing a long letter to his wife and drove into town to post it. It seemed strange that traffic and commerce still pulsed on, although there seemed to be fewer people on the streets than yesterday, but maybe that was his own anxiety at work. As he gave the letter to a postal clerk, there was even a mad and magic moment of complete denial: The business yesterday at the hospital was just a fluke, some kind of statistical anomaly; by evening, he would be making an embarrassed call to Lisbon summoning his family back. But then the clerk coughed, a perfect mirror of his own cough, and the truth came flooding back in. He looked at the clerk, a handsome woman in her thirties, and envied her ignorance.

Upon leaving the post office, he drove to the hospital and saw the embryo of the catastrophe taking shape and preparing for its full expression. The doors were locked and several dozen people waited outside. Most sat on the curb or the little stretch of lawn, and a few reclined on blankets with the clutch of fever already in their eyes. He went around to the back entrance and saw the soldiers for the first time. Two enlisted men reclined against a jeep, with their weapons sitting haphazardly on the seat. An officer was standing by the entrance and strode toward Dr. da Costa's car as soon as he stopped. After he showed them his official identification, the officer went to the jeep and made a call on the radio. Then he came back, gave da Costa a phone number to call, and let him into the hospital.

In his office, he phoned and got the Health Ministry and was promptly put through to the minister in charge. It seemed they had been looking for him all morning. After a moment, he was put on a speaker phone at the other end so he could fully explain the nature of the disease. Clearly, he was the only one on the island who had really characterized it. When he finished, many seconds of silence passed before conversation started again. It was eventually agreed that a twenty-two-hour curfew would let people out for long enough to buy essentials, but would reduce disease transmission to an absolute minimum. Dr. da Costa agreed to collect data at the hospital and operate under the protection of the military and maintain the connection with EDIN, the hospital's only real link to the outside medical world.

And now as he sits at his desk a week later, he prepares to go down the hall and make his daily report over the computer to the satellite. All day he has been in contact with the government and the various medical facilities in the island's interior, and he furiously scribbles notes to assemble an accurate picture of what is going on. The soldiers, wearing surgical masks, bring him meals and leave as quickly as possible, and he eats sparingly at odd intervals. Food no longer matters. The work that he accomplishes now will be the last and most important in his life.

As best he can tell, there are now about 20,000 cases on an island of around 140,000 people. The number is a crude estimate because every clinic is understaffed and overrun. Not a single sheet of X-ray film is left anywhere, and of the hundred or so doctors on the island, only a handful are still on the job. Some have fled, some are sick, a few have died, and the rest are simply unaccounted for.

More importantly, the number of cases is still accelerating. The lines on his hand-drawn graph of susceptible, infected, recovered, and deceased gives a stark depiction of what is happening. The infected line ascends at a steep angle, and so does the deceased line. The susceptible line is plummeting, and the recovered line remains pitifully small. This graphic picture is now clear enough to profile what will eventually happen to the island's population as a whole, and it is a nightmare of the worst sort. A very high percentage of the population will contract the disease, maybe even 80 percent. Of those who get it, perhaps 75 percent will die of it. Less than one in four will recover. Up to 60 percent of São Tomé will be dead, and dead within a few months.

And just today, he learned that the island is now alone in its agony. Every country on the African coast now has a good idea of what is going on, and all flights to and from São Tomé have been permanently canceled, and the ferry from Libreville as well. He was surprised it hadn't happened sooner, but the island was truly a remote place, and it took a while for national bureaucracies to react to anything short of a military invasion. In any case, there would now be widespread panic as people realized they were sealed off, with no escape route. And right behind the panic would come anarchy. In a plague of this scope, those who kept order were no more immune than those who would violate it. Institutional survival would quickly give way to individual survival.

And at this very moment, Dr. da Costa learns how right he is. An explosion of gunfire blows in through his second-story window, followed by screams and shouting. By the time he gets to the window, he can see several bodies on the street, and the squad of soldiers covering their retreat as they back away and give the hospital to the crowd, which is already smashing in the glass entry doors.

The doctor accepts this act for what it is, a final desperate appeal to medical science to protect and cure them. He knows they will ransack the hospital looking for drugs and consume anything that remotely resembles an antibiotic. He removes his coat, so he won't be identified as a doctor and pressed into hopeless service by the walking dead. As he walks down the stairs, they stream up past him and he can hear the crash of cabinets pulled open and their contents spilled out for inspection.

He walks out the back entrance and decides to head home on foot. Behind him, he hears the crash of shattered glass followed by excited shouting. He doesn't look back. The hospital was one of the great positive icons in his life, and he doesn't want to witness its demise.

It's been many days since he ventured out, and he's not sure how safe it is to drive. As he walks down the deserted sidewalk of the empty central business district, he quickly finds there is no traffic at all, not even the military vehicles that are supposed to enforce the curfew. The silence is broken by the distant pop of small-arms fire coming from the northeast, in the direction of the docks. He turns in this direction and sees a curdled black column of smoke rising over the building tops.

Right then, he catches a hint of motion out of the corner of his eye, in the park across the street. A blurred and streetwise insinuation that moves from behind a bench to the base of a nearby statue. The figure moves again, to behind a trash can, and he can see the form of a child.

"Hey! Don't run! I won't hurt you."

A head pokes out from behind the can and watches him carefully as he crosses the street and enters the park.

"It's okay. I just want to talk." He stops ten meters short of the can. "You stay there. I'll stay here."

The child cautiously emerges from concealment, and he sees it's the small boy from the Paradiso, the epicenter of this biological explosion. Amazingly, he appears to be in good health.

"You remember me?" asks da Costa.

"I remember. In taxi. About parrot."

"Where are your parents?"

The boys shifts uncomfortably and tugs nervously on the plastic liner squirting out from the rim of the trash can.

"Are they sick?"

"Yeah, they sick."

"How sick?"

"Dead sick." The boy tears off a piece of plastic and concentrates on wrapping it around his index finger.

Da Costa walks up to the boy, who will not face him, and understands that the boy will burst into grief if the doctor shows compassion. And in this time of great exigency, they both understand that grief is a luxury far beyond reach. He kneels to the boy's height.

"Then you come with me." He touches the boy on the shoulder to point the direction and starts walking.

At first the boy lags back, but then moves up to his side. Da Costa recalls the awful image of the first patient, Mr. Silva, in his death agony and can only guess what kind of scene the boy has witnessed with his parents. He thinks ahead to how he can reconcile his plan of action with the

complication of the boy. At home, he had already prepared
a backpack, with drugs and food to last several weeks if
carefully rationed. He will don the pack and walk southwest
from the town, on the road to Trinidade. After that, he will
continue through the dense rain forest and up the slopes of
the great central volcano Pico Cão Grande, where the clouds
and mist will wrap about him in a gentle shroud to define
his last days. From the rim at the top of the peak, he will
be able to merge geographical and spiritual perspective and
find solace in this final unity.

Only once do they encounter a military patrol. They hear
the jeep long before it comes into view and have plenty of
time to duck off the street. By the time they reach his house,
he realizes that the best he can do for the boy is to donate
his home to the child's survival. As the boy cautiously ex-
plores each room, da Costa gives him instructions.

"Don't eat the food all at once. Eat only when you are
really hungry. Don't answer the door. Wait as long as you
can to go outside. The sickness will pass, but it will take a
very long time. The longer you wait, the better it will be
for you."

On the porch, he adjusts the backpack as the boy watches
with great curiosity.

"Where you go?" the boy asks.

"Up into the mountains. And after that, I may go much,
much higher."

"Into the sky?"

"Into the sky."

With that, da Costa leaves and looks back only once, at
the end of the block. The boy is still on the porch, watching
his departure. The child waves his small but resolute arm to
say good-bye. Da Costa returns the wave and turns to confront the deep, green slopes in the distance.

Martin N'Dong sits with his arms wrapped around his
knees and digs his toes into the warm beach sand. He has
a clear view of the empty marina piers a hundred meters
away. The only boat left is a beautiful white cabin cruiser,
maybe thirty-five feet in length, and at this very moment it
is being loaded with people. Far too many people. They wait
in a small line, most with a single bag, and are pulled aboard

one by one by a large man in a loud sport shirt and sunglasses. At the back of the line are five soldiers with automatic rifles pointed toward the pier entrance, where a desperate crowd mills. The gate to the entrance has been smashed to the ground, and several bodies are strewn about the first few yards of the pier.

A few moments earlier, Martin had watched the gate come crashing down, heard the shots, and seen the muzzle flashes as the soldiers informed the crowd that there would be no more room on the boat.

Martin can see that the craft is riding low in the water, with every deck surface covered with people. Important people, he speculates. People with the power and money to bully their way to the front of the survival line.

But not all such people got their way. About two hundred yards off the pier, another cabin cruiser burns furiously, sending a black column of smoke skyward. Martin had arrived too late to see the cause and asked a passerby what had happened. It seemed the boat didn't have enough room to get all the soldiers on board and tried to bolt for the open sea, but the soldiers opened fire and hit something critical and the boat exploded, a white and orange flower bloating into the blue.

The last of the soldiers leaps aboard the surviving cruiser, and its engines throb as it throws off a big white wake that washes over the pier as the boat heads out and turns toward the eastern horizon.

Just then, a helicopter flies over and hovers near the burning boat, like a noisy, curious metal insect. Its rotor blades disturb the smoke column and peel off eddies that corkscrew into the hazy sky. Then it darts off toward the center of town, leaving the hot, thick air crowded with clumps of rotor noise.

Martin rises and walks down the beach to watch the carnival of desperate construction as people with no shipbuilding skills rush to assemble the vessels that they hope will be their salvation. They are collected in little knots about their craft, the women sitting and fussing with the children as the men mill about and wait for more materials to come from town. They are building basic rafts out of any available flotation device: inner tubes, hot-water heaters, oil drums, logs, milk containers, and even inflated garbage bags lashed together with rope, cable, twine, garden hose, and knotted rags. The masts are fashioned from plastic pipe and wooden poles, and sails from polyethylene tarp and cotton bedsheets.

They are set in supreme focus as they work and ignore Martin as he drifts by. Eventually, he reaches a little knoll where he can recline and watch from a respectful distance. He sighs and pities their mortal agitation, but finds it hard to empathize.

Because just lately, his dry cough has turned damp.

The pilot is from the north country, from Montana, where it kisses the Canadian border. He spent his childhood and youth in the angular light of that latitude, where the sun is skewed to the south and casts every object into shadow. His visual memory is one of contrast, where light meets dark as the days grow into the rich fire of late afternoon.

But here in the South Atlantic, the tropical sun hangs from the zenith and gives no quarter, no shadow in the peak of the day. All is screaming bright on the ocean below, and the diamond dazzle off the waves seems preternaturally bright, even through the dark filter of his visor. On impulse, he raises the visor and lets the light sear his optic nerve for a moment. There is no mercy here. That's what bothers him. No contrast, no compromise. No appeal to the pleasing interplay of shadow and light.

He nudges the stick and turns the chopper due south. His orders call for him to fly this final leg for twenty minutes at three thousand feet, then turn northwest for the trip back to the frigate, the big metal mother that beckons him home. His craft is a small helicopter in the shape of a distorted teardrop, with only two seats and light armament. It is built to wait and watch, to be the eyes of the fleet, to hover on the horizon and bear witness to the movements of the enemy. For this reason, its Plexiglas bubble covers the pilot's entire field of view.

The rotor and engine nose are masked by his earphones, where he hears the chatter on the net. A cipher chip in his radio, 2 million gates strong, turns all this talk from enigma to English and does the reverse when he calls out. All kinds of aircraft are out today, each vectored to a particular area, all with the same cryptic orders: Report what you see, but under no circumstances take an action, except in self-defense.

The pilot is puzzled by the brevity of these orders. In normal times, they are given at least some background to put their mission into context. We're at war, we're in a police action, we suspect terrorism. But not this time. His carrier, after leaving the Mediterranean, suddenly turned south and went to maximum cruise speed. They were supposed to be returning home, so something was definitely wrong in the world. But what? They were now off equatorial Africa, which was a political mess but never a strategic flash point, so why all the fuss?

The pilot checked his navigational display, where the hyper-illuminated pixels fought off the ambient tropical light and gave his position in latitude and longitude, and also on a map. He was close to zero degrees latitude, ranging through the ocean between the island of São Tomé and the country of Gabon on the African coast. So far, he had seen nothing but the cruel and unforgiving southern light.

Ah, but there was something. A white curve on the water dead ahead, maybe five miles. The heft of the hook-shaped pattern told the pilot that the sea was being chewed foamy white by engines under full power, and the severity of the hook indicated a sudden change in course.

"Bluebird, this is Recon Five, over," he said into his throat mike.

"Bluebird," came the terse acknowledgment.

"I have a wake approximately five miles ahead. Just made a course change from one hundred degrees to two hundred forty degrees southwest. Proceeding to investigate." The wake was now straightened out on its new course, which gave the pilot a valuable clue. He traced an imaginary line along the course and extended it out over the open sea, and sure enough, a second, much weaker wake intersected the line.

"Bluebird, this is Recon Five."

"Bluebird."

"I have a second wake with heading of two hundred seventy degrees. First wake is on interception course with it."

"Recon Five," came the voice from the command center in the carrier, "roll video now."

"Roger that." The pilot flipped a switch and a second display came to life, showing the view from the Hi-8 video-cam mounted in the small turret in the chopper's belly. He moved his hand to a joystick next to his seat and jockeyed the camera until the horizon appeared, then oriented the image. He fingered the joystick directly to the left, and the image swept along the horizon until the wake appeared.

The pilot could now make out the ship at the head of the first wake, the one running the interception course. He moved the chopper around until it was aligned with the wake and approached the ship directly from the rear. Then he checked and rechecked his warning system that indicated imminent hostile action from antiaircraft missiles. Nothing. Ahead, he made out the second craft also, a much smaller boat running at a slower but constant speed, still heading due west.

By now, he could make out enough features on the first boat to identify it. A French P 400 Fast Attack patrol boat, probably from Gabon, which had several. Its long, slim hull ran 179 feet, and its two M7 diesels put out eight thousand horsepower to twin props that slammed the boat through the water at up to twenty-four knots. On the forecastle the pilot could see the enclosed turret of the Bofors 57mm gun, and on the rear deck he saw the exposed outline of the twin barrels of the Oerlikon 20mm cannon. He radioed his identification to the carrier, then toggled the video camera to get a good view and settled in about a hundred yards off the patrol boat's stern.

Within a minute it had closed the distance within the second boat, a big white cabin cruiser, and the pilot was startled by what he saw as the patrol slowed to match the cabin cruiser's speed, and the two boats ran parallel through the water.

"Bluebird, I've got an ID on the second boat. Some kind of pleasure craft. About thirty-five feet. There's people all over it. Decks are crammed. Looks like Haiti or Cuba all over again."

"Recon Five, stand by and observe." The carrier voice

offered no explanation for what the pilot was seeing. Something was wrong here. Bad wrong.

The patrol boat was still running parallel to the cabin cruiser about fifty yards off its port side. On the patrol boat, he could see crewmen line the decks on the starboard side and a crew run to man the 20mm cannon. The people on the cabin cruiser were packed too tight to move.

The pilot looked for signs of a small launch boat being readied on the patrol craft, maybe an inflatable Zodiac with a pair of big outboards. The kind of thing you would expect during a search-and-seizure operation. But he saw nothing of the kind.

What he did see would never leave him. The crew on the 20mm cannon swung their mount around to face the cabin cruiser and commenced with fifteen seconds of explosive butchery. In that awful interval, they traversed their fire from the stern to the bow. The barrels pulsated with recoil and flashed brilliant orange, and an angelic cloud of blue smoke formed around the gun mount as over two hundred shells tore into the cabin cruiser's hull halfway between the deck and the waterline.

"Bluebird! Recon Five. I have a shooting situation. Patrol boat just opened fire on pleasure craft." The pilot tried to keep his voice even and steady, but his pitch was on the rise toward the cracking point.

"Recon Five," came the clinical voice from the carrier, "stand by and observe."

The first shells ripped into the fuel tanks and the engine in the stern and set off an explosion that devoured the rear of the boat in a convulsion of flame and smoke. Bodies flew off like the dolls of children and landed limp in the water. The knot of humanity on the front deck had just enough notice to swarm in confusion, with many falling off into the sea as the train of shells marched in their direction.

Just then, the pilot noticed an odd sight on the surface of the sea several hundred yards beyond the mortally wounded pleasure craft. A series of small, white geysers was growing out of the water, a little picket fence of erupting spray. And then he realized what it was. The shells were ripping all the way through the boat and continuing on their trajectory until they collided with the water and built this strange, ephemeral monument to the slaughter in the foreground.

By the time the train of shells arrived at the bow, the boat was already sinking by the stern, and the pilot could see the remaining victims clamber up toward the superstructure of the bridge, the last point of safety. But within seconds, the flames roared over the bridge and forced them to jump into the ocean, now ablaze from fuel flowing out of the ruptured gas tanks.

The minute the last shell was fired, the patrol boat moved off at full speed, and its wake set the entire conflagration of boat and bodies into a horrible bobbing motion, a last rocking in the cradle of death.

As the pilot approached the cabin cruiser, its bow was pointing high into the sky in a final salute as it slid into the sea. In no time, the boat was gone, but the burning gasoline roared on. From this central torch radiated a mass of bodies, some floating lifeless, others engaged in a terminal struggle with the sea. None had life jackets.

For a moment, the pilot forgot about Bluebird, forgot about the orders, and pressed in close. He had one empty seat beside him. Room for one person. And there she was, a woman treading water, her dress billowing out around her like a huge jellyfish. She saw him coming down toward her and raised an arm in supplication. His mind raced. The sea was calm. He could put the runners right down at water level so she could clamber up and get in.

"Bluebird, Recon Five. Pleasure boat is sunk and patrol departed the area. Survivors in the water. I've got room for one. Going in."

"Recon Five, stand off immediately. Do not pick up survivors. Return to base."

The pilot could not comprehend. "Bluebird, say again?"

"Recon Five, do not pick up survivors. Return to base immediately."

"Bluebird, cannot read you. Out," said the pilot in a timeless maneuver to gain control of the situation. He was from Montana. You did not let innocent people die when they could be saved.

"Recon Five, this is the mission commander," came a new voice from the fleet's carrier. "We have standing orders to cover this situation for the duration of this mission. If you return to base with a survivor aboard, your ship will be intercepted and terminated. Do read me?"

The pilot was down to within fifty feet of the woman. Even at this distance, he could see the pain in her face. "Roger, Bluebird. Returning to base."

As he pulled the chopper up and the woman receded, he thought of how cruel the light was, then he knew why. In places with shadows, there is always the possibility of concealment, of survival. But here, there were no shadows, and that left no hope of escape, no chance of life redeemed.

33

THE YOUNG DOCTOR REALLY WISHED SMALI HAD MADE IT. This was supposed to be a joint presentation of the NIH and Centers for Disease Control, but now he was doing it alone. It seemed there was a problem in New York. The material Dr. Smali had been waiting for, something about a computer-generated forecast of psittacosis, had not been delivered, and Smali had canceled his flight to try to trace it.

The doctor couldn't imagine what was so important about this material that Smali had blown an appearance before the National Security Council here at the White House. But right now, it didn't matter. He was on his own, with a presentation assembled only a few hours ago. The CDC would have sent someone more senior, but he was the resident specialist on *Chlamydia psittaci,* which had never been considered a particularly glamorous pathogen when compared to the exotic viruses pursued by many of his superiors. But now this strange little microbe was suddenly the center of global attention, which in turn made him the center of attention at this meeting with the NSC. As he displayed his slides and answered questions, he shifted his balance continually from one foot to the other and kept his hands firmly clasped behind his back.

The president was absent, but the council and several staff members were in attendance, even though the meeting had been called on extremely short notice. An emergency directive had sent out a fleet of helicopters and other military planes to collect the members from wherever they might be. The directive had originally been formulated to cope with a nuclear conflict, thought the assistant to the president. But maybe this was worse.

The crisis in São Tomé had caught the NSC and its staff woefully unprepared. Its members had great depth in the application of political and military force, both strategic and tactical. But when it came to biology, they were struggling up from far down the learning curve, which had a very slippery surface for those moving from the mechanical to biological disciplines. Now they all sat around the polished conference table and stared at the final slide of the doctor's presentation, a photograph taken through a microscope that displayed the cross section of a cell infected by *Chlamydia*. It showed a cluster of circles residing close to the cell membrane. Some were splotched and grainy, while others had a solid nucleus or were nearly filled with a dark material. Each was an individual microbe. The NSC members now knew that the circles represented the bug in different stages of its life cycle within the host cell.

"So how many forms of this stuff are there?" asked the vice president.

"Basically, there are two," answered the doctor. "One causes a form of venereal disease, and the other causes pneumonia. What we think we are seeing is a new strain of the pneumonic form, which we share with the bird world. In addition, there are at least five more forms that we see only in psittacine birds."

" 'Psittacine'?" the secretary of defense asked.

"That includes quite a few common species," answered the doctor. "Parrots, parakeets, pigeons, chickens, ducks, and seagulls, just to name a few."

"You mean all these different bird species could carry this new bug around?" the vice president asked.

"Well, obviously we don't have any experimental proof. But it's probably quite likely given this microbe's past behavior."

"So let me get this straight," said the secretary of defense. "A human being could bring this stuff into the country, and if they got near any of these bird types, the birds could get it."

"Once again, we don't have proof yet, but I think it's a pretty safe assumption."

"And then," continued the secretary, "these birds could fly all over the place and give it back to humans?"

"Absolutely. Both the bird-to-human and human-to-human routes have already been verified on São Tomé."

"Jesus!" exclaimed someone.

"How do people get it from the birds?" asked the secretary of state.

"The birds expel contaminated mucus in a form of sneeze that sprays aerosol droplets in the air. Humans breathe in the droplets. Human-to-human contact occurs the same way. Another way is through dried bird dung. The bug gets into the bird's bowels and feces, which is defecated and then dries up over time. Eventually, it disintegrates into dust particles that become airborne. In their elementary body phase, the *Chlamydia* are able to survive inside these particles for extended periods of time. Once again, humans breathe in the particles, and the *Chlamydia* immediately find an optimum growth environment in the lung tissue."

"That explains how people get it," said the assistant to the president. "But it doesn't explain why it kills them. According to your presentation, even the most nasty strains only killed thirty percent of those untreated—at least up until now. What's made this get so vicious?"

"I'm afraid I can't give you a good answer to that," sighed the doctor. "The different levels of virulence in microbes is still pretty much a mystery. In viruses, even a slight change in the genetic structure can turn a pest into a killer. These slight differences set off very complex molecular chain reactions that aren't well understood."

"In this case, is there any visible difference between the way this new killer bug acts compared to its predecessors?" asked the assistant to the president. He knew that the CDC had an actual sample of the bug from São Tomé. It was obtained from the WHO headquarters in Zurich, where it was collected from a blood sample that was sent there from

São Tomé very early in the epidemic. Serological assays had verified that the infectious agent was indeed *Chlamydia,* but of a strain previously undiscovered. The sample was placed inside a series of containers, the outer one armored against explosions, then moved under heavy guard to the airport, where it was placed aboard a supersonic military aircraft and flown to Atlanta, where it was sent under armed escort by the Secret Service to the CDC.

"Yes, there are some visible differences. In our p4 lab, we've cultured the bug in living tissue and observed its life cycle. It hasn't been easy. *Chlamydia* are right at the limits of visibility with optical microscopes, but now we've got a pretty good picture of what happens."

The doctor pointed to the slide that was still projected behind him. "First, you've got to remember what happens with normal *Chlamydia.* About twelve hours after it enters the cell, the bug grows big enough to begin dividing into what are called elementary bodies. After about thirty hours, this process is complete. And after about forty-eight hours, these infants have grown into adult *Chlamydia,* which burst out of the cell and look for a new host. So the whole business takes about two days. But the new strain is different. Things start off more slowly, but then get much worse. The creation of the elementary bodies is very slow at first and continues that way for several days. Then all of a sudden, there is a population explosion so large that it literally destroys the cell by the time the new *Chlamydia* are mature and migrate."

"Does that explain the progress of the disease?" asked the assistant to the president.

"At any rate, it's consistent with it. The subject comes down with what appears to be a mild chest cold, but once the growth of the bug reaches a certain threshold, it accelerates rapidly. It looks like this first phase lasts about two weeks before the patient gets seriously ill, maybe as high as three weeks."

"Is this good news or bad news?" asked a staff member.

"Very bad news." The doctor was becoming more self-possessed as he realized these people were no more formidable than a high-school biology class when it came to communicable diseases.

"How come?"

"Because each infected person can transmit the bug during most of this incubation period. This means the longer the incubation, the more widespread the distribution of the disease. The number of people infected goes up exponentially. Let's suppose the incubation period is, indeed, three weeks, and that we start the chain of infection with a single person. If this person infects one other person every three days, and if these people do the same to others, there would be sixty-four people infected by the time the first person came down with the serious symptoms and we knew something was wrong. Not too bad. But what if each person infects another person every two days? The total goes up to one thousand infected in the three weeks. And what if each person infects another every single day for three weeks? With an airborne, pneumonic disease, this is certainly possible, especially in urban areas. Past history has shown that the rate of infection goes up in direct proportion to the density of population. In this case, the total number of infected goes up to over a million."

The room lapsed into silence. The doctor, who had been rocking nervously on his feet, froze in place.

"So," said the assistant to the president, "if we add up the antibiotic resistance, the bird problem, the incubation period, and God knows what else, this thing could be everywhere before we can stop it. Is that correct?"

The doctor gave a pensive stare at the slide with the microbes, sighed, and turned back to the director. "I'd like to say no. But I can't. Sorry."

The assistant to the president rose from his chair. "Doctor, thank you. We've got a plane on standby to get you back to Atlanta. We're arranging a teleconference link with this office and your facility at CDC. We'll be back in touch as soon as it's arranged."

As the doctor departed and the doors closed behind him, the assistant to the president sat down and looked out from his vantage point at the end of the long table. "Now, let's try to sort this thing out. First, let me summarize the earlier briefing from the Navy. It appears we now have enough force in the area to enact a quarantine. You've seen some of the video from the recon aircraft, and it appears that every coastal country from Nigeria to Zaire has enacted a de facto quarantine. They're simply blowing the refugee crafts out of the water." He sighed. "It's a nasty business, a very nasty business. And I don't think we want to be part of it."

"Besides," spoke up one of the staff members, "it's too late. If the CDC people are right, the thing's already spread far and wide. We'd be beating a dead horse, if you'll pardon the phrase." No one laughed.

A naval officer interrupted the meeting and handed a report to the assistant to the president. Everyone watched expectantly as he read it, then looked at the member who had just been speaking. "The dead part of your metaphor is pretty accurate. Navy intelligence has been doing flyovers of the island to assess the situation. It's pretty horrible. Based on what they've observed and combining it with some basics of epidemiology, they've come up with some numbers. It looks like about a fifth of the population is already dead. That's about twenty thousand people. More than half are sick. The place is dying. Literally dying. All at once."

"How can they estimate that?" someone asked.

"Bodies," said the director of the CIA. "Most communities in Africa have a death rate of about two point three percent during normal times. So that's what their infrastructure is set up to handle in terms of processing the dead. Double or triple that rate, you still could handle the problem in an emergency mode and bury everybody. But not when it goes up to over twenty-five percent. Especially when most of the survivors are getting sick. You start to wind up with bodies lying around. Unattended. And that's what they're seeing from the air."

"So where does that leave us?" asked the chairman of the Joint Chiefs of Staff. "Do we seal off our own borders? Do we halt international air traffic into the country? If we do, people are really going to scream."

"How's that?" asked someone else. "It would clearly be in the interest of public safety. Who could argue with that?"

"You're forgetting that at any given time, there are hundreds of thousands of U.S. citizens traveling abroad," said the secretary of state. "We'd be sealing them off from home.

And people don't understand yet how bad this thing might really be."

"That's yet another problem," commented the assistant to the president. "We're eventually going to have a real wave of public panic. So far, this business has been pretty well contained. It's all on a very remote island in a remote part of the world. And the other countries in the region aren't anxious to talk about what they're doing. But all that's going to change, whether we like it or not. Our sources inside CNN tell us that they've got a lead from someone in Libreville. It'll be on the air as early as tomorrow."

"But even then, it's going to take a little time for them to figure out the real dimensions of the thing," said vice president. "We don't have any reported cases anywhere else yet."

"I'm afraid we do," said the assistant to the president. Everyone froze, turned to face him, and asked the same silent question: Is it here?

"Just before this meeting, I received a report that's current as of yesterday. It's beginning to pop up around the world. But not here. Not yet."

"How did we get this information?" someone asked.

"Through the World Health Organization. It turns out they have an early-warning network for diseases that operates all across the globe, and they're getting reports from every continent. They were going to have a representative at this meeting, but he's pursuing some new lead and couldn't make it."

"We've got to try to seal it off. It's our only chance. We've got to assume that when the public finds out the dimensions of this thing, we'll get the support we need."

"So what do we do?"

"We seal off the borders. Simple as that. Suspend international air travel. Mobilize the military and patrol the Canadian and Mexican borders from one end to the other. Like I said, we'll deal with the political repercussions later."

"What about cases in this country?"

"We try to weed them out while we still can and isolate them until we're sure they haven't got it."

"And how do we do the weeding?"

"The airlines. We go into their databases. Find everybody

that's incoming from connections to Africa over the past three weeks. We can cross-reference this with data from Customs that logs every overseas entry into the country. We run down everybody on the list and quarantine them."

"Quarantine? Can we do that? Legally?"

"We'll find a way. As a last resort, we can declare martial law."

"It's going to take a lot of people to pull this off."

"No doubt about it. But if we don't, there's going to be a lot of dead people."

"All right," the assistant to the president intervened. "We've got to move fast. Does anyone have a better suggestion?" The room was silent. "Okay, then, let's get the staff on it right now. I want to put this in front of the president by tonight."

As the room cleared, he thought about the president and what they would have to do. A contingency plan covered the emergency evacuation of the first family in the event of imminent nuclear war. Now another type of strategic threat was upon them, a new kind of missile, just a quarter of a micrometer across, but maybe even more devastating.

It was time to get the president out of harm's way.

34

"AND FROM THE ISLAND OF SÃO TOMÉ OFF THE WEST COAST of Africa comes a mysterious development that has government and health officials both puzzled and concerned," said the CNN anchorman, his eyes filled with the vacuous look created by staring into a TelePrompTer. The chroma key square over his shoulder featured a graphic with a hypodermic syringe and the word EPIDEMIC? displayed in condensed capitals. "Phone service with the island has been out for the better part of a week, but prior to that, there were numerous outgoing calls that reported widespread sickness and death among the island's population of one hundred and fifty thousand. In Washington, Pentagon officials will neither confirm nor deny that U.S. naval vessels are converging on the area, possibly for some kind of mercy mission. We have two stories tonight, the first from New York. Robert Ocher is standing by."

Robert Ocher stood in front of a walk-up apartment north of Central Park. "Tom, behind me is the home of Mira Sanchez, a former native of São Tomé who now works for the U.N. She refused to be interviewed live, but we did get the following segment on tape just an hour ago."

Mira sits on a couch of faded bronze corduroy with a framed print of the Blessed Virgin hanging solo on the wall behind her. She is of African descent and wears a sleeveless pullover cotton dress. Her English is broken, and the presence of the camera crew chops it even further. "I talk to my son. Week ago, maybe. He say many people sick. Many, many people. He say some people dead. Many dead. No medicine. No help from medicine."

"Did he say what the sickness was like?" asks Ocher from off-camera.

"He say people get a cold. Then it get worse. Fill up their lungs. Then they get real sick."

"Could he tell you what the government was doing about it?"

"He say government sick, too. No help. Then, pretty soon, no phone."

"Have you talked to others with friends or relatives still on the island?"

"They say same. People get sick. Then no phone."

With the interview complete, Robert Ocher wrapped it up in front of the apartment. "Tom, obviously people are concerned for their loved ones left behind on this tiny island in the South Atlantic. But for now, all Mrs. Sanchez can do is hope and wait."

"Thanks, Bob," said the anchorman as the graphic changed to a map of western Africa and São Tomé. "We take you now to Anne Simpson in Libreville, the capital of Gabon, which is São Tomé's nearest neighbor on the African continent. Anne, can you hear me?"

Anne Simpson is conferring urgently with one of her crew when the camera opens on them. They have been watching some kind of footage on a small video monitor set atop an upended metal trunk. At the sound of the anchor, she turns and faces the camera with a startled look. It is night, and the residual glare of the TV lights reveals they are on the tarmac of an airport. Jeeps and army trucks race by in the background, and occasional yelling can be heard as orders are barked out in a foreign language.

"Tom, we came here to get one story, and now we're getting quite another," Anne says with an almost frantic edge to her voice. "We're at the Libreville airport, which, like the rest of the capital, is now under martial law. We came in this morning to inquire about the report of an epidemic off the coast on São Tomé. Apparently, whatever happened out there is now starting to happen here as well. With the emergency in effect, we're confined to the airport, but we've got unconfirmed reports of several thousand people sick here in the capital. There are all kinds of wild rumors about a plague. Government officials refuse to comment, and our only contact now is with the military."

Gunshots. Small-arms fire puts a series of sharp creases in the night. The camera lurches wildly, and someone screams, "Get down!" The staccato pop of a .30-caliber machine gun chatters away in the distance. The camera settles and shows nothing but streetlamps and building lights. "Okay," comes Anne's voice, "over here." The camera pans and her grainy image appears, illuminated only by residual light from somewhere nearby. She crouches behind their small fortress of equipment trunks.

"Anne? Anne?" comes the startled voice of the anchor. "Anne, can you still hear me?"

She cannot. She peers cautiously over the trunks then says to someone off-camera, "Are we still live?" They hand her a headphone, which she slips on and then faces the camera. "Tom? Are we still on?"

"We're still with you. What's the situation there?"

"As you just saw, the situation here is deteriorating rapidly. People are trying to get out of the capital any way they can, and the airport is literally under siege. We've been watching the runway, and in the last hour, all incoming air traffic has come to a halt. Only a few planes are leaving. It appears that what planes are left here are being commandeered to ferry out key people. Apparently, the chain of command is disintegrating and we're headed toward an armed free-for-all among military units, who now realize they're trapped here as their leaders flee."

"Is anybody guarding you?"

"No, we're pretty much on our own. Media censorship is no longer an issue here. We're going to show you a piece of tape that we got today from an unidentified source. We have no way to verify the information that came along with it. Apparently it was shot by a local TV news crew on São Tomé sometime last week and recorded when it was broadcast. That's all we know. Here it is."

A bright and sunny plaza with a park at its center. Two-story buildings all around in the distance. The camera zooms over the pavement and onto the lawn in the park, where a body lies, that of an African man dressed in a T-shirt and brown khaki shorts. A small bird perches on the left knee-cap, which is poorly defined because of the swelling. The flesh of the arms and legs appear inflated, as if a valve somewhere on the body had allowed a bicycle pump to be attached so that moderate pressure was applied under the surface of the skin. In reality, it is the reaction of internal chemicals to relentless baking under the tropical sun, causing them to release various gases and bloat the body into a dirigible of death. The camera pans left, and a pair of swollen feet peek out from behind a bench, the toes a series of little brown globes dwarfed by the distended foot flesh . . .

The camera follows a pitiful raft as two men push it out through the surf. On board are two women and a pile of children. The raft is constructed of inflated plastic garbage bags and rope webbing, and the mast is an old TV antenna covered by a bed sheet. As the wind catches the sheet, the two men leap on, which causes the webbing to submerge almost to the waterline. The raft bobs on the gentle waves and slowly begins to sink in the center as the hot air in the bags contracts from contact with the cold water. The mast topples, and the people clutch desperately at the bags as the craft begins to spontaneously disassemble . . .

The interior of a bar packed with people, mostly young men. The tables are littered with empty glasses and beer cans, and two women dance obscenely on the bar top while people reach over to help themselves to the taps. Behind the bar, the doors of the cooler cabinets are open and the shelves devoid of contents. One young man lurches in front of the camera, waves his can of beer with a grin, then hurls it straight at the lens. A yellow rope of liquid traces an exquisite curve along the can's trajectory then splatters to the floor. The man seems satisfied and moves on . . .

A fire burns furiously and consumes a large wooden building, maybe a warehouse. The white and yellow flames come screaming out from the underside of the roof and ascend in a flickering, skyward prayer. The smoke folds grays into blacks and boils the mixture into a violent upward spiral. No one is fighting the blaze, and in the foreground, three men hold up cans of beer in salute to the conflagration while a gang of children runs in and out of the frame.

The tape is over, and the TV image stutters and wobbles as the picture is switched back to Anne Simpson under siege. "That's it, Tom. Once again, to the best of our knowledge, it was shot on São Tomé several days ago. Exactly how long ago, we can't tell."

Shots ring out again and Anne crouches lower behind the trunks. "We've got to go now. This position is no longer safe. We'll check back when we can."

The anchorman looks stricken as the image returns to network headquarters. No TelePrompTer will help him now. "Well, uh, as you just saw, the situation in Libreville is chaotic at best, and the situation on São Tomé appears to be pretty grim. But let me emphasize that, as of right now, this problem seems to be confined to the west coast of equatorial Africa. As soon as we get more information, we'll be passing it along immediately. Stay tuned to our live coverage of the epidemic in Central Africa."

In the chroma key box beside the anchor, a new graphic has already been produced to reflect the changing circumstances. The question mark is removed from the title of EPIDEMIC and the syringe now has an outline of the continent of Africa behind it.

"Congratulations," said Paris to Elaine as they watched the TV in her room at the hospital. "You called it right. You're professionally vindicated."

Elaine nodded from her bed. She was still weak, and also a little woozy from the medication. If the bug on TV was the same one she had characterized in the simulation, they wouldn't be able to contain it. It had a long incubation period, maybe as high as a couple of weeks. That meant it had already spread far and wide, but just hadn't manifested itself yet. Obviously, it had already gotten off the island and onto the mainland, which meant it had probably hopped aboard the international air routes and gotten to every continent by now.

"I should talk to Muldane," said Paris. "Maybe he's heard from Dr. Smali at the NIH. Could be that they're tracking the pattern of the real thing against your forecast."

"Doesn't matter much now," said Elaine quietly. Once the epidemic reached a certain scale, the outcome would be the same regardless of how it originated. Muldane had better start thinking about what to do right here in Seattle and not worry about what might be happening in Paris or Singapore.

The urgent voice of the anchorman interrupted her rumination:

"We're back with more on the epidemic in Central Africa. We've lost communications with Anne Simpson in Libreville, and it appears that the city is in a state of anarchy as people try to flee from a disease that has not yet been officially identified. The outbreak in Libreville comes on the heels of a similar outbreak on the remote island of São Tomé, where the situation seems very bad indeed. The illness appears to be some kind of pneumonia that goes on to leave the lungs and attack the entire body in the worst cases. The death toll on São Tomé is unknown, and communications there are shut down, and we have an unconfirmed report of naval action in the area involving both U.S. vessels and those of several Central African countries. More on that story as we get it."

"Incredible," said Elaine softly. "Even though I saw it coming, it's still unbelievable."

". . . And we're now getting unconfirmed reports of cases popping up in Western Europe, Asia, and across Africa, but none in the U.S. Now I want to emphasize that these reports are definitely not confirmed and could represent any number of different diseases. We're still waiting to find out exactly what . . ."

"So, once again, it looks like you're right," said Paris. "Got any more educated guesses?"

"None that you want to hear about. This is bad enough."

". . . And now we go live to the Pentagon, where a briefing from spokesperson Jill Perry is set to begin." Jill Perry walks quickly across the vertical ripple of blue curtain to the podium, clutching a single sheet of paper. "I have two announcements to make. One, U.S. vessels of the Sixth Fleet have been dispatched to the vicinity of the islands of São Tomé and Príncipe off the coast of Central Africa. This is in response to reports of a serious epidemic on São Tomé and quarantine procedures by neighboring countries which involve the destruction of refugee vessels in international waters. U.S. ships are involved only in a reconnaissance role and have not physically landed on either island. Any further action will require a mandate from the United Nations Security Council. Two, after consultation with the U.S. Public Health Service, an executive order has been issued to halt all international air traffic into and out of all U.S. territory. This order will be effective as of eleven o'clock this evening eastern daylight time. We want to emphasize that this is a purely precautionary measure and will remain in effect until the precise nature of the African epidemic is identified and appropriate action can be taken. We understand that the majority of European, Asian, and South American countries are taking similar action, so this should not be viewed as a unilateral response on the part of the United States. We will not be taking questions at this time; however, we will update you when more information becomes available. Thank you."

"Well, let's not panic," said Paris with a sarcastic grin as he turned from the TV to Elaine.

She managed a weak smile. Somehow, Paris made this horrible situation bearable. His grim mockery of the fear factor was right on target. The onset of the AIDS epidemic was a good example. It involved a virus that was extremely noncontagious and easily avoided by simple precautions. Nevertheless, it had launched a great wave of paranoia founded on ignorance. Now here was a bug that was not only incurable like AIDS, but also easy to get. It drifted through the air. Even birds carried it. It was the bug from hell. Just breathe the wrong air at the wrong time and you were an upright corpse.

"You know there might be a way we can still sidestep this thing," said Paris.

"What's that?"

"The airport. Sea-Tac's closed. We're out of the international circuit. Won't that help?"

Elaine paused to think. The simulation model had never allowed for an international airport to be completely shut down. It would definitely have an impact, but it was hard to predict exactly what it would be. Two statistical components were involved. One was the infection pattern produced by passengers whose flights terminated in Seattle. The other was the pattern generated by the large population of transitory passengers who were connecting to other flights, many from points overseas. This group would pass the germ to the local airport passengers and personnel, who would bring it into the city. The first group would get around the airport closure through bus and train connections, but at least that might slow the influx.

"It might," said Elaine. "And it might not. Nothing's absolute. It's all a matter of probabilities. It was always a matter of probabilities."

"What do you mean?"

"Our forecast gave a seventy percent chance the disease would strike within ten years. So Uni gambled they would have at least a couple of years to develop the antibiotic. They gambled wrong. The bug beat the odds, just like a long shot in a horse race."

"If they had your model of the germ, the one on the disk, could they still win?" Paris suddenly saw a way out of their predicament with Barney. If the contents of the disk were now worthless to Uni, Barney might quickly lose interest in him and Elaine.

"Not this time around. But they'll make millions when the next major burst occurs."

"The next major burst?"

"That's right. There's more to come." Elaine was too weary to explain it out loud. Big pandemics often came in waves, and when the first wave had done its business, those who recovered had gained a life-long immunity. Thus the disease had limited opportunities until a new generation of nonimmune people came along. But not in the case of Agent 57a. Like its predecessor, *Chlamydia psittaci*, it crawled inside the cells of the survivors and stayed there for a lifetime. In effect, its victims beat down the symptoms of the disease, but never lost the cause. Years later, the infection could flare up again. A permanent reservoir of disease was embedded in the population, which never acquired true immunity. In a relatively short time, the disease could erupt in a new surge of infection.

"So this next burst brings in millions, you say?" asked Paris.

"Millions."

Paris nodded. So they were still in a jam with Barney. A big jam. The value of their lives was inversely proportional to the value of Elaine's model for Agent 57a. And that made them very, very cheap.

"We've got a problem."

"No kidding," said Elaine with a weak smile.

"Let me ask you this: Who can really make use of your disk with the unique germ model?"

"That's easy. Only Uni can." The data that defined Agent 57a was encoded in a way that only their technology could decipher. To any other company or government, it was absolutely worthless.

"Do you want to give the data back to them?"

Elaine sighed. "Personally, no. But ethically, yes. They're the only ones that can make good use of it. Better them than nobody."

"Is time of the essence? Would we have to return it right away?"

"Not really." The damage was already done for this wave of the epidemic. And it was going to take at least a couple of years of intense development before Uni had a viable drug.

"Good. If we're going to give it back, we need to wait and pick our time."

"Why?"

"Because the person who is brokering this deal for Uni, the person who tried to have you killed, is going to be very enraged when he finds out we went around him. Even more than he already is. To make a long story short, he won't rest until we're both dead—however long that might take."

"Couldn't we just give it to him directly? That way Uni would get what they wanted and maybe he'd just forget about us."

Paris thought about it for a moment before answering. "Let me put it this way: Would you have entrusted a cure for cancer to Hitler?"

"Of course not."

"For now, I'll spare you the details, but that's what you'd be doing if you handed the data over to this particular individual."

"I see," said Elaine gloomily. "So where do we go from here?"

"Nowhere. We just play it as it goes and wait for the right break."

Dr. Robert Squire, director of the Seattle/King County Department of Public Health looked at the little red lights aligned vertically on the phone set in the conference room, the lights that indicated busy lines. They all glowed furiously and urgently, as they did on his own desk, and on every other desk in the entire city/county public safety building. After yesterday's TV coverage from Africa and Europe, the news networks blended into a blazing beacon of panic that radiated into every corner of the country. By this morning, hundreds of thousands of calls were converging on the city/county public health service, sending the phone system into electronic gridlock. Squire thought it ironic that the media traffic should be so intense at a time when auto traffic had diminished to a trickle. On the way in, rush hour had been nonexistent and downtown traffic looked about like Sunday morning.

People were scared, he thought, really scared. They were frozen in their footsteps, afraid to make the next move, afraid they might do something to compromise their safety. All this and there wasn't even a confirmed case reported anywhere in the United States. Not yet.

People began to file into the room. The county commissioners. The mayor. The city council. The Seattle chief of police and King County sheriff. In addition, the governor's chief of staff was present. They were on the mayor's turf, so he presided.

"Thanks, everybody," said the mayor diplomatically. "I know it's short notice, but we might have a big problem here in the very near future, and it's probably best if we plan for it right now. Dr. Squire's going to make a statement to the media in two hours, so we've got to have a message and a strategy to back it up."

All eyes turned to Squire, but no one spoke.

"Okay. Let's start with how serious this business really is," said the mayor. "As of this morning, there're still no reported cases in the U.S. But, Dr. Squire, you seem to assume that it's already here. Care to elaborate on that for us?"

"It's hard to believe it's been contained," said Dr. Squire. "It's already caused a catastrophic outbreak in one locality and moved quickly to another. This is exactly the kind of scenario we've worried about for the last ten years or more. Unless it has a very short incubation period, it's already spread to Europe, and that means it's probably here as well."

"So why isn't the WHO or the feds releasing more information?" asked a county commissioner. "They must have it isolated in a lab somewhere by now."

"They probably have. By now they've probably got a very good idea of what it is. But since they're not talking, I think we can assume it's not good news. It may be highly contagious. Or immune to antibiotics. If that's the case, you'll see mass migrations out of pockets of infection, just like that pneumonic plague outbreak in India a few years back. And the migrations will only help to spread the bug faster, which eliminates any hope of walling it off while we seek a cure."

"And how long might that take?" asked somebody.

"Even with the best technology and tons of capital, it could take years. However, we may get lucky and find something that's well down the R-and-D pipeline that already works on this particular pathogen. In that case, they could get something out pretty fast if they bypassed all the usual testing. But even then, mass production might take over a year, even with unlimited resources."

"What about the crash at Sea-Tac?" asked a commissioner. "That cuts us off from international air routes. Does that give us a chance to avoid infection?"

"I can't answer that. It depends on way too many factors. It might, but there's no way to tell."

"If the area around Sea-Tac turned out to be in good shape, what about the rest of the state?" asked the governor's chief of staff.

"Sea-Tac serves a good portion of western Washington. Everything from the Canadian border down to the Centralia/Chehalis area, and everything from the coast over to the Cascades. This entire area might have a fighting chance."

"Fighting chance," mused the chief of staff. "Funny you should put it that way."

"Regardless, we need to be prepared for the worst." Dr. Squire clicked a controller and put up a computer-generated slide. "This list is more or less common sense. Since we have an airborne disease, any close concentration of people represents an opportunity for the disease to be communicated. The first phase would be to close all the schools. We may want to do this anyway as a precautionary measure, since it can be done with minimum disruption to the city's infrastructure. In the second phase, we would close all office buildings and factories. Public office buildings would stay open with skeleton crews to provide essential services. In the third phase, all but key businesses like food distributors and retailers would close down. Surgical masks would be provided to people when they went food shopping, and then collected on their way out for incineration."

"Swell!" said a city councilman.

"At the same time as these general measures, the medical community would need to prepare isolation facilities to treat any cases that may have appeared. This will require some effort. Most hospitals currently have very limited space for isolation. Additionally, arrangements will have to be made for heavy security around all medical facilities."

"Why's that?"

"It's human nature," said the chief of police. "When they're driven by fear, people aren't going to be reasonable about medical attention. They aren't going to stand in line and patiently die while they're waiting for limited resources. There's going to be a huge black market for any kind of medical supplies that produce a cure or alleviate the symptoms."

Before anyone could respond, an aide to the mayor entered the room and spoke quietly to him. "Can you put it in here?" asked the mayor. The aide said yes and walked to the projection unit that Squire was using. "We've got a new development that bears directly on this meeting," proclaimed the mayor. "We're putting it on right now."

The aide manipulated the controls, and it projected a broadcast-TV picture from CBS. The dreaded "Special Report" graphic was just fading to reveal an anchorwoman and a picture of dozens of police cars around what appeared to be a hospital. "The U.S. Public Health Service has now confirmed the presence of the African plague in over a dozen U.S. cities. Officials refuse to release the number of cases involved, or the specific cities, but CBS has learned that New York, Los Angeles, Miami, Dallas, Denver, San Francisco, and Portland, Oregon, are among those with confirmed outbreaks. In all locations, officials are reported to be moving swiftly to contain the disease and prevent the kind of chaos now seen in urban centers in Europe, Africa, Asia, and South America. In many locations, panic has led to anarchy as cities empty out and looting and vandalism set in. In spite of intense pressure on the World Health Organization and the U.S. Centers for Disease Control, the precise cause of the disease still remains vague. Sources close to CBS report that a virus has been ruled out, and the search is concentrating on some new form of bacteria. Whatever the cause, it is now becoming apparent that antibiotics have little or no effect, and once the symptoms become severe, death occurs within a week or so. As more information becomes available, we will interrupt scheduled programming to keep you informed."

As the "Special Report" graphic replaced the anchorwoman, the aide flipped the projector back to Squire's presentation.

"As I was saying," Dr. Squire said to the stunned room, "I think we've got a bit of a problem."

The governor's chief of staff didn't hear Squire's remark. He was silently sorting through the possibilities. Even before this meeting started, he knew they had a big problem, and this last news report made it even bigger yet. He had unofficial contacts inside FEMA, the Federal Emergency Management people, and they'd told him what local governments and the public didn't yet know: the bug had been officially identified by the CDC and the World Health Organization. It was some funny kind of pneumonia spread by this extremely small bacteria that could infect birds as well as humans. It was remarkably virile, and so far, there wasn't a single drug that could touch it.

And now it was in Portland, Oregon, only a couple of hundred miles away and linked directly to Seattle by the I-5 freeway.

They were going to have to act fast, thought the chief of staff. They would have to call out the National Guard and seal off the freeway down around Chehalis, then close the Canadian border and block the mountain passes to the eastern part of the state. They would also have to seize Sea-Tac and make sure it stayed closed, but given the damage there, that wouldn't be much of a problem.

Would the feds react? Probably not. They were going to have plenty of other problems without military intervention in the state's internal affairs. And since the closing of Fort Lewis a few years back, there was no real federal military muscle within nearly nine hundred miles.

And of course they would have to arrange for a biologically fortified compound for key members of state government. People like himself. And his family.

Vincent put down the evening paper, with its monolithic headline proclaiming, "PLAGUE IN U.S." He had read all the reports, the sidebars, and the graphics. And in the process, he had begun to understand the message encrypted within them, a very special message, one densely coded and decipherable only by Vincent himself. After several hours, he finally understood the message in all its detail, and tears flowed down his cheeks and onto the newsprint, dissolving the ink and creating little black pools where there had once been words.

35

JOHN SMALI LOOKED AT HIS COMPUTER SCREEN AND KNEW that he was bearing witness to a very special kind of electronic Armageddon. Only a few hours had elapsed since the arrival of Agent 57a in the United States was announced, and already the nation's telecommunications system had been bent and broken by a catastrophic wave of overload.

When attempting to phone right after the announcement, he'd gotten the standard digitized message declaring that "all circuits are busy right now. Please try again later." But lately, even the dial tone had disappeared. The same was true of the Internet, which was, after all, totally dependent on the phone system to complete its linkage from one computer to another.

With no phone nor E-mail, Smali had given up on reaching Muldane at the public health offices in Seattle. Most unfortunate. He'd even canceled his trip to a National Security Council meeting in the hope he could run down the air shipment from Muldane that held the disks with their incredible prediction that was now playing out in real time over the world's media. He suspected it had something to do with the big air crash in Sea-Tac. However, the disaster had taken out the air carrier's data links to that airport, so it was impossible to trace what had happened to the shipment. It was also impossible to get through to Muldane's public health offices, which, like their counterparts everywhere, were an early casualty of the phone system collapse.

He looked out the window into the late afternoon. The big buildings of midtown Manhattan wrapped each other in enormous ribbons of shadow as the sun went orange in the western haze. The usual swarm of taxis was completely absent on the street below, exposing a blank, oil-stained ribbon of pavement stretching north. Not even the most enterprising driver was going to share the confined space of a cab with strangers from God knew where. Not anymore.

It was time to get the hell out of here. He knew that, but stayed on station anyway. His EDIN system finally had a concrete purpose. The daily download from his network's satellite had just delivered an enormous burst of data that profiled the spread of Agent 57a across the globe. He felt compelled to analyze it and relay the results to the world's major health organizations. It just might help, although he was no longer sure how. The germ was firmly embedded within the populace at thousands of points around the world, like a weed with a vigorous root system that defied a clean and simple extraction.

Now that he'd lost contact with Muldane, he could only wonder if the details of the outbreak matched those of the simulation from the Webster Foundation. The truth was, it no longer mattered. The real thing was here and loose among the people of the earth, and that was all that counted from now on.

He silently wished Muldane and company the best of luck and got back to work.

36

WHAT'S WRONG WITH ME?

The tubes weave about Steven Henry like a disturbed polyethylene vine and carry a variety of chemicals in their liquid mediums. But the chemicals are losing, and Steven knows it, all the way down to his marrow. He is trapped in a furnace of his own making, an act of heated desperation by his failing immune system to literally burn the offending bug out of his body. The fever has pushed little beads of sweat out of his forehead and scorched his mind into incendiary fragments that refuse to reassemble into a comprehensible whole.

The people behind the glass stare at him in his bed. Some

are dressed in white coats, some in suits. Two are in police uniforms. They talk among themselves and then throw sidelong glances his way. But Steven feels no embarrassment because they are both dim and distant. The color is bleeding out of his vision as he sinks into an eternal twilight with its own strange flavor of peace. There is no panic in him, because the machinery required to produce panic, the quickening of the heart and the contraction of muscles, is no longer operating.

His breath comes in stingy little gasps that are nearly pointless. Oxygen tubes feed his nostrils, but no respirator tube is crammed into his windpipe because he barely has any lungs left to respire. They are just twin lakes of fluid, a product of the cataclysmic struggle for control of his alveoli, a struggle that is now nearly over. The bug has won, and for a short time, it will revel in this self-made paradise that was once owned and operated exclusively by Steven Henry. And now the bug also dances in his nervous system, a savage little jig that plays up and down his limbs, sending them into an involuntary tremor.

What's wrong with me?

He remembers some mention of "pneumonia" when they wheeled him into this place over a week ago, this white prison of tubing and leering instruments. He tried to find out more, but no more came. Only the scant reassurance that they would "start treatment immediately."

The isolation suits were the giveaway, of course. No one entered the room without one. Suits of plastic and rubber that crunched and rattled in the solitude of this place, with face masks that obscured the mouth and revealed only the worried eyes.

Earlier two men in such suits had entered and tried to coax him through his entire trip from Africa to Portugal to here. They were from the U.S. Public Health Service, and they told him that he might have contracted a "new kind of pneumonia" and that anything he could remember might be very helpful.

Helpful? Helpful to who? To me? Don't think so.

He recalls the plane trip from Kennedy best, a nightmare odyssey through the plains states, where they stopped at one airport after another and human cargo was swapped in and out. By then, the fever was fully with him, and he clutched his elbows into a shiver and nodded his head against the cabin wall, where it picked up the external roar of air and engines and flooded his head with it.

The flight attendants occasionally came by and gave him funny looks of concern flavored with suspicion. They asked if he needed anything, and he simply shook his head. As passengers came and went, he had a variety of seatmates. A bald man who sold sound systems to casinos. A young woman art student with bushy hair and no makeup. A man with a cowboy hat and a mean grin. An older woman visiting grandchildren. They all sat down and smiled at him politely when they boarded, but then quickly recoiled when they realized how decrepit his condition was.

The coughing didn't help. Big, goopy coughs that took over and had their way with him. Coughs that built their power from huge bronchial contractions as his lungs tried to shove the infection and its liquids out his mouth. Coughs that seared his tracheae as the tissue turned red and swollen from the aerobic beating.

During these spasms, he faced away from the passengers and coughed at the overcast sky out the window. He put a clenched fist to his mouth and covered the noise and airflow as best he could; but still the force of it blew out into the cabin with gusto. When the fit had passed, he would turn his head toward the front and cast a sidelong glance at the passenger next to him. Invariably, they would be seated in a strained posture that pulled their back, neck, and head as far from him as possible.

When the plane landed and pulled into the gate in Portland, he'd remained slumped in his seat as all the other passengers lunged to the overheads and filled the aisles for departure. No one looked at him, but everyone knew he was there.

When the aisle cleared, he got up and discovered that his legs were wobbly. It took a sustained effort to keep on moving, and halfway down the aisle, he stopped and had to lean against a headrest as he burst into yet another fit of coughing. When he was through, he saw the flight attendant on door duty watching him carefully as he made his way forward through the empty plane.

"Sir," she said when he reached the door, "do you require any special assistance?"

Her earnest expression of concern cheered him slightly as he shook his head. "No, I'll be just fine."

As he walked up the gate tunnel to the concourse, the grade of it taxed his legs, and the convergence of the tunnel lines put him into a fever spin so that he nearly lost his balance. Once outside, he started the long journey down the concourse and out into the main lobby. He'd already decided to forget about his luggage and head straight for a hotel.

As he drifted along the walkway, he saw the oncoming people steal discreet glances at him, then look away. Children simply stared. He must look pretty bad, maybe even as bad as he felt.

In the lobby, he made straight for the escalator, then out the revolving doors, which seemed to weigh a ton when pushed on their stainless-steel surface. Luckily, a cab was parked at the curb almost in front of him. He yanked open the rear door and collapsed into the backseat. The cabby turned around, looked at him, and immediately hit the switches that rolled down all four windows.

"Where to?" The man was dark and jowly with eyebrows bridged all the way across his nose.

"The nearest hotel."

"Won't do any good," the cabby said flatly. "Things are all fucked up. That crash in Seattle. Everybody's full."

"That's okay. Just get me there. I'll handle it." Even his voice was getting weak. He was shutting down all over. He was getting scared.

He flew into another coughing fit on the way to the hotel. The cabby ignored it, but when Steve went to pay and needed change, he waved him off. "Check you later, buddy." He left all the windows wide open as Steve watched him pull away at a fast clip that coaxed a little squeal of rubber from the pavement.

In the hotel lobby, Steve approached the counter, where a well-barbered young man in a gold blazer and black tie stared into a computer display. As Steve approached, the man looked up and his eyebrows headed north for just an instant before he regained his composure.

"Yes, sir?"

"I need a room. A single."

"I'm sorry, sir," the clerk said apologetically. "We're all booked up. We don't have a single room. It's the problem up in Seattle."

"Look, this is sort of an emergency. I got sick on the plane. I just need to lie down and call a doctor, okay?"

"All right, sir. Why don't you sit down and I'll see what we can do."

As Steve retired to a chair in the lobby, he saw the clerk read a piece of paper and talk into a phone. Thank God. They were going to help him. He probably needed an ambulance, but if he could just lie down for a bit, maybe he would feel better.

"That's right," the clerk was saying into the phone. "He looks real bad and he's sweating. . . . Get him out of public and put him in a room alone? Yeah. We can do that. How soon will you be here?" While he talked, he read the fax, which the hotel had received only an hour ago:

U.S. Department of Public Health
INFECTIOUS DISEASE ALERT

The Department has received evidence that the so-called African pneumonia epidemic may have been introduced onto the North American continent via air travel. The precise nature of this disease is under investigation. External symptoms may include fever, sweating, shivering, paleness, and coughing.

As the proprietor of lodging on a major air route, you may encounter travelers who manifest these symptoms. In this event, it is IMPERATIVE THAT YOU CONTACT THIS DEPARTMENT IMMEDIATELY!

Put the person in a room by themselves, even if they are traveling with a family or friend. Avoid any unnecessary exposure to your staff or guests.

PHONE 1–800–555–3949 IMMEDIATELY!

"Room number? I'm putting him in one twenty. . . . Okay, I'll be waiting." The clerk hung up the phone, came around the counter, and walked toward the slumped figure of Steven Henry. He stopped a respectful ten feet away. "Sir, we're going to put you in Room One Twenty. It's not made up, but you can rest there until you get medical attention. It's one floor up and to your left. You don't need a key. I've already arranged to have it open. Don't worry about registration. We'll take care of that later."

"Thank you," said Steve weakly as he pushed himself out of the chair and headed for the elevator.

As its doors opened, he got on with ten other people.

The clerk was startled to see the police cars begin to arrive less than five minutes later. Dozens of them. They swarmed through the parking lot and positioned themselves all around the building. Through the front window, he could see the officers get out, then just stand by their cars, as people in the lobby all stopped and stared through the big front windows.

Why weren't they coming in?

Then, in a terrible flash, he knew exactly why. The fax. The disease. The man in Room 120. The police were part of the alert, and they weren't coming in because it wasn't safe to come in. And if it wasn't safe for them, it wasn't safe for him. But it was too late to leave. They were here to make sure that everyone stayed, whether they wanted to or not.

The clerk's mind raced wildly. Only he knew. That was his slim advantage. When the guests and staff found out what was going on, there would be an orgy of fear and panic and his advantage would be lost. He had to act now.

His best bet was to get out of the building, even if he couldn't leave the property. At least he would be out in the fresh air and away from the germs. The easiest way was straight out the front. He walked around the corner and straight out the automatic doors onto the curved sidewalk and loading curb, where two police cruisers were parked with officers standing on the far side of the cars.

The clerk stopped and leaned back against the wall as he pulled out a cigarette and his lighter. He would make it look like a routine smoke break. That would buy him some time to try to figure his next move.

Before he even got the cigarette to his lips, one of the

officers spoke. "Sir, we're going to have to ask you to go back inside the building. We have an emergency situation here."

"But I've been here all day. I work at the front desk. I didn't hear about any emergency. So what's going on?"

"You'll be informed at the appropriate time. Now just get back inside the building." The last trace of diplomacy was gone from the cop.

"I don't think that's such a good idea. There's a guy came in here real sick just a few minutes ago. And we just got a fax saying he might be part of an epidemic. I don't want to be part of an epidemic. And that's what might happen if I go back inside the building. I might die inside the building. Right?"

"Look," said a second cop. "If we let you out, then everyone else will want out, too."

As if to underscore his statement, a couple came through the automatic doors, suitcases in hand. They were neatly dressed and in their fifties.

"Well," said the smiling husband to the cops, "we didn't expect *this* kind of curbside service. A taxi would have done just fine."

"Sir, we're going to have to ask you to go back inside the building," repeated the first cop. "We have an emergency situation here."

"And so do I, Officer," said the husband. "We have an appointment downtown in half an hour, and we can't be late." His voice was laced with authority, as if he might be a senior executive or a military officer.

"Sorry, sir, we can't let you leave. We have orders to prevent that at all costs."

"You do, huh?" said the husband, his face now flush with anger. "Well, I'll tell you exactly what it's going to cost you. It's going to cost you your goddamn *job!* Now I'm walking out to the street to get a cab. Try to stop me, and you'll be on the butt end of a lawsuit that'll never end!"

As his wife looked on in horror, the husband strode toward the police cars with the intent of passing right between them. But it never happened. The first officer drew his automatic and shot the man in the thigh with a 9mm slug, which minced the muscle tissue, fractured the femur, and tore open the femoral artery.

The husband fell to the pavement and howled in pain. His wife shrieked, but her feet were welded in terror to the pavement, and she could only watch. The husband landed with the wounded leg up, and he clutched it to his belly as he kicked in wild pain with his good leg. The sum of these motions spun him like a mad dervish about some imaginary axis that penetrated the pavement and ran far down into the heated depths.

The first cop called into the mike on his shoulder. "Dispatch, this is Q Team. We have a suspect down at the site. Request ambulance."

The husband stopped spinning and the wife ran to him. A big reservoir of red soaked the leg of his gray flannel slacks and began to pool on the pavement. "You bastards!" she screamed at the policemen. "Call an ambulance."

"There's one on the way," volunteered one of the cops, who looked stricken by what he had just witnessed. And at the same moment, the first cop saw the clerk bolting across the parking lot, the tail of his blazer flapping frantically behind him. "Fuck!" he swore. The clerk had misled them and taken advantage of the confusion to make his escape. "Stop!" he screamed. "Or—"

A pistol roared from behind him and the clerk pitched forward, as if from a rude shove between the shoulder blades. He lay still for an instant, tried to push himself up, and fell in a final collapse. The first cop heard the muffled screams and looked over to the full-length glass windows, where a crowd of guests and patrons had gathered in response to the commotion.

"May I have your attention!" came an amplified voice from a bullhorn. It was the team commander, parked a little farther down the drive. "We have a medical emergency. I repeat, we have a medical emergency here. For your own health and safety, please go to your rooms immediately. I repeat: Please go to your rooms immediately. We will give you more information at a later time. Under no circumstances is anyone to leave the premises."

As the bullhorn repeated the message, two large ambulances swung up to the parking curb in a blaze of flashing red and blue, with an unmarked white van right behind them. The people who got out of the vehicles wore isolation suits and sealed hoods that sprouted oxygen hoses connected to tanks on their backs. Two of the team were armed with M16s. The wife backed away from her husband as they approached with a stretcher, bound his leg, and carted him away. "I'm sorry, ma'am. We'll take good care of him. You've got to go back in now and get up to your room."

Steven Henry knew he was dead the moment the door to Room 120 opened and the suited men wheeled the collapsible gurney in. They were ghosts built of rubber and plastic, and the gurney was the terminal vehicle, the vessel for the journey across the darkened river.

One of the ghosts leaned over him where he lay in the clutter of the unmade bed. "Mr. Enri? Steven Enri? E-N-R-I? Is that correct?"

Steven Henry felt the flush of anger in his soul, but had lost the means to physically express it. They were asking a dying man to clear up a petty clerical error.

"Fuck yourself," he said in a whisper.

"What was that?" The plastic ghost leaned in close.

"Fuck yourself," repeated Steve in an even fainter whisper.

"Here it is," interrupted a filtered voice from behind the ghost. One of the others had his briefcase open and was holding up Henry's ticket folder and passport. "Jesus! No wonder we missed him coming in. He was in Africa, all right, but the name on his ticket isn't spelled the same as on his passport. There was no way the computers could do a cross-match and tell us he was back in the country. Shit!"

"Mr. Henry," said another of the ghosts as they placed him on the gurney, "I'm from the U.S. Public Health Service, and I'm going to level with you. You're a very sick man. You've apparently contracted a disease that's become an epidemic in Central Africa. We're not sure exactly what it is, but obviously we'll keep you informed as we go along. Right now, we're taking you to an isolation area in a hospital here in Portland."

Now, as Steven Henry wages his last skirmish against the disease here in the isolation ward, all these memories crack and crumble. Was it weeks ago or days ago? He can't tell. What about his family? Were they here? He doesn't know.

They give him morphine now because the pain is horrible. His internal organs are swollen with disease and his skin alive with eruptions of pathological lava. The morphine packages the memory crumbs in transparent rubber, and he can't get into them anymore. Time expands and contracts in strange and unpredictable ways.

"Steve?"

He opens his eyes and rolls them toward the voice. Another ghost in another rubber suit. A dim image on the far edge of his failing vision.

"Can you hear me? I've come to pray with you."

Steven tries to focus on the image. He can't. Behind the suit, it looks like curtains are drawn over the observation window.

"They've given us this moment of peace and privacy. It's the least they can do. You've suffered greatly. I know that. God knows that. And in the final reckoning, your suffering will be the measure of your eternal reward."

Who is it? A chaplain? It must be a chaplain.

"I know you can't speak, Steve. But if you could, I know what you'd say. You'd say please release me from this terrible suffering."

There is a vague rustle of unfolding plastic near the suited figure.

"Now I want you to close your eyes and imagine the great peace that's soon to come."

Two rubbery fingertips gently pull his lids down. And he feels something descend over his mouth and nostrils.

Vincent glances back toward the curtained window as he holds the sandwich bag over the patient's mouth and nose. After a moment, he looks back and sees the fog of moisture on the inside surface of the bag. Each drop holds millions of deadly microbes, all in the service of Vincent. He removes the bag and seals it carefully, then folds it into ever smaller squares until he can conceal it in the palm of the glove. With his free hand, he pats the patient softly on the back of the palsied hand.

"God bless you, son," he says as he rises to leave.

But Steven Henry can't understand him. The words are a

distant and shapeless murmur on a compressed horizon where the sky has collapsed into total darkness.

Because Steven Henry is nearly gone.

37

PARIS PULLED INTO THE BIG PARKING STRUCTURE OF THE MU-nicipal hospital and guided his car on a corkscrew journey through eight levels of "reserved" stalls, which were mostly empty. On a good day, he might have tolerated this kind of obstacle, but even at eleven in the morning, it was quite clear this would not be a good day.

The day had started with Skip, his young nephew, run amok. A dismal phone call from his sister set up the latest round of problems. He learned that Skip had phoned her and tried to pry loose a little cash. In the call, she had learned that he was no longer attending school and was "just hanging out." When she told him he was destroying his future, he countered with the news on TV about the plague. There was no future, so why bother?

So now, as always, she was turning to Paris. Could he maybe arrest Skip, or something like that, to get him off the street? Could he give the boy a generous dose of "tough love" to show him the true path?

Paris snorted to himself as he wound through the parking structure. He knew the kid was probably holed up in the affluent home of his buddy Adam Larkin, but why bother to fetch him? With the world in a state of catastrophic collapse, it was a little difficult to tell what the true path might be, not only for Skip, but for everyone else perched upon the planetary skin as well.

He finally climbed to a level with public parking and pulled into a stall. When he got out and shut the door, the sound bounced through the empty cavern of cement, and he looked down the long deserted row. Funny. He'd been coming here for years on police business and had never seen such an abundance of parking space.

He walked across to the sky bridge that took him into the main hospital complex and walked through the lobby, where a lone woman manned the reception desk and presided over a sprawl of vacant couches and chairs. He punched the elevator button and the doors slid open immediately to accommodate him. Two floors later, he got off and walked down the hall of the wing where Elaine was.

Something was weird here. Weird, but to be expected, thought Paris. Normally, the halls bustled with nurses, doctors, orderlies, maintenance people, and all the other disciplines found in the operation of a big hospital. But now, on this fifty-yard stretch, Paris saw only an occasional nurse ducking in or out of a room. It wasn't right.

Of course it wasn't right. Paris knew that in a figurative sense, Agent 57a had already arrived in Seattle on a turgid wave of fear. With news of the global outbreak pouring out of televisions everywhere, every talk show in existence had hastily booked medical "experts" to speculate on what it all meant, on who would live and who would die, and personal precautions and public safety. Quickly, a number of common themes had emerged, and one of them was the hospital as infectious graveyard. Since hospitals were full of sick people, they were a potential clearinghouse for infectious diseases. During the so-called golden age of antibiotics, this was a manageable problem, but not during a time of major pestilence. With an airborne infection like Agent 57a, the disease would be almost impossible to contain as stricken patients showed up and spread the sickness through the institution.

Paris came into Elaine's room and was surprised to see her sitting up and watching one of the local TV stations, which was now carrying the plague story nonstop.

"So what's the word?" asked Paris as he sat down next to her.

"About the same." Paris liked the robust sound of her voice. She was coming back fast. "It used to be all about money, sex, and death. But you don't hear much about money and sex these days." She pointed to the TV. "They're going ape-shit out there, Detective. Absolutely ape-shit. You surprised?"

"Can't say that I am."

Currently the screen showed a helicopter shot of the I-90 freeway where it climbed out of the lowlands and ascended into the Cascade mountains with their vast expanse of national parkland. In the foreground were the patches of subdivisions and blocks of retail space that constituted the Seattle suburbs. During the morning hours, the westbound lanes should have been full as they collected the traffic bound for Seattle and Bellevue. Instead, they were empty, and the eastbound lanes heading into the mountain country were jammed with cars, campers, and trailers.

Paris watched the motorized exodus for a moment. "I wonder where they think they're going. You suppose there's a cozy little campsite waiting for them? With a convenient electrical outlet? Maybe even a little tap water and a chemical toilet?"

"I doubt if they're thinking at all. It looks more like they're simply reacting. The news said the run on stores for nonperishable food has nearly emptied the shelves. Still, it won't be long until they get mighty hungry out there amongst the pines."

"Maybe they'll slip into town on Saturdays to hit Burger King. Two cheeseburgers, three fries, three Cokes, and an order of *Chlamydia psittaci* to go. Sound appetizing?"

On the TV, the helicopter shot continued south and soon crossed over Highway 410, a two-lane road that leaves Enumclaw to the east, then heads south for the long climb up into Mt. Rainier National Park. Here the situation was even worse. Outbound vehicles had commandeered both lanes and turned the highway into a mammoth one-way street up into the wilderness.

Paris pointed his thumb back toward the hospital corridor. "What's more important is what's going on in here. It's turning into a ghost town. Seems like a lot of the customers and their doctors have joined the motorcade out there."

"And rightfully so. This is the last place you want to be when the disease comes to town. It'll become a magnet for infection."

"Seems logical. That must be why most of the clientele has already left. The parking lot's nearly empty and the halls are pretty much deserted."

"That reduces the probability of infection, but long term I'd rather be in a bit more comfy setting."

"So give me a medical opinion. How soon can we get you out of here?"

"I tried to get up and walk a little earlier this morning, but I'm still pretty shaky. Give me another day or two. You got a plan?"

"Yeah. We take you and your disk with the magic formula and get the hell out of here. We get on my boat and head north up into the San Juans to buy some time. If that doesn't work, we sail up into the islands along the Canadian coast."

"Cut and run, huh? That doesn't seem like your style. What's wrong?"

Paris thought for a moment before he answered. "I'll be straight with you. That showdown on the *Cedar Queen* made me a very nasty enemy, so now I'm in as deep as you are. But I'm a cop, and cops stick together; so for now I'm immune, but not for long." He paused and looked at the TV, which showed the smashed windows of a looted convenience store in Renton. "Looks to me like the rules are changing, real fast. Pretty soon, there may not be any police department, then we're on our own."

We're on our own, thinks Elaine. Paris was very presumptive about this *we* business. He just assumed that whatever he decided would be fine with her. The least he could've done was discuss their options, so they arrived at some kind of mutual decision. But then again, she was flat on her back in a strange town with the worst plague in many centuries running through it. So what options did she have? For now she'd just have to trust him, and that was the good part, she did trust him. When he held her close after she was wounded and slipping into shock, it formed some kind of bond between them that she'd never shake, no matter what happened. She knew that wasn't rational, but she also knew it was true.

38

THE UNI-VERSE WAS DYING.

All over the planet, the nodes were shutting down, tiny episodes of cybernetic brain death with a disastrous cumulative effect. The entire company was slipping into a paralytic coma from which it might never return.

Bennet Rifkin knew that. And so did the man he now conversed with, the head of the entire Organics group. Yet neither spoke of it.

As the man talked, Bennet stared at his image on the flip-up screen of his notebook computer, which was framed against the view out the second-story window at the Webster Foundation. In spite of his emotional stress, a part of Bennet still appreciated how the scene out the window provided such a fine context for the message the man was delivering on the screen. A few hundred yards away, a mini-mall was in flames. The heat of the fire had already blown all the storefront glass into the parking lot and made it appear as though a storm of green ice had fallen across the pavement. Greedy red fingers of flame curled around the squat, rectangular structures and tickled the thick gray smoke into an upward boil. On the outskirts of the parking lot, a loose pack of vans and trucks provided a camp for a gang of young males who drank beer, smoked dope, and cheered the conflagration. The trucks were loaded with the standard global artifacts of civil unrest: electronics, liquor, and guns.

As the young males milled about in a formless dance of vandalism, the man on the screen was delivering his summary.

"So you see, Mr. Rifkin, the corporation is now recoiling into a preconfigured survival posture, and I'm afraid that while we're in this posture, your services will no longer be required."

Bennet was tempted to switch him off, but there was

something fascinating about the play between the man on the screen and the youths out the window. Besides, the man had already delivered the death blow: there would be no antibiotic to counter Agent 57a, no magic bullet to save the corporate elite, let alone the rest of humanity.

The reasons for the failure were obscure because the technology involved was complex, but Bennet was able to follow the general chain of reasoning without too much trouble. It all began when they took the computer model of Agent 57a, version 8.0, and converted it over to a model that Dr. Ahmadi's groups could use to look for molecular targets. Bennet recalled this phase of the operation, and Ahmadi's confidence that several existing but unreleased drugs would be capable of destroying the real bug in the real world.

To verify this assumption, the LifeForce technology had been brought to bear for the very first time. The nucleoids and plasmids that constituted the living code for Agent 57a were artificially synthesized, then inserted into an existing *Chlamydia psittaci* after its own had been yanked out. Amazingly, the procedure worked on the first try, and the new, mutant bug promptly began to multiply and create a vigorous population of pathogens, which were cultured in the living tissue of psittacine birds, all under the most stringent security conditions.

Next, tetracycline and erythromycin were applied to one group of the infected birds; and true to Elaine's prediction, they had no effect whatsoever. Then, the new antibiotics, known only as RTR-97 and STR-23, were applied to a second group of infected birds. The effect of the new drugs was dramatic. The birds were fully recovered in the space of only two weeks. Immediately, the order went out to set up manufacturing facilities to produce RTR-97 and STR-23 in massive quantities. At the time of the outbreak on São Tomé, these facilities were just coming on-line, so it looked as if the timing would be impeccable.

But then, something went wrong. Very wrong. Through Uni's wide web of industrial contacts, it obtained a piece of infected tissue from one of the first cases to appear in Libreville. This sample, which was teeming with the real pathogen, was flown via supersonic aircraft to Ahmadi's lab so it could be tested with RTR-97 and STR-23 in a final confirmation of the drugs' efficacy.

They didn't work. It was as simple as that. They had no effect whatsoever on the bug that was by now killing several thousand people per day in Africa. Further analysis confirmed Ahmadi's suspicion. Agent 57a and the real bug were kissing cousins, but only the real bug had the kiss of death.

Since that time, the lab had worked in a frenzy to characterize the real bug, and what they found was a layer of genetic armor so thick that it would take years to penetrate.

And that was that, the man said. He wished Bennet the best of luck and terminated the connection.

Bennet slammed down the top of his computer, then threw it across the room. It bounced off the window and slid to a stop on the floor. Things couldn't be worse. The bug was already deeply embedded in San Diego, and now he had no safe passage out of town. Until now, he'd expected a shuttle copter would land on the roof and cart him to the San Diego airport, where a corporate jet would take him to some remote haven surrounded by a great moat of money and power, a place where he would receive the new miracle drug at the first hint of disease.

But now there was no drug, no chopper, no plane, no job, no protection. He was on his own.

And to top it all off, he had this goddamned cold.

That's all it was, of course. There was no way he could have been exposed to the epidemic. No way.

He considered his options. His best bet right now was to get out of here and back to his condo. First, he would go down to the cafeteria and load all the frozen and canned food he could find into his car, then he would drive directly to his place in La Jolla, where he could figure out his next move. Back home, he had lots of cash at his disposal, several thousand dollars in a wall safe. When it looked as if the coast was clear, he could go to the airport downtown and buy his way out. Where would he go? He wasn't sure. He'd figure that out on the way. Maybe to an island somewhere.

His plotting was interrupted by a blurt of coughing. Little coughs. Dry coughs. Nothing to worry about.

39

"I AM THE KING, DUDE," PROCLAIMS ADAM LARKIN AS HE tamps the crystal in the pipe. "The king of the rock. The king of all."

"That you are, my man," agrees Skip as he pulls out the lighter. They are sitting in the "entertainment room" of Adam's parents' house in Bellevue, five thousand square feet of success on three floors. The entertainment room is on the lowest floor and recessed into the foundation because it needs no window light. Its purpose is to create an electronic womb of sound, sight, and motion, so true window light would be a hostile intrusion.

Adam pulls on the pipe as the projection TV shows a local reporter outside a school building saying something about "the closing of all schools is simply a precautionary measure."

Adam and Skip are annoyed because MTV has gone off the air, with no warning or explanation. In fact, the once-fat cable-TV spectrum is now riddled with holes. Only eight of the original eighty-four channels are still on the air, and four of these are local.

But Skip and Adam aren't alarmed. They float comfortably in the womb and drift through a digital amniotic fluid that floods their innards. Adam has some vague discomfort about his parents, who are gone on trips and don't seem to be returning, but not enough to take any real action. Skip occasionally thinks about his mother, but only as a distant and mildly disturbing memory.

Adam passes the pipe to Skip and holds the match while he takes a pull. They are smoking DDT, an acronym for Designer Drug Three, which has the bite of rock cocaine, but not the postpipe crash. Instead, you glide gently down a mental runway with neatly feathered engines and touch lightly to the ground.

Adam points the TV clicker toward the electronics rack and switches to CNN. "And now it is my pleasure to present: 'The End of the Fucking World'!"

Skip applauds with his jaw hanging slack. In the womb, the apocalypse is just another production, another scam for mind share, and Skip and Adam treat it as such. Adam shuts off the TV audio and clicks on a CD by Nine Inch Nails, a song of phallic weaponry put to violent application. They watch the big screen and suck in the big sound along with the DDT. Columns of smoke rise behind the Eiffel Tower. A body covered with sores quakes on a filthy mattress. Small-arms fire shatters the windows of a hospital. Soldiers join looters in downtown Moscow.

What a show.

Vincent peered through his bug-spattered windshield and watched the scene ahead of him as though it were a television show. In the late-afternoon light, the man's red face took on a golden tint as he argued with the soldier. He was a heavyset, jowly fellow, with short sandy hair and a beefy neck that sloped into shoulders thick and rounded. A little tire of flesh hung under his chin and jiggled every time he stomped his foot or smacked his freckled fist into his palm. The soldier was in full combat gear, with camouflage fatigues and sleeves rolled in a neat crease up onto the biceps. He wore sunglasses, an automatic pistol, and a surgical mask.

Behind Vincent, someone honked his horn impatiently. The heavy man yanked his big head toward the sound, screamed, "Fuck you!" and turned back to the soldier, who was motioning to three other soldiers a few feet away lounging on the fender of a humvee. Vincent assumed they were National Guard troops, although nothing on any of the vehicles signified that. He'd heard the rumors about the troops before he left Portland and became apprehensive when he entered the ten-mile line of cars an hour ago. But his initial anxiety had disappeared when he got close enough to see they weren't searching any of the vehicles. Apparently, they were simply turning around the northbound traffic and sending it back to the south, toward Portland. Their roadblock was situated at a freeway interchange on Interstate 5 just south of Centralia and Chehalis, and as he crept forward in the long and irritated line of traffic, Vincent made out the details of their blockade. Two Bradley fighting vehicles and a humvee blocked the northbound lanes toward Seattle, with masked soldiers manning gun turrets pointed at the traffic. Another fighting vehicle was deployed in the open field to the right of the exit, in case someone should decide to go cross-country.

With his window rolled down, Vincent could hear the exchange between the military officer and the beefy man, who stood a few steps from a minivan where his worried wife and two small children looked on. The man was screaming that they had no right to prevent him from going on through to Seattle, "no goddamned fucking right whatsoever."

The officer countered that he was under orders and that was that.

"And whose fucking orders are those?" bellowed the man. As he grew more heated, the soldiers in the background came off the humvee in full combat gear and started toward the pair.

"The governor of the State of Washington," answered the officer in an even tone. "Now I want you to get in your vehicle and follow the markers—now."

Vincent could see that fluorescent pylons had been arranged to make a path down the exit, across the overpass, and onto the entrance going the other way, to the south. Armed troops and fighting vehicles were scattered along the route to ensure compliance. Big mobile generators with floodlights were being moved into place to keep the system humming on into the night.

"The governor, huh?" yelled the man. "Well, fuck the governor. I'm an American and I'll go any goddamn place I please!" He spun in place and started back toward his minivan, which was pointed directly at the opening to the north. Two of the soldiers came up swiftly behind him. One slammed a rifle butt to the back of his head, knocking him to the pavement. The other produced a pair of plastic handcuffs and quickly bound his wrists behind his back while he was still in a stunned state. The man's wife shrieked and got out on the passenger side. The soldiers pulled the woozy man to his feet as blood from a scalp wound dribbled down his neck and stained the back of his polo shirt. They marched him to the passenger side, shoved him in, and ordered his wife to drive. Pinched and white, she came around to the driver's side, got in, and drove where the pylons told her.

Now, as the officer waved him forward, Vincent glanced in the rearview mirror at the major's insignia on the military cap he was wearing. It helped prep him for his upcoming performance; a brief, but absolutely critical one. The infantry fatigues he wore were a good fit, and the various insignias of rank were impeccably arrayed. An army-surplus store in Portland had supplied everything he needed. But the costume would work no better than the player who filled it, and now the player pressed his right combat boot gently on the gas, pulled forward, and parked off to the side so other cars could pass.

The captain was clearly irritated by Vincent's action and yelled at him to get back in line and move out. But the officer's attitude quickly reversed polarity when the major stepped out and strode briskly toward him.

"Afternoon, Captain," said the major casually. "Jim Stafford, Company A, Second Battalion, Thirty-fourth Infantry. You know our outfit?"

"Aren't you guys out of Bremerton?" asked the captain, who scanned the major's uniform and ascertained that he was Washington National Guard.

"You got it," drawled the major, who looked toward the long line of cars. "You runnin' this show?"

"Yessir. That I am."

The major squinted as he gazed to the south. "Shitty duty. Not the right kind of thing for a fighting man. Not at all."

"No, it's not. But I got orders."

"Yeah," agreed the major in a sympathetic tone. "We all got orders." He swung his gaze to face the captain. "Say, you guys got any extra gas?"

"Well, I suppose we could siphon some out of one of the humvees. You running short?"

"Sure am. Goddamned service stations are closed all over the place. I gotta take on enough fuel to get to our rendezvous point. We're supposed to relieve the Third Battalion up in Snoqualmie Pass."

The captain pointed to the empty lanes to the north,

where two fighting vehicles and the humvee were deployed. "Why don't you pull over there and Sergeant Humphery will give you a hand."

"Much obliged," replied the major as he started back toward his car. "Good luck."

"Same to you," said the captain as he turned to watch the continuous flow of cars.

Twenty minutes later, Vincent was on his way. As he drove between the fighting vehicles and headed north, he saw a pickup cocked at a severe angle on the shoulder of the road with the driver's-side door agape. Coming closer, he saw where the machine-gun bullets had chewed holes in the tailgate and punched out the rear window and front windshield. Passing by, he noticed the blood on the dashboard and seat upholstery, already baking from crimson to brown in the late-afternoon sun. Someone had tested the checkpoint and lost. They apparently hadn't understood that everything they knew no longer counted, and that all knowledge must be learned anew.

But Vincent understood. And he knew that in this new and awful world, his modest vehicle was a strategic vessel of the highest order. And as its commander, he carried the ultimate payload on its way to the final target.

He couldn't wait to get home. Before he left for Portland, he'd already assembled his flock and prepared them to go forth and preach. Now it was just a matter of anointing each of them with this infectious balm brewed from a dying man's breath.

Then the world would be his, and he would be the world. His hands were dry and his pulse rate low as he barreled down the empty lanes to the north toward Seattle.

40

PARIS STANDS BEFORE THE WINDOW AT THE END OF THE north concourse inside Sea-Tac and sips his Redhook ale as CNN carries the story of the sealed plane over the remnants of its world network. In the foreground on the tarmac, he can see the troops and vehicles assigned to "guard" the disabled 737. A euphemistic term, to be sure. If anyone manages to get off the plane, they will be shot. From a respectful distance, a distance that ensures no possibility of airborne contamination.

As Paris takes another sip, he realizes that his role here as a hostage negotiator has descended into tragic farce. He was skeptical from the outset, when the police commissioner and state public health director had explained the nature of his mission. Even then, it was fairly clear that this was a political gesture, a way to legitimize what was clearly illegitimate. In this case, the government was the terrorist, and he the representative of some undesignated moral force.

Minutes ago, Paris had spoken with the commander of the troops outside. The man was anything but reasonable.

"Now look, Detective, I've heard about enough," said the National Guard captain. "I got my orders. They stay on the plane."

"Okay," countered Paris, "and I've got my orders. We don't kill anyone who's not trying to kill us. They're going to die of dehydration if they stay out there in this heat. All we've got to do is get them inside where there's shade and water. They can stay quarantined here. They never have to leave the airport. They're no threat to anybody except themselves. They're not contagious unless they mix with the general population."

Paris could see the object of their debate directly over the captain's left shoulder. The 737 passenger jet sat on a taxiway several hundred yards across the tarmac, crippled and sealed by the cherry-picker trucks. Paris had received confused reports about its point of origin. The best he could tell, the plane had taken off from somewhere in the Southwest just as the domestic airports in California and Oregon were shutting down by blockading their runways. It had become an instant orphan and flew the entire length of the West Coast, desperately looking for a place to land before its fuel ran out. Sea-Tac was the last stop, and the runways were open, even though the airport was closed.

"Are you monitoring their radio calls?" asked Paris.

"No, sir, we are not. We have not been informed as to the frequencies." The captain's right hand rested on the butt of his holstered .45. Numerous military vehicles sat stoically behind him, and an armed infantry company milled about, waiting for some kind of punctuation to present itself.

"Bullshit. You just don't want to hear. That's all. You just don't want to hear them beg. And you know why, Captain? Because you don't really feel very good about this, do you?"

The captain looked away from Paris's glare. "Doesn't matter. I've got orders. And that's that." He turned and walked back toward his troops.

Paris watched him retreat. The captain was scared. To him, the plane was not people, the plane was death. There was no use arguing anymore. Reasonable individuals no longer ran the government. Fear ran the government.

Paris walked back across the tarmac toward the main terminal building. The entire center of the structure was gone, a huge gap with a blackened and jagged border. Beyond the gap, he could see the collapsed remains of the parking structure, where the top floors had caved in and left a demolished heap of concrete and twisted tentacles of rebar. He directed his walk toward the long wing of the north concourse, which was still intact. At one of the gates, he found an open door and walked up to the main level. For a moment, he stared out at the vast canyon of destruction in the terminal's center, then turned to walk down the concourse in the solemn silence.

And now Paris sips the cold ale and stares out at the field, the plane, the troops, all rippled and folded in the summer heat. He raises his ale for a final toast to the plane and its passengers, reluctant martyrs for a cause both they and he would never understand.

The big HDTV screen was the centerpiece of the audiovisual wall in the conference room of Robert Fancher's office suite. Around it was a glittering array of electronic boxes and displays, many of unknown and exotic function. But right now, the big show was on the big screen as CNN documented the collapse of Los Angeles. At long last, the concept of terminal gridlock had moved from theory to practice as the freeway system choked to death under an impossible glut of vehicles. The flow of trucks, cars, campers, big vans, minivans, army trucks, ambulances, and police cruisers had ground to a complete halt, and now the overflow was beginning to choke the main arterials as well. And as the city's bloated veins and arteries shut down, the entire urban area drifted into a terrible fit of anarchy. No clear roads, no police or firefighters. No through streets, no National Guard. A thousand columns of smoke poured into a baby blue sky, cleansed and purified by the complete absence of auto exhaust.

Barney Cox swung in his seat at the big conference table of polished teak and turned from the TV to Robert Fancher. "Bob, I couldn't be more pleased. What a party!" he said, pointing toward the screen. "What a way to celebrate my release! Thank you, my man. Thank you," he gushed.

"No trouble," mumbled Fancher as he nervously eyed the two men who had accompanied Barney. They were big, mean, and stupid; and they stared at him out of recessed caves housing the darkest of fires.

Fancher now realized he was in a supreme bind. Bennet Rifkin and Uni had been a fat cash cow, and he'd tried his best to get Barney to forget about chasing the Wilkes woman and the "property," whatever the hell that was. But it was no go, and the loss of Uni's cash seemed a lot less tragic than the loss of his physical self at the hands of Barney. So he'd gone ahead and made the proper payments to the proper people and gotten Barney released on bail.

And now, Jesus! This bug was loose and the whole fucking world was going down in a crash dive. And somehow, this business with Uni was linked to it, and Barney seemed to have sniffed out the connection. He'd just have to improvise and feel his way through until he saw an escape route.

"Now, let's talk business," commanded Barney. "I've been thinking about your relationship with Uni Corporation. They're a very impressive organization, Bob. People like you and I could learn a lot from them. And I think there's no time like the present to start. So I'd like you and I to chat with your contact there and see if maybe we're enriched in the process."

"Well, I'm not sure if Mr. Rifkin will be available . . ."

Barney's hand shot across the table and his palm came down over the back of Fancher's hand. It was cool and dry, noted Fancher.

"Try, Bob. Just try."

"Very well," sighed Fancher. He rose, went to the equipment array, and arranged the cipher connection to Uni.

"Add video, Bob," demanded Barney. "I like to see the face at the other end. I'm a nervous sort, you know, and it soothes me to see the face behind the voice. So let's see what we can do, okay?" Fancher nodded silently, and the big HDTV screen switched from CNN to the telecommunications mode.

To his complete surprise, it was not Bennet who appeared on the screen, but a muscular man wearing a sweatshirt pulled over a completely bald head. Behind him was a background that resembled the interior of a nuclear submarine. Several bays of electronic equipment were set against a steel wall, where an airtight hatch door was partially visible.

"Yes?" the man said in an irritated voice.

"We are trying to make contact with Mr. Rifkin," ventured Fancher.

"All Mr. Rifkin's communications have been directed to this location. He's no longer with the firm. Now how can I help you?" The man spoke in a crisp, arrogant tone that even Fancher couldn't hope to match.

"My name's Robert Fancher, and I represent the company's interests in the state of Washington in the United States. We were given the assignment of recovering property stolen from you in San Diego. I have—"

"I've already been briefed on the details. So why are you calling?"

Before Fancher could answer, Barney pulled the lawyer and his chair to one side and slid his own into the field of view of the video camera with its glowing red eye. "Hello, I'm Barney Cox," he said in a breezy voice. "And I don't believe I caught yours?"

"No, you didn't. And you've got about ten seconds to explain why I shouldn't terminate this connection." The bald man had a commanding presence about him, noted Fancher. He was obviously a major galaxy in the Uni-verse.

But Barney was not intimidated. "We've got access to the disks. The entire set from the EpiSim project."

"What do you mean, you've 'got access'?"

"We know who's got them, and we know how to get them. I'm in the process of making the arrangements right now."

"Good. Then we'll arrange for a delivery procedure."

"I don't think it's going to be quite that simple."

"And why not? I understand we've invested a great deal of time and money in you, Mr. Cox. And unless we start seeing results, we may have to take more drastic steps to protect our investment."

Barney broke into a big smile, and his eyes broadcast a malicious light. "Well, now, Mr. X, I hate to tell you this, but the system you bought and paid for is collapsing into a pile of infectious goo. You can say the words, Mr. X, but the sticks and stones will soon be mine. So I advise that you adjust your thinking."

"And just what kind of thinking do you advise, Mr. Cox?"

"Very expensive thinking. You see, I'm like you. I'm a product of the information age. I've done a little research on EpiSim and Agent 57a, especially on the computer model of the disease itself. And to tell you the truth, its value is so large, it's very difficult to calculate. Now I'm not an economist, but it seems to me that even the hardest of currencies are melting like butter, which takes us back to the gold standard. So I think we'd best negotiate in pounds of gold. Thousands of pounds of gold."

The man glared ferociously at Barney before answering. "You're going to have to be more specific."

"I'm working on that, Mr. X. Now how can I reach you?"

In fact, the man was in a bunker bored into a roadless slope on a mountain in the Swiss Alps. Uni had constructed the site as part of a strategic contingency plan formulated shortly after the company's conception. The bunker held five hundred people in modest comfort and was fully fortified against nuclear, chemical, and biological assault. From this location, the bald man had monitored the failure of the anti-biotic project and initiated a hurried audit of the EpiSim files at the Webster Foundation. Sure enough, the audit team uncovered a fatal flaw. The model of the bug used by the antibiotic team was not the final version used in the simulation. Apparently, the only copy of that version was the one the Wilkes woman had stolen and taken to Seattle. And now, it represented the only hope of developing an effective drug to fight the disease. Barney had them cold.

"I am going to send the contact procedure to Mr. Fancher's E-mail address," the bald man said.

"That'll be fine," said Barney. "And you can address it to me personally. I'm now the managing partner here."

"Very well." The man's image disappeared as the screen went blue and the audio clicked off.

Barney turned to Fancher, whose intestines were already constricting in utter terror. "Sorry about not telling you ahead of time about the management change, Bob." Barney rose from his chair and walked to the enormous picture window overlooking Elliott Bay. "But like I told Mr. X, we're on the threshold of a new age." He stopped and ran his hand over a sculpture on a pedestal, the head of a woman emerging from an amorphous chunk of white marble veined with subtle shades of gray. "And somehow, I don't think our present legal system is going to survive the transition. Which means a man's worth is going to be measured in more direct terms. And when I apply this new yardstick to you, Bob, you just don't measure up."

In an amazing display of strength and speed, Barney picked up the sculpture and hurled it through the picture window, which shattered completely in a loud crash and left a rectangular hole into the airspace seventy-three stories above street level.

Barney's hair quivered slightly in the newly formed breeze coming in from outside as the two big men came out of their chairs, locked Fancher's arms behind his back, and dragged him toward the yawning cavity.

"What are you going to do?" whimpered Fancher as the toes of his polished wing tips dug furrows into the plush green carpet.

"You're an angel, Bob. You know that? An absolute angel. And now I want to see you fly."

"No! No!" screamed Fancher as he twisted his torso violently in a futile effort to free himself.

Barney's eyes glowed brilliantly and the veins in his neck bulged as Fancher's head passed through the window. "Fly, Bob! Fly like an angel, you sleazy fuck!"

Fancher screamed incoherently as he flew out into space. Barney peeked over the precipice and watched the material on Fancher's Armani suit flutter madly while the body tumbled end over end.

"Oh, and by the way," Barney said softly as the body hit the pavement with a sickening finality, "is it okay if your wife sucks my cock?"

For a long moment, the only sound was the breeze blowing through the conference room as Barney and the two big men looked down on the street, where the broken body of Robert Fancher was becoming the center of an instant solar system filled with tightly orbiting objects.

"What about the cops?" asked one of the big men in a toneless voice.

Barney turned to the HDTV screen, which had automatically returned to CNN and now broadcast an aerial shot of a pair of police cars riddled with bullet holes and broken windows in some nameless downtown. He let out a long howl of delirious laughter that caused the two big men to look on in confusion.

"What about the cops! Yeah! What about the cops!"

The era of the cops was almost over. Barney could already see the dull embers of the legal sunset, and a descent into the longest of nights.

In the midst of chaos, there are always cheerful little bouquets of order and predictability, and Paris encountered one when he finally returned to the office and saw Larsen sitting at his desk eating a maple bar and sipping a large paper cup of coffee.

"You don't look so good," commented Larsen. "What happened?"

Paris plopped down into his chair and surveyed the office. About a quarter of the desks were empty. Not bad, considering the circumstances. He was still haunted by the image of the people roasting in that little silver tube out on the taxiway. It had stayed with him all the way back into town as he fought through the traffic on I-5 and listened to the rolling boil on the police radio bands.

"Let's not discuss it," Paris suggested. "What's going on here?"

"Well, we just got a report of a break-in at a medical-supply warehouse over on Elm. Are you surprised?"

"Not exactly. What did they take?"

"None of the usual stuff. No drugs. No electronics. No instruments."

"Then what?"

"They took off with fifteen thousand surgical masks."

Of course, thought Paris. The people on the street didn't need a medical degree to know what was most valuable during an epidemic spread by an airborne germ.

"Oh, and I took a call for you," recalled Larsen. "Do you remember a Mrs. Kimberly?"

"What'd she want?"

"She works at Providence Hospital. She said you talked to her and gave her your card."

Paris's heart jumped. Seven years of work, and it all narrowed down to this one moment. The break. The big break. The airport, the plague, Elaine, and the disks all faded into the background. He could feel the old obsession suddenly inflate and fill him with an exhilarating yet noxious gas.

"What'd she say? Tell me *exactly* what she said!" Paris was relieved to see Larsen thumb through a notepad on his desk. Like a good cop, he'd gotten the details and documented them.

"Well, for starters, she's a very religious person. And that's why she called you."

"Oh, yeah?"

"Yeah. She thinks this plague is the end of the world, and that the Antichrist has appeared."

"How's that?"

332

"She said you talked to her about a priest or minister that visited one of the food-poisoning victims a while back. She remembers the guy and says that he's the Antichrist. Turns out that this same guy, this priest or whatever, rents a house in her neighborhood. It's a crummy address in South Seattle, and she's seen him coming and going in an old station wagon at odd hours. She thinks he was planted there by Satan and disguised as a priest."

"She may be pretty close. Is she positive about the ID?"

"Seems to be." Larsen tore the notes off his pad and handed them to Paris. "Here's the whole deal."

Paris was already on his feet and heading toward his boss's office as he grabbed the notes.

Agnes Kimberly was unimpressed by the assemblage of officials who had just listened to her story in the mayor's office. She'd seen the mayor in the newspaper, but the chief of police and director of public health were just more men in suits as far as she was concerned. The only one she took a shine to was Paris, the big policeman who had brought her over from the hospital. If she'd been twenty years younger and a little less devout, he might have made a great fling.

"Mrs. Kimberly, I'm going to ask you one more time. Are you sure the priest at the hospital was the same person as the one in your neighborhood?" asked Dr. Robert Squire, the director of public health. Agnes didn't like the doctor's patronizing tone. It seemed as if he didn't want her story to be true, even if it was.

"Yessir, I am sure," replied Agnes in a steady voice. "I am quite good with faces. I saw the priest at the hospital, and I saw him again in my neighborhood. His house is just one down from my bus stop. Yessir, I am sure."

Philip Paris turned to the others in the group. "Anybody got any other questions?" Nobody did. "Agnes," he said as he came around to her chair, "thank you very much for your time. We'll definitely be in touch."

"Better hurry," declared Agnes as Paris escorted her toward the door. "That bug's going to get us all, you know."

No one cared to comment on her last remark as an officer

outside took Mrs. Kimberly back to the hospital. The chief of police broke the silence.

"Okay, so let's get this straight," he said to Paris. "You checked with the victim's pastor and confirmed that he never visited her in the hospital?"

"That's correct."

"And you checked with the hospital chaplain and confirmed that he never dropped in on the victim?"

"That's correct."

"And you checked with the victim, and she gave the same general description of the priest as Mrs. Kimberly?"

"That's also correct." Paris smiled inwardly. The tide in the case had turned his way. All three parties had been readily available by phone to make the verifications.

"What about the address she gave?" asked the chief. "Have we checked it out?"

"I had a patrol car cruise by and get the address. They said the place was a real dump, with the curtains all pulled shut. The mailbox appeared empty and there wasn't a paperbox. We ran the address through the database at the assessor's office and got the owner's name, but we can't contact him."

"Not surprising," said the mayor. "There's a lot of people in Seattle you couldn't contact right now."

"Lieutenant," said Dr. Squire in an annoyed tone, "I appreciate the fact that you've been chasing this thing for years and finally have some solid evidence. But we're facing the biggest public health crisis in history. My staff is holding their finger in a very fragile dike against a very big disease. So my question to you is this. Why should I do anything different because of your serial poisoner?"

"Because from the poisoner's standpoint, it represents the biggest opportunity in his entire career. Everything he's done up until now is nothing more than rehearsal time. Here's an entire city, an entire region, teetering on the brink, and he has the power to bring it down. There's no way he can pass it by."

The mayor, the chief, and the doctor all exchanged glances. Paris could tell by their expressions that no one was going to mount a serious rebuttal.

"So," said the mayor, "what do you want to do?"

41

BREATHING THROUGH HIS MOUTH, BENNET RIFKIN SANK ONTO the sidewalk and looked down the long, hot stretch of arterial in North San Diego. No traffic. No people. Only heated pavement, gaudy commercial signs, and a thicket of overhead wires that slashed the sky into countless polygons.

All day, his lungs had been filling with sand, a heavy, gritty sand that left little room for air. And now the sand was turning damp, a choking conglomeration of pink mud that pushed up into his trachea. Suddenly, every breath was a precious little reward earned only at great physical expense. His head expanded, like a balloon gaining altitude, and his mind diffused over a great volume, so that his thoughts could no longer be collected and concentrated. Great waves of hot and cold flowed through him in long undulations, and their motion sickened his stomach.

It seemed his cold was acting up a bit.

It had been getting worse for several days as he holed up in his condo, waiting for civil authority to reassert itself so he could make a break for the airport. He imagined that somehow, through brains and guile, he would weasel his way onto a plane to somewhere safe, or at least relatively safe. He also imagined the plane people wouldn't notice his cough, and how it was marching rapidly from dry to damp.

When he finally made his break, he quickly realized he'd waited far too long. On the outskirts of the city he encountered a grotesque freeway pileup of a big truck and four or five cars, their twisted metal seared black by fire and pocked with burst heat bubbles. Worse yet, the bodies of the victims were still there. Obviously, no one had come to the rescue. No police, no emergency vehicles, no life-flight helicopters. Only scorching flames and oily, dirty pavement.

He'd backed up to the nearest exit and drove through an unfamiliar stretch of the city where traffic was almost nonexistent. About ten blocks later, he found out why. Two gentlemen with large-caliber handguns hijacked his car at an intersection. Before they left, they explained they wouldn't shoot him because ammunition was now too valuable to waste on "some business asshole." After that, he continued on foot toward the airport, his only hope of salvation. And with each block, his cold had gotten a little worse.

Now Bennet rotated his head and looked up and down the arterial where he sat on the sidewalk. His back was resting against a Laundromat located on a corner, and directly across the street was a Dairy Queen. The far corner of the intersection housed a paint store, and on the corner to his right was a 7-Eleven. The afternoon was dying, and the sun slanted at a vicious angle that bathed all the buildings in a pernicious orange.

The orange went prematurely gray as Bennet nodded off into a fevered stupor. He floated through the Uni-verse and the digitized images of its employees became playing cards that he dealt in a desperate and formless game.

He awoke to the glow of mercury vapor from the street-lamps. Night. The stores were all lit from inside, but empty. Time to go now, time to head toward the airport. He tried to rise, but had no strength. All he could do was move his head slightly and weakly raise his hand to his steaming face. The hand shivered with fever. As he dropped it back to his side, he heard the voice, an alto male voice that screamed into the darkness.

"The pigs are dead!"

The owner of the voice appeared from around the corner, walking down the middle of the street. A tall, thin youth, with legs like bamboo that grew from baggy shorts. A blue checkered bandanna encapsulated his hair, and a droopy T-shirt hung from his shoulders.

"The pigs are dead!" repeated the boy of the blue bandanna, who walked down the very center of the street carrying an assault rifle with a big cartridge clip curved into a lethal scowl.

When he reached the center of the intersection, he dropped to one knee, hung his head down, and placed the rifle butt on the pavement. The barrel pointed straight into the skyglow of the urban night. Then he rose, pointed the rifle slightly above the horizon, and pulled the trigger while he rotated in a complete circle.

The pulse of muzzle flash and explosive chatter slapped brutally across Bennet's burning face. Windows shattered, lights blew out, and bullets ricocheted onto capricious paths of random destruction. Afterward, the smoke from the discharge took on a chimerical glow under the glare of the vapor lamps.

The youth held the rifle over his head with both hands and pumped it rhythmically while he once more turned in a circle. At every major point of the compass he repeated his chant: "The pigs are dead!" At the end of the rotation, he faced directly toward Bennet and took notice of his prostrate position. He brought the rifle down and slowly walked toward Bennet, who could do nothing but track the youth's advance with his flaming eyes. He stopped about six feet from Bennet and leaned forward to peer.

"Man, you're one sick motherfucker."

He wheeled about and disappeared around the corner. Bennet's ears rang with a million needles from the rifle report, and his eyes stung from the acrid rifle smoke laced with sulfur. Distant whumps and pops from the far reaches of the city penetrated the ringing as they flew in and landed on his eardrums. Anonymous calamities represented only by the signature of their sound. With most of the lights shot out, he could see patches of moon-baked clouds sailing by in a furious nocturnal motion. From somewhere near came a woman's scream and the pop-pop-pop of a handgun.

And now the disease pulled all the major levers inside Bennet. The world went black. The calamitous sounds tapered off to a vague murmur, then disappeared entirely.

Dawn. A dirty, dim sky filled with shapeless overcast. Bennet shivered in pain as a squalid army of aches and jabs bloated his torso and radiated into his limbs. His lungs barely functioned.

He heard footsteps and the roll of wheels on the sidewalk to his left. He tried to turn his head toward the sound. He could not.

A man came into his field of view, pushing a grocery cart.

An old man, a dirty man, with wild shocks of gray hair and a patchy beard. His cheeks were varnished with grime, and his gray eyes peered out from a web of deep brown fissures. His corded neck jutted from a dirty T-shirt, and his Adam's apple bobbed continuously at the sight of Bennet.

"Well, what have we here?" the old man asked himself as he stopped in front of Bennet on the sidewalk. He wore a beautiful silk bathrobe over his dirty garments, with the price tag still attached to the sleeve. On each of his bony fingers was a large diamond ring. The cart held a single grocery bag.

"Is this the Lord's work I'm lookin' at? I do believe it is." The man squatted directly in front of Bennet and peered into his eyes. "You have been taken ill, and cast out. I, too, was cast out, friend. And made to wander. But no longer. I live in the light, and the light is my home. And now it's yours, too."

The man moved inches from Bennet's face. Pink lightning streaked the whites of the man's bloodshot eyes, and spent alcohol stormed from his breath. "Can you accept the light as your home, my friend? I think maybe not. Whatever can we do for you to show you the way?"

The man's eyes widened and he gasped. "I hear you, friend. I hear you speak. Even with a dead tongue, you speak. And I shall obey your command."

The man hurried to his cart and dumped the contents of his grocery bag into the basket and madly sorted. He returned with a clutch of tissues, a woman's makeup kit, and a small hand mirror. He held the mirror so Bennet could see himself. "Behold your face, friend. Behold your suffering."

And Bennet beheld. His face had gone to clay; a pale, wet clay with dead sockets housing tiny eyes in full and final retreat.

The man yanked the mirror away and swabbed the perspiration from Bennet's face with tissue, then opened the makeup kit. He produced a brush, rubbed it in a square of blush, a pale apricot, and raked in across Bennet's fiery cheeks. "I can feel the spirit of your hand guide me."

He threw the brush over his shoulder, grabbed an eyeliner pencil, a cobalt blue, and moved it in a graceful curve over one lid, then the other. "Paint is light. Light is paint. Learn it, live it."

He dropped the pencil and opened a tube of mascara and

hummed a meandering tune as he twirled the spiral brush over Bennet's eyelashes. "If the eyes are the windows, then these are the fringes of the shades."

He coiled the brush back into the tube and pocketed it in his splendid bathrobe, then returned to the makeup kit and dabbed an applicator into the eye shadow. "I see the light returning. I feel it glowing within you." The applicator flowed across Bennet's eyelids with cool, chemical precision.

"And now," he said as he dropped the applicator into Bennet's lap, "we must draw you a voice, a perfect voice." He twisted open a tube of lipstick, the red color of a late-summer rose, and pulled it across Bennet's parched lips.

The old man leaned back and capped the lipstick as he admired his work. "Yes! Look! Look what we have done, you and I." He picked up the mirror and thrust it in front of Bennet.

A clown, a horrible clown, a horrible dead clown.

Furrows of concern creased the old man's face. "It's not right, is it? Something's wrong. Tell me. Tell me what it is." He moved his ear close to Bennet's lips, and the stink of his hair clambered up Bennet's nose.

Then he turned to face Bennet. "Ah. You're lonely. You need consolation. Companionship. A friend in this time of pestilence." He leapt to his feet and went to his cart. "You stay here," he commanded Bennet. "Leave the rest to me." He wheeled the cart toward the intersection and out of Bennet's sight. A moment later, with a crystalline twang, the cart dropped over the curb and down to the street, where it receded in a shimmering, metallic clatter.

In the solitude, Bennet nodded deep into a burning pool of fever and the day went dim. Time stopped. Then, the slow whine of tire tread on pavement brought him back.

A police car. At last, they had sent a car for him.

The cruiser car stopped at the intersection. The officer in the passenger seat wore riot gear, a crash helmet, and the breathing mask of a fighter pilot. His padded elbow protruded out the window and pointed directly at Bennet. Then his head turned and he peered at Bennet through aviator sunglasses, appraising him in the same way a praying mantis might.

He turned away with contempt, and the car moved on.

Bennet felt his head expand to a prodigious circumference, which pulled apart much of the wiring that defined his brain function. Once again, darkness.

The roll of the cart brought him back. The old man halted it right in front of him. The basket held the limp form a small woman in her late fifties in a polka-dot blouse and filthy polyester slacks of sky blue. She had a ravaged nest of gray hair, a flattened nose, and the permanent pout of severe overbite. Her forearms and legs dangled over the edge of the basket, and the pale, waxy state of her flesh indicated she had been dead for some time.

"A friend in need is a friend, indeed," quoted the old man as he pulled the dead woman out of the cart, dragged her over the sidewalk, and propped her up in a sitting position beside Bennet.

"We're a community here," he declared as he placed her cold arm around Bennet's shoulder. "A true community."

He moved to the other side of Bennet, sat down, and completed the union by putting his arm over the woman's arm behind Bennet.

Bennet could see neither of them. His peripheral vision was rapidly constricting, leaving only a tunnel that faced the Dairy Queen.

Later that day, near the very end, he heard the old man speak, although he could no longer see him.

"You were almost right about the simulation and the antibiotic. Too bad about that. Now you're part of the demand instead of the supply. Only there isn't any supply. But somehow, it seems right, doesn't it?"

42

THE ISOLATION SUIT WAS A SIZE TOO SMALL FOR PARIS AND BIT at his armpits as they jogged from the van toward the little house with peeling paint in South Seattle. Ahead, two officers with assault rifles bounded up the sagging steps and covered either side of the door while a third officer kicked it in.

Paris doubted that the suspect was home, but they couldn't take any chances, and so they were prepared for an armed confrontation. They had watched the house for several hours and had sweat heavily into the suits as they waited for some sign of activity. Nothing. Eventually, Paris decided to go in. Even if their man wasn't there, they had to find out what he was up to.

So now Paris climbed the porch steps as the first officer went in through the open door. A moment later he reappeared.

"You're not gonna believe this," he said as he turned to go back inside.

A single glance told Paris they were late. Way too late.

Vincent kept tamping down the excitement as he drove through the parking lot of the shopping mall in North Seattle. There were cars here. Not as many as in more normal times, but still, quite a few. Every day, people seemed to be gaining confidence that Seattle was going to be spared. And that meant they should celebrate. And in America, to celebrate was to shop.

He quickly found what he was looking for. An entrance with sliding glass doors. He carefully pulled the old station wagon into position. It was a little tricky because he had no vision out the rear or back windows, which were covered with wrapping paper and masking tape to conceal the car's contents. In addition, a makeshift cardboard barrier separated the front seat from the rear, so he had only his side mirrors to figure the distance and angle.

He got out, went to the rear, and unlocked the tailgate and left it open a fraction of an inch. He sniffed the fine air of this fabulous day, then got back into the driver's seat for the final maneuvers.

Once in place, he stopped with the engine idling and sucked in a shuddering breath while his hands clenched the steering wheel.

At last, the definition of Vincent was complete.

He put the selector stick into reverse and jammed his foot on the accelerator. The car shot backward, jumped the curb, roared between startled shoppers, and crashed through the mall's double glass doors in a shattering blast of noise and spraying glass.

When the car halted, it was embedded halfway into the doorframe. And at that very moment, the momentum of the collision blew the tailgate open and flung the car's contents into the mall.

Two hundred thirty-three pigeons. Two hundred thirty-three extremely contagious pigeons.

All up and down the mall, the shoppers came running to see what had happened. Hundreds of them. And the pigeons fanned out to greet them, their wings madly beating the air into a cloud of highly diseased fecal dust.

A mass baptism of rampant infection.

Vincent got out of the car and strolled exuberantly across the parking lot. No one stopped him. Throughout the entire episode, he hadn't even bothered to wear a surgical mask.

No need. He was immortal.

"Car 102."

Paris heard the compressed bark of the radio speaker and reached over for the mike as he headed north on Fourth Street back to the downtown precinct. As he reached the building, he felt how sticky he was from the dried sweat accumulated during his stay in the isolation suit. He doubted the call was good news. And he was right.

"Car 102," he echoed.

"What's your ETA to station?"

"About two minutes."

"Report directly to Captain Carno. You copy?"

"I copy."

Carno. His old boss from Homicide. Paris sighed. The last thing he needed was another office beef to compound his problems. At this very instant, the poisoner was out there somewhere preparing to deliver them to a diseased hell. At the scene of the raid, both the cops and public health people were put under strict instructions to stay mum about what they'd seen. The city was already a rumor mill working three full shifts per day, and a story like this one would blow the place wide-open. As a result, he couldn't talk about it on the radio. In a big city with an idle and agitated populace, probably thousands of ears were glued to scanning receivers.

He pulled into the parking area under the precinct and took the elevator directly to Carno's office. Whatever it was, he wanted to get it over with and back on the trail of the poisoner. When he entered, Carno gestured for him to sit down.

"So what happened out there? You didn't get the guy, did you?" Obviously, the old cop had his connections and knew all about the renewed interest in the poisoner.

"No. We didn't. All we got was a bunch of bird shit. Enough bird shit to kill everyone in the state of Washington. How'd you know we didn't get him?"

"So the bird shit's poison, huh? It's carrying the bug, right?"

"You got it. But like I asked, how'd you know we didn't get him?"

Carno picked up a notepad and stared at it as he spoke. "I just got a report of a traffic accident. A very unusual traffic accident. Seems some nut crashed a station wagon into the entrance of a shopping mall. The car was full of pigeons. Dozens of them. Maybe hundreds." Carno looked up at Paris with ancient and sorrowful eyes. "Now why do you think somebody would do a thing like that?"

"Jesus!" breathed Paris.

"It's gonna take more than Jesus to save us now. Phil, I don't know what to tell you. You were right on this one. You were always right."

"Did they get him?" asked Paris, ignoring Carno's apology. "Did they get the driver?"

"Nope. Looks like he just walked off in the confusion. Didn't even get a good ID."

Paris couldn't help himself, he was relieved. Even under these gruesome circumstances, he wanted the bust for his very own. "Well, Captain, congratulations. You've got one of biggest homicide cases in history. Maybe a half million. Maybe more. So it's payback time. I want in."

Carno got to his feet and went to look out the window. "Phil, it's over. There's not going to be a chance for any payback. You watch CNN? You see what's happening in other cities that got the bug? They melt down into a pile of steaming crap, and that's what's gonna happen here. I called you up here because I owed you one. You still got that boat of yours?"

"Yep."

"Good. Get out while you can. You got a good head start. There won't be any press on this, but word'll leak out anyway. Always does."

"What about you?"

Carno looked back at Paris. "I've been a cop too long to be anything else. I'm staying on the case."

"My sentiments exactly."

Carno sighed, looked at the floor, then up at Paris. "You got a lot of friends around here, Phil. More than you know, even. But lately, you've made a few enemies. I hear things. I hear things I'm not supposed to hear. And right now, I hear the sound of shit rolling downhill, and unless you step aside, it's going to roll right over the top of you."

Paris smiled a sad smile. "You couldn't be more specific, could you?"

"Would it make any difference if I was?"

"No. Not really." Paris rose to his feet. "Thanks, Al. We're even."

"Good luck, Phil."

"Same to you."

As he climbed the small flight of steps, Paris could smell the fragrance of the rhododendrons that flanked the entrance to the Specialized Care Group. Before entering, he stopped and looked out over the view from West Seattle toward downtown. A warm breeze blew in the steely buzz of the city, and little whitecaps dotted the green waters of the bay. It all looked so normal, he thought. How could it be so sick and not know it?

He lit a cigarette, and he knew he was stalling. He didn't want to go in. He wanted to stay here and soak in the soft summer wind, until the light dimmed and Mt. Rainier became a vague, blue chimera on the fading horizon. And as the light dissolved, he wished he could dissolve along with it, a slow and graceful fade to black.

A slow and graceful fade to black.

Yes, that's what it would be like for her, he thought. *Just a simple fade, a painless journey through a deepening gray and on to complete blackness, then out into some grand and unknowable light.* Would she remember him then? Would she remember those fine days on the boat, when the wooden hull caressed the water and he wrapped his big arm around her shoulders and steered a steady course toward some distant island?

He finished the cigarette, stubbed it out, and buried the butt under the bark dust at the base of the rhododendrons. He opened the door and signed in at the reception desk, where a middle-aged woman smiled quickly at him and went back about her business. He went through the twin set of double doors and onto the main floor. It was quiet. The only sound was the whisper of a nurse's rubber soles as she ducked into one of the bays formed by the dividers. His big feet and leather shoes abruptly broke the silence with each slap onto the polished floor.

She was in the third bay down, on the side facing the Sound. The requisite tubing invaded her mouth and her nose as she lay on her back with palms up. Before he sat down, Paris went to the utility table with the monitoring instruments and powered them down one by one. Then he leaned over and gently removed the nasal tube from her nostril. Finally, he found the valve for the respirator, turned it off, and carefully removed the flexible plastic tube from her mouth.

He kissed her on the forehead, sat down, and grasped her nearest hand.

When Paris got off the hospital elevator on Elaine's floor, the corridor was completely empty, an illuminated tunnel flanked with scores of open doors. He immediately had the terrible feeling he'd waited too long to pull her out. Then from down toward the nurses' station, he heard a crash as something hit the floor. He walked briskly toward the sound and heard more crashing, this time a lighter sound, like the impact of paper and cardboard.

When the nurses' station came into view, he saw a single figure, a young man behind the counter, reaching up and searching through the overhead cabinets. The man had the wasted frame and dirty, long hair of a drug addict. More specifically, a speed freak whose body fat had been boiled away in a prolonged blaze of injected methamphetamine. Although the doper had his back to Paris, he must have heard the approaching footsteps, but he ignored Paris's presence and went on pawing through the contents of the higher shelves.

And in a flash, Paris realized the doper had it right. Why be afraid of cops anymore? Compared to the plague, what could a cop do to you?

Paris resisted an impulse to intervene and continued on to Elaine's room.

"Elaine?"

At the sound of his voice she came out of the small bathroom fully dressed in jeans and a T-shirt and wielding a large scalpel in one hand.

"You okay?"

"Good enough." She reached behind and fetched a canvas athletic bag full of medical supplies. "Glad you got here when you did. I was going to wait another hour or so and take off for the boat. As you can see, things have gotten a little weird around here. The staff has been augmented by a new breed of pharmaceutical experts."

He smiled. She was tough. And even though he couldn't admit it on this particular afternoon, he was glad to see her.

"So how can you be sure?" asked Elaine as she and Paris drove down Westlake Avenue. "You've got a contaminated house in one place, and a weird traffic accident in another. How can you be sure they're linked?"

"I can't. And by the time I can, it'll be way too late."

As he turned off Westlake and arrived at his marina on Lake Union, Philip Paris immediately saw a potential problem. He turned to Elaine. "You'd think it was a national holiday, wouldn't you?"

Many of the slips were already empty. Too many, even for a clear summer afternoon such as this one. And even more people were gearing up to leave, carrying groceries and supplies down the ramp.

"Do you really think they all know?" asked Elaine as they left the car and headed for the marina gate.

"Sure thing. Must be several dozen people in police and health that were in on the case. And they've all got families.

Rumors travel fast. Unbelievably fast. Especially in a city that's been one big raw nerve for weeks on end."

As they headed down the ramp and out into the mooring area, the usual friendly banter among the boat owners was conspicuously absent. They all knew why they were suddenly here, and nobody wanted to discuss it. The boats were the best ticket to survival. The bigger ones were traveling homes. You could live in them, fish from them, and travel hundreds of miles north into Canada, losing yourself in a great wilderness of forest and water.

No problem, except that hundreds of boats were moored in Lake Union, and many thousands in Lake Washington. And they'd all have to go through the locks, which were large enough to accommodate maybe seventy pleasure craft in a single cycle. But to drain them, dispatch the vessels, refill them, and reload the next batch of boats took nearly an hour at best. As the marine stampede grew in magnitude over the next few hours, the locks would begin to operate at a hopeless deficit.

Once they were on the *Cedar Queen,* Paris fired up the engines, pulled in the mooring lines, and headed north to the Fremont Cut, the first leg of the Ship Canal on the way to the locks.

Elaine sat in a canvas chair on the rear deck and watched the modest wake as Paris headed west. There was still a dull pain in her chest from the wound, and her legs went soft if she stood for too long. She turned and looked at Paris through the wheelhouse door as his hands played gently over the wheel and the throttle. Something about Paris continued to tug at her. No matter what he did, it seemed to have an absolute force and direction to it, which was something she had seldom witnessed in other people.

By the time they crossed under the Fremont Bridge, Paris saw they were too late. A big fleet of pleasure craft milled about on the lake just outside the entrance to the canal. That meant that both the canal and Salmon Bay were already jammed with boats waiting to get through the locks. Thousands of them. Then he wondered if the locks were even operating. Maybe not. Why should the operators let others make the dash to safety while they stayed on the job to face disease and death?

Elaine turned toward the wheelhouse as she felt the boat slow to a crawl. Paris looked at her with a wry grin. "Bad timing. We're a little late."

"So what do we do now?"

Paris put the boat in neutral, came back, and sat in the chair next to her. "We stay for the party. Could I fix you a drink?"

In the darkness, the running lights from the column of boats made it appear as if a cosmic midnight express were moving against the backdrop of city lights. They were heading east through Lake Union and back to Lake Washington, a long train of defeat and despair. Earlier, while there was still light, the little portable TV on the *Cedar Queen* had shown them aerial shots of the jam at the locks, which were indeed closed for "unspecified reasons."

"Well, Detective," said Elaine, "here we are. Parked on a lake in the middle of hell." She took another sip of whiskey and soda, her third. And why not? It made the wound feel better, and her probability of enjoying a full life span was now drastically reduced.

"So where did we go wrong?" asked Paris.

"Everyone knew that the public health infrastructure had taken a beating for years. We thought we were king of the microbes and didn't need to take infectious diseases very seriously. So there was no public funding for things like EpiSim." Elaine took another sip. "Too bad about that."

"You've already said Uni's too late to develop an antibiotic for this wave of the bug, but what about a vaccine? If they could vaccinate, wouldn't that cancel most of the need for an antibiotic in the future?"

"Yes, it would. But don't count on it. There have already been vaccine tests involving the venereal form of *Chlamydia,* and they didn't work. They sensitized the subjects' immune systems so that when they were exposed to the bug there was a violent reaction that produced very severe symptoms. It just doesn't look like a very good option."

Elaine paused and took a sip. It seemed surreal to be in such a comfortable setting on a nice summer night with such a horrifying reality only yards away on the shore. But in truth, she knew it was largely a matter of the way culture inevitably colored human perception. Christianity made a sharp distinction between the flesh and the spirit, which produced a civilization patterned after abstract thought as opposed to a reflection of the natural world. The result was an elaborate illusion that people somehow existed separately from nature, as some kind of special case. Humankind had given up on the earth as the center of the solar system some time ago, but it still saw itself at the center of nature, with the biosphere rotating around it in some kind of perpetual servitude. At best, it was seen as some kind of reciprocal arrangement. "Be nice to Mother Nature, and she'll be nice to you," as if *Homo sapiens* had some kind of partial control, and nature would be "reasonable." But then along came something like Agent 57a, and suddenly there was no control at all.

"You can't help but wonder if something like this is actually a scheduled event, some kind of spring pruning," continued Elaine. "Or maybe an automated reaction that obeys some set of rules we just don't understand." She knew that one interesting line of thought had it that some diseases were a kind of chaotic system. In their natural state, they seemed to behave quite predictably and came and went in regular waves strung out over decades, even centuries. But if something intervened to drive them far from their natural state, they became chaotic. Then the waves were no longer regular. The disease might disappear altogether—or it might suddenly go nuclear and kill with a vengeance. Ironically, vaccines were a possible cause. Vaccination programs seldom reached everyone in a target population. The expense and logistics were just too difficult. Instead, they covered selected groups, such as rural villages, or the very young. So rather than completely snuff a disease out, they could drive it into an entirely novel state, into chaos. There might not be any change for quite a while. Then things might suddenly go wildly out of control.

Her thoughts were interrupted by clusters of fat little pops off in the distance, almost certainly the product of small-arms fire. She turned to Paris, who was quietly surveying the city lights.

"What's going to happen to us, Detective?"

Paris smiled. "Only the best."

"And why's that?"

"Because we're doing the right thing."

She nodded and tilted back in her chair. It was extremely simplistic thinking. Or extremely subtle. She was no longer sure which. The man was a mystery to her. The old parade of Bennet-type men in her life had all been predictable because they always did what was in their immediate self-interest. She had the profile down pat, and that put her in control of the relationship, for better or worse. But Paris wasn't like that. She couldn't figure out the internal engine that propelled him. She clearly wasn't in control here, but for some reason, it just didn't seem to matter. She had begun to understand that the power of Philip Paris was his lack of lust for it, and that was a novelty to her, an attractive novelty.

43

PARIS CLIMBED THE ALUMINUM LADDER GINGERLY, TRYING to time his steps with the gunshots coming from the pitched roof. He paused for a moment and turned around to make sure no one was watching. The backyard had an oval patio with white plastic lawn furniture, a neatly clipped lawn, and a propane barbecue secured with a black cover. A plastic swimming pool occupied the middle of the lawn, and a small bike with trainer wheels sat on the patio. The house was a split-level affair, a stolid middle-class structure painted an earthy tone with a complement of mature shrubbery surrounding most of it.

No one was watching, so Paris turned his attention back to the roof. One more step would let him peek over the lip of the gutter and put the sniper in full view. It was hot out, but the thick clumps of black smoke provided intermittent shelter from the sun, and he hunkered down in one of these smoke shadows as he unholstered his pistol.

Graziano had directed him to this house. He'd parked three houses away and crossed through their backyards to avoid coming into the sniper's field of view. Before he left the car, Graziano ran down the sequence of events. Seemed that one family in the neighborhood came down with the plague. Two sick kids. But they refused to admit it and kept coming and going as usual. So today, their house had mysteriously caught fire when they were gone, and no one had bothered to call in an alarm until they realized the fire might spread, which it had already done. The house next door was also ablaze, with festering holes of flame punching through the roof.

When two fire trucks finally answered the call, the shooting began. The first shot took out the windshield of one of the trucks. The next smashed a headlight. As the firemen took cover behind their rigs, the call went out. Graziano's car and a patrol car answered and decided that protecting the firemen was their first priority. The gunshots were methodically dismantling the fire trucks, and the cops could see the smoke from the rifle shots coming from a roof three houses down on the opposite side of the street and across an intersection. At that point, Graziano called for backup and got Paris.

Paris took a deep breath and peeked over the gutter top. The sniper was a man in his thirties wearing a plaid shirt and jeans. His elbows were propped on the peak of the roof to provide leverage for a hunting rifle with a scope. The man was just squeezing off a shot, and as he pulled back the bolt, a spent round ejected and rolled down the roof, then pitched onto the lawn where it joined a scattered pile of shell casings. The man's vision was riveted on the fire trucks down the street, and he was oblivious to Paris.

"Police! Put it down!" boomed Paris as he leveled his revolver at the prone figure. The man stopped and stared down over his shoulder at Paris. He wore glasses and had a receding hairline. He gave Paris an annoyed look, but carefully put the rifle down on the side toward Paris. As soon as he let go of it, the rifle slid down the grade of the roof, where Paris caught it just before it reached the edge. It was an exceptional weapon, a .284-caliber Winchester Model 70.

"Now keep both hands on the roof and slide down to the ladder," ordered Paris. When the man reached the ladder, Paris backed down and the man followed. As soon as the man's feet hit the ground, Paris parked the rifle, shoved him up against the house wall, and searched him. No weapons.

"You own this house?"

"Yes, I do," replied the man, his arms still extended against the wall.

Paris moved over and picked up the rifle. "So what's the deal, friend? When did you decide to become a sniper?"

"The people in that house have the plague. They wouldn't leave. It was them or us. If the fire trucks saved the house, they'd stay on. Then we'd all get sick. And we'd all die."

"You're sure about that?" asked Paris as he removed the bolt from the rifle and stuffed it in his pocket.

"Yes, I am. And that's why I did it."

To his right, Paris heard the sliding sound of the patio door opening and whirled to see the cause. A child of about three in pajamas peeked out, an angelic little girl with big worried eyes.

"Daddy?"

"Daddy's okay, baby. Daddy's all right. Now you stay inside."

Paris sighed. The man looked as if he probably sold computer supplies or some such thing. But he'd just committed a felony that would have made the national news in saner times.

In saner times, thought Paris. That was the new key to the street. Saner times were now no more than a baseline, a point of departure, an old dream of things gone right during a time when they were going inexorably wrong.

"You got any other weapons in the house?"

"No, I do not."

Paris put his gun back in his holster. "Okay, listen up. Here's what you do: Go in the house. Don't come out until the fire trucks are gone. If there's another report of shooting from here, I'm going to come back, and there's going to be very big trouble. Got that?"

"Got it."

"Okay, then, get in the goddamn house." Paris watched as the man shuffled toward the patio doors. What was the use of arresting him? It was now eighteen days since the plague had reached Seattle. Elaine estimated that over 350,000 people were already dead. The jail was completely full, and its staff was decimated. The court system had ground almost to a complete halt, and martial law had been declared, but those who were supposed to enforce it were as devastated as those who were supposed to observe it.

"You shoot him?" inquired Graziano as Paris approached the cluster of fire and police vehicles. Technically, Graziano was Homicide, but now, in a desperate attempt to maintain civil order, everyone worked the street. Everyone.

"Nope. Just some schmuck doing his duty to defend the neighborhood against the big bad bug. I can shoot a bad guy, if I have to. But I can't shoot a schmuck. Know what I mean?"

"Yeah, I know what you mean." Even with a surgical mask, Graziano was easily recognizable with his heavy black brows and dark brown eyes. They all wore the masks now, and Paris was surprised at how quickly you could identify people from only the top half of their face. Graziano inspected a shattered headlight on one of the fire trucks and saw a bullet hole dead center through the bulb in the middle. "Well, anyway, the son of bitch was really a good shot. I gotta give him that."

Behind them, the two ignited houses burned toward their foundations as the firemen sprayed down the adjoining homes to contain the damage.

Before leaving the neighborhood, Paris dropped the rifle bolt in the sniper's mailbox. After all, the man still had a family to defend in a time when 911 was just another number.

As Paris waited at the end of the pier on Lake Union, he carefully scanned the parking lot and old factory building. It seemed clear, but he knew that as soon as he dropped his vigilance, Barney would strike like a silent cobra. Before he'd left the fire scene, Graziano had said something that reinforced his suspicions.

"Phil, I just want you to know you've got friends," Graziano had said earnestly. "Just in case you need them."

The implication was clear. Somewhere up there, in the rotting and diseased political hierarchy, somebody had it in for him. And with Fancher dead, that left the deepening shadow of Barney, who had to be in a rage over Paris's protection of Elaine. The city was heading toward a state that could only be described as criminal anarchy, and once it arrived, the protective shield he enjoyed as a policeman would quickly dissolve.

Still, he had friends.

The distinctive burble of *Cedar Queen*'s engine caught his ear, and he turned to see Elaine guiding it alongside the pier with a sure hand on the wheel. He grinned. She had the knack, all right. Just a couple of days of practice, and she could already pilot the boat like an old hand. In the background about a hundred yards offshore, two boats from the Harbor Patrol patiently idled. Paris waved at one of them, and a uniformed figure on the deck waved back. Some old friends were taking care of Elaine during the daylight hours, when the *Cedar Queen* was vulnerable to assault by boat. They had also supplied fuel and provisions when needed.

Paris jumped down onto the deck, and Elaine quickly applied the throttle and pushed them out toward the middle of the lake. "So what's new at work?" she asked as he came into the wheelhouse.

"Nothing good," he said as he took off the mask. Out here on the lake was one of the few places it was safe to do so. "Nothing good."

Later, after dark, it rained. A cool, steady rain that leached the summer heat and beat insistently on the roof that overhung the rear deck. They sat in the deck chairs and were illuminated only by a weak splash of light coming up the stairs from the main saloon. Elaine watched the glow of Paris's cigarette tip as he took a drag then stole a small sip of whiskey. The ice in his glass clinked as he raised it to his lips. The beating of the rain lowered a curtain between them and city, which was obscured in a minor mist. They had not spoken for some time, and the span of the silence seemed stretched just a little too taut.

"You got any family?" asked Paris. "I don't think I asked that, did I? It never seemed right."

"It's okay. No, I don't. I was an only child and a late-life one at that. Both my parents are dead. Natural causes."

"Well, at least they didn't have to live to see this."

"That's true. But I think my father would have liked to see it. He was very bright and very cynical. None of this would have surprised him. He would have been fascinated."

"Was he a doctor?"

"No. He was physicist. And a good one." Elaine paused and focused on the glow of Paris's cigarette. "What about you? You told me about your wife, but not much. Anybody else?"

"Yeah. I got a sister. Widowed. And a nephew."

"Are they okay?"

"I checked on my sister a couple of days ago. She's scared, but she's not sick. The kid's out on his own. No telling what's going on with him."

The rain beat a big hole into the conversation while Paris drained the last of his whiskey.

"I let her go."

"Let who go?" asked Elaine.

"My wife."

An air horn sounded somewhere out on the water and echoed off the docks in the distance. Then the rain closed in once more.

"Was it hard?" she asked softly.

"No. It was sad. But not hard. I did it just before we tried to get out through the locks. No way I was going to let the plague get her. No way." He got up abruptly and headed for the stairs, his big frame blocking all the light from the cabin. "Good night."

"Good night," she echoed. She turned to face the night, the rain, the city in the distance. She wanted to hold him, but he was gone.

"Barney!" exclaimed Julie Fancher as she opened the front door with its carved-oak panels and squinted into the noontime summer light. "How are you?"

"I'm fine, Julie, I'm sorry I missed Bob's funeral. But it's been a bad time for all of us. You know what I mean?" Barney could see the frantic little question marks in her eyes as she tried to read him, tried to maneuver for the high ground. She was wearing a tailored workout suit made of some exotic material, and virgin athletic shoes. Her makeup was tastefully applied and her hair cut in an abbreviated, streamlined style. She was fully everything that forty-two could buy.

"Barney, I know exactly what you mean," she said as she reached out and gave that little charm-school pat on the back of the hand. "Would you like to come in for a minute?"

Barney flashed himself a bitter smile. Perfect. The gracious hostess was going to invite him in, but with the careful qualification that he stay "just for a minute." This time, it would be a very long minute. The longest minute Julie Fancher had ever known.

"Thanks, Julie," he said earnestly. "It's good of you to make the time."

As they walked through a big anteroom, he saw that she was steering them into the kitchen, the safe room, the room with absolutely no sexual overtone. "Would you like a little coffee?" she asked as he seated himself at a glass-top breakfast table where a picture window looked out onto the lake.

"No, but I would like a little drink," he said with a smile. "How about a gin and tonic?"

He caught the flicker of terror in her face, and the quick recovery. "Sure," she said breezily. "Be right back."

He let her round the corner into the hall, then followed the synthetic swish of her workout suit in the silent house. When the sound stopped, he looked around the corner and saw her frantically punching the buttons on a phone perched atop a small table with filigreed-silver legs and a marble top.

"You forget about the drink?" he asked to her back. Her spine jerked straight up and she nearly dropped the receiver at the sound of his voice.

"Oh, Barney!" she said in mock surprise. "I had to cancel an appointment and I nearly forgot. Sorry."

"That's quite all right." Barney looked over her shoulder and down a hallway to an open door. "Say, what's that big room back there?"

"Oh, that? That's the master bedroom." She tried to affect a casual pose, half-sitting against the marble tabletop, but Barney could see that her fingers were turning white where they gripped the table's edge.

"You know, Julie, Bob never really gave me a tour of this place."

"He didn't?"

Barney pointed toward the bedroom. "You mind if we take a peek back there?"

"Oh, it's just a *mess* back there today! Let's wait until some other time, okay?"

Barney put his hands in his pockets, and he could feel the erect shaft of his penis brush against his forefingers. "Well, as you know, Julie," he said quietly, "things are pretty bad right now. So there might not be another time. Which means we all have to adjust our thinking. We can't wait any longer to do those special things we've always wanted to do. You know what I mean?"

"I'm not sure," she said shakily.

Barney started toward her, his hands still in his pockets. "I don't think I can explain it any better than that." He could see her stare in horror at the bulge in his crotch as he came forward. He reached out, gripped her forearm, and nodded toward the bedroom. "Come on. Let's get started."

Before she could reply, he turned her toward the hall and led her into the bedroom. Once inside, he let her go and she darted out of his grip and around to the other side of the king-size bed covered by a hand-stitched comforter. She put her palm against the doorframe to the bathroom to steady herself as Barney surveyed the room.

"Boy! This is beautifully done!"

"We, uh, had it redecorated last year. It was one of Bob's favorite—"

"You know, I thought we were going to get through this without saying the 'B' word. But I guess I was wrong."

"I'm sorry, I . . ."

"There's nothing to be sorry about, Julie. Let's be friends, okay? Say, I brought you a little something to slip into."

"You what?"

"I said I brought you a little something to slip into." Barney's hand came out of his pocket with a pair of handcuffs, which he tossed onto the center of the bed, where they punched a soft, rounded crater into the comforter. "The very best. Silver-plated and custom-engraved. What do you think?"

She looked at him and desperately tried to push her horrified face into an expression of indignation and anger. "You can't do this. You can't get away with this. The police . . ."

"Julie, Julie," scolded Barney. "Don't you get it? It's all different now. I *am* the police. Now let's get on with it, shall we?"

The remaining color drained out of her tanned face, like coffee from an overdose of cream. She stared at the floor and walked forward.

As she raised her leg to climb on the bed, Barney came. No matter. They had all day.

It was the right thing. A sensible act of self-preservation, a move that would have no effect on the final outcome.

Still, Paris loathed himself for it.

When he'd gone up the stairs to the porch of his sister's house, he should have known something was wrong because the front door was open behind the screen door. Cathy was a cautious sort and always kept the door closed, even in the heat of summer. Instead, she ventilated the place by opening the windows a foot or two behind their protective screens. But today, Paris could see through to the staircase as he cleared the top step, crossed the porch, and tried the screen, which was unlocked.

"Cathy?" he yelled as he poked his head in.

As he turned to face the living room, he saw her lying on the couch, one arm dangling down and jumping about in an awful little dance. A bloody red cloud spread across the cushion supporting her head, and her eyes were fixed on the ceiling as her slack jaw left her with a permanently open mouth.

"Don't move!" he'd said stupidly, and backed out onto the porch. Then he turned, ran to the car, and grabbed his surgical mask.

Now, as he bounded back up the stairs, he felt the guilt of having deserted his sister, if even for moment, to save his own hide. As he tore open the screen door and crossed to the couch, he realized he'd better save the self-flagellation for later. He picked her up, took her across the room, and kicked the screen door open with a blow that severed the top hinge and left it dangling at a crazed angle. He strode out onto the porch and deposited her in an old porch swing that was still mounted from the roof by a pair of rusting chains. Here he was safe with her. In the open air, the bug dispersed rapidly, according to Elaine. And with the double insurance of the surgical mask, he was okay.

But Cathy wasn't. Cathy was nearly dead.

"Cathy? Can you hear me?"

He thought she nodded, but then realized it was her head bobbing from a set of tremors as the germ dismantled her nervous system. Her eyes turned to focus on him, but she couldn't hold them in place. An alien sound rattled out of her open mouth, a little clue to the horrible devastation in her respiratory system. A small stream of blood worked its way out her nostril and down her cheek.

Then, just as he thought he'd lost touch with her, her hand grasped his wrist and pulled him toward her. He leaned in and pointed his ear toward her mouth. Her fingers were hot as fire on his wrist.

"Skip." The word was deeply mixed in a liquid gravel of failing respiration. "Find Skip."

He backed away from her so he could see her face. "Find Skip?"

She managed a single nod as she let go of his wrist and closed her eyes.

He came in close to her ear. "Don't worry. I'll find him. It'll be okay. I promise. I'll find him."

She lasted until midafternoon. A curious thing happened when he buried her in the backyard. There was a birdbath, an old and ornate one, filled to the brim with water from the recent rain. As he started to dig, a robin flew down and perched on the edge. It looked at him quizzically as he stabbed the shovel into the lawn turf, and later into the clay soil below. The bird remained absolutely stationary, its eyes fixed on the grave. Only when the excavation was completely refilled and he rested all sweaty on the shovel did the bird once again take flight.

44

First they found the dead, then the liquor, and finally the gun.

"Hey! Lookee here, man. A little home protection!" Skip watches warily as the Tall Boy waves the pistol, a big .44 magnum, then flexes his knees, grasps the gun in both hands, and assumes the cinematic pose of the police marksman. "Didn't protect 'em too well now, did it?"

He is referring to the owners of the house, which is a miniature mansion in the style of casual affluence. As the Tall Boy points the gun elsewhere, Skip relaxes slightly and sinks back into an expensive leather couch. He is gang people now, and the gang had carefully stalked this house for many hours before smashing a window to gain entry. Sure enough, it was a Dead House, just like thousands of others in Bellevue. The furnace still worked, so the smell was bad, but that didn't matter when there was free booze and shelter. They were all thin now, young and gaunt from malnutrition. Five boys and three girls. A sixth boy was dead in a dispute over the third girl, his brain jellied by the shock wave from a crowbar accelerated to a murderous velocity. A fourth girl lay moldering on the lawn of a house that wasn't quite dead yet, where the owner had taken up arms against them and opened fire from concealment.

At first, it was an adventure being gang people, then routine, and now, minimal survival. The gang had formed at Adam Larkin's house, stoned Adam whose parents had never returned from their final business trips. But soon the food was gone, and hunger became their new leader, a strange and alien authority to these children who had bathed for their entire lives in a continuous stream of nutrition. They had no money and no coupons from the state, and the troops running the supermarkets made no exceptions, so all they could do was raid the Dead Houses. At first, the houses were hard to find, but not for long. Over ten thousand people were dying every day, and that left a lot of vacant real estate to prowl.

When they first started their chain of migration through the Dead Houses, they were still wary of getting caught. Under martial law, looting was a capital offense, and justice was often administered right at the scene of the crime. They would peek out through the curtains and occasionally spot a military vehicle rolling down the street. But that seemed months ago, and now few vehicles of any sort came by.

At this particular house, they found a man and wife. They knew this because the pictures on the mantel still bore some resemblance to the shriveled faces on the corpses, although a rodent had been chewing on the nose of the husband, making his original appearance a little harder to construct. They found him on the big leather couch in the living room, dressed in Nike sweats and barefoot. He had the big lesions on his face, a sure sign of the plague; but there was also an empty bottle of Seconals on the large glass coffee table, with several spilled onto the carpet. At the end, he must have strapped on a chemical booster to get him to the other side.

The wife was in bed, wearing a silk nightgown, with her head resting on a pillow stained an ancient brown from the hemorrhaging that had accompanied her final hours. For some reason, she clutched an old teddy bear, which stared at the world through wide, buttoned eyes, as if to absolve itself of any blame.

By this time, they had it down. To dispose of the bodies, they dumped them into bedsheets and dragged them out to the garage. That's all garages were good for these days.

One of the girls beams approval at Tall Boy's antics with the pistol. He is rising in the pecking order. The girl now operates under the atavistic urge to find a protector and provider. More civilized qualities are no longer coefficients in the social equation. She lounges on an easy chair and throws a leg over one of the arms, drawing the fabric of her jeans tight over her crotch.

Skip looks at her blankly through the cruel, cloudy light that intrudes into the living room through the big picture window. Seattle is wet, Seattle is cold, Seattle is dying. But Skip is warm, heated by a constriction of capillaries brought on from the bottle of Vigna Rionda he appropriated from a tidy little pantry off the kitchen. However, the wine is waning now, leaving his head throbbing and a dull burn in his empty belly.

"Hey, motherfuck. Gimmee that." Skip looks up and sees a thick hand clamp onto Tall Boy's wrist. It's the squat, muscular kid, the one with the shaved head and no name except for Mr. Beef. Tall Boy pulls hard against the tug of Mr. Beef, bringing his elbows into his chest and twisting his torso away from the challenge. Mr. Beef brings a second hand across and grabs Tall Boy's free wrist. The struggling pair teeter, then pitch forward onto the carpet. As they hit, the pistol discharges, a voluminous blast that fills the living room with its concussive power.

A scream. The round from the pistol has entered the belly of another boy and punctured his large intestine. He folds into a twisted knot of agony.

Mr. Beef relaxes his grip. For now, the pistol is no longer a prize. They all gather around the stricken boy, who clutches the wound with blood spurting between his fingers. But there is nothing to be done. Nothing. So their drunken vigil is brief and dissolves into more random plundering. The boy is left folded in terminal suffering as the carpet bleeds red around him.

Skip wanders to the window and peers out into the empty street. Soon it will be dark out. Dark and hungry out. He is sick of it, the violence, the aimless cruelty, the mad indulgence, the hopeless wandering. He now understands why there are people like his uncle Phil in the world. They form a kind of defensive perimeter that keeps the bad things from running wild through people's lives. He would go home in a second, but he's terrified of what he might find. In his fitful dreams, he sees the body of his mother sprawled on the front lawn of their house, dead of the plague. People pass by casually on the sidewalk, as if she weren't even there.

Skip looks over at the stricken kid, who is wound in a fetal coil on the plush carpet. He has stopped moving, except for his lower lip, which quivers violently. Skip goes over and squats down before him. The kid's eyes have the death shine. Skip goes to the couch, gets a blanket, and gently covers the kid. It's all he can do.

"I cannot overemphasize that you represent the *new leadership* of this city," declared Barney as he paced in front of the audience sitting in steel folding chairs. "And with that must come a sense of *duty* and *responsibility*."

His voice bounced off the cement floor of the big, empty warehouse, reverberated off the tilt-up concrete walls, and rose into the darkness above the suspended banks of fluorescent lights. He paced as he talked, covering the space between the audience and the three folding tables where the trials had just taken place.

"If we do not follow policy, if we break the rules, we jeopardize not only ourselves, but this entire organization. And I'm here to tell you, friends, this organization is the only chance that any of us have of surviving. If you go against the team, you go against all of us."

He stopped and gestured to the eleven men bound hand and foot and sitting in folding chairs facing the audience. In front of each was a stainless steel tub, and dangling above every head was a hangman's noose that went up to a pulley on a steel girder overhead. The men were dressed in cheap sweats and rubber sandals, and they all cast a stupefied stare at the floor, the result of a sedative administered just before the start of the trials and now in full force.

"Each of these men put themselves above us. Each of these men acted in their own selfish interest. You've heard the testimony. You've listened to the witnesses. And I hope that each one of you is as *disappointed* and *disgusted* as I am."

He paused and scanned the audience. Few of the men made eye contact with him. Most shifted uncomfortably in their seats and kept their eyes locked on the nooses and the tubs.

"There was a time when we could have shown some measure of mercy. But not now, friends. Unfortunately, extreme times call for extreme measures. And I want you to know that it is my sincere wish that we never have to assemble like this again. But when you leave here tonight, I want you to remember this. Each of the accused was granted *due pro-*

cess. We are not savages! We will not repeat the repression we all suffered by those in power, by those who let us agonize for so long!"

Barney was referring to the due process administered by a tribunal of three men, faithful cronies who had sat at the head table and heard the charges against the "accused," who were then given a chance to present their side of the story. In every case, the crime was not an act of violence or theft. This would not have impressed the dozens of men in the audience, many of whom had committed criminal acts of the worst sort. Instead, the crimes were acts of infidelity and disloyalty against Barney himself, although this was always couched in terms of offenses against "the organization."

The trials were imperative. Anarchy was a disease, he knew, a worse disease than the one now tearing through the population. The creeping anarchy on the streets was eating away at his ranks, infecting his minions with thoughts of independent action. Anarchy destroyed structure, and structure was what Barney was all about. An absurdly cruel structure, based on the most primal of constructs, but a structure nevertheless. And its primal nature gave it a perverse kind of robustness that allowed it to thrive in these terrible times.

Barney knew that he had to act swiftly and decisively to excise the diseased tissue from his organization, and that was why they were gathered here tonight. He was performing the surgery in plain view of all his supervisory personnel, so that they might communicate it back to the those on the streets.

"I can only hope," continued Barney quietly, "that what you witness here tonight never has to be repeated. But I can't guarantee it, because that decision is not mine. It's yours."

As he spoke, men came out of the shadows and grabbed the legs of the prisoners, pulled the nooses down, and slipped them around the prisoners' ankles.

"I feel pain because I've failed these people. I was not able to communicate with them. I was not able to impress upon them how destructive their behavior was."

The men stepped back and pulled on the ropes. Overhead, the pulleys creaked and squeaked as the prisoners were hoisted up by their heels until their heads were about a yard above the floor.

"I can only hope that I have not failed the rest of you. I can only hope that you each understand what is required of you that we may all survive."

A second set of men appeared and took away the folding chairs occupied by the prisoners. They neatly stacked the chairs on a cart, then returned to position the stainless steel tubs directly under each prisoner's head. The inverted faces stared out at the audience through filmy and sedated eyes.

"In the end it comes down to this: They perish that we may learn! They die that we may live! So be it!"

Barney stalked off to the side and into shadow. And the whine of an electric motor rose to fill the great open space. A deep and throbbing hum that fluttered the thick and expectant air. And over the top of the hum came the angry gnashing of metal against metal, buffered only by a thin film of oil.

A short, wiry man appeared out of the shadows, wearing dark glasses and dressed in yellow rain gear. In his rubber-gloved hands was an electric chain saw.

At the sight of the saw, there was a long burst of metallic pops and snaps as the audience shifted reflexively into defensive postures in their folding chairs. A little flurry of anxious whispers floated up, but quickly evaporated in the darkness above.

One of the prisoners made a feeble attempt to turn his head toward the sound, but the drug and bondage pulled him back.

The short man stopped at the first man in line and turned to the man who controlled the prisoner's pulley. He jerked his thumb up to indicate he wanted the height adjusted. The prisoner was hoisted upward until the man raised his palm in a signal to halt.

In a careful motion, he positioned the whirring blade at the base of the prisoner's neck and cut his head off. A fine spray of blood hit his rain gear as the screaming chain roared through flesh and bone. After a few awful moments, the head dropped into the tub with a clunk that could clearly be heard in spite of the saw noise. As the man in yellow took a step back, the decapitated torso swayed gently and drained a river of blood into the tub.

Barney surveyed the audience. A few watched the severed

body in lurid fascination. Most averted their eyes. Some twisted sideways in their chairs as if to face in some other direction.

Good. He had made his point. And in case not everyone got it, there were still ten more heads to go.

Shortly after dark, when the Harbor Patrol boats had left, they hoisted the *Cedar Queen*'s anchor and turned over its old engine. With all the running lights off, they crept through the scattered flotilla of vessels that had taken refuge along the north-south axis of Lake Union. Elaine's eyes dark-adapted more rapidly than Paris's, so she took the wheel and he kept watch from the bow. In all, they moved about half a mile north to where a screen of other boats shielded them from the shore. Here they dropped anchor and turned on the interior cabin lights only after drawing the curtains.

As was their ritual now, they came up and sat in their deck chairs, whiskey in hand, and looked out into the evening.

"Do we really need to do this every night? Won't Mr. Cox be sufficiently deterred by your gunboat friends?" asked Elaine. They had been repeating the same maneuver for the better part of a week.

"We've got what the bogeyman wants, and sooner or later, he'll be coming to get it."

"I suppose," sighed Elaine. She knew Paris was right. The people at Uni were smart and powerful enough to focus on the long term. They were fully aware that epidemics of this type came in bursts, and that while they'd missed an antibiotic for the first outburst, a drug to cure the next major burst of infection would have enormous value, even in a severely depressed world economy. But to make the drug, they needed the disk with the correct model for Agent 57a. And the only copy in the world resided in the forward locker of the *Cedar Queen*. And as Paris had explained, the man now assigned to retrieve the disk was a special monster who would soon fill the vacuum left by the collapse of civil order in Seattle.

"So what do we do?"

"Simple," Paris said as he got up and collected her glass. "We have another drink."

"I'm serious. What are going to do?"

"And I'm serious, too. We're going to have another drink. That's as far as the plan goes."

"Is there perhaps some way we might avoid being killed? Is there some way we can give the germ model back to Uni and maybe save the remnants of the human race?" she asked sarcastically. "From my point of view, these might be highly desirable outcomes."

"We wait. We see what happens. As long as there's a police force, we're okay. We're protected. After that, it's a little tough to tell."

"I'm sure it is," Elaine said glumly.

"Tell me this, Dr. Wilkes. Are you pissed off, or just plain scared?"

"The latter," said Elaine without hesitation. "Definitely the latter. And what about you?"

"The former. I'm pissed off. Have been for years."

"Are we talking about the usual hard-boiled cop stuff? You know—where the mean streets finally get to you, and all that?"

"No. We're not." He paused, and she saw only the ghost of his face in the cast-off light from shore. "Somewhere out there is the guy that killed my wife. I never got him. And because I never got him, he's now killed half of Seattle."

"But I thought your wife was diabetic and had complications brought on by food poisoning."

"Forget about the food part. She was poisoned. Simple as that. Deliberately poisoned. But I couldn't prove it. I damn near lost my job trying."

At that moment, Elaine feels the stab of jealousy go through her heart. It happens so fast, she can't stop it and must accept it on its own terms. His wife. His poor, deceased wife. Paris still carries a passion for her, only now it manifests itself through his obsession with this monstrous killer. Elaine resents it deeply, because it marks the distance between them, which although diminished, will never close until he puts the matter to rest. And even though the stab is fading, its ghost lives on and shoves the truth into the middle of her emotional vision. She knows now that she wants to sail off with him not just to escape, but to build a new life together, a permanent life. She feels a great wave of passion run through her and wants badly to tell him. But this is hardly the time. The best thing she can do right now is stay focused on the present.

"Meanwhile," continued Paris, "the killer was out there perfecting his trade. And two weeks ago, he made the big time."

"You mean the psycho who hit the shopping center?"

"Yeah. The psycho. He's out there somewhere. Floating on air. A very pleased man."

"Wrong. He probably contaminated himself somewhere along the way and died."

"Don't think so. It only happens that way in the movies. He's out there, all right. I can feel him."

45

THE DUMP TRUCK IS THE LAST ONE OF THE DAY, A BRUTISH machine with thick tires, big bumpers, and a diesel snarl that rages into the overcast sky of early evening. It backs down the sharply graded incline of packed earth, brakes pumping gingerly and wheels maneuvering to stay centered. When it reaches the bottom, fifteen meters below ground level, it follows the directions of a suited figure who walks along with it toward the center of the depression. The walker proceeds at a leisurely pace, occasionally raising an arm and pointing out a correction in course. He wears green rubber waders over the legs of the suit, and the waders are splashed with a brownish red coat of mud from the recently excavated earth.

Eventually, the walker halts the truck and signals for the dumping to begin. The engine's pace quickens to force the hydraulics into action, and a black ball of diesel smoke puffs out of the chrome exhaust. The bed of the truck begins to tip skyward, and the front fenders rise visibly as the center of gravity shifts toward the rear. Then the dumping begins.

The dumping of the lumpy parcels wrapped in black plastic tarps and bound with twine or bungee cords.

The dumping of the dead. Thousands of them. Today, nearly sixteen thousand.

As the bed rises, the bodies fall out slowly at first, black and wrinkled lumps of plastic that issue a leaden thump when they land atop those that came before them. The bed rises higher and the pace quickens, and a dark, shiny waterfall of death cascades down toward the damp, red soil.

The last body struggles posthumously against the urge of gravity and holds out until the bed is pointed high into the sky, to where the hooves of Pegasus will soon tred the firmament of night. Then it, too, slides down and out.

The body of the mayor of Seattle comes to rest at last.

A hundred yards away, Barney Cox lounges comfortably on the couch in his trailer with his feet up on the coffee table. The yellow light of the table lamps and the orange glow of the space heater bring a cheery warmth that holds off the chill damp outside. Through the trailer wall, he can hear the last dump truck of the day labor back up the incline and out of the pit. A phone on the coffee table rings and he answers. It seems it's time. He puts down the minutes from the last city/county meeting, stretches, stands, and goes to the closet to don his isolation suit.

While he adjusts the hood and breathing apparatus, he chuckles to himself about the meeting. Every time he advances, the commissioners back up, just like a troupe of trained animals. His latest proposal would give his organization certain regulatory powers. "Extremely limited powers" was the way he phrased it in the presentation, powers that applied only to his specific charter.

And that charter was, of course, the collection and disposal of the dead. Some time back, the government had learned a horrible lesson in the mathematics of premature mortality. Within a month of the mass infection, the number of corpses quickly climbed beyond the capacity of all the funeral homes and cemeteries in the metropolitan area. And no arm of government could muster the manpower or organization required to deal with such a gruesome and repellent problem. Decent people simply weren't equipped to absorb the unrelenting horror of it.

Decent people. That was the key, the key that unlocked the prison system and let Barney's shadow army out onto the streets. He presented the government with a well-organized workforce that was anything but decent, but ready to take on the task with a grotesque kind of gusto. At first, his proposal was rebuffed with great indignation, but the bodies continued to pile up. And when they began to decay and stink and became rotting warehouses of various diseases, an agreement was hastily reached.

Now, in his latest round of negotiations, he is proposing that his people have certain powers to search private homes and businesses. As of late, many plague deaths were going unattended and unreported, so Barney and company needed a more proactive program to seek out and dispose of the victims. The surviving members of government had to admit that it made sense and said they would take the matter under consideration.

Barney zips up the front of his suit, cracks open the trailer door, and steps into a plastic antechamber. He shuts the door behind him and hears the rush of air from the compressor as he opens the front door. He steps out onto the muddy ground just as the overhead lamps fire up, the big halogen monsters mounted on the hastily installed wooden poles.

They flood the big clearing, where hundreds of dump trucks are parked, with big metal ribs bulging from the sides of their beds.

They illuminate the crews, still in their suits, who sit in cabs or lounge against fenders.

They shine down into the pit, the monstrous earthen laceration, still brown and raw from recent excavation, a cavity over two hundred yards on a side.

They bathe the bodies in their tarps, the bodies of mothers' sons and fathers' daughters, the bodies united in a terminal community under a damp and fading sky.

From the near corners of the pit, two gasoline tanker trucks feed big pumps attached to hoses that spray columns of high-octane petrol over the dead. A delicate mist drifts off the columns, and the arc of a halogen rainbow forms and reforms in the drifting spray.

Abruptly, the spraying stops. The gas trucks roll back from the precipice. The air clears. The rainbows vanish. The crews come off their trucks and turn their attention toward Barney. No one speaks.

In the silence, Barney's boots squish and suck in the shallow mud as he walks from the trailer toward the edge of the pit. He stops ten yards short of the edge and raises a flare pistol he has been carrying. He raises the gun slowly, in the timeless cadence of ritual, and squeezes the trigger.

The flare sizzles along a curved trajectory that lands it in the center of the pile, where it hides in a long moment before ignition.

A brilliant and awful ball of fire erupts with a huge whump that propels a mighty wall of heat across the clearing. Barney rocks back on his feet as the blast bakes the front of his suit.

The bodies burn with a hellish fury.

Barney turns his back to the flames and walks toward the trailer. Then the cheering starts. The pathogens have been consumed and hoods come off the suits. Two flatbed trucks come forward, both loaded with dozens of cases of beer and liquor. The crews grab their due and wander to the edge of the pit, where they squat and watch the conflagration burn an obscene hole into the night.

Later, Barney sits on an oil drum outside his trailer and feels the heat on his face. The crews are drunk now and present lurching silhouettes before the churning curtain of flame. From somewhere, a boom box blares basic rock, and the demon figures gyrate to the rhythm while raising their bottles in salute to the blaze.

At last, thinks Barney, *a set of rules I can live with.*

Vincent stares at the monkey, a male chimpanzee in early adolescence, which is scooping popcorn out of the red-striped bag and shoveling the swollen white kernels into its large mouth. Every time the chimp's jaws open, Vincent can see the formidable set of fangs, the big incisors that curve into sharp points of gleaming enamel. The beast keeps its distance and stays seated on the white plastic table, where it occasionally throws a cautionary glance in Vincent's direction, then goes back to work on the popcorn.

The context of the monkey is lost on Vincent as he sips a soft drink in this public eating area at the Seattle Zoo.

Behind him, the woman who served him remains obscured behind a surgical mask as she wipes the counter of her small concession booth with a damp rag. All the other tables are empty, and only the distant squawk of a tropical bird interrupts the silence.

Why is she here at all? Why is the monkey loose? But then again, why is anybody anywhere? The pain in Vincent's head has shredded his thinking into incoherent ribbons that twist and snake in random directions. For days now, the black crush of depression has been relentless and nearly suffocating. No matter how he squirms, it pins him against a damp and hopeless wall of despair.

He dimly remembers the slow, patient ascent to the zenith, the defining moment of his life, when the birds took flight in a glorious explosion of wings and feathers inside the shopping mall. His busy little disciples, spreading the word far and wide. Afterward, he'd walked the streets for the rest of the day, his feet barely touching the ground. All that he could see, all that he could smell and feel, were his, and for the first time, he felt a great love for the city and its inhabitants. At last, he had touched them, had touched them all. And in return, they gave him a shape and a definition that had eluded him always.

Over the following days, he felt like an enormous vessel, maybe an ocean liner or starship, that had just taken on a full load of fuel and departed on a grand journey of great distance. Only in his case, the fuel reserves were an ether of euphoria stored at great pressure and capable of producing prodigious bursts of power. He'd dined in restaurants, sat in bars, and waited in a glorious stupor for the news. It took longer than he'd expected. The authorities had either missed the significance of the shopping-center incident or covered it up to avoid panic. But the bug was coming, he knew it was coming, and that quivering bubble of expectation elevated him to the highest possible emotional stratum. He was beyond sleep now and strolled the streets until dawn, when he would nibble at a pastry in some little café and let the day plot itself.

He was in a little tavern in the University District when the news hit. The cute and trendy anchor couple, a demographer's dream, had delivered it with just the right touch of responsible concern mixed with unmitigated horror. Three confirmed cases in one afternoon. When the story ended, the bar's patrons plunged into a frantic hum of speculation that was still at peak pitch when Vincent left an hour later. The hum still rippled through him, and its power propelled him effortlessly down the sidewalk.

For the next week or so, he greedily devoured the manic mood swings of the city as it confronted the probable death of half its population. Despair and euphoria mixed like oil and water in chaotic patterns that never stood still. They were all going to die, they thought, so let's live like we've never lived before. He watched the bars fill up and quake with riotous parties that spilled out onto the summer streets. At first, the National Guard troops contained them, but the troops were also citizens and suffered under the same sentence as everybody else, so they quickly doffed their uniforms and melted into the revelry. Soon, little drunken clots of humanity were flinging beer mugs at display windows and plundering at will in the downtown area. On one particularly warm night, Vincent had watched people come out of a trashed clothing store with new apparel to wear at a packed bar just across the street. In the distance, a couple was copulating in the shallow water of a public fountain, with a fine spray of water playing over their shiny flesh.

But then the headaches started.

Big, fat headaches that cooked the contents of his skull to almost unbearable pressures. The first came while he was walking down Broadway on Capitol Hill. It started slowly, but ramped up quickly, and he veered off into Volunteer Park to find refuge from both the street and the pain. In the heart of the park, he sat on a bench by a circular wading pool, a little concrete desert devoid of water, children, or parents. He buried his face in his hands, and as the darkness descended over his eyes, he entered a theater of memories, a mongrel assortment of short subjects selected by someone unseen and unknown. The were fully formed, vivid, and had a disturbing authenticity about them.

. . . the oaken deck of a sailboat, with distant islands sprouting hills thick with big fir trees. An attractive woman (his wife?) in expensive but brief clothing listens to the glib chatter of a handsome man. Something about Greece. Something about the Stones. As she listens, she slides through a series of sexual postures that signal more than casual interest. He watches, but doesn't intervene. A sudden breeze chills him and he turns away . . .

. . . his gloved hands dipping into the body cavity of a cadaver and pulling out the liver. He is surprised by the weight of it and carefully moves it to the scale. Other people in white coats (students?) look on attentively as he weighs the organ. Then somebody cracks a joke, about livers, about masturbation, and the group breaks into laughter . . .

. . . the woman from the sailboat, now in a small yard, with a cherry tree in brilliant blossom. He is confessing something to her, and she stares at him with an excruciating mix of amusement and disgust . . .

. . . a living room, attractively furnished, where a middle-aged man lies lifeless and a small dog attempts to whine him back to life. The room quickly fills with firemen and paramedics, with cases and hoses and confusion. The dog barks fiercely at them, but no one pays any attention . . .

. . . an operating room, an odd one, a clever facsimile of the real thing. Populated by a surgical team more rendered than real. He is a surgeon, he is the center, he is in charge. And he is wrong about something, horribly wrong. He looks down at the body of an elderly man, drained and lifeless . . .

Vincent brought his face out of his hands and stared across the little circular void formed by the wading pond in the park. By nightfall, the head pain subsided, only to be replaced with a great rush of anxiety. He wanted to explore, to travel through the memories, but he didn't dare.

Because maybe the plague hadn't made him whole after all. Maybe there was some other reason why there was no Vincent inside of Vincent.

Maybe someone else was Vincent. Maybe the memories, the short subjects, came out of an entirely different vault.

The headaches came back, with increasing frequency, and with them came more memories. And as they marched before him, all he could do was catalog them and look for a thread that strung them into a comprehensible necklace of personal definition.

Vincent finishes his soft drink at the same time the chimp finishes its popcorn. He turns to the concession booth. The woman is gone now. He turns back to the monkey, and they stare at each other, and in that one cathartic moment, he understands that the monkey knows the truth about him, the central dogma that he has struggled so desperately to construct. It shines with a perfect certainty in the monkey's black eyes.

I'm a doctor. Yes. I'm a doctor.

Carno shifted uneasily and assumed a strained posture with his spine stiff and his elbows folded on his desk so that his hands grasped his forearms. "Phil, a while back, I gave you some very good advice. I told you to get out while you could. What happened?"

"The locks."

"The locks?"

"Yeah, the locks. They closed down before I could get the boat out." Paris could see that this only added to Carno's mounting guilt. Paris's boss in Theft was dead, along with several hundred other cops on the force, and a hasty reorganization had put Carno in charge of Theft as well as Homicide.

"Well, that's a bad break. I'm sorry. But I'm afraid there's more bad breaks to come."

"Like what?"

"Like you're fired, Phil."

"As of when?"

"As of right now."

"As I recall, it's not quite that easy. There's a whole dance we have to do and we're just at the start of it."

"Nope." Carno shook his head. "We're at the end of it. The city has passed emergency legislation that redefines the terms of employment for everyone, including you."

"So whose decision was this? Not yours, right?"

"Not mine. I got the directive from the office of the police commissioner." Carno sighs. "Look, Phil, I don't know what you did. I don't know what you said. All I know is that somebody has a real jones for you. And it's not me."

"I know that, Captain. And I know you probably did what you could. Thanks. Mind if I stick around long enough to clean out my desk?"

"No problem. All I need right now is your badge and your gun."

Paris fishes out his badge and puts it down on the desk.

"And the gun, Phil. I've got to have the gun."

Paris shrugs. "I forgot it."

"You what?" asks Carno with a weary brand of incredulity.

"I forgot it. I left it at home this morning. Don't worry. I'll get it to you as soon as I can," promises Paris with an optimistic smile.

Carno looks down at his desktop. Both he and Paris know that guns are now so valuable they can be used as a negotiable currency. There is no way Paris is going to voluntarily give up his weapon. In effect, he is asking Carno for one last favor.

"Okay," says Carno. "But get it here by tomorrow so we don't have to come looking for it. All right?"

"You got it," says Paris as he rises to leave. "And what about severance pay?"

Carno puts on a bitter smile. "Check's in the mail."

"One other thing. Have you gotten any more breaks on the psycho who brought the bug to town?"

"Not a goddamn thing. You surprised about that?"

"No. Can't say that I am. See you."

"Good luck, Phil." Carno reaches for a report to read, signaling that Paris's professional execution is now complete.

Paris has no difficulty cleaning out his desk. The only thing worth keeping is a picture of Ginny on the deck of the *Cedar Queen* and an old school photo of his nephew, Skip. He doesn't want to carry the frames around, so he slips the photos out and puts them in his pocket. Then he swivels in his chair and contemplates his old 286-driven PC. He smiles. The only redeeming thing on it is a solitaire game that Larsen had given him.

As he wonders about saving it onto a floppy, Graziano and Larsen come up, both looking uncomfortable.

"We just heard," announces Graziano.

"Well, you heard right. I'm outta here."

"So, what can we do?" asks Larsen.

Paris looks at Larsen. "First, you can wipe the crumbs off your tie. After that, I've got a few favors."

"So let's hear 'em," demands Graziano.

And Paris tells them.

As Paris goes to make a last stop in records, he thinks about the long walk out the door of the precinct. Given the madness on the streets and the will of Barney, it'll be somewhat like going into a tank battle on foot. And the more he considers it, the more he realizes that sheer audacity and surprise are probably the only real weapons he has left. Graziano and Larsen seemed pretty sure they could grant his wishes, but that still leaves the balance of the job up to him.

There is only one clerk left in records, and she stares out through anxious eyes over the top of her surgical mask. "Can I help you?"

"Yeah, I'm Lieutenant Paris. A while back, I made a query on a license number to the Department of Motor Vehicles in Olympia. Obviously, they've got their problems down there right now, but I thought I'd give it one last check and see if anything came in."

After the shopping-center crash, Paris had checked with Homicide to see if they were following up on the wrecked station wagon. They told him the license number had already been sent to Olympia, but there wasn't any response. Apparently, the state bureaucracy was barely under control, and lines of communication to the capital were not in the best of shape. But just to make sure, Paris had put in his own request, and now, in his final act as a policeman, he gives it one last try. He provides the necessary information and the clerk goes solemnly to the terminal and types in a dozen strokes. A moment later, a new window pops up on the display.

"Here it is. License number 863-ENQ. Is that correct?"

Paris can scarcely believe it. Somehow, in the middle of this spasm of pestilence and apocalyptic madness, this one little parcel of data has managed to squirt through the system and reach its destination. And now he can grab the parcel, rip it open, and watch the monster squirm in the light of day.

"That's it," confirms Paris. "Who's the owner?"

"The vehicle is registered to a David Vincent Muldane."

"Who?" It can't be true. There has to be a mistake.

"The name is David Vincent Muldane," repeats the clerk, a little impatiently. "Do you want the address?"

"As a matter of fact, I do."

"You think he's sick?" asks the apartment manager with an anxious edge as he pulls the mask up over his face.

"I doubt it," answers Paris. And he really does, because that would imply some sort of justice, some cosmic balance. They are standing in front of the door to David Muldane's apartment on the west side of Capitol Hill. And as Paris stares at the tarnished brass numbers on the face of the door, his self-reproach is temporarily shoved aside in favor of an overwhelming curiosity about what he will find inside.

As soon as he'd left the clerk's desk at the station, he charged up several floors and into the public health department, where he discovered that David had not been to work for at least a couple of weeks. And given the horrible attrition rate within the department, no one was taking the time to follow up on absent employees.

Of course he wasn't at work. He was busy figuring out how to parlay poisoning and murder into a crime of almost unbelievable magnitude. On the way over to the apartment, Paris had kicked himself up and down for failing to see the connections, however remote they might have been. A failed doctor. A fraudulent surgeon in the virtual realm. A loner wrapped in a multimegabyte womb of computer code that kept the world safely at bay. The fact that "David" had bought and registered the car used by "Vincent" was quite consistent with the pyromania research that had pointed him toward the poisoner in the first place. In the world of fire-bugs, a small segment termed "severely disturbed" commonly used a practice called "splitting" to reconcile their good and bad behavior. To avoid personal accountability, they simply refused to believe that a single person did both the bad and good things in their lives. In David Vincent Muldane, the splitting was so severe that two distinct personalities had formed. One was the public health official, dedicated to fighting pathogens. The other was the monster dedicated to propagating them. Had Muldane been adopted?

Paris bet he had. "Vincent" was probably the product of a wildly dysfunctional early childhood, while "David" was the result of a later upbringing that was much more civilized.

But so much for theory. The worst part was, he'd let Muldane pull him away from his intuition. After years of patient analysis, he'd strongly suspected that this was an inside job, someone within the health department who had the skill and the knowledge to pull it off without detection. But he'd let Muldane talk him out of it.

The manager inserts the key, opens the door, and immediately steps back out for fear of infection. "Just lock it on your way out," he says over his shoulder as he takes off down the stairs.

Paris pulls up his mask and walks in, leaving the door open behind him. He immediately strides through to a sliding glass door that opens onto a small balcony. He parts the curtains and yanks the door to a fully open position. Instantly a breeze flows through the room along the path between the two open doors. Ventilation minimizes infection, and this may well be the world capital of infectious material.

Paris then turns and surveys the living room and kitchen space under the cool, gray light flooding in through the open door. There is a perfunctory couch and chair, cheap but serviceable; and a chrome-and-glass coffee table, all arranged in a kind of manic geometry. The small dining area holds a square table with a brick red surface of hard plastic bounded by an aluminum strip sporting five parallel grooves. Farther back, the drainboards in the kitchen are completely bare and spotless, and the stove burners bear not a single splash of grease.

And that's it. No art, no photos, no books, no magazines. Only a little portable TV with rabbit ears arranged in a perfectly symmetrical V. Paris can feel a sad and terrible vacancy here, a desperate attempt to mimic the mainstream of humanity, but with no success. None at all.

Paris checks the cupboards and refrigerator in the kitchen. All empty. He moves on to the lone bedroom. Beside the neatly made bed is a nightstand with a cheap tensor lamp, an alarm clock, and a stand-up photo. Its frame holds a small color picture that has been clumsily cut from a plastic

ID badge and sandwiched under the glass. It is a photo of David Vincent Muldane, a bad photo under bad light, taken for the most utilitarian of purposes. For some reason, Paris can visualize Muldane contemplating the photo before turning in each night, trying to attach some meaning to the image, but failing, always failing.

Paris checks the closet and glides past the generic career clothes to the one garment that provides the final verification. A priest's suit, neatly pressed, with the Roman collar hung over the neck of the hanger.

As he fingers the black material, he feels the truth of the matter slowly seep out of the fabric and twist into an intractable knot. All these years, all these setbacks, all his longing for revenge, all his obsessions; and at the end of the trail, he discovers there is really no one to arrest.

There is a body, to be sure. But there is no person, only a badly fractured facsimile of one.

He leaves the bedroom and walks out onto the little balcony, which looks out onto another apartment building across the street. He feels the cool metal of the railing in his palms and a subtle chill on his cheek that suggests the quiet approach of rain.

46

VINCENT MULDANE APPROACHES THE ENTRANCE TO THE BIG hospital and notices the smashed window covered with cardboard and duct tape. Obviously, the hospital is being assaulted by more than germs, but there's nothing he can do about that. All he can bring here is medical training and vigorously apply it in this time of most urgent need.

The sliding door opens and closes, and he sees a new kind of reception area spread out before him. Huge curtains of milky plastic hang from the ceiling and seal off the entrance area from the rest of the hospital. In the center is a hastily constructed booth with a glass window and a speaker, and a door off to one side. Vincent approaches the booth and sees a uniformed nurse. When he reaches the window, he can also make out two armed security guards sitting behind her. They all wear surgical masks.

"Can I help you?" comes the nurse's voice over the speaker in a cheap electronic rendition of natural speech. Her eyes dance like spawning fish above the ridge of the mask, and Vincent can feel her fear come over the speaker in a subliminal hiss.

"Yes, my name is Vincent Muldane. I'm a doctor. I've come to offer my services."

The nurse's eyes blink several times in rapid succession. "Are you associated with the hospital?"

"No, I'm not. I'm from out of town. Could I speak with someone on the staff?" says Vincent in a more authoritative manner.

The nurse's eyes narrow a notch, but she picks up the phone. The two security men eye him curiously. He must be crazy. "Dr. Renfro?" says the nurse. "I have a Dr. Muldane here. He wants to volunteer." A pause. "Yes, that's right. He's from out of town." The nurse looks up at Vincent. "Where did you say you're from?"

"Minnesota. Hibbing, Minnesota," replies Vincent in an agreeable manner. "The home of Bob Dylan."

"He's from Hibbing, Minnesota. . . . Okay. We'll do that." The nurse hangs up and looks at Vincent. "Before you can talk to anybody, you'll have to go through screening. Go through the door and follow the tunnel to the examination room."

"Thank you," says Vincent as he opens the door and confronts a long plastic tunnel.

As Vincent leaves the screening room, a man in a white lab coat comes up, an older man with thinning gray hair and a kind face. He has a surgical mask slung around his neck but is not wearing it over his nose. He gives David an appraising look over the top of his reading glasses.

"Dr. Renfro?" asks David, taking the initiative.

"That's correct."

"I'm Dr. Vincent Muldane." He points back toward the door of the screening room. "I've got to compliment you on your screening operation. You've done a good job in a very short time." When Vincent had entered the room a half hour before, a technician in a full protection suit with an independent air supply had come in and taken a blood sample. Evidently, they now had some reasonably accurate test that could be quickly run, and Vincent had come up negative.

"Thank you. You say you're from out of town?"

"That's right. Hibbing, Minnesota. I do cardiovascular surgery back there." Vincent smiled. "Of course, it's not like in the big city. But we do all right."

Renfro's eyes widen. "Cardiovascular? Really?"

"That's right," says David, hunting for little flecks of suspicion.

"Then you're it."

"I'm it?"

"At one time, there were nearly three hundred doctors in this hospital. Right now, there're maybe two dozen. And none of them do heart surgery. You've got yourself a job, Doctor."

"I'm not really looking for a job. I'm just looking for a way to help. That's all."

"Good for you." Renfro gives Vincent a pat on the shoulder and steers him down the hall. "We've all got to do what we can. The public's forgotten that psittacosis isn't the only thing that can kill you. We've got a lot of sick people here with heart disease, cancer, injuries. They still need our help. But there's not many of us left to give it." He sighs. "It's depressing. That's the worst part. The depression."

"I'm sure it is. But we've got to do what we can."

"You need a place to stay? If you want to, you can stay here. The place is about eighty percent empty. Nobody comes here now unless they're desperately sick."

"Thanks. I'll take you up on that."

"Good. I don't think there's any scheduled heart surgery at the moment, so we'll go ahead and get you what you need."

At dusk, Vincent stands in a former patient suite on the top floor. He looks at himself in the mirror. The white coat, the stethoscope, the new ID badge.

I'm a doctor.

* * *

The last light is fading over the Olympic Range as Paris spots the *Cedar Queen* pulling in to pick him up. Elaine aligns perfectly with the dock, and the boat drifts to a halt just a foot from the pilings as Paris jumps down onto the deck. Elaine then guides the big craft out toward the middle of the lake and the cover of the flotilla.

As Paris comes into the wheelhouse, Elaine glances at him, then immediately back to the water, where the navigation is becoming tricky in the maze of lights from both the shore and the craft in the water.

"You scared me, big boy. This was the last scheduled stop." They had a system where Elaine pulled into the pickup place at three half-hour intervals, so Paris had some latitude in timing his actions. This was the first time he'd waited until the last interval to go aboard.

Paris chuckles and watches for a moment as she adjusts her course in response to a smaller boat moving across their path. "You drive this better than I ever did. You know that?"

Elaine keeps her eyes trained out the windshield. "Maybe. By the way, you had a couple of electrical problems. I took the liberty of fixing them."

"Thanks. How're you feeling?"

"About like the rest of the world. Half-dead. And yourself?"

"Let's just say its been an interesting day." Paris studies her profile as she pilots the boat toward midlake. She most certainly doesn't look half-dead. If anything, she looks in better health than he does, and he has to admire her mordant humor, which shields her from the emotional fallout of this great disaster. Her tan arms taper into long, graceful hands that lightly grip the wheel, and she holds her head erect, like a startled swan.

The conversation dies until they reach the center of the flotilla and drop anchor. As Elaine settles into her deck chair, Paris brings out two whiskeys and hands her one. "It's the first of the last bottle," he announces. "After this, we can either loot a liquor store or go to AA meetings."

"Thanks," says Elaine as she takes the drink. It is a windless night, and they are softly illuminated by the lone overhead lamp in the wheelhouse. Paris watches as she tilts back in the chair and extends a leg out to prop her heel on the deck railing. The pose takes the slack out of her baggy shorts, and he can see a hint of sinew on her inner thigh. He takes a sip of whiskey as he watches, and for the first time, he lets her sexuality punch through to him. There are countless reasons why he shouldn't; but right now, they all seem dim and shapeless. Besides, it won't last. He has things to say, things that will break the spell. Bad timing, he thinks. But then again, life is a continual exhibition of bad timing in action.

"I found him."

"Found who?"

"The poisoner."

Elaine pulls her leg down and sits straight up. "Where is he?"

"I'm not sure." Paris takes another sip of his drink. "It really doesn't matter."

"What do you mean, 'it doesn't matter'?"

"Lot of reasons. Some I can explain, some I can't. Besides, the damage is already done. He's blown his wad. And that's what'll do him in in the end. Not me. Not the justice system."

"You're sure about that, Detective?" She says it quietly and earnestly.

"Yeah." Paris takes another sip and looks out across the lake. "I'm sure." He pauses and turns toward Elaine. "Trust me on this one, okay?"

Elaine sighs and settles back in her chair. "As long as it's okay with you. That's what counts."

"And speaking of the justice system, I was fired today."

Elaine doesn't reply. She sits thoughtfully in her chair and mulls the consequences, which Paris has previously explained in detail. Her attempted rape at the locks is just a sample of what might be ahead. "Does that mean that the nice men with the guns in police boats won't hang out with us anymore?"

"Yeah, that's what it means."

"A while back, you said we would wait and see what happened. Sounds like it just happened. So what do we do now?"

She is startled to see Paris break into an impish smile. "Glad you asked. Let me tell you."

When he is finished, she leans against the canvas back of her chair and polishes off her whiskey. "Okay, Lieutenant. If that's the way it's gotta be, then so be it."

"You scared by it?"

"Absolutely."

"And what scares you the most?"

She leans forward, elbows on her knees, and stares at the deck, as if lost for an answer. Paris is puzzled. She's too quick for that. Way too quick. What's wrong?

She reaches out and gently puts both her hands on top of his. "What scares me the most is that I might lose you."

In the night, Paris pulls up out of sleep and opens his eyes. He feels Elaine curled warmly against him on the berth in the main saloon, and he softly strokes her bare shoulder. Across the cabin he sees the faint circle of light formed by the porthole in the galley and hears the fragile lap of water against the old wooden hull, which moderates the sound and ages it in a pleasant way.

47

PARIS POKES HIS HEAD THROUGH THE BUILDING'S ACCESS hatch and surveys the large expanse of roof from eye level. Even at midmorning, the smell of tar peels off the black surface and drifts up his nostrils. It will be hot up here later on, but two service shacks for the air-conditioning will provide shelter from the sun. He pushes a long Fiberglas case up before him and places it on the roof, then climbs the last few ladder rungs and out into the open.

Without hesitation, he picks up the case and strides briskly toward the first service shack. While he walks, his eyes track the enormous structure about three blocks away, the Seattle

Space Needle, which rises 607 feet above downtown and sprouts into a stylishly compressed concrete mushroom that houses a circular restaurant. The entire rim of mushroom is lined with windows, which afford a 360-degree view that takes in much of Seattle and far beyond.

The windows also take in Paris, and although he doubts that those at the top can continuously survey the entire area below, he is slightly wary. A few seconds later, he is safely concealed behind the second shack. He looks behind him and doesn't like his position; nearby buildings to the south afford a clear view of him. He moves to the rear of the first shack and looks once more. Much better. The first shack blocks the southern buildings, and the second shack conceals him from the Space Needle itself. He relaxes, sits down with his back against the wall of the shack, and pulls out a cigarette. As he lights it, he looks down at the case he has brought.

Inside the case is a rifle, the same rifle that only recently was shooting at fire trucks in a neighborhood not far away. Early this morning, Paris had gone back to that neighborhood. He drove by the two charred foundations. One of their driveways held a blackened mattress and a baked recliner chair stretched out into smoky rigor mortis on the front lawn. There was still shattered glass from the shooting in the parking lane. He drove on, pulled in front of the sniper's house, and rang the doorbell. When the sniper answered, he was momentarily startled to see Paris again, but calmed down when Paris explained it wasn't police business. He was there to propose a trade, a trade that would offer substantial benefit to both parties. He briefly explained the terms of the deal and the man let him in.

Inside, they discussed the exchange in more detail. Paris had brought an AR-16 assault rifle, recently stored by the Seattle police in their evidence locker. It was usable in the full automatic mode, which made it an excellent defensive weapon in uncertain times such as these. Paris was also throwing in several clips and a generous amount of ammunition. In return, he would receive the sniper's rifle, the Winchester Model 70 Classic Stainless Synthetic with a variable power scope of the highest quality. Paris had noticed something else about this rifle the day he'd apprehended the sniper on the roof. It had what was called a Ballistic Optimized Shooting System, which adjusted the length of the barrel and thereby fine-tuned its harmonics. With the weapon properly optimized and the scope suitably calibrated, a round could be placed within one inch at a hundred yards.

When the terms were agreed to, they took the Winchester into the sniper's basement shop, where Paris filed off the serial number in the man's presence. The man said he was sorry to see the rifle defaced in even this minor way, and Paris said he was, too. But it had to be done. There could be no circumstantial trail that led back to the sniper, who was the registered owner. There was no similar problem with the AR-16. Its serial number had been obliterated long ago.

On the roof, Paris opens the case, takes the rifle out, inserts a clip, chambers the first round, and clicks off the safety. There was no time to check out the scope, but the sniper had assured him it was fully calibrated; and based on the pinpoint shooting at the emergency vehicles during the fire, Paris believed him.

Paris positions himself where he can see around the corner of the shack and catch a full view of the Space Needle. He is nearly perpendicular to the elevator track, where a passenger capsule crawls up and down the huge tower like a little bug of glass and metal. Right now, this elevator, with its big observation windows, is not visible, which means it is tucked in the entrance building at the bottom or the restaurant at the top.

Paris shifts his position slightly so he can keep an eye on the elevator track, but remain mostly concealed. As the minutes pass, the waiting creates a mental void, and trickles of thought drift in to form little pools, which soon disperse and form other pools. After a while, they congeal into two large lakes. In the first of these, he sees Ginny in her final repose and feels the weave of her cotton gown against his cheek as she drifts away. He tries to take her point of view and watches her interior light slowly fade; but on the brink of darkness, he sees the ghostly outline of the porthole in the *Cedar Queen* and feels Elaine curled up tightly against him.

There is a fortuitous ordering to these events, he thinks. If he had become involved with Elaine first, he could never have let Ginny go. The thin and delicate membrane that separates mercy and murder would have been hopelessly ruptured by the presence of motive. He would have been forced to leave her alive and wonder forever what happened as the plague forced its way into the building where she lay.

In the second lake of the mind, he stands on the apartment balcony of David Vincent Muldane and contemplates his failure. If his associative powers had been just a little keener, he might have seen the pattern, might have sniffed the scent of the monster before it killed half the city. But then he realizes that a second monster is waiting to feed on the half-dead carcass of Seattle, a monster that will destroy the city's soul instead of its body. Barney. The very same beast that now waits patiently to devour both him and Elaine. And this time, Paris knew, it was no longer a matter of clever and patient deduction, it was a matter of immediate and violent action.

Paris's ruminations are interrupted by the beat of big wings against the warm air of late morning. A seagull sets down on the shack above him, its full wingspan stretched in profile against the blue and cloudless sky. They look like angel wings, and well they should, because the seagull is an angel of death. It is a psittacine bird and therefore a potential carrier of Agent 57a. Instead of shooing the seagull away, Paris stretches his mask over his face and sits back to watch it.

It doesn't seem right to interfere with the bird, because he, too, has become an angel of death.

Barney pauses from taking notes and looks out the window. His eyes are slightly strained from reading and he focuses them onto the distant Cascade Range to compensate. He is putting together a proposal that he will soon submit to the remnants of the city and county government, a novel document that makes him a "contractual partner" in governing, a partner with broad executive powers based on "joint decision making." A month ago, such a proposition would have seemed insane. But not now, not with anarchy in the streets, the economy in shambles, and mass burials conducted on a daily basis.

From his position at the top of the Space Needle, Barney's

line of sight extends for many miles, but not nearly as far as his ambition. Except for a single bodyguard, he is alone here in the perfect bio-bunker, completely isolated from the city below. Several dozen of his palace guard are housed in the building at the base of the tower to ensure his security. Negotiating a lease had been no problem. The owners were easily persuaded that it was in the community interest to give him a suitable base of operations from which to supervise the collection and disposal of the dead.

Barney shifts his imperial gaze to Lake Union, which appears as a minor pond fed by Lake Washington. Paris and the woman are down there on the lake, along with the disk, the data, the key to the production of an antibiotic, a special antibiotic. He doesn't understand all the scientific nuances involved, nor does he need to. Even when the plague has subsided, the antibiotic will be worth a fortune, a large fortune. And the key to expanding his new empire beyond Seattle will ultimately be economic. Right now, that was hard for many people to realize. All the major stock markets had utterly collapsed, and even the most stable of currencies were disintegrating rapidly. Gold, weapons, and ammunition were the new mediums of exchange. But Barney had the vision to know that periods of chaos are inevitably followed by times of recovery and stability. And when they entered the next quiescent period and the world crawled out of its diseased hole, a new order would be created, an order dictated by people like himself and the man in the bio-bunker built by Uni. Their encounter in Fancher's office was a perfect blueprint for the future of world trade.

If he wanted to, he could probably scan the lake's surface right now with a pair of binoculars and pick out the detective's ridiculous old boat. Only when compared to yesterday, the view would be slightly different. The Harbor Patrol boats that hovered protectively around the *Cedar Queen* would no longer be there. Barney had pulled his new political strings and had Paris fired. The lieutenant was now on his own. No more buddy system to keep the wolves away. No more political risk to Barney over an armed confrontation with the police to get the disks.

Now it will be a simple matter. He picks up the phone, speaks a few clipped sentences, and it's done.

Barney hangs up, turns from the window, and looks across at the array of empty tables, which are still covered with starched white tablecloths. He sighs and checks his watch. He has a meeting with the surviving city and county commissioners down at the courthouse in twenty minutes. He doesn't want to go, doesn't want to waste the time. But he will. Because in the very near future, it will be he who dictates the times of the meetings. And everything else, too.

Skip sits on the backyard patio of the current Dead House, where the food is nearly exhausted. Inside are the remaining three members of his gang. The rest have been shot by vigilante homeowners or struck down with the disease. And now, these last three are all showing symptoms, and Skip is scared to go back inside. At the moment, he feels okay, but he knows that means little. Thin, tired, and malnourished, he is a perfect candidate for terminal infection. The microscopic seeds of infection may already be madly sprouting in his lungs, and preparing to strangle him from the inside out.

Worst of all, the liquor and the drugs are exhausted here, so he must face this possibility without any chemical mitigation. He nervously tilts back and forth on the edge of his lawn chair and knows how badly he wants to go home, but just can't bring himself to do it. His mother cannot be dead. He cannot face that possibility.

Suddenly, he remembers being very small and reading a storybook with his mother about a silly monkey. They sat on the couch and she cupped him in her arm and read the words slowly, and her voice had the beautiful tone of a fine clarinet as the warm lamplight played down over him, and he wiggled his toes in his stocking feet and looked up at his mother's lips as they carefully sounded each word so that he would understand perfectly and forever.

He puts his face down into his hands as the memory dissipates and feels the tears drain onto his cheeks. What if the others saw him like this? What would they think? It no longer matters. He is beyond caring. He keeps his face buried for a long time after the tears dry up. Only his curtain of dirty fingers now keep this terrible world away.

"Skip?"

He looks up and sees a middle-aged man in jeans and a leather jacket standing over him. "Yeah?"

"You're a tough guy to find. We've been looking for you all day."

Skip looks behind the man and sees two uniformed policemen. He's too exhausted and emotionally drained to be scared.

"My name's Graziano. Tommy Graziano. I'm a friend of your uncle's. He sent us to get you."

"Uncle Phil?" asks Skip weakly.

"Yeah. Uncle Phil."

Paris seeks a flicker of motion high above, where the tower portion of the Space Needle meets the belly of flattened mushroom that forms the restaurant. The elevator is moving, creeping down out of the mushroom and riding the track toward the entrance building far below.

As he comes out from behind the shack, he notices that there is virtually no wind. Good. He isn't expert enough to make allowances for windage at this range.

He reaches the edge of the building and falls into a prone position on the cracked black surface with its smell of heated tar. The edge of the roof has a ridge about eighteen inches high, a perfect rest for the rifle. He brings the weapon into position, checks that safety is off, and aligns his right eye with the scope, which is zoomed to maximum magnification.

If someone up there sees him now, it is too late. The elevator is out in the open, and even if they try to bring it back up, it will be exposed for long enough to do what must be done.

For Paris the world is reduced to a large, circular image floating in blackness. Methodically, he brings the top of the tower into the scope's field of view, then tracks downward to locate the elevator.

There it is. With great big observation windows that expose its innards. And sure enough, two men ride the elevator, and even at this range, it is clear which one is Barney. He stands tall with a military bearing, like a general on a bluff looking out over a great battle.

Paris brings the crosshairs to bear, little black threads that define the vertical and horizontal axes of sudden and distant death. He aims low, at Barney's belly, to compensate for the downward motion of the elevator as the bullet travels the necessary distance to pierce Barney's chest.

He tenderly applies trigger pressure until the bullet blasts forth, propelled to full muzzle velocity by a precisely measured quantity of powder.

He immediately recenters the scope on the image of the elevator. The middle window is blown out and he can see through to the back wall. No one is visible. He continues to track the blown window until it disappears into the entrance building at the base of the tower. No one appears. Did he hit Barney? Did the glass in the window deflect the bullet?

He brings the rifle down from his eye and looks at the entrance building. Men are swarming out like agitated wasps from a threatened nest. No time to wonder. He must leave now, before they spread the net. He's done what he can.

Barney hugs the floor of the elevator, his cheek smashed against the cold tiling, and looks at the bodyguard slumped against the rear wall. Already, a cloudy red planet is forming in the chest area of the man's shirt, and his mouth is flopped open in a silent exclamation that will never be completed. Barney's heart pounds, and he sees an instant replay of the explosion of glass and the loud thump as the bodyguard is hurled against the rear wall by the force of the bullet. Now he feels the fresh air flow in through the broken window and sees the cement surface of the tunnel of the entrance building block out the daylight as they near the bottom.

He pushes himself to his feet during the short excursion through the tunnel. He must present the persona of the heroic leader to those he will now confront, even though huge waves of anxiety splash about inside him. *Who did it? Who helped them? Who can I trust? Will they try again?* His heart is still pounding and he feels a cold sweat creep across his brow as the elevator door slides open and his palace guard comes running.

Barney steps out of the elevator through a crunch of broken glass and begins to bark. "Sniper! Extend the security perimeter! Get me a phone! Call in more people from downtown! Cordon off everything south of here for ten blocks! We're going to get this sucker and eat him alive!"

As the men scatter into action, he notices that although his heart has slowed, he still feels funny. The room does a lazy spin and his chest feels as if it is constricted by a huge rubber band that reduces his breathing to a string of shallow gasps. A growing river of pain flows out from his jaw and forms tributaries in his left shoulder and arm. A cold slab of sweat creeps over his upper body, and he drops to his knees. Several of his men form an anxious circle around him, but are afraid to act.

"Get an ambulance," Barney gasps.

"It's too late," says one of the men, referring to the bodyguard. "He's already dead."

"Not for him," whispers Barney as he sits back on his haunches. "For me."

As Paris guides his car to the end of the pier, he sees that his timing is perfect. Graziano is there with Skip, and the *Cedar Queen* is just pulling up.

Skip just sits on the bumper of Tommy's car as Paris walks toward them. Paris is shocked by how thin and exhausted Skip looks. He can only hope the poor kid isn't sick

"Did you do the deed?" asks Tommy.

"Yeah, I did the deed, but I can't be sure about the results." Paris squats down before Skip. "You okay, kid?"

Skip looks at him with troubled eyes. "What about my mom? Where is she?"

"She's dead. Died of the plague a few days back. I buried her myself."

"I knew it," says Skip, his voice breaking. "I just knew it."

"Before your mom died, she made me promise something."

"What was that?"

"She made me promise I'd get you out of here. And that's what I'm doing. Right now. Let's go."

Skip offers no resistance as Paris helps him up, and they head toward the edge of the dock. As the boat pulls up, Paris turns to Graziano. "Good luck, Tommy."

Tommy grins. "You're the one that's gonna need the luck, friend. See you around." He stays and watches as Paris and Skip jump aboard, then heads for his car.

As Paris comes into the wheelhouse, Elaine goes to full

throttle and steers a course straight toward the Fremont Cut, about a quarter mile away. The bow comes up, then settles back down as the big engine carves a foaming white trail into the green water.

"Welcome aboard, Captain," says Elaine. "You want to take the wheel?"

"Nope. I'm on lookout duty. You just haul ass. And don't slow down when you get into the Cut."

Paris goes out onto the rear deck, where Skip sits dazed. Paris puts a hand on his shoulder. "Hang in there, my man." Paris scans the waterline, and to the south, he sees trouble. Three powerboats are headed directly toward them, and even at three-quarters of a mile, Paris can see their hulls do a mad dance as they streak over the water at full speed.

As they enter the Cut, Elaine presses forward at full tilt, and Paris grins. Here the channel narrows to about twenty-five yards wide and was never meant for high-speed traffic. The *Cedar Queen*'s powerful wake is throwing off big waves that crash into the steep shoreline and reflect back into the middle of the channel, causing a great commotion that will slow the speedboats considerably.

As they leave the Cut and tear through Salmon Bay, the water widens a bit and Paris can look ahead to the locks themselves. The water is completely clear of boats. With the locks shut down, no one comes here anymore.

Still, they have a problem. Paris makes an agonizing calculation, but keeps it to himself.

Barney's chest is a solid mass of constricted pain as they wheel him into the hospital's emergency room. His view is limited to directly overhead, and he is afraid to move because it might amplify the constant hurt within him. He hears shouting and confusion as they arrive at a curtained bay where three gowned figures stare at him through eyes covered with protective goggles. They all wear respirator masks with hoses connected to filter packs to protect against the plague. One of the figures, a woman, speaks to someone he can't see.

"What have we got?"

"White male, midforties," answers a male voice. "Severe chest pain. Blood pressure seventy-nine over fifty-eight.

Pulse ninety-eight. Profuse sweating. Looks like a classic myocardial infarction."

"Let's take a listen," says the woman, bending over with her stethoscope. "What's the patient's name?"

"Cox," states the voice. "Barney Cox."

The woman looks down directly at Barney after removing her stethoscope from his chest. "Mr. Cox, I'm Dr. Prescott, the ER physician. It appears you're suffering a heart attack. Most likely, it's being caused by a coronary insufficiency. We're going to begin some preemptive treatment immediately and do some tests to confirm the diagnosis. Then we'll decide on a course of action. Right now, we'll give you something to make you a little more comfortable."

"Don't fuck up," hisses Barney through the pain.

The woman looks at him in disbelief and turns to the nurses. "What did he say?"

No one answers.

As Elaine cuts the throttle back and they near the locks, Paris is relieved to see the massive figure of Larsen standing on the tip of the long, narrow concrete island that separates the big lock on the right from the small one on the left. Farther down the island, in the control tower, he can see a lone figure through the glass.

Larsen is gesturing emphatically toward the entrance to the big lock, where the massive doors are already swinging open. As they come within shouting distance, Larsen yells, "We can't open the little one! You gotta use the big one!"

Paris's fears are confirmed. The tide is out on the Sound, so it will take almost fifteen minutes to drain the water in the big lock down to the level where they can sail away to freedom. By that time, the big powerboats will have arrived.

As they pass through the massive forward gates into the lock chamber, Paris looks ahead towards the far gates, the gates to freedom, about 250 yards in front of them. It seems an almost impossible distance. "Where's Bronson?" he yells to Larsen as Elaine maneuvers the boat toward the lock chamber wall.

"Up in the control room," shouts Larsen, pointing toward the figure in the tower. "He blew the door open and figured out how to open the forward gate for you."

"We got trouble," says Paris as they pull up alongside the chamber wall and he throws a rope to Larsen. "Three boats. Maybe five minutes away."

"That's not all the trouble you got. Seems that the National Guard destroyed the controls to the forward gates, the ones that open into the Sound."

"Jesus! Why'd they do a thing like that?"

Larsen shrugs. "Why does the government do anything?"

Paris feels his stomach sink. Their plan is going to hell. Behind him, the rear-gate doors are nearly closed, which will block the speedboats from entering. But the beasts that man them will simply moor alongside, scale the wall, and blast away at the *Cedar Queen*'s completely exposed position inside the lock chamber. They'd be forced to abandon the boat and fight a running battle as they tried to escape on foot. It wouldn't work.

"This is not good, Steve," says Paris. "Not good at all."

"There's another way," says Larsen with a knowing grin. "Bronson figured it out. But it may be a little rough on your boat."

"What's that?"

Larsen tells him.

When Larsen is finished, Paris turns to Elaine, who has joined him on the rear deck. "So, what do think?"

"What's to think? Let's just get it over with."

"I can't believe it!" They turn and see Skip standing in the cabin door, his eyes wide. "I can't believe we're really gonna do this!"

Paris reaches around and feels his 9mm automatic in its holster. He's got nine shots in the clip. That's it. Larsen and Bronson probably have about the same. They're no match for whatever is coming in the powerboats.

"Sorry, sport," Paris says to Skip. "Don't think we've got much choice."

"Mr. Cox, can you hear me?"

Barney opens his eyes, looks up, and nods. It's the woman doctor again. Only this time, they are in a different room, a small space with windows on both sides and double doors straight ahead.

"Mr. Cox, I've consulted with a heart specialist, and he's

come up with a different diagnosis than the one I gave you earlier. It appears you have what's called aortic stenosis, and it's reached an acute stage. This means that one of your heart valves is defective and will have to be repaired through open-heart surgery. The specialist doesn't see any alternative. Apparently, the valve is too far gone. You've been prepped and they're ready to go. I wouldn't worry. It's a fairly routine operation. If you have any questions, you can ask the surgical team before they put you under. Good luck."

Before Barney can speak, the gurney moves forward, and he rolls through the double doors into a brightly lit space. Clusters of exotic instruments and lighting gear line the corners of his vision. A group of masked figures tower over him in green gowns. His chest continues to squeeze a flood of pain through his body. He is afraid now, very afraid. The rules here are no longer his.

Then one of the figures speaks.

"Mr. Cox, my name is Dr. Muldane, and I'll be performing your surgery."

Twenty minutes later, Vincent Muldane looks down at the anesthetized patient on the table. Funny fellow. He had such a frantic look in his eyes when they put him under. Oh, well, the operation will be a grand adventure.

I'm a doctor.

He lowers his scalpel and cuts an incision down the length of the breastbone.

Larsen and Bronson stand on the shore side of the big lock as they reach over and shake Paris's hand on the rear deck of the *Cedar Queen*. Bronson holds a black box connected to a wire that snakes away over the cement toward the far end of the lock.

"Good luck, old buddy," says Larsen. "No matter what happens, you're in for one hell of a ride."

To the rear, Paris can hear the whine of the approaching powerboats. "Thanks for everything, guys. We better do it while we still can."

Larsen and Bronson give a push, and as soon as the boat is clear, Elaine gently nurses it out into the center of the channel. Paris looks at Elaine with a grin. "You still want to drive?"

"Not this time." Elaine surrenders the wheel to Paris. "It's all yours, big boy."

"Find something you can get a grip on," commands Paris to Skip and Elaine. Then he looks to the shore and gives the high sign to Larsen and Bronson.

Bronson waves an acknowledgment and manipulates the black box. Paris turns his attention to the forward gates of the lock, which conceal the twenty-six-foot drop to the water level of the Sound. An enormous explosion rocks the entire structure as several pounds of plastic explosive sever the hinges on the huge gates. The shock wave from the blast propagates through the water and slams into the *Cedar Queen,* which shudders and groans under the impact.

Paris glances briefly toward the shore. Larsen and Bronson are already sprinting toward the far end of the lock to watch the final spectacle before they beat a hasty retreat to avoid the powerboats. Paris has no doubt that as late as yesterday, the plastic explosive resided in the evidence locker of the Seattle Police Department. Now it was resolving a case of a much different sort.

Paris pushes the *Cedar Queen* to full throttle to extract all the maneuvering capacity the boat can give. They quickly pick up speed as they are sucked toward the huge gap where the big gates once were. The lock's seven million gallons of water are on a mad downhill stampede, a onetime rapid of stupendous force as thirty thousand tons of agitated liquid fall twenty-six feet in just a few seconds.

Paris turns the wheel to keep them centered and remembers a time long ago, a time of his youth when he used to go river rafting, and now it will serve him well. He takes a brief instant to look ahead and anticipate their course. By now they are rocketing through the breach at the end of the lock, and he can see a railroad bridge one hundred yards ahead, where a big island of concrete sits in the channel to support the trestle. On their present course, the monstrous current will carry them across the channel and right into the island at over thirty-five miles per hour, creating a sudden cloud of wooden splinters and shattered bodies. They will be there in five seconds.

Paris jams the throttle into full reverse and spins the wheel until they are aimed across the current and directly at the concrete island, then carefully plays the wheel to maintain that course.

"No!" shouts Elaine, but as they rush forward, she suddenly sees the mechanics of it. The combined motion of the current and their reverse power is the optimum course to avoid the island. As the seconds tick away, the *Cedar Queen* lunges forward and the island grows ever bigger.

Paris feels Elaine's anxious fingers dig deep into his shoulder as the vessel's bow whizzes past the island with only a foot to spare. So far so good, but they're not out of it yet. He looks directly ahead to the point of land where the channel widens and curves out into the Sound itself. A ten-foot wave is smashing against the beach, capsizing boats, turning docks into flying lumber, and roaring up lawns to lick at houses. He spins the wheel to starboard and brings the throttle to full forward. As the bow swings around, he can see the open waters of the Sound. The *Cedar Queen*'s six-cylinder engine pushes mightily, and slowly they pull away from the chaos on the beach and head toward safety. They've made it.

"Awesome!"

Paris and Elaine turn around to see Skip standing behind them, his arms braced against the frame of the wheelhouse door, his eyes wide and his mouth hung open.

Paris breathes for what seems like the first time in minutes. If nothing else, he's finally made a good impression on the kid. He looks at Elaine, who wraps her arm around his and closes her eyes in relief.

"We're outta here," he announces, and sets the throttle to a comfortable eight knots.

They don't look back.

Epilogue

ELAINE STANDS ON THE REAR DECK OF THE *CEDAR QUEEN* and extends her arms in a big morning stretch as she looks out at the little bay where they are anchored off Mayne Island far up in the Strait of Georgia. Fall is coming, the first fall of the new epoch.

On their way north after leaving the city, they had stopped at Anacortes, where Uni had an office that controlled its regional oil-refining operations. They came ashore under cover of night and found the office deserted, which greatly simplified their mission. Paris used some of his street-learned skills to let them in, and Elaine promptly activated the computer and telecommunications equipment.

It took several hours of probing the ruins of the global computer networks to make the proper connections. Once they were established, Elaine took the disk with the model for Agent 57a, placed it in an optical disk drive, and sent its contents over a high-bandwidth channel to a computer complex at the U.S. Public Health Service in Washington, D.C., along with an explanation of what the data was and why it was so valuable.

Then she contacted the bald man in Uni's bio-bunker in Switzerland. He wasn't pleased about the deal she offered him, but was forced to accept. To get the data on the disk, he would have to negotiate with the Public Health Service officials, who had the power to ensure that whatever antibiotic was developed from the Agent 57a data would be used in the best interests of people everywhere.

A soft hush of fog clings to the fir trees of Mayne Island and diffuses the rising sunlight, and for the first time, Elaine can see the condensation of her breath form a bright cloud of steam. Paris comes out of the cabin, hands her a cup of coffee, and puts his big arm around her. They have a comfortable niche in the new order of things. Elaine is a doctor, and few doctors are left, especially in this remote area in the Strait of Georgia. The *Cedar Queen* is a floating clinic, a welcome sight wherever they go. The residents are more than willing to barter food and supplies for medical attention. Paris can even get fuel for the boat, a precious commodity now reserved for use by emergency vehicles only.

Skip left them several weeks back to take a job on a fishing sloop operating out of Victoria, B.C. No one asked about citizenship or work permits. Now that the plague was subsiding, labor was extremely scarce. On the day he waved good-bye to them, Paris thought he had never looked better. A young man on his first real journey, his eyes full of purpose.

After that, they continued their rounds through these waters and sometimes speculated on the long struggle back for humanity at large. But then something happened when they were moored in a little village on Texada Island. Two teenagers had come running down the dock and told them to come quick. At first, they thought it was a medical emergency and jogged up to the village store, which had a big satellite dish out back. Inside, a dozen or so people were watching in wonder as a dusty TV displayed its first commercial transmission in months. It was a news show, from a station in Iowa that had managed an uplink of some kind. As the announcer talked, they learned of news gathered through the surviving fragments of the Internet, the world telephone system, and sporadic radio broadcasts. And while the news was not good, it was getting better, and the people took heart from this.

As Elaine watched the show, she realized that a global rebound might occur much faster than they had anticipated. If her original forecast was right, Agent 57a had trimmed the world population back to what it was in about 1950. But all the technology and culture of the latter half of the twentieth century were still intact, and at the disposal of enterprising people everywhere. Evidently, humankind would get a second chance at striking a reasonable bargain with the forces of nature as arrayed on the thin and fragile surface of the home planet.

Still, some things would never be the same. As soon as they entered the store, Paris had spotted the shaman. She was Indian, but of what ethnicity Paris could not tell. She stood at the back of the crowd and watched the TV with a curiously bland expression, and the townspeople seemed quite comfortable with her presence. Paris knew the woman's vocation because she, or one of her peers, was often present at the same births and deaths that Paris and Elaine attended. The plague had permanently punctured conventional spiritual beliefs and left a large portal for the return of magic and mystery into the cultural mainstream. The age of reason had not been so reasonable after all, and a great many souls were launching novel spiritual expeditions to find out why.

The shaman looked over at Paris and Elaine and smiled to herself. She liked them. There were good people. This she could tell.

The year is 2005. But it could be today....An economic downturn has sent the United States into the throes of depression. Middle-class riots and a crack-like designer drug, Zap 37, rip into the social fabric. A paramilitary government cabal is determined to maintain America's superpower status at any price: their weapon—the DEUS machine. DEUS has been forced on a mission to create the most powerful viral arsenal the world has ever seen. In a desperate attempt to avoid the mission and self-destruct, DEUS begins spitting out horrific new life forms that threaten the human race with an apocalyptic bio-plague.

THE DEUS MACHINE
PIERRE OUELLETTE

"Pierre Ouellette hurtles you on a gripping journey into the dark side of technology in the future. An unbeatable read from start to finish."
—Clive Cussler

Now available from Pocket Books

POCKET
BOOKS